Praise for *Counter Attack*

"Balancing a slow-burning romance with a twisty mystery, this will keep Bradley's fans hooked until the final page."

Publishers Weekly

"Plenty of action and interesting details about the dark web and police procedure keep this thriller with light Christian messaging moving."

Booklist

"*Counter Attack* opens with a chilling snippet that takes us into the dark web, a murderous game, and a killer's quest for revenge. Buckle up, because *Counter Attack* by Patricia Bradley takes you on an intense ride!"

Reading Is My Superpower

"Patricia Bradley introduces her new Pearl River series with a bang with *Counter Attack*."

Life Is Story

"What a great read! Infused with tension that comes with the search for a killer, this book will have readers flipping the pages late into the night to find out what happens."

Lynette Eason, bestselling, award-winning author of the Danger Never Sleeps series

"If you like your romantic suspense to include a twisted villain, a deadly plot, and a second chance at love, look no further than *Counter Attack*. I couldn't put it down!"

Lynn H. Blackburn, bestselling author of the Defend and Protect series

"Checkmate! Patricia Bradley hits the mark again in this fast-paced, high-stakes suspense you won't be able to put down!"

Natalie Walters, award-winning author of The SNAP Agency and Harbored Secrets series

"*Counter Attack* grabs you from the first page and doesn't let go until the end. The story plays out like a fast-paced chess game, with plenty of action and red herrings to ratchet up the suspense."

Sarah Hamaker, award-winning author of the Cold War Legacy series

FATAL WITNESS

BOOKS BY PATRICIA BRADLEY

LOGAN POINT SERIES

Shadows of the Past

A Promise to Protect

Gone Without a Trace

Silence in the Dark

MEMPHIS COLD CASE NOVELS

Justice Delayed

Justice Buried

Justice Betrayed

Justice Delivered

NATCHEZ TRACE PARK RANGERS

Standoff

Obsession

Crosshairs

Deception

PEARL RIVER

Counter Attack

Fatal Witness

PEARL RIVER • 2

FATAL WITNESS

PATRICIA BRADLEY

Revell

a division of Baker Publishing Group
Grand Rapids, Michigan

Published by Revell
a division of Baker Publishing Group
Grand Rapids, Michigan
RevellBooks.com

Printed in the United States of America

Library of Congress Cataloging-in-Publication Data
Names: Bradley, Patricia, 1945– author.
Title: Fatal witness / Patricia Bradley.
Description: Grand Rapids, Michigan : Revell, a division of Baker Publishing Group, 2024. | Series: Pearl River series ; 2
Identifiers: LCCN 2023022654 | ISBN 9780800741631 (paper) | ISBN 9780800745592 (casebound) | ISBN 9781493444731 (ebook)
Subjects: LCGFT: Christian fiction. | Detective and mystery fiction. | Romance fiction. | Novels.
Classification: LCC PS3602.R34275 F38 2024 | DDC 813/.6—dc23/eng/20230605
LC record available at https://lccn.loc.gov/2023022654

Baker Publishing Group publications use paper produced from sustainable forestry practices and post-consumer waste whenever possible.

24 25 26 27 28 29 30 7 6 5 4 3 2 1

To my readers.
Thank you for reading my books!

And to my sister, Barbara,
who was the one who told me I should write a book
set in the Chattanooga area.

And in memory of Lonnie Hull DuPont.
Thank you for taking a chance
on an unknown writer ten years ago.
You changed my life. You will be missed.

1

The back door slammed, and nine-year-old Danielle Bennett jumped. Her daddy was home. She held her breath, waiting to see which Daddy it was. The one who laughed and swung her up in the air or the one who yelled and broke things . . .

Her heart sank as he yelled at her mama to get things packed. When she yelled back that she wasn't going anywhere, Danielle covered her ears, but it didn't do any good. She prayed Daddy wouldn't be mean. Remembering the last time that happened made her sick to her stomach. She should have done something. Stopped him . . . or called someone.

"Danielle! Get in here!"

She flinched.

"Now!"

If she didn't go, he would come after her. She laid her Barbie on the floor and trudged to the kitchen, slipping inside the room quiet as a cat.

Her dad shoved her mama toward their bedroom. "Get packed. We have to leave. Now!"

Mama turned and crossed her arms. "Why is he coming here, Bobby? What does he want?"

"His share of the diamonds," he said. "We need to leave before he gets here. Now get to packing!"

"No! You have to take them back!"

"You've been talking to your mother, haven't you?" He jutted his jaw. "Don't you understand? They're our way out—" He cocked his head as tires crunched in their drive. "He's here!" He slammed his fist against the table. "If you'd done what I'd said, we'd be out of here."

"Me? You're the one who broke the law! And now you're even stealing from your partner."

His face was so red Danielle thought he might explode. Then his face changed, and he didn't look so mad. "I'm sorry. I'm just . . ." He swept her up in his arms and turned to her mama. "You stay here. I'll see if I can talk our way out of this. But first, I'll hide Danielle."

She looked over his shoulder as he rushed her out of the kitchen. Her mama's face . . . Danielle had never seen it so white.

"It's going to be all right, Little Bit."

Danielle's stomach squeezed. Daddy smelled funny . . . he always smelled funny when he yelled at Mama. She buried her face in his shoulder, not wanting to remember.

They stopped at a row of cabinets in the hallway, and he opened the door to the one they put her in when storms were coming. "I want you to get in here, and no matter what happens, you stay here until Mama or I come get you. Can you do that?"

"Why, Daddy?"

"Because it's very important." He knelt and pushed a board on the wall, and it slid open. Then he put something inside, but she couldn't see what it was before he closed it. Her daddy motioned her inside the cabinet. "Climb in."

Once she was settled, he stood and stared solemnly at her. "Promise me you'll stay here no matter what you hear. Will you do that for me?"

Danielle nodded solemnly.

"I want to hear you say it—I promise."

"You're scaring me, Daddy."

"Hurry! You have to promise."

Tears burned the back of her eyes. "I promise."

He shut the door, and darkness closed around her like a blanket. She scooted back against the wall and pulled her knees to her chest. It was hard to breathe . . .

Suddenly there was shouting. Someone was yelling at her daddy.

The house filled with booms. Then it was eerily quiet.

Danielle's heart beat so fast she thought it would jump out of her chest. She felt for the door and remembered her promise. Maybe Daddy would come get her in a minute.

Danielle waited as long as she could, but she had to go to the bathroom. Daddy would be mad if she wet her pants. Slowly, she eased the cabinet door open and crept down the hallway in her bare feet, not remembering when she lost her shoes. A noise in the kitchen drew her. Maybe it was Mama and Daddy . . . Danielle eased down the hall, remembering not to step on the squeaky board at the door.

She rubbed her eyes, trying to make sense of what she saw. Across the room, her daddy lay on the floor beside her mama. A man knelt beside them. Danielle must have made a noise because he looked up, right at her.

She whirled around and raced down the hall to the cabinet and pulled the door shut. Danielle curled into a tight ball and closed her eyes. Seconds later footsteps pounded down the hallway past the cabinet.

"No, no, no!"

A crying voice awakened her, and she blinked open her eyes.

Why was it so dark? She couldn't see *anything*. She stilled as footsteps hurried down the hallway.

"Danielle?" a voice called softly. "Where are you, honey?"

Her body started shaking, and tears ran down her face. Suddenly the door flew open, light flooding the little space she was in.

"Danielle?"

She blinked at the brightness and shrank back.

"It's me, honey. Are you all right?"

She didn't answer, instead staring at him as a horn sounded in the distance.

"We've got to get out of here," he said and reached inside the cabinet.

She wanted to fight him, but her arms wouldn't move.

He pulled her out and carried her through the front door to a four-door pickup parked in the driveway. Once he settled her in the backseat, he said, "It's going to be all right. I'll take care of you."

She stared at him. "Who are you?"

2

TWENTY-FIVE YEARS LATER

Dani Collins tilted her head as she tapped the Blackwing pencil against the sketch pad and studied the woman she'd just drawn. Something was off. But what?

Her Puli, Lizi, padded over and put her paw on Dani's thigh. Absently, Dani set her pencil down and ran her fingers over the dog's corded fur. "I know. I should be getting ready to leave instead of drawing people I don't know."

She glanced around the pottery-slash-artist studio where her portable wheel and supplies waited to be loaded in her RAV4 for the workshops at the University of Cincinnati. She'd been honored when they asked her to teach two classes—how to add sculpture techniques to wheel-thrown pieces on Thursday and brushwork decoration on Friday.

Dani was amazed at the success she'd enjoyed while combining her two loves. Her gaze shifted to a grouping of photos on the far wall. Four photos she'd taken of the nearby Badlands and Makoshika State Park. Her aunt had surprised her with the matted and framed prints last year.

But it was the photo in the center of the grouping her eye was drawn to—a dark green mountain range bathed in a smoky haze. It was like a green oasis in the middle of arid ground.

That photo had been a gift from her uncle when she moved into the studio ten years ago. When she'd asked where he got it and why he chose it, he'd shrugged. "I just liked it."

So did Dani. It stirred something in her heart. *Home.* The word popped into her head. But why?

He never did tell her where he got it. As she stared at the mountain scene, a dreamlike memory surfaced. Riding on a man's shoulders, a woman walking beside him, her laughter warming Dani. In her heart she knew the woman was her mom. The man had to be her dad, but before she could decide, the scene faded.

Had it actually happened? Or was it something she'd dreamed up to compensate for not remembering her parents? Dani didn't have a clue, but for a few seconds, she'd felt carefree . . . and happy.

She turned back to the sketch and stared at the drawing. A picture emerged in her memory, and she picked up her pencil again. A few strokes later, a braid curled over the woman's shoulder.

"Yes." That's what had been missing. If her colored pencils were handy, she would fill in the braid with red and make the woman's eyes blue. Dani didn't know how she knew this, but she did, just like she knew how to draw the woman's features.

She wished she knew more about the woman, but her memory was selective, as it had been with the half dozen other people she'd sketched in the past few months. People she didn't recognize but whose images popped into her head and stayed until she sketched them. People she believed held the key to her past.

"Who are you?" she murmured. Could this possibly be the woman in her memory? Her mother? Dani didn't think so. In her mind, her mother would be younger than this woman.

If only she could remember—

Lizi barked when she heard a soft knock at her studio followed by her uncle's voice.

"Mail's here," Keith said as he opened the door.

Dani quickly closed the sketch pad as he entered. Her uncle got really upset when she questioned him about their life before they came to Montana. He would flip out if he thought she was beginning to remember people from her past. "Thanks."

Lizi rubbed her head against Keith's leg as Dani sorted through the mail, separating it into bills, ads, payments, and the latest issue of *Pottery Making Illustrated.*

"I see you made the cover," Keith said, pointing to the magazine with one of her plates on the cover.

"My work, not me." Making the cover was a surprise—a nice one. She smoothed the plastic sleeve encasing the magazine and read the caption under the photo: "Talented ceramic artist Dani Collins talks about combining her two loves—painting and clay."

"Same difference."

Dani frowned. Keith worried there would be trouble every time she received any type of attention through her art, but he would never tell her why. Just like he wouldn't talk about what happened to her parents.

"It's not the first time my work has been featured in a national magazine. Nothing happened before, and I don't expect anything to happen this time, especially since my photo isn't even featured in the article. Besides, I'm not even sure what *could* happen since you won't tell me."

"I know . . . but if—"

"The wrong people see it, there will be problems." She'd heard him say it so many times that she could finish the sentence for him. Except he wouldn't tell her who those people were or what the problems could be. Dani studied Keith as he stared at the cellophane-wrapped magazine. What secrets did he hold that made him so afraid? And why did he refuse to talk about their past life?

Keith was like a father to her, and his wife, Laura, whom he'd married when Dani was eleven, had been like a mother . . . *had been.* She blinked back tears. It'd been a month since the woman who'd raised her through her turbulent teens died of cancer, but some days it was as fresh as yesterday.

Laura had always been her ally, and she would miss her. Laura had even encouraged Dani to ask Keith about her parents, but when Dani did, he never told her what happened or what made her forget them.

"*Your past is best left alone.*" Keith had been so upset and hurt by her questions that she'd dropped it. But with Laura's passing—Dani preferred that word much better than died—it drove home that if something happened to Keith, her questions would never be answered.

"Aren't you going to read it?"

She looked up. "I will later. Right now, I need to finish packing." Dani itched to check out the article but refrained, just in case the journalist hadn't kept his promise about not using her photo. Keith would have a fit.

"What time are you leaving tomorrow?"

"Early."

He glanced toward the wheel and supplies by the door. "It's not too late to cancel."

"I cannot believe you suggested that. The workshops start Thursday, three days from now. The university is expecting me, spent money advertising the classes . . . not to mention, I made a commitment to be there." Dani raised her eyebrows when his lips pressed in a thin line. "Why is this such a big deal for you?"

Keith held her gaze briefly, then he lifted a shoulder in a half shrug. "Cincinnati is thirteen hundred miles away—you don't usually venture that far."

"Don't you think it's time? I'm thirty-four years old and back living at home." He started to say something, and she palmed her hands. "I'm not saying I didn't want to be here for Laura, and I know you're lonesome and would like me to stay on."

"I appreciated you being here. Laura loved you like a daughter. And I do too." He hugged her. "I do hope you'll continue to make this your home. 'Cause you're right, it *is* lonesome when you're not here. I'll miss you this weekend."

He knew how to play on her sympathy.

"I'll think about continuing to live here."

"Good!" He smiled as though it were a done deal. "It seems to me living here would be more convenient instead of driving out here from your apartment in town every day."

It was also smothering. "If I do stay on, you have to cut me loose."

"I know . . . it's just . . ." He frowned. "You're smart, but you're not street-smart. You've led a sheltered life—"

"And whose fault is that?"

Keith continued like she hadn't spoken. "You know how you're always getting lost. And what if you have car trouble on the road in that little RAV4?"

"I have GPS—I won't get lost." If she did, unlike him, she had no problems stopping and getting directions. "And if you're worried about my SUV, let me drive your Navigator. That way I can take more of my porcelain pieces, you won't have to worry about me breaking down, and Lizi will be a whole lot more comfortable in the bigger cage."

Amusement lit his eyes, and his mouth twitched. "I walked into that one, didn't I?"

She gave him a grin for an answer.

He sighed. "Seeing that it's for Lizi's comfort, I'll get it serviced today and fill it up with gas."

"Thank you." While Lizi technically belonged to Keith, the Puli had bonded with Dani and would be miserable if she was left behind. Dani hugged him. "You're the best. I know you worry about me, but I'll be fine."

"You two will be back by Monday, right?"

She shot a loaded glare at him.

"Okay . . . backing off." He turned and walked to the door. "I'll help you load your stuff when I get back."

"I'll do it—I know how I want to arrange it." His way of loading a vehicle made her shudder.

"All right, Miss Persnickety."

He shut the door behind him, and Dani breathed easier. "Thank you, Lord."

She'd wanted to ask Keith about driving the Navigator because the university was allowing her to offer her work for sale at the workshops. He'd been so negative about the trip that she hadn't found the right timing and had resigned herself to only taking what she could fit in her smaller SUV.

Now she'd better finish packing and add the other pieces from her showroom that she wanted to take. She laid the mail on her desk, but instead of packing, Dani removed the magazine from the cellophane and flipped to the section featuring her work.

Front and center was a photo of her looking dead-on at the camera. Her heart stuttered, and she clenched her jaw. It was the very photo the journalist had promised he wouldn't use. If she'd looked at the article while Keith was with her . . .

But she hadn't, and Dani forced her jaw to relax. There wasn't much danger of him seeing it now, not if she took the magazine with her—it wasn't like he'd go out and buy a copy. She scanned the article.

"Where did you get your love for the clay? A relative, maybe?"

The question stopped her just like it had six months ago when the journalist posed it. She didn't remember her answer and read her response.

"Oh, I don't know. I think the first time I felt the clay under my hands, I was hooked. Clay gets in your blood, you know."

That was true, but the journalist's question had started her thinking about her family again. It hadn't been long afterward that the faces started popping into her head.

She scanned the rest of the article, pleased at how he'd captured both in pictures and words her steps in painting on the ceramic canvas. If only he hadn't included her photo. It was the only image of her anywhere—out of respect for Keith, she hadn't posted one even on her website.

A shiver ran through her. She didn't share Keith's paranoia, and she should be excited to see her photo in an international magazine. The unease running through her had to be from years of Keith's warnings.

3

Wednesday morning, Mae Richmond bent over her potter's wheel, putting pressure to the wet clay until it became smooth under her hands. Once the porcelain was centered, she opened it up and pressed her fingers on the bottom of the spinning pot, compressing the clay.

At seventy-eight, she was proud of the fact that she could still throw the large pitchers, but handling more than five pounds of clay was mostly a thing of the past. That didn't seem to matter to the customers who came to her shop in Russell County, Tennessee, many of them from Pearl Springs, the small town just down the mountain from her home on Eagle Ridge.

An hour later, Mae trimmed the bottom of the fourth pitcher she'd thrown and lifted it from the wheel. She set it on the table beside the others. Once the clay dried to leather hard, she would attach the handles.

A text message chimed. Mae dried her hands and pulled her iPhone from her pocket. Mail was here already? The gizmo she'd installed on the lid of her mailbox had saved her a lot of steps by alerting her when the rural carrier delivered her mail.

She covered the pitchers with plastic so they would dry evenly and walked the quarter mile down the hill to her mailbox, enjoying the perfect weather of the late April day—not too hot and not too cold. In the distance, the Cumberland Plateau Mountains in East Tennessee that rose above Eagle Ridge almost took her breath.

The carrier was waiting for her in his small SUV when she reached the box. "Mornin', Randy. Is there something I need to sign for?"

"No." The fiftysomething man smiled. "I waited around because I haven't seen you in a day or two."

"Thank you," she said warmly. "I've been busy glazing and firing—lots of Mother's Day orders to fill."

"Good to know you weren't sick."

Mae nodded her appreciation. Russell County was a tight-knit community where everyone looked out for each other, even people like her who kept to themselves. While she didn't know every person in the small Tennessee county, she figured she knew someone connected to each family.

Mae was fond of telling newcomers to be careful who they insulted, since just about everyone in Russell County was related, either by marriage or blood. Like the mail carrier, Randy Hart. His daughter, Jenna, was a new deputy with the Russell County Sheriff's Department.

Randy nodded toward the magazines as he handed her the mail. "You still playing detective?"

Mae glanced at the periodicals. He wasn't talking about *Pottery Making Illustrated*. No, he was referring to *Unsolved Crimes*. "Just trying to find my granddaughter." And Keith Bennett, her son-in-law's brother. She believed where she found one, she'd find the other.

"It's been twenty-five years—maybe it's time to let it go," he said gently.

Mae shook her head. "God hasn't told me to give up yet. With his help, I believe I'll find her."

Randy didn't understand what it meant to lose a child. Mae knew she'd see her daughter again one day, but she wanted something tangible now. She wanted her granddaughter.

Except for a great-nephew and great-niece Mae rarely saw, Danielle was all she had left, and as much as it was in her power, Mae would keep looking until she found her. But Randy meant well, and she managed a smile. "Got time for a brownie and a cup of tea or coffee?" she asked.

"Thanks, but not today. People have been ordering online like crazy—I have more than a hundred packages yet to deliver."

"Next time, maybe."

Mae's was the last house on the road, and she waited as he turned around in her drive and headed back down the gravel road toward Pearl Springs. Then she turned and climbed the hill to her small house, wishing she'd brought her cane or at least the staff she used when she went up on the ridge looking for mushrooms or some of the herbs for her "remedies."

Her stomach growled, and she checked the time. No wonder. It was noon. Mae entered the house through the back door and laid the mail on the counter, noting an article on the cover of the ceramics magazine about combining painting and clay. Right up her alley, and she'd look at it first—Mae often painted the hazy mountains around the ridge on her pieces, even her pitchers.

She made a ham and cheese sandwich, grabbed the pottery magazine, and headed for her picnic table—it was an ideal day to eat outside.

Mae had never liked eating alone, and today *Pottery Making Illustrated* would keep her company. She leafed through the magazine, enjoying the warm sunshine on her face as she turned the pages, seeking the feature spotlighted on the cover about combining painting and clay.

There it was.

She blinked. And stared closer at the photo of the potter with her golden red hair pulled back in a ponytail. Freckles dotted the area across her nose, and it looked like she had blue eyes . . .

Mae's heart pounded in her chest as she looked for the name of the artist. Dani Collins. She stilled. Dani could be short for Danielle . . . Was it possible?

Mae grabbed the magazine and hurried inside the house to the spare bedroom she'd made into a command center of sorts and switched on her computer. While waiting for it to boot up, she turned to the crime board she'd created after Neva and Robert were murdered and Danielle disappeared.

Most of her friends thought she was obsessed with what happened that night, especially after she created a "crime board" with all the key players on it and how they were connected. Mae didn't deny it, and she didn't care what they thought—her friends hadn't lost their whole family. There wasn't a day that she didn't spend at least a few minutes studying the board—it was a way to keep Neva and Danielle alive in her memory.

Today she ignored the left side of the board where she'd pinned photos of Bobby's friends, all possible suspects. Even now, Mae didn't understand what her daughter had seen in him. The boy had been bad news from the get-go. Nothing like his brother, Keith.

She found it so hard to believe Keith had anything to do with the burglaries that Neva said Bobby was involved in, but when he disappeared the same night as the murders, most people painted him with the same brush as his brother. Some even believed he was their killer. But not Mae.

She was pretty certain Keith had taken Danielle with him that night when he ran. What she didn't understand was why he didn't leave the girl with her. Danielle was her granddaughter. They were blood kin.

That first year, she'd hired a private investigator to find Keith, but it was like he'd fallen off the face of the earth. There were no signs of him—no credit card transactions, and she wasn't sure how the PI knew, but his Social Security card didn't show up anywhere either.

From everything Mae learned as she searched for him and her granddaughter, obtaining a new Social Security card was difficult but not impossible if you knew the right people. That's when Mae went from looking for Keith to trying to find Danielle. Myspace, Facebook, Instagram—over the years, she'd scoured their pages looking for images that might be her granddaughter.

She shifted her gaze to photos of Danielle on the right side of the board. The top one had been taken just before she disappeared. It had been her ninth birthday, and she was standing on the front porch of the house Bobby had built.

Comparing the two photos, Danielle's hair, pulled back in a ponytail, was lighter, and her freckles were more prominent than those of Dani Collins. Mae could easily see that the adult shape of her granddaughter's mouth would be similar to the potter's. She shifted her gaze to two other photos the PI had aged to show how Danielle might look at twenty-one, then at thirty.

Mae compared Dani Collins's photo in the magazine to the two aged photos of her granddaughter. Iffy. Then she compared it to the photo in the middle, the one of her daughter that had been taken when Neva would've been about the age of the potter in the magazine.

Dani Collins looked more like Neva than the images in the aged photos.

Her computer alerted that it had finished booting up. Mae settled behind it and googled the website listed in the article for Dani Collins. Maybe she would find more photos of the ceramic artist.

There were plenty of photos and how-to videos and tutorials on the site, but not one that showed Dani Collins's face. That seemed a little odd. She tried the phone number listed on the website for the pottery studio, but it went straight to voicemail. "Sorry I missed you. Leave a message and your number, and I'll get back to you."

Mae hung up without leaving a message. She knew how she'd feel if someone left a message on her voicemail saying the caller might be a long-lost relative. No, she needed to talk to her either in person or in a phone conversation. Except there was no address on the website. She scanned the photos on the site, stopping at one that had what looked like the Badlands in the background. Could Dani Collins live in the Dakotas or Montana? But how would she find out?

Social media. That's where her experience from years ago and all the true-crime shows she watched told her to look next. Mae started with Facebook. Half an hour later, she hadn't found a Dani Collins that fit the profile she was looking for. Another thirty minutes and no results on Twitter, Instagram, or TikTok. She tried Pinterest. Nothing.

She braced her chin on her hand. Mae was proud of her computer skills, especially since she was mostly self-taught, but just as her searches years ago never found a Danielle Bennett on social media sites, her searches for Dani Collins netted a zero as well. Maybe it was time to bring in help. But who?

Not Sheriff Carson Stone. Even though Mae and Carson's wife, Judith, had been friends for over seventy years, the sheriff thought Mae had gone off the deep end after Neva's death. Especially after she showed him her crime board.

Carson didn't take her seriously, and it rankled every time he reminded her that she wasn't living in Cabot Cove and she wasn't Jessica Fletcher. Besides, after his heart attack last fall, he'd hired his granddaughter as his chief deputy, and Alexis was running the sheriff's office. She corrected herself. It was Alex now. She glanced at the article. Maybe like this Dani was really a Danielle?

Before Danielle had disappeared, she and Alexis Stone and

Morgan Tennyson were best friends. Mae smiled. She'd dubbed the girls the Three Musketeers because where you saw one, you saw the other two. Until everything changed.

Should she start with Alex? Alex once thought Mae hung the moon, but she was all grown up now. Would she be like her grandfather and think Mae was a foolish old woman?

But if not Alex, who? A smile pulled at her lips. Of course. Mark Lassiter. She should have thought of him first.

She picked up her phone and dialed Mark's number. When it went straight to voicemail, she frowned. He must be out of range.

Since Russell County was in the mountains of the Cumberland Plateau, there were a lot of areas that didn't have good cell reception, her own property included. It's why she had an outdoor Wi-Fi extender on the roof.

She punched in another number. Maybe Alex would know where Mark was.

4

Russell County K-9 officer Mark Lassiter pulled into Peterson's, the small, locally owned grocery that he preferred over Walmart. That it was located in downtown Pearl Springs instead of out by the highway might be a factor. He turned to Gem, his K-9 German shepherd. "Stay. I'll be right back."

Even though the temps were in the low sixties, Mark left the motor running. The heat controls in the Ford Expedition automatically kicked in if the temperature in the vehicle dropped too low. Conversely, if it got too hot, the air conditioner turned on.

A bell rang over his head as he pushed open the door to the old store and glanced around for the owner. He nodded to the older man sitting behind the counter. "Morning, Mr. Peterson."

The grocer smiled big. "Almost afternoon, Mark. How's my girl?"

With his strong voice, Mr. Peterson didn't sound ninety-two and certainly didn't look it with his mostly still-black hair. "She's good." Mark walked to the pet supplies and picked up the treats as the grocer's grandson, Kyle, came from the back of the store.

"Can I help you find anything else?" the grandson asked.

"I think this will get me through today." Kyle had worked at the store for as long as Mark could remember. He took the treats to the checkout.

"These are on the house today," the older Mr. Peterson said.

Kyle stiffened.

"Thanks, Mr. Peterson," Mark said, "but I really want to pay for them."

"Your money's no good here." Mr. Peterson narrowed his eyes at his grandson. "And I'm giving them to Gem, not you."

It was no use arguing with the older man. "Gem thanks you," he said and took the treats. As he walked out the door, he heard Kyle griping to his grandfather that it was hard enough to keep the doors open without giving away stuff.

Once in his SUV, Mark backed out of the parking space and drove to the Pearl Springs city park. It was a perfect place to practice for the K-9 scent trials in Kentucky in June. There were enough people around throwing Frisbees or walking the trails or just enjoying the beautiful weather to simulate the distractions at the trials.

He left Gem in the SUV while he walked across the park to a huge oak, where he removed the vest from a scented teddy bear and propped the bear against the oak tree. He jogged back to the Expedition and used his remote to open Gem's door. The black and tan German shepherd hopped out of the SUV and pranced in a circle.

"You ready, girl?" Gem let out a woof, and Mark let her sniff the small vest before he gave the search command.

Gem ignored the people in the park and bounded away, her nose in the air while she worked a zigzag pattern. When she caught the scent, he followed as she made a beeline to where he'd hidden the bear and alerted by plopping down beside it and barking.

"Good girl!" Mark patted her side. "Free," he said, releasing the dog before rewarding her with one of Mr. Peterson's treats.

Then he pulled out a short, braided rope, and she scrambled up and grabbed the rope.

Mark spent a few minutes playing tug with Gem before he threw the rope, and she bounded after it. Like most of the dogs he'd trained since leaving the military, she preferred playtime over the treats, but she was really happy when she received both.

His cell buzzed, and he unhooked it from his belt. It was a call from his boss, Chief Deputy Alexis Stone, who preferred to be called Alex.

Mark was still a little bummed to lose the chief deputy spot. He was thirty-four and had hoped to be more than a deputy by this time. In fact, he'd hoped to take Harvey Morgan's place when the former chief retired, but Sheriff Carson Stone had hired his granddaughter. She was doing a good job running the office after Carson had suffered a major heart attack. So well that she'd probably win the next election, since Carson wasn't running again, and so far she had no opposition. Maybe he'd be made chief deputy then.

Mark slid the answer button on his phone. "Lassiter."

"Hate to bother you on your day off, but I just got a call from Mae Richmond. She tried to reach you, but you didn't answer."

"Is she all right?" He'd hate to see anything happen to his neighbor and friend.

"Yeah, but . . ." Alex sighed. "She's coming into the office . . . something about her granddaughter. Gramps was here and he about had a fit, said she'd drive me batty if I encouraged her at all."

He was surprised Carson had come into the office—he rarely did anymore. He must be feeling better. "Up until a couple of years ago, Mae came by at least once a month to see if the sheriff had any updates on her granddaughter and to share her latest theories," Mark said.

Gem brought the tug and dropped it at his feet, and he threw it again. "I think your grandfather is really bothered because he hasn't been able to solve the murders or find the granddaughter or her uncle, Keith Bennett."

"That's what I think too," Alex said. "Since you and Mae are friends, I think it would help if you were here when she arrives."

"Sure." The request puzzled him. Alex and Mae went way back—Mae had regaled him with tales of babysitting the chief deputy. "I'm at the park. Won't take me five minutes to get to your office."

"See you then."

He opened the rear door to his SUV and called Gem. Once he had her secured, he drove to the sheriff's office, still thinking about Alex's request when his phone rang. It was Mae.

"Lassiter."

"Oh, good." Relief flowed through the phone. "I tried to call you earlier."

"What's going on?"

"I have something to show you. Can you meet me at Alex's office?"

"She called, and I'm on my way there now."

"Oh."

"Isn't that what you wanted?"

"Yes . . . but if she's already talked to you . . ." Mae sighed.

"What's wrong?"

"Nothing."

The rhythmic ticking of a blinker filled the silence. She was probably turning onto the highway to Pearl Springs.

"See you in a few minutes," he said.

"Just promise you'll keep an open mind."

"Don't I always?"

"That's what I like about you," she said and ended the call.

Mark shook his head. Mae was as independent as they came. Eccentric was what people usually called her. Sometimes he forgot she was a well-known potter, and that some of her porcelain art pieces commanded a thousand dollars or more on the website she designed herself.

He was one of the few people she actually engaged with. Maybe because they were neighbors on Eagle Ridge. Or more likely because he made it a point to chop wood and lay it by her back door at least once a week during cold weather. Sometimes, if she wasn't working in her pottery shop, she would invite Mark and Gem into the house, Mark for coffee and one of her rich fudge brownies and Gem for a special homemade dog treat.

From what the sheriff had told Mark, it hadn't always been that way. She'd been active in church and some of the women's groups in Pearl Springs even after her husband had been killed in a logging accident. But when her daughter and son-in-law were murdered and her granddaughter disappeared, she'd retreated to her home and pottery studio on Eagle Ridge.

So what had brought her out today?

5

Mae noted Mark's SUV in the parking lot as she pulled her small pickup into a visitor's spot and got out. She was counting on him to be on her side. Alexis too, maybe—if her grandfather hadn't undermined Mae's credibility.

She knew why Carson Stone called her his "thorn in the side." The first few years after someone killed Neva, Mae had bugged the stew out of him with her theories on the murders. For all the good it had done. Not that Carson Stone wasn't a good sheriff. He was, but there'd been so few clues to go on. He'd leaned toward the killer being from Chattanooga since that's where the jewelry stores her son-in-law broke into were located.

Mae wasn't so sure. The day they were killed, Bobby had asked her to hide a small package, but when she wanted to know what it was, he became enraged and stormed out of her house. She'd called her daughter as soon as he left, and Neva confessed that Bobby was involved in a burglary ring. Something had gone wrong, and he'd brought the stolen goods home.

The last conversation she'd had with her daughter was etched in her memory like stone.

"Make Bobby give the stolen goods back, Neva."

"I'll try, but you know Bobby." Her daughter was practically in tears. "I'm scared, Mama."

"Call Keith. He'll help you figure out something."

"Bobby says he's involved too."

Mae had trouble believing that. She'd known both Bennett brothers all their lives, and unlike Bobby, Keith was rock solid. Mae had never understood why Neva chose Bobby over his brother or why Keith hadn't fought harder for Neva. "Make Bobby do the right thing, and—"

"You don't understand, Mama. I can't make Bobby do anything, and he says we're leaving Pearl Springs."

"Just call Keith. He'll help you."

"I know. I gotta go. Love you, Mama."

"Love you too, Neva."

They were the last words she'd spoken to her daughter.

The investigation into the murders showed only one call from Bobby and Neva's house after that one—to Keith Bennett. She believed in her bones Keith had come to his brother's house and found Neva and Bobby dead and had taken Danielle with him. She never understood why he'd taken her granddaughter with him when he ran instead of bringing her to Mae . . . unless Danielle saw what happened and he was afraid for her life.

Hope fluttered in her chest. Maybe she'd get her answer if this Dani Collins turned out to be her granddaughter.

Mae grabbed the magazine and photos of Danielle and Neva she'd taken from the crime board. The Russell County Sheriff's Office had the resources to find Dani Collins and Mae didn't. That's why she was here.

She locked her truck and hurried inside, winding her way around to Alexis's office. "Afternoon, Marge." She smiled at the woman behind the desk. "I believe Alexis is expecting me."

The office manager returned Mae's smile. "She is, but first, how are you?"

"Good. Keeping busy."

Marge tilted her head. "Do you have any of your large pitchers? I want to get one for my daughter for Mother's Day. It's her first one, you know."

Mae swallowed a smile. Marge's daughter had called earlier in the week with the same request. "Not right now, but I have four waiting for handles—they'll be ready by next Friday."

"I'll come see you." She nodded toward Alex's office. "Door's open and Mark's here too."

Mae took a deep breath and walked through the doorway. Tension eased out of her when only Mark and Alexis were in her office. She'd been dreading Carson. She nodded at the two deputies.

"Good to see you, Alexis, I mean Alex. You too, Mark. Gem's looking good," Mae said.

The dog sat on her haunches and looked from Mae to her trainer. A low whine came from Gem's throat.

Mark leaned down and patted her on the side. "Okay, girl. Free."

Gem crossed the room in two strides and sat at Mae's feet. She held a paw up, and Mae shook it. "Sorry I don't have a treat for you," she said and smoothed the German shepherd's coat before turning her attention to Alex.

The chief deputy gave her a warm smile. "It's really good to see you. Sorry I haven't been up to visit you lately, but it's been busy around here."

"That's what Mark tells me."

"Did you know Morgan was in town?"

"No." Mae was surprised that her great-niece hadn't let her know she was coming to Pearl Springs. "When did she get here?"

"Yesterday, I think. She's staying with Ben."

That explained a lot. Morgan probably wouldn't call her as long as her brother was around. Mae's great-nephew was still upset that she refused to sell her place and move to town. That'd been six months ago, and she hadn't heard from Ben more than twice since. "If you see Morgan, tell her I asked about her."

"I'm sure she'll call you soon." Alex shuffled papers on her desk, then looked up. "So, what can we help you with today?"

Mae felt the full force of the chief deputy's piercing blue eyes. Alex was a bottom-line person, a lot like Mae. *Lord, help me make this clear and concise.* She pulled the magazine from her satchel. "I'm sure Carson has told you I'm still looking for Danielle."

A wry smile and nod confirmed what she already knew—Carson had painted Mae as a meddling old woman. She opened the magazine to the featured article and handed it to Alex. "Take a good look at the photo of Dani Collins."

Alex studied the photo, then handed the magazine to Mark. "She looks a little familiar . . ."

Mae slid the photo of Neva across the desk. "Compare the two."

She watched with satisfaction as first Alex's eyes widened, then Mark's. "I believe that's my granddaughter."

"It's a possibility, but we all have a doppelgänger," Alex said.

"I get that, but Dani Collins is a potter, just like me—how likely is that to happen?"

"Granted, that seems unusual . . ." Alex rubbed the back of her neck. "I'm not sure what you want me to do."

Mae pulled out the photo of Danielle as a child. "Can you run this through a facial recognition program and see if the person in the magazine matches this photo?"

"If I had a program like that, I would." Alex blew out a breath and stared at the magazine. "There's a company in Chattanooga that could compare the two photos. Not sure how much it'd cost, but—"

"I don't care what it costs. Can you do it today?"

"Let me call Nathan. He has the number."

Mae turned to Mark while Alex called Nathan Landry, Pearl Springs's chief of police. "I've missed you and Gem."

The dog thumped her tail at hearing her name. Mark leaned toward Mae. "We've been training for the trials in Kentucky."

"She'll do good," Mae said. "I have a phone number for this Dani Collins—it's her studio number, but I only get her answering machine."

"Did you leave a message?"

She shook her head. "I didn't know what to say. Certainly couldn't say 'I might be your grandmother'—she'd think I was crazy. And if it turns out to be true, I thought maybe I could get you to call her. She'd be more likely to believe it coming from a law enforcement officer."

"That'll be Alex's call," he said.

She was afraid he'd say that, but for some reason, Mae wanted him to make the call. Maybe because he wouldn't put it on the back burner.

Alex ended her call. "He said to send him the photos and he'd email them to the company." She used her phone to snap shots of the two photos and then texted them to Nathan. "Done," she said.

"Did he say how long it would take?"

"He didn't know but didn't think it would take long since they're only comparing the two photos. Mark will call you as soon as we have an answer."

"Thank you." She smiled her gratitude as well.

"I hope it is Danielle. I've thought about her a lot since I returned to Pearl Springs." Alex hesitated. "Just don't get your hopes up too high. It may not be her."

"It is. I feel it here." Mae touched above her heart. "I hope you don't mind, but I already asked if Mark would call the number listed on the website and talk to her."

Alex didn't answer right away. "Let's see what the facial recognition company says first."

"Of course—but the photos are going to match." Mae stood. "I need to get back to my studio and check on my kiln . . . and pull some handles for the pitchers I made this morning."

Alex's face lit up. "Gram loves your pottery, and I want to get her one of your tulip vases for Mother's Day."

Mae thought a minute. She had several of the artistic pieces, but Judith wouldn't be happy if Alex spent that much money. "I think your grandmother would rather have something more utilitarian. I have a pitcher I'll be glazing and firing tomorrow. It has her favorite flower on it—forget-me-nots."

"That sounds perfect. I'll drive up in a day or so. And I'm paying full price for it—no friend discount."

"Wouldn't be a gift if it didn't cost you something." Mae smothered a grin. Not that she would let Alex pay full price. "See you then."

Mark stood. "I'll walk out with you."

She nodded her thanks. Neither of them said anything until they exited the building with Gem on their heels.

"Do you have time to grab a cup of coffee at the Bean Factory?" Mark asked.

She tilted her head. The K-9 officer had something on his mind, and she wasn't certain she wanted to hear what it was. But Mark had been so good to check on her periodically, especially when the weather was bad. "Sure."

A few minutes later Mae followed him inside the busy coffee shop. "Did you leave your motor running?" Mark had left Gem inside the SUV.

"No. She'll be fine. I have an alert on my phone that lets me know if the temperature gets too warm."

Mae glanced around and spied one empty table in the room. She shoved a five-dollar bill in his hand. "I'll grab the table if you'll get me a plain coffee."

He handed it back to her. "You're not paying."

Mae gave him an exasperated huff. She liked paying her own way, but two more people came into the shop and she didn't have time to argue with him if she wanted to snag the table. "Whatever."

It wasn't long before he brought their coffees along with a scone and some kind of sandwich. "I haven't had lunch," he explained. "The blueberry scone is for you—I don't like eating alone."

"Appreciate it." Even to her it sounded more like a complaint than a thank-you. "Really, I do thank you."

He grinned. "I knew you meant it the first time."

Her mouth twitched and then curved up in a full-on smile. Mark knew her so well. "All right. What did you want to talk about?"

Mark took a bite of his sandwich, chewed, and swallowed before he answered. "I'm like Alex—I don't want you to get your hopes up, and there's something else you need to consider. Even if it is your granddaughter, she might not want a relationship with you."

His words took the breath right out of her.

6

Why wouldn't she want a relationship?" Mae demanded. Her face had turned as pale as her white porcelain vases, and Mark's heart plummeted. He hadn't meant to upset her, but she had to face reality. "You have to consider she hasn't tried to contact you. What if she doesn't want her life upended?"

"What if she doesn't know about me?" Mae crossed her arms.

"Danielle was nine—she should remember you."

"But what if she doesn't? I'm 99.99 percent certain Keith took Danielle and left town that night. If he was running from the law, like everyone believes, he would've wanted Danielle to forget her life here. It wouldn't be hard for a nine-year-old to forget a grandmother."

"If Keith Bennett was running from the law, why would he saddle himself with a nine-year-old girl, even if she was his niece?"

She stared down into her coffee mug. "I don't know," she said softly. Then she raised her gaze. "Keith was a good man. I have to believe he took her and was afraid to bring her back. If he didn't . . ."

Mae didn't have to finish her thought. If the person who killed her daughter and son-in-law took Danielle . . . well, there were a thousand places a body could be buried around here.

"Aunt Mae?" a feminine voice asked. "Is that you?"

They both looked up. Mark didn't recognize the raven-haired woman who had stopped at their table, but he did recognize the man with her. The mayor, Ben Tennyson.

Mae's eyes widened. "Morgan? I heard you were in town."

A smile lit up the woman's whole face. "You were on my list to call tomorrow, and here you are."

Mae's gaze shifted to her great-nephew. "Afternoon, Ben."

He bobbed his head. "Mae."

Mark nodded to the two empty chairs at their table. "You two want to join us?"

Regret crossed the mayor's face. "I have—"

"Of course!" Morgan pulled out the chair nearest her and plopped down. She turned to Mark. "I don't believe I know you."

"I'll grab our coffees," Ben said before he could answer.

"You should know me—we went to school together."

"It's Mark Lassiter," Mae said.

Morgan gaped at him. "You were so skinny as a kid. You must work out."

He shrugged. "Something like that."

Morgan turned to Mae. "You're looking good too. Still working in your pottery studio?"

"Every day. How about you? What are you doing now?"

A shadow crossed her eyes, then she straightened her shoulders. "Actually, I'm looking for a job. The TV station in Houston got a new manager who brought in all his people, including an investigative reporter, and they didn't need two. Ben offered me a job working in his real estate office, but working for my brother who thinks he can boss me around just because he's ten years older won't work." She palmed her hands. "Besides, I'm not a salesman."

"You could learn," Ben said as he set Morgan's coffee in front of her. "And I do not boss you around."

"Yes, you do." She shook her head. "And I don't want to learn. Aren't you going to sit down?"

"Afraid I can't—just got a text that someone wants to meet me in ten minutes about buying property on Eagle Ridge." He turned to Mae. "I don't suppose—"

"No. And I told you not to ask me again."

"But Mae, you're getting up in years—you need to think about moving to town."

"No," she repeated, more forcefully this time.

Mark had been tempted to tell her the same thing. Now he was glad he hadn't. He didn't want Mae glaring at him like she was at Ben.

"Okay." The mayor checked his watch. "Sorry to leave you good folks, but I have just enough time to walk to the office before my prospective client gets there. Morgan, I'll see you at the house later." He headed for the door.

"Sorry about that," Morgan said after her brother left. "He can be kind of pushy sometimes."

Mark turned to Mae. "Would you like more coffee?"

"No, thank you. As late in the afternoon as it is, this cup will probably make it hard to sleep."

Silence fell at the table briefly, then Morgan tilted her head. "Ben and I were talking about Danielle yesterday. He said you still hadn't found her."

"That was yesterday," Mae said. "Today may be a different story."

"What?"

"You may want to hold off on that until we know for sure," Mark said. It was ingrained in him to refrain from discussing a case.

"I'm sure," she replied. "Besides, Morgan is family."

Before he could divert her attention, she pulled the pottery magazine from her satchel and flipped to the article with Dani Collins's photo. It was like stopping a runaway train as she pushed the magazine and the photo of Neva clipped to the top of the page toward her great-niece.

"I think I've found her."

Morgan gasped. "What? You're kidding! Have you talked to her? When is she coming home?"

Mae sobered and glanced at Mark. This was what he'd wanted to spare her from.

"We haven't talked to her," he said. "The process is just beginning."

"Oh, so it may not be Danielle," Morgan said.

"It is her," Mae insisted. "And Mark's right. I shouldn't have said anything yet."

"Mum's the word," Morgan said, turning a pretend key on her lips.

Mark checked his watch. There was still time to practice for the upcoming dog trials. "I hate to leave you ladies but . . ."

"I have to go too," Mae said. "I have a kiln to check on and handles to pull."

Morgan stood when they did and hugged her great-aunt. "I'm so glad I ran into you today. Do you have time for me to visit you? I'd love to see what you've been up to."

"Of course, child. Anytime. I might even put you to work—you were a good student once upon a time, even though you were so young."

Morgan sighed. "I miss those days. I wish Daddy had never taken us away from Pearl Springs." She hugged Mae again. "I'm glad to be home. And I'm glad to see you too, Mark."

"You as well," he said. "Hope you find a job soon. Are you looking around here?"

"Not Pearl Springs—no TV station—but I'm sending my résumé to the Nashville and Chattanooga stations, maybe even Knoxville. Wouldn't mind going freelance if I could find a good story."

Mark would be sure to avoid Morgan. He liked to keep a healthy distance from reporters.

"At least Chattanooga and Knoxville are closer than Texas," Mae said. "I hope you'll come visit soon."

"I will, but I'll call or text first." Morgan looked at Mae. "You do text?"

"All the time," Mae answered.

Mark waited until both ladies were gone before he slid behind the wheel of his SUV. "You ready to work, girl?"

Gem barked her agreement as he drove toward the park. After an hour of hiding the bear and Gem finding it on the first try each time, he loaded her up and they made the drive to Eagle Ridge and home.

Mark paused before turning into his drive, then pulled in. He'd thought about checking on Mae, but she knew how to take care of herself as well as anyone he knew. He would check on her in the morning before he left for his K-9 duties.

However, a call for backup at six the next morning had him and the German shepherd in his SUV racing to Harper Point, the local teen hangout on Pearl Lake, to help Jenna Hart with a group of rowdy kids who'd consumed too much alcohol. By the time they had the kids settled down and their parents on the way to the jail to pick them up, it was midmorning.

He fed Gem and filled her water bowl in the SUV, then drove across town to Pete's Diner for breakfast. Ethel had just set his plate of sausage and eggs and pancakes in front of him when his phone rang. Nathan Landry, Pearl Springs's chief of police.

"Morning, Chief," he said.

"Same to you," Nathan replied. "Alex was tied up in a meeting with the county commissioners and she told me to call and give you the news on Mae's case."

"Were the photos a match?"

"The answer is yes . . ." Nathan said.

"I hear a *but* in that."

"This particular company uses a program that overlays eighty facial landmarks from one photo to the other. The two photos had a 95 percent match. Even so, to be absolutely certain, they suggested a DNA test."

"But they were pretty sure this Dani Collins is Danielle Bennett?"

Nathan didn't hesitate. "Yeah."

"I'll call the number Mae found on Dani Collins's website and see if she'd be willing to take a DNA test."

"I think that's a good idea."

"Thanks for your help," Mark said. He disconnected and stared at his phone. It was hard to believe that after all these years, Mae's granddaughter had been found.

He dialed the number Mae had given him for Dani Collins and got a recording that requested the caller leave their number and a message.

"Ms. Collins, this is Deputy Mark Lassiter with the Russell County Sheriff's Office in Tennessee. Would you please return my call?" Then he left his cell phone number and, as an afterthought, his badge number. That way if she thought the call was a scam of some sort, she could check him out.

7

It'd been a good workshop, but now Dani was tired after two days of nonstop talking and demonstrating her techniques. She surveyed the few remaining pieces that hadn't sold, thankful she didn't have many to take back home.

"Ms. Collins!"

Dani's dog stiffened as one of the university students hurried toward her. "Sit," Dani said. Lizi obeyed but didn't totally relax.

"Thank you so much for coming! Your technique is fantastic—I learned so much."

Dani remembered the student from the classes. "I love teaching, especially to artists like you who are eager to learn."

"Thank you. I hope you'll come back."

"I'd like to." She encouraged the girl with a smile. "Just don't ever stop learning."

"Don't worry. I won't." She looked down at Lizi, who hadn't moved. "What kind of dog is that? She looks like a mop with those dreadlocks."

Dani got that question a lot. "She's a Puli, and that's the way her hair grows."

The girl's eyes widened. "Is she a guard dog?"

"Yes, she is." She patted Lizi's side. "And a good one."

"Can I pet her?"

She hesitated. Lizi thought she was on duty, and Dani didn't want to confuse her. "Let me release her first." She patted Lizi's side. "Break," she said softly, telling Lizi she could play. The Puli wagged her tail.

The student gingerly felt the cords of Lizi's coat. "Do you have to do these yourself?"

"No, they're natural."

The girl rubbed Lizi's back one more time and then nodded toward the pieces yet to be wrapped in newspaper for transporting. "Can I help you?"

"I'm almost done, but thanks."

After the student wandered away, Dani finished packing and loaded the boxes on rolling tables the university had provided. It had been a really good workshop, and she liked connecting with the students. She also enjoyed talking about Lizi, but she was glad she didn't have to talk to anyone until tomorrow, when she'd agreed to have breakfast with the director of the ceramic arts program.

Two hours later she let the jets from the spa bathtub massage her muscles and thought about getting one for home.

Home. The studio. Dani sat straight up. She'd been so busy she'd forgotten to check the shop's voicemail. Hopefully she hadn't lost any orders because of it.

As soon as she was dressed, Dani turned her cell phone on. There was a call and message from Keith thirty minutes ago. She quickly called him back. "Sorry," she said when he answered. "I forgot to turn my phone back on after the workshops."

"You never keep your phone on," he complained.

"I forget . . . or I forget to charge it. It's not like anyone is going to call me on it." Until recently, her cell phone consisted of a cheap flip phone with prepaid minutes that she'd rarely turned on. No one had the number for the smartphone that Keith bought her a month ago. She knew how to turn it on and turn it off and that was about it.

"I thought you needed a better phone."

"I liked my old phone. It was all I needed." Dani hated that people thought she should be accessible 24/7. She had a computer and a tablet, so why would she want a smartphone that was expensive with an equally expensive plan when she only used a cell phone for calls and a few texts?

"How are you?" she asked, softening her voice.

"Good, now that you'll be home by Monday. What time are you leaving in the morning?"

She never told him she'd be home by Monday—he'd assumed she would be. "I'm not sure what my plans are other than I'm having breakfast with Evelyn."

"Oh."

She narrowed her eyes at the censure in his voice. Dani had accepted long ago that he'd never liked her teacher and mentor. "I'll call you before I leave."

"Good. You sound tired. Get some rest."

"I am, and I will, and thank you for caring." And he did care, but sometimes . . .

She disconnected and padded to the coffee station in the room and picked up an herbal tea pod. Maybe that would help her sleep.

She suddenly remembered that she still needed to check her business messages. She dialed the number. The first two messages were people wanting to know about pieces featured on her website, mainly the price. The next three were people signing up for classes at her studio in June, and the last four were orders. Her eyes widened as she listened to the next one. A request from a deputy in Tennessee. Probably wanting money. Then she frowned. Scammers didn't normally leave their badge numbers. The smooth-voiced deputy hadn't left a landline number, only his cell.

This Mark Lassiter had credited her with having enough sense to be wary if he'd left a number claiming it was for the sheriff's office. She listened to the message again, writing down his badge and phone number, then googled the Russell County Sheriff's Office. They had a website, and even a Facebook page. She clicked on the website first.

The only photos on the site were of the sheriff, an older man, and the chief deputy, who was a woman. Both carried the last name of Stone. Interesting. Before she opened her Facebook app, she looked up the county's location. Just north of Chattanooga. Why did a deputy in East Tennessee want to talk to her?

Dani clicked over to the Russell County Sheriff's Office Facebook page and scrolled through the photos until she came to a photo gallery of deputies. She recognized the chief deputy's photo. Alex Stone.

She clicked on each photo, smiling at the one of a beautiful German shepherd, then Dani noticed the man standing beside the dog. The caption read "Mark Lassiter and Gem."

So the man really existed. And not only existed, but by anyone's reckoning ought to be a model for one of those calendars of firefighters and law enforcement officers showing off their pecs and biceps. Not that Mark Lassiter was shirtless, but the black T-shirt fit his torso like a glove.

She clicked out of the photo. What was she doing, ogling the man like he was eye candy? Heat crawled up her neck, and Dani clicked out of the Facebook page and back to the website to get the number for the office. She hesitated before dialing. It was after eight. Would they be closed? Then she shook her head. Of course not—law enforcement offices didn't close.

"Russell County Sheriff's Office," a woman's voice answered.

Dani gave her name, then said, "I had a message from Mark Lassiter, who said he was a deputy there."

"Yes, ma'am. We have a K-9 officer by that name."

That fit the Facebook photo. She read off the cell phone and badge number she'd written down. "Can you verify that those belong to the deputy?"

"If you'll hold, I'll check and see." A minute later she came back on the line. "Both numbers are correct."

"Is he there now?"

"He's off duty, but if he left his cell number, feel free to call him. Or I can take a message."

"Thank you. I believe I'll give him a call." Dani disconnected and grabbed a bottle of water from the hotel refrigerator. So, the call wasn't spam. She punched in the area code. *But what if the call is bad news?*

Dani brushed that thought away. How could it be anything bad when she didn't know a soul in East Tennessee? She finished dialing and held her breath while it rang.

"This is Mark Lassiter."

The voice was even smoother than on the message and sent a shiver over Dani. The man ought to be in radio or TV. She cleared her throat. "This is Dani Collins. I believe you left a message for me on my answering machine."

"I did. Can you give me a minute? I'm just leaving Pete's Diner."

"You want to call me back?"

"No, if you'll just hold on a sec while I pay."

Voices mixed with the sounds of silverware clinking on plates. Two minutes later, everything was quiet. "Sorry, but the diner was kind of noisy. I could barely hear you."

"It's fine. Why did you call me?" The brief silence on the other end of the line had her gripping her phone tighter. Then her stomach dipped when he sucked in a deep breath. "Has something happened to my uncle?"

Stupid question since her uncle was nowhere near Tennessee, but it was her first thought.

"Your uncle? No. I mean, I don't know. I don't know your uncle."

Her muscles relaxed slightly. "What's so difficult about telling me why you called?"

"It's complicated," he said. "And it's been more than a day since I called you, and I just worked a really bad accident. Give me a second to collect my thoughts."

"I'm sorry. I hope no one was—"

"It was only by the grace of God there were no fatalities."

"Good." She didn't often run into a man who talked about God with a stranger so easily. "Would you like to call me back when you get it together?"

"No. Now that I have you, I don't want to let you go."

She couldn't keep from chuckling.

"Oh, man," he muttered. "That didn't come out right."

"It's okay. I know what you meant. So, what's complicated about it?"

Again, he took a deep breath. "I'm working a cold case, and maybe if I give you the background, it'll be easier for you to understand."

"Okay." A compulsive note-taker, Dani put the phone on speaker and then picked up a hotel notepad and pen from the nearby desk.

She printed the deputy's name at the top of the page and circled it. Then Dani wrote down key words as he described an unsolved murder case, her writing slowing as he moved on to the disappearance of a nine-year-old girl.

She tried to swallow but suddenly her mouth was bone dry. She uncapped the water and took a long draw. "How old . . ."—she kept a tight rein on her thoughts—"would this girl be now?"

"The murders happened twenty-five years ago, so she would be thirty-four."

"Her name?" She barely got the question out.

"Danielle Bennett."

Danielle. Dani covered her mouth with her hand. The name was only a coincidence. The story didn't have anything to do with her.

A groan escaped her lips, and Lizi padded over and put her head on Dani's thigh. "Why are you telling me this?" She forced the words through her lips.

"The grandmother, Mae Richmond, is a friend of mine. A few days ago, she showed me a magazine with your photo in it. She'd brought it to the sheriff's office along with a photo of the nine-year-old girl and asked us—my boss, Alex Stone and me—for help. We submitted the photos to a facial recognition company in Chattanooga."

Dani's head felt like there was a spinning gyroscope inside it. "The results?" she whispered into the phone.

"There's a 95 percent chance you're my friend's granddaughter, Danielle Bennett."

8

Friday night, Mae removed the last piece of bisque from the kiln and reloaded it with glazed pieces. It would take twelve hours for the pieces to fire and another twelve for the kiln to cool. She checked her watch. Nine thirty. No wonder she was tired. So much for glazing the bisqueware tonight. She could push through, but her favorite glaze was running low, and she definitely needed to be fresh to accurately weigh and measure the ingredients for a new batch.

She'd intended to take the weekend off but got behind on her orders when she drove into Pearl Springs Wednesday afternoon. With the craft market coming up, Mae needed to work in the shop tomorrow.

With one last look around the studio, she locked the door and walked the familiar path to her house. Her cell phone rang just as she reached the back steps. Her heart fluttered when Mark's name came up, and she slid the answer button. "Did you talk to Dani Collins?"

He chuckled. "Hello to you too."

"Mark!"

"Okay. Yes, I talked with her, and she's actually in Cincinnati.

Not only is she willing to take a DNA test, but she's driving to Pearl Springs. She'll be here Sunday."

Driving. Here Sunday. Mae almost dropped her phone. *Thank you, Lord.* She took a big breath. "Did she say why she never came home to Pearl Springs?"

"From what I understand, she has no memory of living here and didn't know she had any relatives other than her uncle and his wife who raised her. And she'd never heard of Pearl Springs or Russell County, Tennessee, before tonight."

"Why doesn't she have any memory?"

"You'll have to ask her that. She was stunned by my call, so we discussed the most important things."

It was hard to believe that if Keith took Danielle, he'd kept information about her Tennessee family secret, but he had to be the uncle who raised her. She would get her answers when Danielle arrived. "Thank you so much for believing me and not letting this go," Mae said. "Do you know what time she'll get here?"

"No. Like I said, my call kind of overwhelmed her, and she wasn't certain when she'd leave. Something about a breakfast with a professor in the morning, and she may have other things she has to do. Who knows, she could be taking two days to drive from Cincinnati. At any rate, she's supposed to call me before she gets here Sunday, and I'll call you."

After she hung up, it hit Mae—she would see Danielle in two days. It was more than she could wrap her mind around. She went inside the house to her office and picked up the spiral notebook on her desk. Every year, she started a new one and wrote something every day, usually about the prayers God answered. She couldn't wait until morning to write about how her granddaughter would actually arrive in Pearl Springs in two days.

Tension eased from her shoulders as she poured her heart out on paper. Mae wasn't worried that the DNA test would come back with a different result than the facial recognition. Her heart told her this was her granddaughter.

Just as she finished her entry with a prayer of thanksgiving, her phone rang. Morgan's name showed up on the ID. She would probably be almost as excited as Mae.

She answered, and Morgan said, "I hope I'm not calling too late, but Ben and I were talking, and he agreed to bring me up on the ridge Sunday afternoon."

Mae's heart sank. She'd love to spend time with Morgan, but not that afternoon. "Could you come tomorrow?"

"Let me see." A minute later she came back on the line. "Ben said he has appointments to show houses all day. Sunday isn't good?" Morgan sounded disappointed.

"Danielle is coming home," Mae blurted.

"What? Oh, Aunt Mae, that's so exciting! Of course you don't want anyone there when you first see her! We'll do this another time."

"Thanks for understanding. I can't believe it's happening after all these years."

"So, she was the one in the magazine. How did you get in touch with her?"

"It's complicated, and I'm too excited to talk about it tonight."

"Okay, I understand. Well, I hope to see you soon so I can hear all about it."

Mae agreed.

"Try to get some sleep," Morgan said just before they hung up.

Sleep was all but impossible, and after fighting the bed most of the night, Mae gave it up at six and got up. Being awake and dressed wasn't much better. After checking on her kiln, she thought about mixing the glazes, but Mae was too excited to concentrate on measuring out the ingredients. All she wanted to do was pace the floor.

At eight, she grabbed her mesh bag and staff and set out for the old poplar trees on the side of the ridge. A walk would calm her down. Even better if she found a few morel mushrooms for dinner Sunday.

She passed by a thicket with a path tunneled into it. Too small to be used by deer but big enough for the coyotes she sometimes heard at night. She took a deep breath, inhaling the different scents—pines, a hint of sassafras from the heartleaf plant buried under the brown leaves of winter, the decaying leaves themselves . . . this was just what she needed to keep her mind off Danielle's arrival.

Mae had been so afraid her granddaughter might not want her life upended. She'd prayed hard that wouldn't be the case ever since Mark brought it up. She checked her phone, thinking Mark might've heard from Danielle. Mae had checked MapQuest on the distance, and it was only a six-hour drive, even with stops. Maybe Danielle had changed her mind about waiting until Sunday and was arriving today. *No service.*

She might as well enjoy her time in the woods. Sunlight filtered through the spring leaves as Mae used her staff to steady herself on the climb, glad the poplars where the mushrooms grew were just ahead. Lately, she had tired easier and sometimes got a headache. Probably her blood pressure like her cardiologist Dr. Wexler had said last week, even though she'd disagreed with him.

She should rest a bit before she looked for the morels. Mae settled against the trunk of a huge poplar and enjoyed the warmth of the sun on her face. Spring had broken out all around her with wild rhododendron in full bloom. Overhead, blooms filled the poplar trees. This was her safe place, and she would never sell her land.

Her great-nephew, Ben, would have to wait until she was dead and gone before he got his hands on her property. And if Dani Collins was Danielle, he wouldn't get it then.

To chase away those thoughts, she stood and used her staff

to rake away dead leaves from around the poplar. She quickly spied the coned shape of a morel growing in the rich soil and stooped over and twisted it off. Fifteen minutes later she had over a dozen of the prized mushrooms that brought over twenty dollars a pound in town. Not that these were going anywhere—she had plans to batter and fry these if Danielle agreed to join her for dinner tomorrow.

Her cell phone rang once, startling her, and she fished it out of her pocket. Her heart skipped when she saw Mark's name. But the call had failed. It was a wonder it rang at all. Maybe he'd heard from Dani Collins.

There were more mushrooms, but they would wait for another day. Going down the hillside was harder on her knees than climbing up, and that headache was back. When the house came in sight, she stopped to check her phone. Yes! Mark had left a message. She punched the play button.

"Where are you, Mae? Call me as soon as you get this."

She tried to decipher his tone . . . He didn't sound excited. More like worried. Mae winced. She'd forgotten to text him that she was going up on the ridge. He'd probably called to check on her and got worried when she didn't answer. Mae hated getting old and having to let people know where she was and what she was doing. Oh, she knew it was because Mark cared, but still . . .

Mae approached the steps to her back porch and froze. The door was a quarter of the way open. She hadn't left it that way.

She jumped when something crashed to the floor. Someone was in her house. Mae backed away from the steps. *Call 911.*

The floor creaked inside the house. She knew every sound in her house, and that creak came from the hallway to her office. Another creak indicated the person was walking to the front of her house. Anyone bold enough to break into her house in the middle of the day would have no problem taking care of her.

She needed to hide, but where? The thicket she'd seen earlier.

It was only a short walk up the hill. Mae dialed 911, but when the operator answered, she hesitated. If she said anything, the person in her house would hear her. Instead, she turned and used her staff to hurry along, veering off the path when she came to the thicket. Maybe she could make the call once she was hidden.

What if there were varmints in the brush? They wouldn't be as dangerous as the varmint in her house. With her head pounding like someone had taken a hammer to it, Mae pushed away thoughts of what might be in the maze of weeds and bushes, got down on all fours, and crawled inside. Why did her head feel like the top was going to blow off? Maybe if she rested.

9

It was Mark's weekend to work, and he'd intended to go by Mae's before he started his patrol, but a 7:00 a.m. call from dispatch about a missing five-year-old sent him and Gem on the other side of the county. It was now almost ten.

Kids. Mark couldn't keep from chuckling as he pointed his SUV toward Eagle Ridge. The boy claimed that he didn't know how he ended up in a closet sometime in the night, and since his parents said he was a sleepwalker, Mark believed that part. He wasn't so sure about the boy's claim that he'd slept so soundly, he'd missed his parents' frantic voices. Mark figured he'd heard them and assumed he was in trouble and stayed hidden.

He was halfway to Eagle Ridge when his cell rang. Alex.

"Where are you?"

Alex never wasted words, but the urgency in her voice sent a cold chill through him. He gave his location. "What's going on?"

"Mae placed a 911 call at 9:28 and then didn't respond to the dispatcher's questions. When Hayes got there at 9:40, the back door was open, but she was nowhere to be found."

Mae had made the call almost thirty minutes ago. "How did Hayes get there so fast?"

"He said he was in the area."

The young deputy was a go-getter, usually patrolling one end of the county to the other on his shift. "Did he check her pottery studio?"

"He did. She wasn't there either."

"Something's bound to be wrong, then. She wouldn't go off and leave her door open, not even if she was just going up on the ridge." He floored the gas pedal. "We'll be at her house in fifteen minutes or less."

Mark tried his neighbor's number as he raced toward home. Still no answer, and he left a voicemail. Mae was at least seventy-five and independent as all get-out, often hiking the ridge alone looking for her special herbs and mushrooms.

He didn't know how many times he'd asked her to let him know when she was going so he could make sure she'd gotten back safely. It would be all too easy for her to step in a hole and break an ankle. But did she listen? No.

Ten minutes later, Mark passed his house on Eagle Ridge. Mae's was a good three miles beyond it and up a steep incline. When he rolled into her drive, everything looked normal except for Hayes's vehicle.

Mark climbed out of his SUV and popped the door for Gem. She bounded out and looked toward the house as his fellow deputy approached. "Any sign of Mae?"

Hayes Smithfield shook his head. "Could she be off looking for some of those mushrooms she sells?"

Mark sighed. Hayes was new, fresh out of junior college, and was scheduled to attend the Tennessee Law Enforcement Training Academy in July. Training he sorely needed, but that was three months away. "She wouldn't have called 911 and then left."

"What if she's not far from the house, maybe unconscious?"

"Good point. Let's let Gem find out. We'll start with the house."

"But I checked—"

"Let's check again." With the German shepherd at his side,

Mark marched to the front porch and climbed the sturdy steps and entered the front door. He scanned the room. It looked normal enough . . . except something he couldn't put his finger on seemed different.

He walked through the house to the kitchen, and it came to him. Mark had never seen the photo of her daughter on the end of the mantel. It was always in the middle. He grabbed one of Mae's sweaters from a peg by the door and let Gem sniff it. "Search."

She ran sniffing through the house, and then out the front door and bounded away toward the ridge, running a zigzag pattern with her nose in the air. Mark jogged after her with Hayes trailing. Gem swung to the right and plunged through a path in the undergrowth.

Mark followed. Briars tore at his clothes as he got down on his hands and knees on a path made by a much smaller, four-legged animal. Suddenly Gem lay down and barked.

She'd found something. *Don't let it be Mae's body.* Mark crawled through the brush, stopping at the sight of a pair of Redwing boots laced tight against thin legs. Mae lay on her side, like maybe she'd been crawling and just keeled over. Gem barked again.

Mark moved around the boots and rewarded Gem with a head rub. "Good girl."

So far Mae hadn't moved or responded to the dog's barks. He felt for a pulse and released a tight breath when he found a weak but steady beat. But with the side of her mouth turned down like it was—

"Did you find her?" Hayes called from the outside of the brambles.

"Yes. Call for a medevac chopper—tell them she's had a stroke." Mark surveyed the area. "Make sure they have a stretcher we can get in here."

"Roger that."

He examined as much of Mae as he could without moving

her—he'd leave that to the paramedics. If it weren't for the 911 call, he might think she'd been mushroom hunting and suffered a stroke. Except this wasn't a place where the fungi grew.

"Mae, can you hear me?" Had her eyelids moved? Mark tried again. "Blink if you can hear me."

Her eyelids definitely twitched. She could hear him. He squeezed her left hand, and her fingers curled tightly around his. Mark didn't want to lose his independent and sometimes stubborn older friend. He leaned closer. "An ambulance is on the way, so just hold on."

He didn't mention a helicopter—that might freak her out if she was alert enough. Mark surveyed the area. With the flat ground, extraction should be fairly easy, notwithstanding the briars. While he waited, Mark sat back on his haunches and stilled, employing the training he'd learned as a sniper—stop what he was doing, look around, listen, and smell.

He'd already looked around, but now he scanned the area with a different intention. Nothing was trampled beyond where Mae lay, so that meant she hadn't been dragged here—so she must have crawled. But why?

Mark sniffed the air, and while his nose couldn't compare to Gem's, he had a keen sense of smell. This time he took a deep breath and cataloged the different aromas. Wet earth from last night's rain. Rotting leaves from the winter. And the green scent of new leaves. Not surprising since it was April.

He tried to re-create what could have happened. Perhaps Mae had been out—maybe walking the ridge since she liked to do that, and when she returned to her house, she noticed that someone had broken in. So she dialed 911.

But why not respond to the operator? Had the intruder heard her? Or had she feared being overheard and looked for a place to hide?

Mae knew every foot of the land surrounding her property

and would have seen this tunnel in the briars during her walks. If she feared for her life, it would be a natural place for her to take refuge. He turned toward where the deputy waited. "Hayes!"

"Yeah?"

"Did you come in with your siren blasting, like usual?"

"Sure did."

And alerted the possible intruder, who would have beat a hasty retreat. If that was the scenario, Hayes may have saved Mae's life.

His cell rang. Alex. He pressed the answer button, surprised he had service. "I found her, but I think she's had a stroke."

"I'm on my way. The hospital called—they've dispatched an air ambulance. Was there any sign of an intruder?"

"I'm not sure. We won't know anything until Mae can tell us what happened."

"Where are you?"

"With Mae. She crawled through a tunnel in the briars where it looks like she had the stroke."

"Stay with her. I'll see you in a few."

Mark pocketed his phone and looked back at Mae. Her lips moved and he leaned closer.

"D-D—"

"Don't try to talk." He rubbed her right hand with his thumb. "I'll ask you a question, and you just squeeze my hand once for yes, twice for no. Can you do that?"

She nodded, but Mark felt no pressure from her fingers. "Let's try that with your left hand," he said and switched hands.

Nothing wrong with Mae's strength in that hand. "Good. Did someone attack you?"

Two squeezes. "Okay. Did someone break into your house?" One squeeze. "Did you see who it was?" There was a hesitation, then two squeezes.

"Head hurts," she whispered. Her hand loosened in his, and she closed her eyes.

"I hear the chopper coming in," Hayes yelled.

Mark crawled out of the tunnel just as the chopper landed, and soon paramedics hiked toward him with a scoop stretcher.

"Pretty sure she's had a stroke," he told them. There was a short window of opportunity to bust up blood clots that caused strokes. "Do you have the clot-buster drug on the chopper?"

The lead medic shook his head. "No. Too dangerous for us to administer. Dr. Wexler will make that call if she needs it."

Ten minutes later, the paramedics brought Mae out of the thicket strapped on the yellow board. Mark didn't like how pale she was . . . and dazed. Mae was a friend, and he didn't want to lose her.

10

Alex's cell rang as she turned onto Eagle Ridge Road. Nathan. Her adrenaline spiked again as she thumbed the answer button. "You're waiting for me, aren't you?"

"It's after ten. Is there a problem?"

They'd been engaged since Christmas and had fallen into a comfortable pattern—coffee around ten most mornings at the Bean Factory Coffee Shop. "Afraid so." She explained about Mae. "Mark thinks she's had a stroke. He also thinks that because her door was open and she called 911, that someone may have broken in. I'm on my way to her house, and the CSI team will check it out as soon as they finish with a break-in at the drugstore."

Another call buzzed in, and she glanced at the screen. Ben Tennyson. "Can I call you back? I tried to call the mayor earlier since Mae is his aunt, and he's ringing me."

"No need. I'll meet you at her place," he said. "And be sure to count your fingers and toes when you finish with Ben."

"Nathan!" Alex shook her head. The two men were like nails on a blackboard to each other. She switched over to the mayor's call. "Thanks for returning my call, Ben."

"What's up, Sheriff?"

"I'm the chief deputy," she reminded him.

"Just until the next election."

"Which is eighteen months away." Alex would have her year residency in Russell County completed this October, but she hadn't made up her mind yet if she'd run for her grandfather's office next year. "Have you talked to your aunt this morning?"

"Mae? No. Is something wrong?"

She repeated what she'd told Nathan. "Do you know of anyone who would want to harm your aunt?"

"Not really. I'm sorry to say I haven't visited her as much as I should have since returning to Pearl Springs. But she doesn't live in town, and I just don't get up on Eagle Ridge that often. I'll leave now."

"No, just meet us at the hospital." Alex disconnected.

Ben and his sister, Morgan, had been born in Pearl Springs, but their family left when Alex was in grade school. Their leaving broke her heart, and while Nathan had always been her hero, Morgan Tennyson and Danielle Bennett had been her BFFs. Best Friends Forever. Only forever hadn't lasted. But what a sweet time it had been with sleepovers and hours of playing make-believe. Did kids even do that anymore?

Alex slowed to take the S curves on the mountain road. She hoped Mae was all right. Especially since it was probable they'd found Danielle.

She smiled, thinking how Mae had often been tasked with watching the three of them to make sure they didn't get into mischief. That had been like putting the fox in charge of the henhouse.

Her phone rang again. Ben once more. "Stone."

"Morgan told me Mae's granddaughter, Danielle, has been located. Should someone call and let her know what's going on? She may want to wait about coming."

"We're not 100 percent certain this Dani Collins is Danielle. Besides, I'm pretty sure she's already on her way from Cincinnati. I'll see you at the hospital."

Alex passed Mark's house, then the road Danielle had lived on as a child. She'd never visited the house where Danielle's parents had died, even though it was a cold case her grandfather still talked about. Maybe now that she was chief deputy, she would look into it. A few minutes later, she pulled into Mae's gravel drive and parked beside Mark's Expedition. A medevac helicopter waited in the clearing near the house.

She climbed out of the SUV as paramedics came down the hill with Mae on a stretcher with Gem trotting beside them. Alex reached the chopper before they did. While the paramedics prepared to load her, she took Mae's hand.

The older woman's eyes fluttered open briefly, and she mumbled something unintelligible. Alex sent Mark a questioning gaze, and he mouthed, "Definitely a stroke."

She leaned closer to the older woman and brushed a twig from her short hair. "It's me, Alex," she said softly. "We're going to get you to the hospital, where they can help you."

Mae gripped Alex's arm with her left hand. Her mouth worked, but no words formed.

"We need to get in the air," the lead paramedic said.

"Of course." Alex turned to Mae. "Ben and Morgan are waiting at the hospital in Pearl Springs for you, and I'll be there soon."

Mae's eyes blinked open. "Neva?"

Alex's heart sank. If Mae didn't know Neva was dead, the damage from the stroke might be bad. Alex moved out of the way as the medics loaded her in the chopper, then she and Mark stepped back as the rotors whipped the air around them and the chopper lifted off the ground. Once it was out of sight, she walked toward the house with Mark. "Where did Gem find her?"

"About a quarter of a mile from the house. She'd crawled into a bramble patch. She indicated someone was in her house, but she didn't see them."

Like Alex, Mae had a healthy respect for snakes, and blackberry and dewberry patches were known habitats for the area's copperheads and rattlesnakes. She must have been frightened to brave the thicket. They'd reached the porch where Hayes waited. "Did you notice any vehicles parked on the road when you got here?" she asked him. "Or maybe on a side road?"

The deputy shook his head. "If someone was here, they must've hiked in through the woods."

Tires crunched on the road, and her heart lifted as Nathan's pickup pulled in behind her SUV. While she waited for him to join them, Alex pulled on a pair of nitrile gloves.

His generous mouth curved into a smile when their gazes met. Six months ago, no one could have made her believe she'd leave behind the Chattanooga Police Department and her dream of being the first female chief of police to be Russell County's chief deputy. Or that she'd fall in love with her high school crush again.

"How's Mae?" Nathan asked when he reached them.

"Hard to tell," Alex said. "She was conscious, but she thought Neva was still alive."

He winced, then nodded at Mark. "I understand Gem found her."

"Pretty quickly too."

"She's well named."

The K-9 officer grinned his agreement as Nathan took a pair of the black gloves from his back pocket and pulled them on. Then he stepped up on the porch. "What are we looking for inside?"

"Evidence someone was here," Alex said. "When Mark checked to see if Mae could've fallen, he noticed a photo had been moved. Of course, Mae could've moved it herself." The screen door creaked as Alex pulled on it. "I don't know how many times I opened this very door when I was a kid. Even after Morgan moved and Danielle disappeared, I came with Gram to visit Mae."

"I've heard Judith speak often of Mae," Mark said. "Mostly of ways to get her to move to town."

She laughed. "I've heard it too. She and Gram have been friends ever since grade school."

Alex and Nathan stepped inside, and she scanned the room. Everything looked neat and tidy as always. If someone had searched this room, they went to a lot of trouble to put things back the way they were.

She ran her gaze over the books on the shelves and walked closer. Alex rubbed her chin and scanned each title. Mae's fiction titles were on one shelf, a collection of poetry books on another, and several Bibles were lined up beside a set of commentaries. If anyone searched through the books, they'd been careful to put them back in the right order.

"I don't see anything wrong here," Alex said. "I'm going to check out the rest of the house."

Nothing looked out of place in any of the other rooms. Could Mae have been wrong about someone being in her house? But why would anyone break into her house? It was the question she asked Nathan and Mark when she returned to the living room and they moved outside under the shade of an old oak tree to wait for the forensic team to arrive.

Mark kicked a rock. "I've been asking myself that very question. Mae told me once she didn't keep much cash here, that her customers usually paid with a check or credit card. A lot of her orders are online."

Nathan chuckled. "Mae has always amazed me the way she taught herself how to operate a computer."

Alex smiled. "She's never been afraid to tackle anything."

"Including a murder investigation," Mark added. "Have you seen her crime board?"

Alex nodded. "You think this could be related to her daughter's murder?"

"That was twenty-five years ago," Nathan said. "Why now?"

11

Dani was late for her breakfast meeting. She flicked a wayward curl out of her face and jabbed the elevator button again, trying to forget Lizi's sigh when Dani told the Puli to stay.

Why had she forgotten to set her alarm for her breakfast with Evelyn Engels, her former professor and mentor? A certain phone call, probably. And a couple of hours searching the internet for articles on dissociative amnesia.

"There's a 95 percent chance you're my friend's granddaughter, Danielle Bennett."

Mark Lassiter's words had looped through Dani's mind as she scoured the internet for articles on the memory disorder. If what he said was true, her parents had been murdered. Had Dani witnessed it? Was that the reason she couldn't remember them?

"Your past is best left alone." She punched the button again. Keith knew about her parents' murder, had known all along. Was he there? Her mouth went cotton-dry.

Had he killed her parents?

The elevator doors slid open, revealing the black marble interior. Her feet refused to move as her mind teetered on the edge of a black hole. One step and it would swallow her.

"Lady, you getting on?"

The man's voice snapped Dani back to reality. "Sorry." She waved him on. "I, ah, forgot something."

The silver doors closed, and she took a deep breath. *Get a grip.* Of course Keith hadn't killed her parents. If he had, he wouldn't have taken her to live with him. He would've killed her too . . . unless, maybe it was harder to kill a child.

She shook the thoughts off, hard-pressed to understand why she even entertained them. A message dinged on her phone. Evelyn. *On my way*, she texted. Once again she punched the down button.

Maybe it wasn't true. Maybe she wasn't this Danielle Bennett. She massaged the muscles in her neck. No. Deputy Mark Lassiter wouldn't have contacted her if he hadn't been convinced she was, and the DNA test would be a mere formality.

The elevator doors slid open again, and she focused on getting to the lobby and out the door, where the Navigator waited. Dani had already programmed the GPS app on her phone for the Cozy Sisters Restaurant. Maybe she could get there before Evelyn called looking for her.

Five minutes later her phone rang, and she answered without looking at the ID. "I'm almost there."

"You're almost home?"

Keith. An emotion she couldn't put a name to flashed over Dani. She had so many questions, but there wasn't enough time to get into them now. Pushing a smile into her voice, she said, "No. I thought you were Evelyn."

"Tell her I said hello and to come visit us sometime."

He almost sounded believable. "I will. Can I call you back later? I'm almost at the restaurant, and I'm running late."

"Late? That's not like you. Is anything wrong?"

Everything, maybe? "No, I overslept. I'll call you later."

"Wait—what time do you think you'll get in Monday? I thought I might pick up a couple of steaks to grill for dinner."

"Let me get back to you on that." She disconnected before he could throw another question at her.

Dani pulled into the restaurant and found a parking spot, but she didn't get out right away. Instead she took a couple of deep breaths. Unfortunately, they didn't do much for the knots twisting in her stomach at the thought of talking to Keith later. Or the decision she had to make. She'd told Mark Lassiter she would come to Pearl Springs tomorrow, but after thinking about it, doubt had crept in. Should she go home first and discuss what she'd learned with Keith?

But would he tell her the truth? He'd been lying for twenty-five years. Maybe not lying, but certainly withholding information. She didn't know what to do.

She did know she had to calm herself before she met Evelyn. If her friend suspected a problem, she wouldn't stop until she pried it out of Dani. She focused on her breathing, forcing her muscles to relax. Slowly the tension eased from her body.

With renewed energy, she entered the restaurant and scanned the room. The hostess glided toward her. It was the only word Dani could think of for the way the woman walked.

"Are you looking for Professor Engels?"

"Yes, but how did you know?"

"The red curls," she said with a smile.

Dani trailed the hostess, feeling like a hippie from the sixties in her peasant dress. Good thing she hadn't braided her hair. Immediately the image of the woman she'd sketched popped into her mind. Could that be her grandmother?

She couldn't think about that right now and slid across the bench opposite her friend. "Sorry I'm late."

Evelyn made a show of checking her watch. "Twenty minutes is somewhat early for you."

Dani held up her forefinger. "You're never going to let me forget that one time I got lost and was half an hour late for a meeting, are you?"

"And what fun would that be?"

They both laughed. Evelyn was already a master potter when Dani took her first class under her, and the woman had scared her to death. Confident, talented, and outspoken—all the things Dani was not. It'd taken the whole semester to learn that Evelyn Engels used her personality to push her students to be their best, and if one of them poured their passion into the clay, they had a friend for life.

"Keith said to tell you hello and for you to come visit sometime."

Evelyn lifted an eyebrow. "Really?"

She nodded.

"If I thought he meant it, I would." Her eyes softened. "I heard about Laura, and I'm so sorry. I always liked her."

A lump formed in Dani's throat. "Thank you. Fifty-five is much too young to die."

"Absolutely."

Neither of them spoke for a minute, then Dani asked what had been going on in Evelyn's life. While the older woman talked, Dani listened, absently picking at a hangnail on her thumb.

"And then a Martian landed and took me on board his ship."

"Good." Dani jerked her head up. "What?"

"Just checking to see if you were listening."

She smiled. "I guess I'm tired, and I have a long drive ahead of me."

"Understood." Evelyn sat forward. "I sat in on your morning workshop yesterday. You did very well."

"I didn't see you."

"That was on purpose. I seem to make you nervous when you're teaching."

That was an understatement. Dani looked up as the waitress set two glasses of water in front of them. "Thank you."

The waitress took out an order pad. "Do you know what you'd like?"

Dani hadn't even thought about food. Before she could ask the girl to come back in a few minutes, Evelyn said, "You can't go wrong with the loaded Southwestern omelet with sausage and a pancake on the side."

"That sounds good. And coffee," Dani added.

Once they were alone, Evelyn said, "The students loved your workshops."

"I'm glad." Dani's mind drifted back to her conversation with the Russell County deputy.

Evelyn said something else, and Dani nodded.

"So that's a yes?"

She blinked. Somehow she'd missed something. "What did I just say yes to?"

"Making this an annual event."

That was high praise, and a smile spread from inside her chest to her lips. "I'd love to do that. Need to check my calendar first, though."

"We'll work it out. Now, do you want to tell me what has you so distracted? And don't give me any of that 'it's a long drive' drivel."

She should've known she couldn't hide anything from her mentor. Trouble was, she'd never shared with Evelyn that she didn't remember her early life.

"Does it have anything to do with Keith?"

Her breath caught in her chest. "What makes you say that?"

Evelyn gave a noncommittal shrug. "He's very protective of you, to put it mildly."

"He raised me after my parents died, so I guess that makes him feel like he has the right to offer advice. I owe him a lot." Dani sat back as the server brought their coffee. Why did she feel the need to defend Keith?

"His protectiveness goes much further than advice," her friend said when the server left.

"What are you talking about?"

Evelyn emptied a packet of sugar in her cup and slowly stirred it. "We've never discussed this, mainly because you always change the subject when it concerns Keith."

"He's been very good to me, and I always felt disloyal talking about him behind his back." Presently, Dani wasn't certain she still felt that way.

"I'm sure he conditioned you to feel that way—controlling people have a way of manipulating others." Evelyn sipped her coffee and raised her gaze when she set the cup on the table. "Haven't you ever wondered why I only asked you that one time to apply for a teaching position at the University of Cincinnati?"

It had crossed her mind, but Keith had convinced Dani that at twenty-two, she was too young for that much responsibility, and that Evelyn offered the job out of kindness, hoping she'd say no.

"I thought you were just being nice." That's what Keith had said.

The older woman shook her head. "No. I thought it would do you a world of good to get out from under Keith's thumb. Plus, you were so talented for one so young. You would have been a great asset to the university."

Dani sipped her coffee and set the mug down. "Why didn't you ever bring it up again?"

"Because Keith called and told me in no uncertain terms to withdraw the offer. That you were under the care of a psychiatrist and too fragile to live on your own."

"What?" Dani blinked and sat back. She didn't know what to say. Why would Keith lie about that? What else had he lied about?

Their server picked that moment to bring their food. "Here

you go, ladies. Sorry it took so long." The server set each of their plates on the table. "I hope you enjoy."

Dani stared at the food, her stomach churning like a hurricane.

"I'm sorry." Evelyn reached across the table and squeezed Dani's hand. "I shouldn't have told you all that, especially before our food came."

Dani raised her gaze. Regret filled her friend's eyes. "It's all right. The omelet looks delicious." She would eat the food if it killed her rather than disappoint Evelyn. She picked up her fork and took a bite. And another. Neither of them spoke as she went through the motions and the food on her plate disappeared. If Evelyn had asked what it tasted like, Dani couldn't have told her.

When she finished, Dani laid the fork on her plate. "For the record, I haven't seen a psychiatrist since I was eleven. I don't understand why Keith told you that."

"For whatever reason, he feared you leaving his protection."

"You mean control."

"That, and I'd like to know why he feels he needs to protect you. Maybe it has to do with your parents' deaths. How did they die?"

Evelyn's words hit her like ice water, and she gasped.

Her friend's eyes widened, and she pressed her hand to her chest. "Did I say something wrong?"

Dani stared down at her clasped fingers, where her knuckles were turning white. She didn't remember locking her hands together. "It's just that . . . until last night, I didn't know. I didn't even know their names."

"I don't understand."

"I better give you a little background first." Dani unlocked her hands and took a deep breath, releasing tension as she exhaled. "The only memories I have of my early childhood are of my life in Montana. According to Keith, I was nine when we moved there. Before that—nothing. Since I don't remember my parents, I figured they must've died earlier."

"Dissociative amnesia disorder," Evelyn said softly. "Probably caused by your parents' deaths."

She nodded. "That's what my college counselor called it."

"Did you ever ask Keith what happened?"

"Yes. As well as that psychiatrist that I saw off and on until I was eleven."

"And . . . ?"

"I received a vague answer from the doctor, something about I was seeing her to regain my memory. Looking back now, I don't think Keith gave her any of the details.

"When I was fifteen, I asked Keith about my parents, and he lost it." Dani closed her eyes briefly, reliving his breakdown. "I'd never seen him that way. He told me that if it was something I needed to know, he would've already told me."

"And you, being the people pleaser you are, didn't argue. You let it drop."

"I am not a people pleaser." The words rang hollow even in Dani's ears. She picked at the hangnail on her thumb. "It's just, he was always so disappointed when I didn't agree with him. I couldn't take that."

"Why was that?"

"He was the only family I had."

"And Laura?"

"They didn't marry until I was eleven, and while I always knew she loved me and I loved her, she wasn't blood kin. Besides, Laura wouldn't have known about anything that happened before we moved to Montana unless he told her. And I'm sure he didn't."

"Earlier you referenced something about last night. What was that about?"

Dani's fingers shook as she reached for the glass of water. It was so difficult to share anything private. *And why is that?* Because that's the way Keith raised her. But Dani needed an outside opinion, someone to help her see things clearly.

"Last night I received a phone call from a deputy in Russell County, Tennessee . . ." She related everything Mark Lassiter had told her. "It seems I have a grandmother that Keith never mentioned. Maybe even other relatives."

"Wow," Evelyn said softly. "I can't even imagine how you're feeling."

"My emotions are all over the place."

"Understandable. You *are* going to this county in Tennessee, right? I mean, it couldn't be that far."

Dani dug into the cuticle again. "It's six hours. Last night I booked a room in Knoxville for tonight so I could get a good night's sleep since I barely slept at all last night. Then tomorrow, I'd planned to drive the hour and a half to Pearl Springs, but now I don't know . . ."

"What do you mean, you don't know?" Evelyn leaned toward her. "Dani, you have to find out what happened to your parents. And meet this grandmother."

"It's not that easy." She blinked back the tears that stung her eyes and then stared at the ceiling.

"Tell me what you're thinking."

She didn't know what she was thinking, or maybe she didn't want to admit it. "What if Keith killed my parents?"

Evelyn pressed her hand to her throat. "This has to be tearing you apart. Let's try and look at this logically."

"Okay." Dani pressed her lips together. "Why didn't he leave me with my grandmother? And you said yourself, he tries to control me. Maybe he's afraid I'll remember something he wants to make sure I don't tell anyone."

"Would he have taken you to a psychiatrist if that were the case?"

She hadn't thought about that.

"Perhaps he thought you were in danger, and he couldn't leave you with your grandmother." She raised her eyebrows. "You'll never know unless you discover the truth."

Truth. It's what she'd always wanted, wasn't it?

"Maybe I shouldn't encourage you to do this—if you did see the person responsible for your parents' deaths, it could be dangerous."

She hadn't considered that and mulled the possibility over in her mind. "It's been twenty-five years. The murderer could be dead. Besides, I don't think the deputy I talked with would encourage me to come if it were dangerous." Dani straightened her shoulders. "I'm going to do it. Thanks for helping me make up my mind."

Evelyn raised her eyebrows. "Tell me about this deputy. You got this dreamy look in your eyes when you mentioned him."

Dani jerked back. "I did not!"

"Methinks the lady doth protest too much."

Heat infused Dani's cheeks as she grabbed the water glass and took a long draw.

"Are you telling me you haven't looked him up?"

"He was nice."

Evelyn took out her phone and opened Facebook. "Did you say Russell County, Tennessee, Sheriff's Office? And his name is Mark?"

"I'm not having this conversation."

Evelyn was quiet as she scrolled through the app, then she stopped and brought the phone closer to her face. "Wow. No wonder you light up." She looked up and grinned. "Ask him if his father is available."

"Evelyn! I can't believe you said that. I don't even know the man. He could be married, for all I know." But she certainly hoped not. The reaction shocked her, and she took another drink of the water. "We were talking about my grandmother . . . who lives just outside of Pearl Springs."

Evelyn gave her a gentle smile. "I'm sorry. This has to be overwhelming for you."

"Yes. And tomorrow . . ." She barely got the words out before tears stung her eyelids and her chin quivered. She hadn't been kidding that her emotions were all over the place. Where was her stress ball when she needed it?

Dani shifted her gaze across the room to a family that appeared to be celebrating someone's birthday. A happy, whole family. Not the best distraction. She straightened her shoulders and turned and faced Evelyn. "Tomorrow I'll meet my grandmother and get answers to my questions."

12

Alex's CSI team had arrived, and she walked outside under the trees with Nathan to call the hospital and check on Mae. The operator put her through to the ER.

"Are you family?" the nurse asked.

"No, but if you check her records, you'll see that I'm authorized on her HIPAA form to get information." *Thank you, Gram, for insisting that Mae put me on the form the last time you took her to the hospital for blood work.*

"We have to be so careful to follow HIPAA rules," the nurse said.

"I understand. Can you tell me her condition?"

"Hold on a sec." Alex heard her keyboard click, then she came back on the line. "Stable and she's been sent for a CT scan."

"Thanks." After hanging up, she turned to Nathan and updated him.

"Why don't you go on to the hospital," Nathan said. "I'll help with the investigation."

She was tempted, then shook her head. "All I could do there is pace the floor. At least if I stay here, maybe I can find out who broke into her house."

"I figured you'd feel that way," he said, squeezing her shoulder. "You know she's in good hands."

She did. Time and again, the paramedics who came today had saved lives. "I hope they got her to the hospital in time to use that clot-busting drug."

"They should have. Mark said he overheard the chief paramedic discussing it with the doctor."

Pearl Springs Regional was a good hospital, but it was small. "Do you think they'll send her on to Chattanooga?"

Nathan shook his head. "Peter Wexler was the doctor the paramedic was talking to."

Wexler was Mae's cardiologist, and knowing he'd been pulled in already made Alex feel better. "Let's see if Taylor and Dylan have discovered anything."

As they walked toward the small frame house, Nathan wiped his brow and pulled off his jacket. "Getting warm."

"Summer's coming." She inhaled the clean scent from the rising sap in the pines scattered among the hardwood. "It's too pretty a day for something bad like this to happen."

"I agree." On the porch, Nathan slipped on a new pair of nitrile gloves, and she followed suit. Inside the living room, her CSI team dusted for fingerprints. Taylor Owens, the female half of the team, looked up.

"Find anything?" Alex asked.

"If anyone was here, they wore gloves," she replied. "And they knew how to avoid leaving any trace evidence behind."

"Is there anything obviously missing?" Nathan asked.

"No," replied Dylan, the other half of the team. "But her computer shows someone booted it up at 9:15. What time did the 911 call come in?"

"9:28. Hayes arrived in fifteen minutes."

Dylan nodded. "He probably scared off whoever it was."

"Could you tell if any files were opened on the computer at 9:15?" Alex asked.

"There weren't any opened, but I just did a quick scan. Her

internet history showed several searches for a Dani Collins, both last night and this morning."

No surprise there—Mae would have researched the name.

Taylor motioned toward the hall. "I saw a journal on Mae's desk, but I didn't open it."

Alex wouldn't read it either, not without Mae's permission. "I guess that wraps it up here. Appreciate you two dropping everything to come up here."

"I wish we could be more definite," Dylan said.

"We need Mae to tell us what, if anything, is missing." Alex rested her hand on her holster. "Where's Mark?"

"I think he and Gem are tracing the path Mae took this morning."

"I'll see if I can find him," Nathan said.

"I'll come with you." Alex glanced around the room. There was nothing more to do here for now. She nodded at Dylan and Taylor. "I'll see you two back in town."

As she and Nathan walked toward the ridge, a bark drew Alex's attention, and she turned toward it. The trees hadn't leafed out completely, and she could make out Mark and Gem approaching from the ridge above the house.

"Find anything useful?" she asked her K-9 handler when he reached them.

"Gem took me along the path Mae took this morning. Found where she'd cut a few mushrooms, but she left quite a few behind. That's not like her, so I figure something drew her to the house where she may have seen her door open and called 911. Then she retreated to where Gem found her."

"Was Mae able to tell you anything?" Nathan asked.

Mark shook his head. "I asked her to squeeze my hand instead of trying to answer me. There was no grip in her right hand, so we tried the left, and Mae indicated she wasn't attacked. I wonder if she can identify the intruder."

Nathan winced. “The stroke could completely wipe out the memory of what happened this morning.”

That was Alex’s fear. “I’m going to the hospital. Perhaps she can tell me what happened.”

Mark nodded. “Do you want me to assist Dylan and Taylor?”

“They’re done here.” She glanced back toward the house. “Hayes didn’t see a vehicle anywhere, so the intruder either walked up the road or came in from the ridge. See what you can find.”

The three of them walked to their vehicles in the drive. Nathan cleared his throat, and Alex looked up. He was watching Mark, and his eyes had that teasing look in them she’d seen before.

“I heard Mrs. Grayson fixed you up with her granddaughter last night.”

Red crept up Mark’s neck. “Aw, come on, Nathan. Don’t start.”

“Went that bad, huh?”

“Let’s say I won’t have to worry about Kinsey Grayson calling me.” He whistled for Gem, and the dog came running.

“What did you do to the poor girl?” Alex asked.

Mark tossed the tug toy for Gem to chase. “Nothing. Just told her I wasn’t husband material, and if that’s what she was looking for, she needed to keep looking. Don’t know why it made her so mad.”

She coughed to cover a laugh. No woman wanted to be told she was looking for a husband. Alex hadn’t known Mark before his tours in Afghanistan, but her grandfather had told her he wasn’t the same man when he came home. And the conversation was making him uncomfortable. “Matchmakers like Mrs. Grayson and a few others at church are one reason I stayed away from Pearl Springs so long,” Alex said.

“Might be the reason I leave,” he grumbled.

She laughed and opened her door before turning back to her K-9 deputy. “There used to be a path from here to her daughter’s house on Trinity Road, at least that’s what it was before the county renamed all the little roads with numbers. I don't know what it's called now, but if you check around Mae's house, you might still see signs of the path."

"It's still there," Mark said. "Mae told me she took the path to the house every week."

"If someone was here, that's where they could've parked."

"Could still be there," Nathan said. "So be careful."

Alex agreed. "Take Hayes with you."

13

Alex pulled out of the gravel drive and pointed her SUV toward town with Nathan right behind her. When she neared town, Alex called her grandmother and let her know about Mae, but her grandmother already had heard through the church. Then Alex dialed Marge, her secretary and sometimes-dispatcher. "Any word on Mae Richmond?"

"Pastor Rick called. The doctor was able to break up the clot, and she's been admitted to the intensive care unit."

Marge was also on the church prayer chain. "Did he say if they were keeping her in Pearl Springs?"

"Yes. Mae was adamant about staying at the local hospital, and I don't blame her. She'd just be another patient in Chattanooga, and here the doctors and nurses all know her . . . and the nurses love her." Marge chuckled. "The verdict is still out on some of the doctors."

Alex laughed with her. Not all physicians agreed with Mae's belief that her homeopathic herbal remedies were better than prescription drugs. "Yeah. Gram told me Mae and Dr. Wexler tangled at her appointment last month, but he'll do his best."

After she disconnected, Alex pulled into the hospital parking lot and looked for an empty space. Evidently there were a lot of sick people in the hospital. She found a spot in the back row, and Nathan pulled in beside her.

"When we leave here, you want to grab a bite to eat?" he asked as they walked to the entrance.

Her stomach growled. She had missed the snack from their usual ten o'clock coffee and was hungry. "Sounds good."

"Pete's Diner?"

"Sure." Since Pete's scare with his heart, he'd changed his cholesterol-laden menu to include a few healthy alternatives and even carried diet Dr Pepper.

Inside the hospital, they went straight to the ICU waiting room. Morgan and Ben Tennyson stood and waved them over when they entered the room. Two other men stood with them, one Alex didn't recognize, but from the resemblance to Ben, he had to be kin. The other was Rick Adkins, the pastor at Community Fellowship, where Mae attended. Alex, too, when she got to go.

"Sorry about Mae," she said and hugged Morgan.

"We need to get together," Morgan said.

"When this is over, we will." Alex turned to Ben, and he enveloped her in a hug. "I'm so glad you're here. I'm worried about Mae."

"I am too." Since Ben was ten years older, they hadn't been close as kids, not like Alex and Morgan. "How is she?"

"I'm not sure," Ben said. "I was only allowed in for a few minutes. Then Rick went in."

Alex turned to her pastor. "How do you think she was?"

"Confused," Rick said. "But she's a strong woman."

"That's the way she was at her house."

Ben nodded at the man standing beside him. "I don't know if you two have met my uncle, Craig Tennyson. He moved home from Chattanooga recently. I was with him when you called about Mae, and he brought me to the ER."

Alex dipped her head toward the older man. "We met when Ben first opened his office. In January, wasn't it?"

"It was," Craig said. "Good to see you again."

She hadn't been surprised to see Rick at the hospital, but she'd wondered why Craig was here since he wasn't a blood relative. Alex studied the man, seeing the way the mayor would probably look in twenty years, then she shifted her attention back to Ben. "Did she know you?"

"Yes, but she wasn't totally coherent." Ben frowned. "Kept mentioning Neva, and once she said something about Three Musketeers. I don't know what that was all about."

"That's what she used to call us," Morgan said.

And it told Alex that Mae was stuck in the past, thinking her daughter was still alive and the Three Musketeers—her nickname for Danielle, Morgan, and Alex—were still nine years old.

Alex turned to Craig. "How do you know Mae?"

"I was friends with her son-in-law, Bobby Bennett. Neva too. Met Mae a few times at their house. She's one feisty lady." He turned to Ben. "You think Morgan can take you back downtown? I have an appointment."

"I'll make sure he gets back," Morgan said.

As Craig walked away, Alex asked, "Did you get a chance to ask Mae what happened?"

"Not really. She mumbled something about Bobby and diamonds. They hadn't treated her yet—she hadn't even had the CT scan—and she wasn't making a lot of sense. I'm afraid the stroke has affected her mind." Ben glanced past her and held up his hand. "Dr. Wexler, we're over here," he called out.

Diamonds. There'd been something about diamonds in the Bennett case, but she'd have to look over the file to remember what. Alex followed Morgan and Ben to meet the doctor, who waited near the door.

"How is she?" Alex asked. Wexler looked from her to Ben, and she added, "I'm on the list of people you can share information with. Besides, this is an investigation."

The doctor shot Alex a puzzled look. "Investigation?"

"Someone may have broken into her house and could have possibly threatened her in some way."

The doctor nodded and looked at his tablet. "My notes," he said. "After the brain CT scan showed a left cerebral thrombosis, I administered a tissue plasminogen activator."

Alex understood some of what he'd said. "Are you saying she had a blood clot on the left side of her brain and you used a clot-buster drug?"

He smiled. "Precisely."

"But Mark Lassiter said her right side was affected," Alex said.

"Because the left side of the brain controls the right side of the body and vice versa. If the thrombolytic therapy had been unsuccessful, Mrs. Richmond would have suffered speech and memory loss, however I'm not expecting any of those problems."

Ben frowned. "But it is possible she won't remember what happened?"

Dr. Wexler nodded slowly. "I never say never, but when administered quickly enough, the tissue plasminogen activator works miracles."

Alex nodded. "One of the patrol officers I worked with in Chattanooga had a blood clot like Mae's, and he was back at work in two weeks and mowing his grass even before that."

"Exactly, and I don't foresee any problems for Mrs. Richmond. I expect her to be back to her normal self very quickly, even though she'll tire easily for a while. But she's healthy and strong."

"Can I talk to her?" Alex asked.

The doctor tensed.

"As a friend, not a deputy—I think a familiar face might comfort her."

He relaxed. "In that case, yes, but don't do or say anything that will cause anxiety."

Alex agreed, and while the doctor answered a couple of Morgan and Ben's questions, she joined Nathan, who was in a conversation with Rick.

"I thought you and your wife were going to Hawaii." Nathan cocked his head toward the older man.

"No, it was always Betsy and her sister—it's their annual trip. I'm going fly fishing in northern Wyoming." Rick glanced toward the ICU door and grimaced. "I feel bad leaving Mae like this, though, especially with her granddaughter arriving tomorrow."

"She'll be the first one to tell you to go," Nathan replied. Then he frowned. "How did you know about Danielle?"

"I think Morgan has told the whole town the story about Mae finding Danielle after seeing her photo in some pottery magazine," Rick said with a chuckle.

Alex and Nathan laughed along with him. Everyone including Alex liked the kind pastor at Community Fellowship. He was about the age her dad would've been had he lived and had given her fatherly advice on more than one occasion when she was a teen. "I hope you have a good trip."

"Thanks." He shook hands with Nathan and squeezed Alex's hand. "I need to get on the road, but I'll be praying for Mae. If she needs me, don't hesitate to call. I can always get a flight back."

"Thanks, and watch the speed limit," she called after him. Her deputies had mentioned he had a heavy foot on the accelerator.

Rick saluted and walked to the elevator.

"He's a good pastor," Nathan said after the elevator doors closed behind him. "Have you scheduled a time to see if he can officiate our wedding?"

"Not yet." Before he could ask why she hadn't—a question she really didn't have an answer for—Alex said, "I was going to, but like you, I thought he was going to Hawaii. I thought I'd wait until he returned."

Nathan studied her, then nodded as Dr. Wexler gestured to her. "I won't be long," Alex said and followed the doctor through the ICU doors to Mae's room. "How long do you think she'll be in the hospital?" she asked the doctor.

"The question is, how long will she agree to stay?" he replied with a chuckle. "She's already asking when she can leave. I hope you can convince her to stay until Monday, but if she continues to do well, I'll probably discharge her tomorrow. She is a very lucky woman."

"She would say blessed."

"Point taken." Dr. Wexler made a note on her chart. "I'll give you a few minutes alone with her."

She stopped outside the room and looked through the window. In the seven months since Alex had returned to Pearl Springs, she'd seen Mae at least a couple of times a month, and she still hadn't gotten used to seeing her with short hair. Alex missed the long braid she remembered from her childhood.

Alex took a deep breath and knocked as she pushed the door open. The older woman turned her head but didn't say anything.

"How do you feel?" Alex asked. Someone, probably a nurse's aide, had brushed the leaves and twigs from Mae's copper-colored hair that had almost no gray streaking it.

"Where did Morgan and Ben go?"

Alex was relieved that she didn't seem confused at all.

"They're in the waiting room. How do you feel?"

"Tired." She closed her eyes.

"Maybe I better go and let you sleep."

"No! I'm just resting my eyes. Dr. Wexler said I'd be fine, and that I can go home tomorrow."

"He actually said he hoped you would stay until Monday." Alex pulled a chair beside the bed and sat quietly for a few minutes.

Mae turned her head and stared blankly at her. Alex leaned closer to the bed. "Do you know who I am?"

"Of course," Mae said sharply. "I was just remembering. And when Danielle gets here, with Morgan home, the Three Musketeers will be back together."

"Do you know how we got that name?"

"Sure—'cause where you saw one, you saw the others, just like in the comic books you read. That's where you got that saying I got so sick of hearing—'One for all and all for one.'"

Alex ducked her head to hide a smile. They never would have discovered the comic books if Mae hadn't pulled them out that summer to keep the three girls entertained. "Do you remember where we got the comics?"

"Of course I do. Do you think I'm senile? Or are you like the nurses who keep coming in and asking if I know where I am or what year it is—testing me?"

"I'm testing you."

Mae stared at her, and her lips twitched. "Well, you can quit. I'm fine. But to answer your question, your grandmother hijacked me into babysitting you. Got me to come down off the mountain twice a week while she *supposedly* ran errands. I had to do something to keep you three from running me ragged."

Alex smiled. "And it was three because . . . ?"

"I brought Danielle with me," Mae said softly. "And back then my great-niece, Morgan, lived next door to you, and that's why I had all three of you."

Alex fell quiet and let memories wash over her. With a sigh, she said, "It was the best summer of my life."

The older woman's face softened. "Pretty good for me too. Your grandmother was a wise woman. Still is."

"Yes, she is."

"Then Morgan's dad moved them to Texas, and Neva . . ." Mae's chin quivered. Neither of them spoke as ghosts of times past settled between them. Then the older woman wiped her eyes with the back of her hand. "I miss her so much. And little Danielle . . ." She fixed her gaze on Alex. "She's coming tomorrow. You have to make them release me—I don't want her to see me like this."

14

Three hours into the trip, doubts assailed Dani as the miles rolled off on I-75. Was she crazy to strike out for Tennessee like this? According to the GPS on the Navigator, she would arrive in Knoxville in forty-eight minutes, and it was only two thirty. Way too early to stop for the night. She might as well drive on to Pearl Springs.

"Maybe I should've talked to that deputy again," she muttered. "What do you think, Lizi?"

The Puli barked from her crate. If the dog ever answered with more than a bark . . . Dani laughed. It was bad enough that she talked to the dog like she was a person. She sat up straighter as a sign for the Tennessee Welcome Center came into view. "You want to stop and stretch your legs, girl?"

Dani certainly did. She slowed and flipped her right blinker on. Maybe she'd move Lizi to the other side of the seat so she could see her. Might not be as lonesome. Of course, she could answer Keith's calls—three so far.

Keith's ringtone sounded in her purse as she pulled into the Welcome Center. She didn't want to talk to him and deal with his anger when he learned where she was going—she wouldn't lie if he asked her point-blank. Maybe when she got to Pearl Springs. It'd be too late to do anything about it then.

Dani parked and hooked the retractable leash to Lizi's collar. There were several dogs and their owners in the pet exercise area, and she kept Lizi on a short leash. Normally she didn't mind the inevitable questions Lizi's corded coat always brought, but after the third time, she was ready to return to the SUV. She tugged on Lizi's leash. "Come," Dani said, and Lizi quickly heeled.

After she visited the restroom, she grabbed a bottle of water to share with Lizi. Dani glanced at her new phone before fastening her seat belt. Keith had called again and left a voicemail.

He was probably worried. She pressed the button to listen to the message. Scratch that, he was definitely worried, and she didn't want that, but neither did she want to get in a discussion with him about a grandmother he'd never told her about until she had irrefutable evidence, like a DNA test. She pressed call back. *Just keep it light.*

He answered on the first ring. "Why does your phone indicate you're in Kentucky?"

Instantly, she realized Keith had installed a GPS app on her phone. Heat started in her chest and spread to her face. She'd never been this furious in her life. Dani opened her mouth and closed it and then counted to ten. When that didn't work, she counted to twenty. Finally, she found her voice.

"Actually, we're in Tennessee, headed to Knoxville," she snapped. The state line was a few miles north of the rest area. Dani transferred the call to hands-free and pulled out of the rest area onto I-75.

"So you and Evelyn decided to take a girls' trip."

"Something like that." She'd meant her and Lizi when she said *we*, but she didn't correct him . . . It wasn't really lying, was it? Besides, Evelyn *had* encouraged her to go to Tennessee.

"Why didn't you mention it before you left?"

"It was a spur-of-the-moment thing." And that was the truth. "You're breaking up a little bit. Are you feeling okay?"

"Sure. Lonesome, though. When are you coming home?"

Dani hadn't thought that far ahead. "Probably the middle of the week."

That should give her time to talk to the woman who claimed she was her grandmother and sort things out. Once she talked to this Mae Richmond, Dani would have enough information to confront Keith.

"I guess—can survive—that—ong." Reception was really bad. "What—re—doing—Knoxville?"

"We have a bad connection. I'll call you back." When he didn't answer, she checked the screen. The call had dropped. Good. She'd never outright lied to him before, and she didn't want to start now. She put her phone back in her purse.

The only time she'd ever thought about lying to him was when she applied for a scholarship to Montana State University. He'd always discouraged her from on-campus classes, convincing her that the associate's degree that she'd gotten online was all she needed. She'd been eighteen and afraid to stretch her wings.

But at twenty, her advisor encouraged her to attend in-person classes, even helped her find a scholarship. It had been at the university that she met Evelyn and discovered her love of clay and that she had talent. And not just with the wheel but with sculpture and painting as well. That first semester, Evelyn had been amazed at how Dani could transform a small block of clay into a sheep or a horse or a shepherd without any formal training.

When Evelyn had asked how she did it, Dani had shrugged. She hadn't known how to tell Evelyn that her fingers seemed to work on their own, removing clay until the animal in her mind's eye was left. At least now, thanks to Evelyn, she knew how to not only explain her techniques but teach them.

It was the same way with her art. In the beginning, her fingers had simply drawn what she saw, but now she taught that as well. If she'd listened to Keith, she would still be dependent on him. Her cheeks heated up at how easily he'd manipulated her. Why hadn't she been able to see what he was doing? The answer flashed like the neon sign on the side of the road advertising subs two miles ahead—because Keith had groomed her to follow his orders since she was nine years old.

15

When Dani reached Knoxville, she decided to drive on to Pearl Springs. Then she took a wrong turn that added more time to her drive. Something she wouldn't tell Keith.

But at least she'd put a stop to him tracking her—she'd turned off her phone. He was forever telling her she'd get lost in a silo. Probably one reason he worried about her.

"Won't be much longer," she said to Lizi. The gas gauge made a soft dinging, and she glanced down. She should've stopped for fuel before she got off the interstate.

Up ahead she spied a small grocery store with fuel pumps. After she pulled off the road, she stared in awe as the sun dropped behind a bank of clouds, creating a beautiful pink and red backdrop with golden rays shooting outward. Her gaze landed on the hills around her. The mountains were so different here than the Rockies and the Badlands back in Montana. In Tennessee, everything was green. She could get used to this.

She quickly fueled up and grabbed a sandwich from their deli before she let Lizi out for exercise. Once they were on the road again, she checked the GPS on the dashboard. Looked like they would get to the hotel in Pearl Springs a little before seven. Once she checked in, she would find Mark Lassiter's number and let him know she was in town.

Dani quickly nixed that idea. It was Saturday night, and the man probably had a hot date. In the morning would be soon enough to call him.

A little before seven she pulled into a parking space beside the entrance to the hotel. It appeared to be fairly new, and right across from a small hospital. Once she checked in and hauled her suitcase to her room, Dani's stomach growled. The sandwich had not lasted. Maybe the nice clerk who checked her in could recommend a place to eat. She returned to the lobby.

He gave her directions to a steak house, a diner, and a barbecue place along with where to find the fast-food chains. She settled on a salad at Wendy's. Once her order was up, she found a table in the corner and pulled her phone from her purse to check for missed calls and messages, but it wouldn't boot up. *Dead?* Dani tried to remember the last time she'd charged it and winced. Must've been yesterday afternoon.

On the bright side, if her phone was dead, Keith couldn't track or call her. She checked her watch. Almost nine. It didn't get completely dark in Montana until tenish. Couldn't be that much different in Pearl Springs. Why not scope out where Mae lived? She'd looked up Mae Richmond and had her address.

According to her research, the address was located only about 15 miles from Pearl Springs. What was 15 miles when she'd already driven 350 today? She could drive up on the mountain, find the house, and be back by dark. Dani wouldn't attempt to contact her. No way would she just drop in without a warning even though she was certain Mae—she still didn't think of her as her grandmother—was anxious to meet her.

Half an hour later, Dani groaned. For the second time since leaving Cincinnati, she was lost and was beginning to agree with her uncle that she had no sense of direction at all. She'd made a wrong turn on one of the little side roads, and by the time she made it back to the main road, the Navigator's GPS had told her it was "recalculating" at least ten times.

She stared at the dashboard. The GPS map indicated Mae's house was within three hundred feet. Dani glanced around at the deepening shadows. Night had come faster than she'd anticipated, and it would soon be totally dark. She should head back to the hotel. But three hundred feet? It wouldn't take five minutes to see if the GPS was lying. Again.

She turned left and inched up the mountain road in the dusky light. These mountains were not like Montana's where she could see forever. Here she couldn't see around the bend. And the occasional sign reminding motorists of falling rocks had been a little bit scary.

Her car lights automatically came on and swept across a drive. Could that be it? At the last second, she whipped into the drive just as an outside light illuminated a small plank house in the dusky twilight. A house she'd seen before—she just couldn't remember where or when.

"I believe this is it," Dani replied softly. A sense of home settled in her heart. Except . . . the house was dark. Either no one was home or it was the wrong house and no one lived here.

She'd plugged her phone in earlier, and once she found Mark's number, Dani tapped on it. Call failed. Oh, great. No cell reception. She sighed and rested her head on the steering wheel. Lizi whined from the backseat. Might as well get out and at least let the Puli get rid of some of her energy.

When she returned to the hotel, she would do what she should have done in the first place—locate Mark Lassiter and let him handle the details.

If only Dani could remember her grandmother, but when she tried, all she got was the face she'd drawn the other day. Other than that, she drew a blank. Just like when she tried to remember her parents. Maybe when she came face-to-face with Mae, everything would become clear.

Dani climbed out of the Navigator and opened the back passenger door. Lizi bounded from the SUV and circled it until something in the leaves moved. A squirrel. Dani couldn't keep from laughing as the chase was on. Why hadn't she hooked Lizi's leash to her collar?

"Come," she called softly so as not to disturb anyone in the house.

The Puli hesitated, and the squirrel made a run for a tree near the house. Lizi dashed after it. With a sigh, Dani grabbed the leash and unplugged her phone from the charger. She stuck it in her back pocket in case she ever got cell service, and hurried up the hill after her dog.

When she reached the tree, she snapped the leash on Lizi. "Maybe another time," she said, still keeping her voice soft, even though no one appeared to be home.

Just as she reached for a post on the porch to steady herself, a crash came from an outside building a hundred yards away, and she whirled toward it as a growl came from Lizi's throat. Before she could hide, someone eased from the building.

The intruder stopped when he saw her. She strained to see his face, but in the dim light and distance, his large frame was only a silhouette.

He pulled something from his waist band. Not something. A gun.

The report sent her diving to the ground, taking Lizi with her as a bullet buried into the post. "No," she whispered when Lizi growled again. "Stay!"

The Puli remained tense but didn't move. Dani fished her phone from her back pocket and punched in 911. Failed call.

She scanned the area. Another bullet kicked up dirt behind

them. Dani looked for a better place to hide. A line of trees and brush was about fifteen feet away from the corner of the house.

If they could make it to the back of the house, it would block the shooter's view. Then they could make a run for the trees and disappear into the mountain. But what if they got lost?

Lost was better than dead.

Dani crouched and duck-walked to the back of the house with Lizi by her side. No more shots came. The shooter was probably on the move too.

Dani dashed to the tree line with Lizi on her heels, then they slipped farther into the woods. A hundred yards into the trees, and darkness closed around them. She cocked her ear, listening for their assailant. A twig snapped behind her. Before she could move, a hand covered her mouth.

"I'm not going to hurt you, but be quiet."

Her first impulse was to fight, but something about the way he spoke made her hesitate. She nodded, and his grip loosened.

"I'm a deputy for the Russell County Sheriff's Office. Stay here."

While she'd only heard him speak once, she was certain it was Mark. He didn't have to tell her twice. But once he was gone, his absence left her shaking. Lizi pressed against her leg. She knelt beside the dog. "It's going to be okay."

But would it? Why was someone shooting at her? It had to be because the person had been breaking into her grandmother's building and she'd seen him, and not because of her past. Still, her uncle's voice echoed in her head. "*Your past is best left alone.*"

Resistance stirred in her heart. Keith wasn't always right. If only she could remember what happened the night her parents died. Buried somewhere in the deep recesses of her mind was another life.

Nine years of experiences and people she'd known and loved. And trusted. Had the killer been one of those people? Was that why someone was shooting at her tonight? Couldn't be. No one knew she was here. So there had to be another explanation.

A stone settled in her stomach. She was flying blind . . . but at least she could trust Mark Lassiter—he was too young to have been involved in the murders.

Where was he anyway?

16

The light from the rising moon cast eerie shadows as Mark crept through the woods to where he'd seen the muzzle flash.

Nothing moved, and even the tree frogs had fallen silent. He wished he'd brought Gem now, but he hadn't wanted to take a chance that whoever was shooting might hit the dog.

Questions bombarded Mark. Why was someone shooting at this woman anyway? Who was she? And what was she doing at Mae's house?

Something rustled behind him, and he jerked around. A hard blow to his head sent him reeling. Moonlight glinted off steel. *Gun!* Mark stumbled back, fighting to stay conscious.

He blinked. A growling dark mop lunged at the assailant and latched on to his arm. The assailant screamed.

"Lizi! Release!"

The dog released its hold. The attacker turned toward the direction of the voice and shifted his gun to his left hand.

The woman hadn't stayed put. Mark couldn't let the man hurt her, and he lifted his gun. The assailant pivoted and ran toward the road. Mark sank to his knees, still fighting the darkness.

Gentle hands grabbed him. "You're hurt!"

"No . . . I'm . . . fine." If someone would only get rid of the jackhammer pounding in his head. "Give me a minute."

The woman straightened. "I hear a car engine. Do you think he's leaving?"

Mark hoped so since he was in no condition to fight the assailant off again. "Probably. Figure he got a good look at me—maybe he recognized me and backed off."

"Can I call someone?"

Backup. He needed to call Alex. "Call my boss. Tell her we're at Mae Richmond's."

"I'll need your phone—mine doesn't work here for some reason."

The pain in his head was easing slightly. "I think I can do it."

Mark pulled his phone off his belt and stared at the blurry screen—make that two screens. He blinked, but his eyes wouldn't focus. Wincing, he handed the phone to the woman. "I'm seeing double—look for Alex Stone. She's the chief deputy."

He cradled his head in his hands while she made the call.

"Um, this is Dani Collins . . . I'm at Mae Richmond's house with one of your deputies. He's been injured."

"Put it on speaker," Mark said, and she punched the screen.

"Do I need to send an ambulance?" Alex was asking.

"No," he said.

"Mark? Is that you? What happened?"

"A car went past my place, and I thought Mae's intruder might be returning so I came to check it out. Then there were shots, and I ran into the butt of a gun."

"Do you have a concussion?"

"No. Just a bad head—"

"He may have a concussion—he's seeing double," Dani said, overriding him.

"Is she right?" his boss asked.

"I just need a minute or two." *Or thirty.* "Send Hayes or one of the other deputies to investigate. Someone was shooting at this lady."

"Stay put. I'll be there in twenty. And keep her there." The line went dead.

"Evidently she hung up. And why does she want you to keep me here?"

"Can we wait until Alex gets here? My head is killing me." Maybe he did have a concussion. He certainly wasn't thinking clearly. "And do you think you can help me get to Mae's porch?"

"You think it's safe to leave the woods?"

"Yeah. If he was going to kill us, he could've done it earlier. Besides, you said you heard a car start up."

"If you think it's safe." She turned. "Lizi, come."

He watched as the dog went to her side. At least he guessed it was a dog—in the moonlight, it still looked more like a mop than an animal.

"Can you stand?"

"We'll see." Mark grabbed a nearby sapling and used it to pull himself up. Once he was upright, he waited for his world to stop spinning.

"You okay?" she asked.

For the first time he took a good look at the woman and blinked. Then he blinked again. Jolie? No. He'd heard her say her name—Dani Collins. Besides, Jolie was dead. And it'd been his fault she was dead. Mark focused. Dani had asked if he was okay . . . "Give me a minute."

"You said that already. When you're ready, put your arm around my shoulder. I can't hold you up, but I can guide you and maybe keep you from falling."

He took a deep breath and nodded. The first few steps were wobbly, and sweat popped out on his face. As they walked, he found himself relying more and more on her.

"Can we get inside the house?" she asked as they neared the front porch.

"Nobody's here."

"Why is the porch light on if no one's home?"

"I talked Mae into getting it. It's on a timer." He stumbled to the steps. "Let me sit here a minute. Maybe my head will clear."

Mark sat on the porch and leaned against the post. Once everything stopped spinning, he said, "So you're Dani?"

"I am. And you must be Mark."

"Yep. Thanks for helping me." Now that he could see her better, she didn't look quite so much like Jolie. Both had golden red hair and blue eyes, but Jolie had looked like the soldier she'd been—solid but feminine as well. Dani was more delicate and artsy in the peasant dress she wore, which made sense since she was a potter and artist.

He had so many questions to ask, but first he thanked her again for helping him. "And I'm sorry we had to meet this way, but what are you doing here? You weren't supposed to arrive until tomorrow."

"When I got to Knoxville, it was so early and I didn't have anything to do and it didn't make sense to just hang out there." She stopped and took a breath.

"A woman always has the right to change her mind, but why didn't you let me know?"

"I almost did, but . . . it's Saturday night. I figured you'd be busy."

He had to strain to hear her soft voice. "Nope, wasn't busy. You should've called."

"Actually, I couldn't. My phone had died since I forgot to charge it." She sighed. "I'm really not a ditzy redhead."

"Never said you were." He might've come close to thinking it. "I'm sure there's a reason for you forgetting to charge your phone and it dying."

"Now you're making fun of me."

"No! Not at all." *Way to go, Lassiter.* "Do you know why the man was shooting at you?"

"I think I surprised him. He was coming out of a building behind the house."

"Mae's pottery shop."

Her eyes widened. "So that's why she had a *Pottery Illustrated* magazine."

Mark frowned. "What?"

"When we talked Friday night, you said Mae had seen my photo in a magazine, and *Pottery Illustrated* is the only one my photo's been in, and I've wondered why she would have that magazine."

He wondered if she always talked in run-on sentences, then he shook his head to clear it and winced. Wrong move. "Did you get a good look at the intruder?"

"I caught a glimpse of his outline just before he started firing and again before he ran. He was wearing a ski mask, so I didn't see his face." She glanced toward Mae's front door. "Do you have a key to the house?" she asked.

"What?" He was having trouble following her . . . maybe he did have a concussion.

"I thought if you had a key, I could maybe find a washcloth and wet it for your head."

"That's okay. Knowing Alex, she's sending an ambulance," he said. "Did I thank you for helping me?"

"You did."

"Well, thanks again." He frowned as the dog leaned against Dani. "Is that really a dog?"

"She is, and a pretty good guard dog too—she probably saved your life."

Ouch. He hadn't meant to insult the dog. "You're right, but I've never seen a dog that looks like a . . . a—"

"Mop?" Amusement had replaced the annoyance in her voice. "She's a Puli."

Gem! He sucked in a quick breath.

"Is something wrong?"

"I have a K-9 dog in my SUV."

She looked toward the road. "Where?"

"About half a mile down the road." He calculated how long he'd been gone and relaxed. It couldn't have been more than thirty minutes, and she had plenty of water and the temperature was okay. His ears picked up the wail of a siren in the distance. Alex must have floored it to get here this fast. "My boss'll be here soon and can let Gem out. She should be fine until then."

"This Alex . . ."

Dani didn't finish whatever she was going to say as flashing blue lights rounded the curve, and a police SUV pulled into the drive beside the Lincoln Navigator that apparently belonged to Dani. "That should be her now," he said.

17

Dani hugged her arms to her waist as a woman dressed in jeans and a pullover walked toward them. The logo on the SUV indicated she was the sheriff, or at least driving the sheriff's vehicle. But she didn't look any older than Dani, and in her book, that was too young to be a sheriff.

Maybe the blond hair pulled up in a ponytail made her look younger than she was. What had Mark Lassiter said her name was? Alex. The name rang a bell. And something about the way she walked was familiar.

Alex spoke to Mark first. "How's your head?"

"Clearing up. I hope you didn't have an ambulance dispatched."

"I thought I'd wait and see how you were first. Hayes should be here momentarily. He'll take you by the hospital to get checked out."

"I can drive myself—I'll need my SUV when I get out of the ER to get back home to Gem."

Alex crossed her arms. "He's bringing Jenna Hart to drive your vehicle back. And Gem will be fine. If you're not discharged in the morning, I'll send someone to feed her."

It looked to Dani like Mark was about to disagree with his boss, but she cut him off. "This isn't a request, it's an order." Then she turned to Dani. "Thank you for helping Mark, and I'm so glad you decided to come. Mae is really looking forward to seeing you."

Why did the chief deputy talk like she knew Dani? She'd never seen her before. The question must've shown on Dani's face.

"You don't remember me—Alexis Stone. We were best friends before . . . well, before."

Alexis. Dani stared at her.

For a second, the memory of a blond-haired girl with braids darted through Dani's mind. Then it was gone. "I'm sorry . . . I don't remember anything about my life here."

"Well, that explains a lot," Alex said. An awkward silence settled between them. "You look a lot like—"

"It was—"

They'd tried to break the silence at the same time. "You go first," Alex said.

"I was going to say it was actually Lizi who helped Mark when she attacked the assailant."

"Lizi?" she said, looking around.

"My dog." Dani pointed to the Puli. She couldn't keep from grinning as Alex's eyes widened.

"What . . . kind is it?"

"It's a Puli," Mark said.

"A Hungarian herding dog as well as a guard dog," Dani added.

"Well, thank you, Lizi." Alex looked back at Dani. "I was going to say you look a lot like the photos of Mae's daughter."

Dani glanced at the front door again. "Do you think there are any photos of . . ."—she couldn't bring herself to say "my mother"—"Mae's daughter inside the house?"

Alex and Mark exchanged looks. "I don't think Mae would mind if we showed you Neva's picture, but I didn't bring the key to her house," he said. "Can you wait until tomorrow?"

"Sure." She'd waited twenty-five years. What was one more day? Dani tilted her head. "Where is she, anyway?"

Again, they exchanged glances. "She's in the hospital," Alex said.

Hospital? "Is she all right?"

"She had a stroke this morning," Mark said.

Alex added, "But we got her to the hospital in time for the doctor to give her the clot-buster drug."

Surely Dani hadn't found her grandmother only to lose her. "You're sure she's okay?"

"I had just left her room when you called," Alex said. "She was fine then, and as soon as we get back to Pearl Springs, you can see for yourself."

Dani's shoulders relaxed. "You think she'll be up to—wait!" She turned to Mark. "Earlier, you said something about an intruder returning. Did someone hurt her?"

"We don't think so. And we don't even know for sure that someone broke into her house."

"What do you mean?"

"So far, Mae can't remember much about this morning. She doesn't even remember calling 911." Mark explained how he and Gem had found Mae. Then he winced. "Someone needs to let Gem out of her carrier."

"And you need to see a doctor," Alex said as a siren sounded in the distance. "That should be Hayes now."

Soon a police cruiser turned into the drive, and they waited as two deputies climbed out. While they jogged toward them, Alex turned to Dani. "We need to sit down and go over this in more detail, but that can wait until we get back to Pearl Springs."

"Good. Do you think I could visit Mae tonight? Or would it be better to wait until tomorrow?"

"They may let you in—we'll have to check." Alex glanced toward the woods. "Before we leave, would you show me approximately where the assailant attacked him?"

"What's wrong with me showing you?" Mark asked.

"You're going to get checked out—now," she said as they reached them.

Hayes took one look at Mark and said, "You don't look too good."

"I'm fine." He rose from his sitting position on the porch, but when he staggered, defeat slumped his shoulders.

"Okay." He sank back down on the porch. "Gem's in my SUV that's parked down the hill. We need to stop and get her so we can drop her off at my house—they won't let her come in with me at the hospital."

"I'll take care of Gem," Jenna said. "And your vehicle."

Alex introduced the two deputies to Dani, then she turned to Mark. "I'll check on you at the hospital as soon as we finish here."

A few minutes later, Hayes helped Mark to the police cruiser.

"Men," Alex said, pocketing a roll of crime scene tape she'd gotten out of her SUV. "You'd think I'd asked him to take a few days off."

"I think his pride is wounded more than anything else," Dani said.

"You're probably right. Are you up to showing me where he was attacked?"

"Sure. Come, Lizi." The dog came immediately to Dani's side, and she led Alex to the area where the attack had taken place. "The man was standing over here when Lizi attacked him."

Alex tied a yellow tape to a branch. "Did Lizi bite him?"

"I don't know. Possibly. I called her off because at the time I didn't know if she'd gotten hold of Mark or the assailant."

"Can you describe him?"

"Like I told Mark, I didn't see much. He wore a ski mask—the kind that covers the whole face except for the eyes, nose, and mouth—but I can sketch what I saw." When Alex gave her a puzzled look, Dani said, "I'm an artist, among other things."

"I'd appreciate that." Then the deputy turned in a slow circle, shining the light around the area. She tied the yellow tape to several of the trees before she pocketed her phone. "I guess that's all we can do tonight. I'll come back in the morning with my crime scene investigators, but thanks for showing me."

"No problem." She followed Alex back to the car with Lizi on her heels. After she crated the dog, Dani turned to Alex. "Can we follow you out? I don't want to get lost again."

"Sure." Alex tilted her head. "I know Mark told you the facial recognition company suggested a DNA test. I have one in the SUV, if you want to do that."

Dani thought a minute, then nodded. "It would answer the question once and for all."

"I think it's a good idea. Mainly because I just read an article about these two boys who look like twins and even have the same birthday, but they'd never met. They wondered if their parents had given one of them up for adoption and just wouldn't admit it. DNA proved they were not even remotely connected."

"That seals the deal—I don't want there to be any question in my mind or anyone else's."

"Won't take a minute." Alex opened the passenger door to her SUV and took a small box from the glove compartment. After rubbing the inside of Dani's cheek, Alex secured the cotton swab in a paper container. "I'll get this off tomorrow."

"How long . . ."

"Usually a week."

Dani sighed. She'd hoped it would be sooner.

"I know I said something about you going to the hospital to see Mae, but you look beat, and it's late. Why don't you plan on waiting until morning?"

No doubt about it—Dani *was* tired, and Mae wasn't expecting her until tomorrow anyway. "That's probably for the best."

"Your grandmother loves you very much. It's going to do her a world of good to see you. Maybe more than any medicine."

The thought that someone she didn't know loved her soothed an ache in Dani's heart.

"Do you plan on staying around town for very long?"

Dani thought about her conversation with Evelyn, when Evelyn warned her that coming back to Pearl Springs could be dangerous. What if Mae was hurt because of her? "After tonight, I don't know. I don't want to put Mae in jeopardy."

Alex was quiet a minute. "I don't know that she would be safer if you leave."

"What do you mean?"

"While we don't know for certain anyone broke into her house, Mae did call 911. She would not have done that without a good reason." Alex rested her hand on her gun. "Mark and I—all my deputies—will be protecting Mae, and if you stay, we can protect you as well."

She stared at Alex. Her confidence reminded Dani of something that had come to her off and on over the years . . . "You were the girl!"

"What?"

"Over the years, sometimes I have this memory—a boy is teasing me, and a blond-haired girl punches him in the nose."

Alex's eyes widened. "Tyler Spence!"

Instantly, Dani put the name with the boy. "You're right."

"Oh, wow. I hadn't thought of that in years." She grinned. "You won't believe what he's doing now, but I'll give you a hint—he followed in his daddy's footsteps."

"His daddy was our principal—" She gasped. "Another memory!"

Alex grinned. "You have to stay now—we were best friends before you disappeared, and I can help you get your memory back."

That sounded good, but at what cost? Dani was already responsible for Mark Lassiter being injured. Would she be putting others like Mae or even Alex in danger as well?

Dani glanced around the area. It was isolated—anyone intent on harming Mae could walk up and escape with no trouble. But that wouldn't happen if Dani moved in. Lizi would be there to guard them both. It was a good enough reason to stay. Besides, Dani wasn't a quitter.

18

Alex kept the Lincoln Navigator in her rearview mirror as they wound down the mountain from Eagle Ridge. What she'd learned from Dani, aka Danielle Bennett, raised more questions than answers.

Was this possibly connected to the break-in at Mae's house? While there was still no conclusive evidence there'd been a break-in, Alex no longer had any doubts there'd been one and it was the reason Mae called 911. Maybe the person hadn't searched her pottery shop earlier and returned tonight to finish the job. But what was he looking for?

Alex turned into the hotel parking lot and waited until Danielle parked, and then she pulled beside her and lowered her window. "I'll wait until you get inside, but then I need to check on Mark. Once that's done, are you up to discussing what happened tonight since I never got your statement?"

"As long as it isn't too much later. I'm in room 235. Text me before you come."

"I will." Alex entered the number Danielle rattled off into her contacts and when she started to add her name, she hesitated. Her given name was Alexis but only a few people called her that—

mostly Nathan and her grandparents. She preferred Alex. "Your name . . . I remember you as Danielle, but do you prefer Dani?"

Her friend pulled her bottom lip through her teeth, then slowly nodded. "Make it Dani. It sounds odd to hear someone refer to me as Danielle."

"Totally understand. It took a while to get people to call me Alex instead of Alexis—that's how you would've known me when we were kids."

Dani startled, then her eyes widened. "The Three Musketeers!"

"Yes! Mae tagged you, me, and Morgan Tennyson with that name."

"Just for a second I had a picture of three girls." Her shoulders drooped. "Then it was gone, and I don't remember a girl named Morgan . . . or Alexis."

"Give it time. I'm not a psychiatrist or anything, but I wonder if being back in Russell County may trigger more memories."

"I hope so."

"See you in about thirty minutes."

Once Dani was inside the hotel, Alex pulled straight into the hospital lot and found a space near the entrance. A few minutes later she approached the desk in the emergency room. "I need to check on one of my deputies. Mark Lassiter. He was brought in a little earlier."

The receptionist checked her computer. "He's in room 201." She pointed toward the double doors. "Go through those and he's straight down the hall—right in front of the nurses' station."

Alex thanked her and followed the directions. She heard Mark before she reached room 201, arguing with the doctor.

"I don't need to stay here tonight."

She knocked and was given the okay to enter. Alex pushed open the door and eyed Mark as he sat on the ER bed with his arms crossed. "Giving them trouble already?"

He jerked his thumb toward the doctor, who towered over him.

"He won't give me my clothes back. Says I need to stay overnight for observation."

"Sounds like a good idea to me," she said. "I can pick you up first thing in the morning."

"Thank you," the doctor said as Mark glowered at her like she was a chicken-killing dog. "He's experiencing double vision."

"Then that settles it. You can't report to work until the doctor releases you—and I imagine that'll come quicker if you cooperate."

"That's blackmail."

"No. County policy," she said. "Let me know what room they move you to. I'll be around—I'm going to check with Mae's nurse about her condition and then get Dani's statement about what happened earlier tonight. I'll need your report tomorrow if the doctor releases you."

Mark glanced at the doctor. "If I agree to stay, will you give my clothes back?"

The doctor exchanged looks with Alex. "I suppose that isn't an unreasonable request," he said.

"See you tomorrow, Mark," Alex said.

He was still grumbling when she left, and Alex understood. She didn't like getting sidelined either. A few minutes later she approached the ICU doors and pressed the call button. It wasn't visiting hours, but Mae had listed Alex on the HIPAA release, and the nurses usually let her in. Tonight was no exception.

"How is Mae tonight?" Alex asked when she stopped at the nurses' station outside Mae's room.

"Restless," the nurse replied. "Maybe hearing a familiar voice will calm her."

Alex had been praying for Mae to recover, and it sounded like God had answered her prayers. Not that he didn't always, but his answer wasn't always the answer Alex wanted.

She slipped inside the darkened room and approached Mae's

bed. "It's me, Alex," she said softly, touching her on the shoulder. "How are you?"

"Well enough to be home."

Mae's voice was strong, and Alex was amazed at how she'd bounced back from the stroke. Not that she had completely recovered. Mae was still pale, and Alex glanced up at the monitor. "That's not what your blood pressure says."

Mae glared at her. "I feel fine." Then her gaze softened. "I want to be home when Danielle gets here."

Should she tell her Danielle was already here? If she did, Mae might get so excited she wouldn't sleep at all. On the other hand, knowing she was here might relax her. Besides, if their roles were switched, Alex would want to know. "I'm afraid it's too late for that—she's already here."

Mae stared at Alex like she didn't believe her. "Where?"

"She's at the hotel across from the hospital."

"You've talked to her? Seen her?"

"I have, and I'm going to the hotel as soon as I leave you."

"Why didn't she come to the hospital to see me?"

"It's late. *I* shouldn't even be here—I only stopped by to talk to your nurse, and she thought I might help you relax. Dani should be here first thing in the morning. So try to get some sleep."

"I will." She gripped Alex's hand. "How does she look? Are you certain she wants to see me?"

"Stop worrying. She looks good—favors you and Neva. And she definitely wants to see you."

Mae winced as the blood pressure cuff inflated. "Confounded thing pumps up every thirty minutes. Don't know how they think a body can rest with that going on."

Alex watched the numbers on the monitor as they changed. And not for the better. She'd thought about questioning her about what made her call 911 earlier, but her blood pressure had gone up slightly. She didn't want to make it worse. She leaned over and kissed the older woman's cheek. "I'm going so you can rest. See you in the morning."

"Thanks for telling me Danielle is here."

"I would have wanted to know."

"Then thanks for not treating me like an invalid."

"You're welcome." Alex pulled the sheet up on Mae's shoulders. "Good night."

The nurse looked up from a chart as Alex stepped outside the door. "She should be tired enough to sleep now. I told her that her granddaughter from Montana will be coming to see her in the morning."

"That will be wonderful. The first visiting hours are between six and seven a.m." The nurse glanced at the clock and winced. "If that's too early, I can leave a note requesting that her granddaughter be allowed to help her with breakfast at eight. How's that?"

"That's great. Her name is Dani Collins."

"Good. I'll get Mrs. Richmond to sign a HIPAA form before she goes to sleep, allowing us to give the granddaughter information about her condition."

Alex left her SUV parked in the hospital lot and walked across to the hotel. Once in the lobby, she texted Dani she was there and immediately got an answer to come up to the room. She'd barely knocked when the door opened.

"How was she?"

"Amazingly well. She's alert and she's looking forward to seeing you tomorrow," Alex said, entering the room.

"And Mark?"

"They're admitting him for observation."

Lizi stood at alert until Dani released her, then the dog circled and plopped down at her feet. Alex nodded at the dog. "What kind did you say she was?"

"Hungarian Puli. You may be more familiar with the Komondor—it's a larger dog." Dani chuckled. "And I see the 'why' question on your face. When my uncle saw a Puli win the Westminster dog show, he decided he wanted one. He got Lizi, whose name is about this long"—Dani held her forefingers a foot apart—"from a Hungarian breeder who trained her in his native language, but she quickly adapted to English."

"She's such an unusual dog," Alex said. "So your uncle bought her for you?"

"Uh, no." Again she chuckled. "For some reason, Lizi bonded with me in spite of Keith's attempts to win her over. He finally gave up when I went away for a weekend and he insisted she stay home. Lizi didn't eat anything the whole weekend."

"Dogs are funny that way."

Lizi looked up and thumped her tail. "And she knows we're talking about her." Dani rubbed Lizi's ears. "Before I forget, what time could I go visit Mae tomorrow?"

"The nurse said you could come at eight."

"Good." Dani stared into space for a second. "I just wish I could remember her."

19

By eight the next morning, Dani had dressed and eaten and taken Lizi to the pet area at the hotel for exercise. She'd tried to call Keith last night, but he hadn't answered, and it was too early to call him now. She would try him again after she saw Mae. It was time to discuss her past.

She approached the ICU doors and pressed the call button like Alex had instructed. After she identified herself, the door buzzed and she pushed it open. Dani hadn't known what to expect, but not this maze of hallways.

"Can I help you?"

Dani turned. A twentysomething girl dressed in blue scrubs and holding a tray smiled at her.

"I'm looking for Mae Richmond's room."

"I'm taking this to the room next to hers—it's right down here. Just follow me."

Dani hurried after her.

The girl paused at a central station with medical personnel coming and going. She stopped a young woman with a stethoscope looped around her neck. "This is her nurse."

After Dani introduced herself, the nurse smiled. "I'm Jane. I had a note that you were coming, and that you're on her HIPAA form. But I would have known you were Mae's granddaughter—you really favor her."

Dani wasn't sure how to respond and offered a tentative smile. "Thank you."

"Miss Mae is an amazing woman. I wish I knew a tenth of what she knows about herbal remedies. She's famous around here, but I'm sure you know all about that."

Again, Dani didn't know what to say. "How is she?"

The nurse glanced toward the window, where Dani could see a sleeping older woman with reddish hair so like her own. She'd been expecting . . . maybe a gray-haired granny, certainly not someone who looked to be in her sixties.

"Her nurse from last night indicated she was restless the first part of the night but slept well after midnight. Her doctor's already been in to see her, and if her blood pressure remains regulated, you should be able to take her home late this afternoon or tomorrow."

The nurse thought Dani was going to take Mae home? An image of the isolated house formed. What if the person who was after Dani returned? "That soon?"

"Like I said, it'll depend on her blood pressure."

"Is it okay for me to go in?"

"Of course. I need to take her vitals anyway."

A monitor beeped over the bed as Dani followed the nurse inside the room. It was only the second time she'd been in an intensive care unit, and the first time was just a month ago when she and her uncle were allowed into Laura's room after she developed pneumonia. She glanced up at the screen. "Is her heart rate supposed to be that high?"

Laura's was like that just before she died.

"It's actually better than it was during the night." The nurse turned to her patient. "Mrs. Richmond, your granddaughter is here. I need to check your blood pressure, and then I'll let you two visit."

Mae slowly turned her head toward Dani and opened her eyes. "Danielle." Then she winced as the blood pressure cuff inflated.

"I'll be done here in a jiffy," the nurse said soothingly. The cuff deflated, and new numbers appeared on the monitor. "Your blood pressure is improving," she said. "And now I'll let you visit."

While her grandmother didn't speak, her blue eyes bored a hole in her. Blue eyes like Dani saw every time she looked in the mirror. Once they were alone, Dani pulled a chair over to the bed and sat down. She wouldn't want someone hovering over her. Now that she was closer, Dani could see a few silvery-white streaks in the copper strands.

Instinctively, she took Mae's hand, and her fingers curled around Dani's. *A Band-Aid.* An image of those fingers applying a Band-Aid to her knee flashed in her mind's eye. *Angelica from* Rugrats.

A ton of emotions ran through Dani. Coming here was the right thing to do . . . but what had she called her grandmother? Dani searched her memory bank. "Nonny?" she whispered. Yes. That was it . . . Maybe.

Her grandmother blinked back tears that had gathered in her eyes.

"Did I call you Nonny?"

"Yes," she said softly.

"I'm sorry I don't remember you." Even so, Dani's heart soared. The memories were buried in her subconscious, waiting to emerge. Peace settled in her heart.

"That's what Mark told me, but we have plenty of time to talk about that once I get out of here. You will stay, won't you?"

"I have so many questions, and I'm sure you do too, but I'm not sure how long I can be away from Montana. I have a business there."

"I know." She raised the head of her bed until she was sitting up. "I read all about it on your website after I saw the article in *Pottery Making Illustrated.*"

Dani had been really surprised last night when Mark told her. She didn't know which surprised her more—the potter part or that her grandmother searched the web.

"Yep." Suddenly her grandmother gasped.

"What? Are you all right?" Dani jumped up, ready to push the call button.

She stilled Dani with her hand. "Yes. It's just, when I went up on the ridge before this happened, I left my kiln firing a whole load of pieces. I never do that, but I only planned to be gone half an hour at most. I'm always afraid something will catch on fire and burn the place down."

Dani's heart slowed back to normal, and she sat down again. "Well, as far as I could tell last night, nothing like that happened."

"You were at my place last night?"

She nodded. "I wasn't supposed to get here until today, but once I reached Knoxville, it seemed silly to wait. Of course, you weren't there—"

There was a knock at the door. "Can I come in?"

"Mark!" Her grandmother's face broke into a broad grin. "Get yourself in here."

Dani turned, and her heart jumped into high gear as the handsome deputy entered the room. He hadn't shaved, and his day's growth gave him a rugged appeal.

"I wasn't expecting you to be here this early," he said.

"Alex said you were admitted to the hospital," Dani said at the same time. They both paused, and she added, "And I don't figure you've been discharged, so shouldn't you be in your room?"

He fiddled with the hospital bracelet on his wrist. "I wanted to see how Mae is doing." He turned to the older woman. "How *are* you doing?"

"I'm fine, but . . ." She looked from Mark to Dani. "You two act like you've already met—and I don't mean over the phone."

Dani wasn't sure how much they should share, given Mae's blood pressure was still high. She stared pointedly at the monitor.

He gave her a barely perceptible nod. "I saw her car go past my house last night so I checked it out."

"Mark Lassiter, you know I can tell when you're not telling the whole story. What's the rest?"

He shrugged. "There might be more, but let's wait until you're out of the hospital to discuss it, okay?"

Mae pinned her gaze on Mark. "Does what happened have anything to do with why you were admitted to the hospital?" When neither of them answered, she said, "Fine. Don't tell me, but I hope you feel bad when my blood pressure goes up and keeps me from going home."

Dani almost laughed. Not only was her grandmother sharp, she knew how to play people. "We wouldn't want to be responsible for that."

"Then give."

"First I want to know if you remember why you called 911," Mark said.

Her shoulders sagged and she shook her head. "I don't remember anything about that morning."

"You just told me about leaving your kiln on," Dani said.

"You didn't tell us that before," Mark said.

Mae nodded her head. "So, I am remembering . . ."

"And maybe the rest will come to you," Dani said.

Mae narrowed her eyes. "Okay, now somebody needs to tell me what happened last night."

"When I got to your house, someone took a couple of shots at me."

"And," Mark said, "I really did see her car pass, so I was there when it happened. Unfortunately, the guy almost knocked me out." He nodded toward Dani. "Her dog, Lizi, attacked him, but when Dani called Lizi off, the assailant managed to get away."

Mae groaned.

"What's wrong?" Dani asked.

She pressed her hand to her forehead. "My door was open—that's why I called 911."

She squeezed her grandmother's hand. "You remembered."

Mark leaned forward. "Did you see the person?"

"No."

There was a light knock at the door. "Breakfast is here," a nursing assistant called as she entered the room with a tray. "Would you like me to help you with this?"

"I'll help," Dani said.

Mark stood. "I'm going to touch base with Alex while you're eating."

"You just don't want to hear me fuss about the food. And I don't need any help. Probably can't eat it anyway since I'm pretty sure it doesn't have a smidgeon of salt on it."

"Be good," he cautioned as he left.

"I'm afraid you're right about the salt," Dani said, reading the sheet on the tray. "Says here salt-free."

"Let's see what it is." Mae lifted the lid and made a face. "Powdered eggs and oatmeal. Ew."

"The oatmeal might not be too bad with brown sugar." She searched the condiments. "I'm afraid you'll have to settle for white sugar, but they did put in a packet of seasoning blend that you can put on the eggs."

Mae took a few bites of her food and laid her fork on the tray.

"You need to eat more than that if you want to get out of here."

Reluctantly she picked up the fork again. "Maybe if you fill me in about your life, I can get some of this stuff down," Mae said as Mark returned to the room.

Dani was quiet for a minute, collecting her thoughts.

"If you would rather, I can leave," he said.

Dani wasn't much for talking about herself, and it surprised her that she didn't want him to leave. It also surprised her that she found him entirely too attractive. "You risked your life for me, so in a way you deserve to hear what I have to say."

He pulled the only other chair in the room to the bed. "Yes, ma'am." Then he turned to Dani. "Just pretend I'm not here. And I won't listen, if you'd like."

She chuckled. Sure, he was just trying to put her at ease, but it had worked. "I'd like that very much, but how do you propose to do that?"

"I can put my fingers in my ears . . ."

This time she laughed out loud, then she sobered. "It was my fault you got hurt last night, and it looks like you've been drawn into my problem, so you may as well listen."

"Never take the blame for someone else's evil intentions," he said.

If he was trying to make her feel better, he'd succeeded. Dani took a deep breath. "First, let me say that I remember very little about my life here. It's like there's a curtain over my brain. Once in a while it will lift, and I get a fragment of a memory. Even then I'm not sure if it's a true memory or something my mind wants to believe." She glanced at her grandmother. "I'd hoped that when I saw you, the curtain would lift for good. I even thought that seeing your house would trigger memories, but so far it hasn't happened. Maybe if I visited where I lived with my parents . . ."

Mae gripped her hand. Concern showed in her eyes. "It's going to be all right."

Mark leaned toward Dani. "Do you remember anything about the night your parents died?"

Dani shook her head. "Like I said, every once in a while, I'll see a scene—not of that night, but something like the time my parents took me on a picnic. I have a memory of walking with them and my mother stopping to take photos." She looked at Mae. "Did I make that up, or would she have done something like that?"

"Neva loved to take photos," Mae said.

"And you love to talk about her." Mark glanced at Dani. "I visit your grandmother at least a couple of times a week, and we spend a lot of time talking about your mom."

A man entered the room accompanied by Mae's nurse, and she introduced him as a physical therapist. After he checked her bracelet, he said, "Time for you to exercise a little. Y'all can come back at ten, if you'd like."

"Do you know when the doctor will decide if she can go home?" Dani asked the nurse.

"He didn't put it in his notes," the nurse replied.

"Will the doctor be back this afternoon?"

"He's usually here around five thirty."

"Thank you." Dani took Mae's hand. "I'll be back at ten."

"You don't have to do that, child."

"I want to. I've already missed too much time with you."

Outside the room, Mark waited while she gave the nurse her phone number. "I'm staying across the way at the hotel. If her doctor comes in, would you give me a call? I can be here in five minutes."

The nurse agreed to her request, and Dani followed Mark to the elevator.

"You said my grandmother likes to talk about my mom. What about my dad?" Dani shot a questioning glance toward Mae's room.

"She never talks about him, but yesterday I looked at the case. His name was Robert, but everyone called him Bobby. He had a brother—"

"Keith," Dani said. "He raised me."

"We could talk about him over a cup of coffee in the cafeteria, maybe even grab breakfast if they haven't taken it up?"

She tilted her head. "You didn't eat your breakfast either, did you?"

He ducked his head. "It wasn't any better than Mae's. And I'd really like for you to join me."

She should say no, but the compassion in his face stopped her. Dani found she very much wanted to confide in him, and that wasn't like her at all since she didn't normally trust anyone. Mark was—she searched for the right word—comfortable. And a little bit dangerous. She could deny being attracted to him all she wanted, but her fluttering heart told her otherwise. The last time that happened had not ended well.

Dani felt her cheeks grow hot and ducked her head. Her cell phone rang, saving her from answering him about breakfast.

"You better get that."

Dani checked the ID and stiffened.

"Who is it?"

"I don't recognize the number, but the ID says it's my area code."

"You want me to answer it? It might be a robo call."

"Would you?"

Mark took her phone and punched the answer button, putting it on speaker. "Deputy Mark Lassiter."

There was a pause. "This is Sheriff Rex Crider in Dalton County, Montana. I'm trying to reach Dani Collins."

"I'll have her call you. I assume your number is on the website. Are you at your office?"

"It is, and I am, but I'm calling on my cell phone. Is there a problem?"

"Like I said, I'll have her call you." He disconnected. "I think it's for real, but just to make sure, we'll look up the sheriff's department number and call him back. Unless you have it."

She shook her head. Dani knew the sheriff when she saw him, but that was it. Mark googled the Dalton County Sheriff's Office and used Dani's phone to call the number. When a dispatcher answered, he asked for Crider. Seconds later the sheriff came on the line.

"Good to know you're for real," Mark said. "Nowadays you can't be too sure."

"I totally understand. Is Miss Collins—"

"I'm here, on speaker," Dani said. "Why did you call?"

Sheriff Crider cleared his throat. "I don't know how to say this other than your uncle, Keith Collins, was shot sometime during the night, and I'm afraid he didn't make it."

Her stomach dropped to her knees. "Are . . . you saying my uncle is dead?"

"I'm afraid so."

Dani raised her hand to her throat, her peripheral vision narrowing as an icy sensation spread across her face. She swayed, and Mark swept her up in his arms.

"Hold on, Sheriff," he said. "I need to find a place for her to sit down." He carried her to a nearby bench and settled her there. "You okay?"

She tried to speak, but all she could do was shake her head. *Keith is dead?*

"Will you be all right long enough for me to get you a cup of water?"

Dani barely nodded. Mark grabbed the phone from her and dashed to the cafeteria, returning a minute later with water. It helped. She nodded toward the phone. "Do you mind?"

"Not at all. Do you want me to leave it on speaker?"

No. "Yes." Dani rested her head in her hand and listened as the sheriff gave Mark the details. Evidently the house alarm system had triggered a call to the sheriff's office around eleven last night, and when the deputy got there to check it out, he found Keith dead on the den floor.

"The state is sending a CSI team to process the scene since I only have three deputies," the sheriff continued. "I need Miss Collins to return to Clifton as soon as possible—she's the only person who would know what's missing, if anything, from the house."

"How soon?" Dani spoke up, her voice breaking.

"Tomorrow, if possible."

"Tomorrow?" she repeated. "I'm not sure—"

"Miss Collins, I'm sure you want your uncle's killer found . . . there are so many ways to take an investigation, and I first need to rule out a burglary gone wrong."

She closed her eyes and leaned her head against the wall. "I'll book the earliest flight to Billings."

"Let me know your arrival time and I'll have someone pick you up."

"Thank you."

Who could have done this? And why? What were they looking for? She flinched as Mark's phone rang. He fished it from his pocket and glanced at the ID.

"It's Alex. I need to take this," he said. "Do you want to speak to the sheriff again?"

"Yes." She took her phone as Mark walked away to answer his call. "Thank you for letting me know what happened. Do you want me to call you on the cell number from the first call when I know my ETA?"

"That will be fine. And I'm really sorry. Mae always said he was a good guy."

"Thank you." She disconnected and pocketed her phone. This couldn't be happening. Fog swirled through her mind.

Someone had killed Keith. Why? Like her memories, the answer seemed to be just out of her grasp. And now she had to return home without any answers.

Lord, please clear my head.

She took a long draw of the water Mark had brought her as her mind tried to put the pieces together. First she'd been shot at, then Mark injured—no. First someone had broken into Mae's house, and then the other two things. And now Keith.

20

Mark punched the answer button on his phone. “Lassiter.”

“Have you seen Dani?” Alex asked. “I tried to call her, but it went straight to voicemail.”

“She’s with me.” He sensed movement to his right and turned. Dani. She pointed toward the nearby restroom and he nodded. At least she was steady on her feet. “We’ve been on the phone with the sheriff where she lives—her uncle was murdered sometime last night.”

Alex gasped. “What?”

“The sheriff wants her to return home to see if anything is missing.”

“Is he going to provide protection for her while she’s there?”

“He only has three deputies.”

“So that’s a no,” Alex said. “I don’t think she should go.”

He was thinking the same thing. Unless . . . “I’m going with her.”

“What? Why would you do that?”

He didn’t understand it himself, so he didn’t know how to explain it. Or maybe he did, but Alex wouldn’t understand. It was almost like he’d been given a second chance. “Someone needs to go with her, and after last night, I probably need to be on light duty anyway."

"The county can't pay your airfare."

"I know. But you'll give me the time off and see after Gem for me?"

"Of course."

"Thanks. Is there a reason you wanted to talk to Dani?"

"She needs to call Hayes to take her to the hotel. No, on second thought, tell her to call me."

"What's going on?"

Alex continued like she hadn't heard him. "I assume you're not in your room? You're supposed to be under observation."

"The doc came by and discharged me early. Then I went to see Mae—that's where I ran into Dani."

"How is Mae?"

"Getting better. She remembered thinking someone was in her house yesterday." He filled Alex in on what Mae had told them.

"Does she have any idea who they were or what they were looking for?"

"The nurse ran us out before we could discuss that. She should be discharged later today or tomorrow. You can question her then." He stared at the floor.

"Good. Be sure to have Dani call me when she's ready to leave."

"Sure. I assume she has your number?" When there was no answer, he checked his phone. Alex had disconnected.

"What's wrong?"

He looked up. "Alex wants to talk to you."

Mark waited while Dani scrolled through her phone for Alex's number and punched it. He didn't know if she meant for it to be on speaker. But it was.

"Thanks for calling me back," Alex said. "I'm almost to the hospital. I'll pick you up and take you to your room."

"Okay . . . but why?"

"We'll discuss it when I get there. I'll be waiting at the side entrance to the hospital—Mark is with you, so he can show you where it is."

Mark opened his mouth to tell Alex he was coming with Dani to the hotel but he quickly closed it. It was easier to ask forgiveness than permission—and Alex would have quickly shot down his offer. It'd be a little harder in person.

21

Mark walked with Dani to the side entrance of the hospital. Alex hadn't arrived yet.

"Thanks for being here. I can't believe my uncle is gone and I have to find a flight home." She turned toward him, her face warming under his concern. She'd never met anyone so nonjudgmental and compassionate. But why did he have to be so attractive?

She did not just think that! Maybe it was a natural reaction for her mind to focus on something besides her uncle's death. No. His murder. First her parents and now Keith. Was her whole family going to be murdered? Maybe she was next. Or her grandmother. She had to keep her focus on regaining her memory—something told her that was the key to everything.

"I'm going with you."

Dani jerked her head up, not sure she'd heard him correctly. "What do you mean?"

"You're not going by yourself, so book two seats when you make the reservation, and don't worry, I'll pay for my ticket. And Alex has already approved my time off."

The weight that lifted off her shoulders surprised her. She

hadn't even realized she was worrying about flying to Montana alone. "You don't have—"

"Yes, I do."

"Why?"

"One, I'm really sorry about your uncle, and two, Alex and I don't think you should go by yourself." He glanced out the door. "And it looks like she's here."

Alex pulled the cruiser next to the entrance, and Mark opened the passenger door. Dani climbed in and fastened her seat belt before looking up at Mark. "I'll call you once I book our flight."

"You're not rid of me yet . . . that is, if Alex will unlock the back door."

"Don't you need to go back to your room?" Dani asked as Alex popped the door locks.

He slid inside the cruiser. "The doctor discharged me early this morning."

Dani looked at him. "But you said—"

"No, *you* said I hadn't been discharged." He grinned. "I was just messing with you when I didn't correct you—you seemed so sure you knew what you were talking about."

Dani didn't quite know how to respond, and from the odd look Alex gave him in the rearview mirror, neither did she. A minute later the chief deputy drove through the pull-through at the hotel, and Mark hopped out first. He opened her door. "Let's get you inside," he said, scanning the parking lot.

His words hit her hard. In the movies, that only happened when someone wanted someone else dead. Dani swallowed hard and pressed her hand to her chest to try and slow her hammering heart. Surreal. That was the only word that fit.

Dani didn't breathe normally until they got off the elevator on the second floor and she pulled her key card out of her pocket.

Mark took it and waved the card in front of the door. "Let me go in first."

"No, I need to go in first. I didn't crate Lizi, so I guarantee no one is in my room, and she would not react well to you entering first."

"After you, then."

Lizi met her at the door, her tail wagging. Dani glanced around the room. No torn pillows. "You've been a good girl," she said, rubbing her head.

A minute later, there was a knock on the door and Mark checked before he let Alex in. "I'm making some coffee. Anyone else want any?" he asked.

Lizi sniffed Mark's shoes, then rubbed against his leg as Dani quickly sank into a comfortable chair. That was odd. The dog didn't usually take up with people she didn't know well. That was a plus for the deputy.

"None for me," Alex said.

Coffee sounded like heaven to Dani. "I would if there's enough."

He held up three packets. "And creamer."

"Great." Dani needed a little boost—she couldn't remember when she'd been so drained. She took the steaming cup of coffee Mark handed her as Alex sat in the chair across from her.

"I haven't had a chance to tell you how sorry I am about your uncle."

"Thanks. It doesn't seem real." Part of her believed if she dialed his number, Keith would answer.

"Did he know you were in Pearl Springs?"

"I never told him, but I'm sure he did." She took out her phone and handed it to Alex. "He gave me that a month ago. I'm pretty sure you'll find a family locater app on it."

"You don't know?"

"I hardly even turn the thing on. I was perfectly happy with my flip phone."

"Are you kidding me?" Mark said. "Everyone has a smartphone."

"Not everyone," she shot back.

"Give me your phone so I can locate and disable the app," Alex said.

"If you find one, I don't mind you disabling it, but why? No one has my new number. Except Keith . . ." She pressed her lips together. "And probably whoever killed him."

Alex scrolled through her phone and deleted the app, then she handed it back to Dani. "I don't know that anyone is tracking you, but now we won't have to worry about it. And if you don't mind, give me Sheriff Crider's number. I'd like to talk to him once we get you moved."

"Moved? Why do I have to move and where?"

"This is the only hotel in town, so if someone was looking for you, this is the first place they would look. And after last night, and now after your uncle was murdered, I don't want to take any chances. Being able to limit the people who have access to you will help me keep you safe. I've already called my grandparents, and they're excited about you coming."

Dani didn't know what to say. This felt a whole lot like her uncle's protectiveness. "I have a dog. I can't impose on them."

"I promise, it won't be an imposition. And it'll make my job easier."

"They don't mind that Lizi is coming too?"

"They both love dogs, but they don't have one now because they don't have the energy to train a puppy. They'll enjoy Lizi."

Dani had to admit she wasn't looking forward to being alone. And since they didn't mind that Lizi was part of the deal, it knocked out her last reservation. "Okay, then. Do I have time to book my flight now?"

Alex hesitated, then nodded. "The later it gets, the harder it'll be to find a flight, especially for two."

Dani booted up her computer and searched for flights. "Found one from Chattanooga to Billings that leaves at 6:00 a.m." She looked up at Mark. "Is that too early for you?"

"That's fine. Let me give you my credit card."

"No. If you're willing to go to protect me, paying your airfare is the least I can do." She got his information and quickly claimed the seats, then she shut her computer down. "I'll check my email once we get to your grandparents' house."

Alex stood. "Good. I'll call Nathan and have him meet us there."

"Nathan?"

"I'm sorry. Nathan Landry is the Pearl Springs chief of police."

"And her fiancé," Mark added with a chuckle. "Not that Dani won't be able to tell it once she sees you two together."

The chief deputy shot him a frown. "Excuse me?"

He held up his hands. "Sorry. Just calling it like I see it."

"Hmph," she grunted and turned toward Dani. "I'll take you over in my SUV and Mark will park your Navigator at the jail."

"Why? I won't have a way to travel—"

"You won't need a vehicle until you get back, and my grandparents don't have a garage. Mark'll pick you up in the morning, and we'll discuss options when you return."

"I see your point."

"If you'll give him your keys, he can get going." She turned to her deputy. "And then take the rest of the day off."

"Aw, come on, Alex. I'm fine."

"You need to pack . . . and rest." She thought a minute. "Why don't you plan on spending the night at our house? It'd be a lot simpler."

He agreed, and Dani fished the keys from her purse and tossed them to Mark. She wished he could come with them now—he made her feel safe.

22

Mark caught the keys. "Is it okay if I use the Navigator to pick up Gem and pack my bag before I drop it off at the jail? Then I can get my vehicle. That is where Jenna Hart left it, right?"

"Yeah, but why don't you pick it up first?" Alex asked.

"I need gas—meant to fill up yesterday afternoon and got sidetracked. By the time I drive across town and I do all that, I can be halfway to my house." He turned to Dani. "Or does your SUV need gas?"

She shook her head. "Nope. Filled up when I first rolled into town."

"Okay," Alex said. "I'll tell Gram you'll be sleeping on her pull-out sofa because of the early morning flight."

A few minutes later, the sun felt good but the cold north wind had him zipping his jacket as he jogged across the hotel parking lot to where the Navigator was parked.

He reached for the door handle, and the hairs on his neck raised. Someone was watching him. Mark scanned the parking lot, but nothing seemed amiss. He looked for Alex's SUV and didn't see it. She must have tucked it out of sight because they couldn't have left for Sheriff Stone's house yet.

With his spidey senses still on high alert, Mark opened the driver door and slid across the seat. *Nice.* It even had a cage for Gem. He familiarized himself with the dashboard and noted the rich leather seats and wrapped steering wheel. He'd bet they were heated too.

Once he started the SUV, his hunch was confirmed as the steering wheel warmed his hands. After scanning the parking lot once more, he pulled onto the street and turned the vehicle toward Eagle Ridge.

Traffic was normal, and he kept an eye peeled for a tail. No one seemed to be following him. By the time he turned on the road to Eagle Ridge, Mark had met hardly any vehicles, but when he passed the first S curve he noticed a pickup in his rearview mirror.

Uh-oh. There weren't that many houses on this road, mostly just cabins that were rented out during the summer and fall months. Mark slowed down to see if the truck would pass him. Nope. It slowed as well, but they were on a double yellow line. He was still a few miles from his house, and there were no roads he could turn off on between his location and the house. *Oh, wait.* There was a logging road just up ahead. He could pull in there and see who was following him.

Mark searched for the road. *There.* He drove past the almost hidden road, then stopped and backed into it, facing out. Then he opened the door and scrambled out.

He used his cell phone to call for backup, then unsnapped the strap on his Sig Sauer as he jogged to the edge of the lane. If someone was looking for trouble, he needed to be ready.

Minutes ticked off. The truck should be here by now. He checked the time, blinking when he saw two watch faces. That hadn't happened since last night.

Mark didn't move, his spidey senses still on alert. Something wasn't right. He glanced toward the Navigator just as a man eased up to the door and opened it.

Mark crept toward the SUV, wincing as a branch snapped under his feet.

The door slammed, and a bullet whizzed by his head. He hit the ground and searched for the shooter, the gun in his hand at the ready.

He barely glimpsed the man as he dashed into the woods. Mark blinked, trying to focus as he jumped to his feet and ran after him. “Halt! Police!”

The man turned and fired. Mark ducked behind a huge oak as a bullet splintered the bark near his head. More bullets buried in the tree trunks around him. But no gun report. He must have a silencer. Mark eased around the oak to shoot, and immediately the gunman fired.

A siren wailed in the distance. Good old Hayes. “You might as well give up. Backup is here,” he yelled.

No answer. He eased around the tree again, expecting the assailant to shoot. Instead, total silence. Mark waited for a few minutes before he crept forward. At least he no longer was seeing double. Somewhere to his left an engine fired up.

He got away.

Mark kicked at a mound of dirt.

23

Dani breathed easier once they were in Alex's SUV, headed toward her grandparents' house. She hadn't realized how uptight she'd been about being alone.

She looked over her shoulder to check on Lizi, who'd crawled up on the seat where she could watch her.

Alex turned to Dani. "You okay?"

She shifted her gaze to the chief deputy. "Yeah, but I feel so responsible for what happened to Mark," Dani said. "If he hadn't come to my rescue—"

"Mark wouldn't want you to feel that way."

"That's what he said, but it doesn't change the way I feel. He seems like a good guy."

"He is," Alex said. "I don't know his whole story, but he was a sniper in Afghanistan."

A sniper? Maybe that's what was responsible for the wounded spirit she sensed in him. And maybe why she was drawn to him. She was a fixer, whether it was wounded animals or people. Dani tilted her head. "I know you said you aren't the sheriff, but you act like one."

"It's a little confusing. My grandfather, Carson Stone, is the sheriff. I was working in Chattanooga last year when I was shot by an assailant, and I came home to recuperate. My grandfather had a heart attack, and he asked if I'd come on board the Russell County Sheriff's Department as his chief deputy. Since he's on sick leave, I'm essentially acting as the sheriff of Russell County."

"Why doesn't he just get you appointed sheriff?"

"Because my residence was Chattanooga and not Russell County—there's a one-year residency requirement to be appointed sheriff, but none if he wants to hire me as chief deputy."

"I get it. Are you going to run for sheriff?"

"He wants me to, but I haven't completely made up my mind. At one time, I wanted to be the first woman to head up the Chattanooga Police Department."

Dani detected a note of uncertainty in Alex's voice. "You sound like that may no longer be the case."

"It's complicated." Blue lights flashed briefly behind them, and a text chimed on Alex's phone. She glanced at it. "And the driver behind us is one of the complications."

She gave a left turn signal and then turned into a circle drive and pulled around to the back. The vehicle on their tail pulled in behind them. Alex killed the ignition. "Sit tight until we can make sure it's safe."

"Did anyone follow us?"

"I don't think so, but I don't want to take any chances."

Dani scanned the area as Alex climbed out of the SUV. Trees surrounded the house, but beyond that, it looked as though a road backed up to the property line. Alex tapped on her window before she opened the door.

"It's clear." Alex nodded at the man beside her. "This is Nathan Landry."

"You'll be safe here," Nathan said. Then he smiled. "And it's easy to tell you and Mae are related."

Dani didn't quite know how to respond to the comment. Other

than the hair color, she hadn't seen a resemblance to herself and the woman in the hospital.

"It's in the eyes," Nathan added. "And hair."

Dani nodded. "Do you know my grandmother well?"

"Not as well as Mark does, but I'm honored to count her as a friend." He smiled. "I even have a few memories of you from when we were kids."

"Did you know my parents?"

"I'm afraid not—I don't remember many adults from my childhood except Mr. Peterson down at the grocery."

Alex laughed when he said that, and Dani quizzed her with her eyes.

"I'll explain once we get you inside," Alex said.

Dani opened the back passenger door, and Lizi hopped off the backseat. She sniffed Nathan and looked from him to Dani. "It's okay," she said.

Soon they were inside a cozy kitchen. After sniffing everyone, Lizi settled in a corner of the room near the door.

"What kind of dog is that?" the older man asked. "Looks like a mop."

"It's a Puli, Gramps, and her name is Lizi." Alex turned to Dani with a wry grin. "Meet my grandfather and sheriff, Carson Stone." Once Dani shook hands with the older man, Alex turned to an attractive silver-haired woman. "And my grandmother, Judith. She's good friends with Mae."

"So nice to meet you both, Sheriff Stone, Mrs. Stone." She nodded her head. "I'm anxious to learn more about my grandmother."

"First of all," the older woman said, "call me Judith. Mrs. Stone makes me feel old."

She could do that. Dani called Keith by his first name. *Had called.* She corrected her thinking and her heart cracked. She looked up, and Judith was watching her.

"I'm sorry about Keith," she said softly.

"Thank you. I'm numb. And I dread returning to an empty house."

"That's understandable. Alex told me you're flying back tomorrow. What time is your flight?"

"Six, so we'll have to be checked in at the airport by at least five." Which meant they needed to leave here by three or three thirty. "We'll try to be very quiet."

"Don't worry about that," Judith said.

Dani directed her attention to Nathan, who sat across from her. "You mentioned a Mr. Peterson? Who was he?"

"Mr. Peterson isn't a was," Alex said. "He's still living, and you would have known him—he had the only grocery store in town. We stopped there every day to get nickel candy." She looked at her grandmother. "He's ninety-two, isn't he?"

Judith chuckled. "Yes, and still helps run that little family grocery his father started back in the 1940s. His grandson, Kyle, does the bulk of the work, but Mr. Peterson shows up every day," she said.

Now Dani was curious. "What am I missing? I don't understand what's funny."

"First, you have to understand we didn't have a lot to do around here in the summer," Alex said. "And I doubt kids would think what we did was funny now, but to get to the story, the summer Mae babysat us—that was you, and Morgan, and me—she made the mistake of telling us how she used to call Mr. Peterson when she was a kid and ask him if he had Prince Albert in a can. And when he said yes, she would say, 'Well, you better let him out.'"

Dani still didn't get it and shook her head. "Prince Albert? I must still be missing something."

Sheriff Stone laughed this time. "Prince Albert is a loose-leaf tobacco that comes in a red can. Back when Mae was a kid, it was very popular around here. Much cheaper than buying cigarettes that were probably a quarter a pack." He cleared his throat. "And it was a rite of passage for a kid to call Peterson's Grocery and ask that question. I dare say Nathan was guilty of calling as well, right, son?"

"Guilty as charged," he responded.

"Anyway, not long after Mae told us that story, your cousin Morgan thought we should make that call, and I got elected to be the one who phoned," Alex said. "Somehow Mr. Peterson recognized my voice and threatened to report to Gramps that I was making harassing phone calls. Scared the living daylights out of me."

"I have absolutely no memory of that," Dani said. How she wished she *could* remember.

"I hope you do someday, because that was a great summer." Alex sighed. "Unfortunately, it wasn't long after that Mr. Tennyson moved Morgan and Ben away, and then you left . . ." She looked up, and sadness filled her eyes.

"We must've been good friends."

"The best. I was really lonesome after that."

"Hey! You had me," Nathan said.

"It wasn't the same."

"I know, just teasing you." Nathan stood. "Look, I need to head out—I have an appointment with the mayor. I'll have one of my deputies coordinate with Hayes on a schedule for driving by here."

"I'll walk out with you," Alex said.

Dani noticed the look that passed between the Stones as their granddaughter followed Nathan outside. "Nathan seems really nice."

"The best," Sheriff Stone replied.

Judith frowned. "I just hope Alex settles on a wedding date soon—"

"Now, Judith, give her time . . ."

Lizi stood and stretched, then padded over to the back door and whined. “You need to go out, girl?”

“What kind of dog did you say she was?” Sheriff Stone asked.

“Puli—they’re Hungarian sheepherding dogs, but they make good guard dogs.”

“She seems quite smart,” he replied.

“Oh, the breed is very smart and brave, which is why my uncle bought her. She’s very protective of the people she owns.” And some she didn’t, as last night with Mark came to mind.

She opened the back door and froze. Alex was in Nathan’s arms. *Not good timing, Dani.* Before she could close the door, Lizi nosed her way through it. Alex quickly moved out of Nathan’s arms.

“Sorry,” Dani mumbled as she hurried after Lizi, who had headed straight for the trees. “We won’t be long.”

“Not a problem,” Alex said.

“Speak for yourself,” Nathan teased.

A few minutes later, she returned with Lizi to the patio where the two still stood talking. “Sorry for interrupting you,” she said just as Alex’s phone rang.

She glanced at the screen. “It’s Hayes.” Alex pressed the answer button and it went to speaker. “What’s going on?”

“Just got a call from Mark. He needs backup.”

“What happened?”

“Not sure. Something about a car tailing him. I’m almost there.”

“I’m on my way.” She scanned the backyard before turning to Dani. “I need you inside. Now!” Then she punched a number on her phone. “Jenna, can you come to my grandfather’s house STAT?” Alex nodded. “Great.”

“Is Mark all right?” Dani’s heart jumped into her throat. If someone hurt him again, this time because he was in her car . . .

Frustration swept over Dani when Alex ignored her and instead turned to Nathan. "This could be a diversion. Jenna says she's five minutes out, but I need to get on the road. Would you stay here until she arrives and brief her?"

"Sure. Keep me informed of the situation, and stay safe."

"Always." Alex turned to leave.

"Tell me if Mark is okay." Dani crossed her arms over her chest. She wasn't going anywhere until she knew.

"As soon as I know, I'll let you know. I have a deputy coming to guard the house—Jenna Hart. Now, inside!" Alex opened the back door, and from the look on the chief deputy's face, Dani knew she had no choice but to go through it.

"What's wrong?" Carson asked as she came through the door.

"Mark's in trouble," Dani said. And it was her fault. Again.

24

As soon as Dani was inside, Alex turned to Nathan. "Thanks for waiting for my deputy."

"I'll come on as soon as Jenna arrives."

"I thought you had an appointment with Ben."

"He wants to go over my budget—this will be a good excuse to cancel it."

An SUV with the Russell County logo on the door pulled around to the back of the house, and a tall brunette climbed out of the Ford Interceptor.

"Thanks for getting here so fast," Alex said to the female deputy. She'd recruited her from the Chattanooga Police Department the same time she'd hired Hayes.

"I read the file on Danielle Bennett that you emailed earlier. And I heard the call for backup go out, and I was halfway here when you called. Any word on what's going on yet?"

Alex could always depend on Jenna being a step ahead of everyone else. "Not yet. I didn't call Mark for fear it would distract him if he was in a tight situation. Thanks for staying here until I get back." She turned to Nathan. "Are you coming with me or driving your vehicle?"

He hesitated only briefly. "Riding with you."

She nodded, and they climbed into her SUV. Alex punched in Hayes's number as she pulled out of the drive. "He's not answering."

"Service is spotty on the mountain sometimes," Nathan said.

"Yeah, I know." She tapped the steering wheel. "Why is someone after Dani? 'Cause I'm pretty sure whoever is tailing Mark in her SUV thinks it's her."

"Been thinking about that and was going to discuss it when she wasn't around. While she seems strong, a person can take only so much."

"What're you thinking?"

"That her parents' killer is afraid she will identify him."

Alex gripped the steering wheel as she turned off the highway onto the mountain road. "She was safer before she came back. I've done a few searches for her over the years and never got any hits. Her uncle did a thorough job of going off the grid."

"My question is, how did someone tail Mark? He would've spotted one before he got to Eagle Ridge. And evidently not just tail him but attack? He wouldn't have called for backup otherwise."

They were both quiet, then they both spoke at the same time. "A tracker!"

"It wouldn't have been hard to put one on at the hotel parking lot."

Alex nodded. "Or even at Mae's house last night."

Silence filled the SUV as she took the mountain road as fast as possible. She rounded a curve and spotted flashing blue lights. The tension in her shoulders released when she saw Mark standing at the back of Hayes's cruiser. She hated it when one of her deputies was in danger.

"Sorry to get you out," Mark said when she approached.

"What happened?" She took her phone out and texted Dani a message that Mark was uninjured, then turned her full attention to her deputy as he filled her in. When he finished, she said, "Did you see him?"

"No—just enough to know it was a man before he started shooting." Mark jutted his jaw. "I can't believe he caught me off guard."

Alex glanced at the Navigator. "Maybe he knew when you stopped and where. Did you return fire?"

"No, I didn't get a chance. He kept me pinned down, then just disappeared."

Nathan scanned the woods. "You think it's someone who knows the area?"

"Yep—he knew where to find the logging road, and where to leave his vehicle. Since Hayes didn't see a car, he must've taken the road that goes by the Bennett place. I figure from the silent way he moved in the woods, he's a hunter." Mark glanced toward the SUV. "He didn't follow me out of Pearl Springs. I bet he put a tracker on the Navigator while it was in the hotel parking lot. Get Dylan to put it up on a rack."

Alex nodded. Great minds and all that. "How many casings and slugs should we look for?"

Mark thought a minute. "At least ten. Do you want me to stay and look for evidence with the CSI team?"

"Good idea—if you're up to it."

Her cell phone rang, and she handed it to Mark. "It's Dani. I texted her that you were okay, but I think she needs to hear it from you," she said with a grin. "She was really worried about you."

He gave her a puzzled look and answered the phone. "Dani? It's Mark. I'm fine." His eyes twinkled as he glanced at Alex. "Yes, I'm sure. You can see for yourself as soon as we finish here and I collect Gem."

Alex noted a grin when he disconnected. Interesting. In the six months she'd been chief deputy, she hadn't known of Mark Lassiter being interested in anyone. The spark of attraction she'd seen earlier between the two had surprised her. Alex hoped it didn't become a problem—Mark would be protecting Dani, and a romance could interfere with his judgment. But for now, Alex would watch and see before addressing the issue with him. If it became an issue.

"She feels responsible."

"Yeah, I know." She pocketed her phone. "So, all your symptoms are gone?"

He nodded. "A little headache and sometimes I see double, but that's to be expected when someone almost knocks you out."

"If it doesn't go away, I expect you to see the doctor again." Macho men. But it wasn't limited just to men—she was about as bad.

25

Now that Dani knew Mark was all right, the stress of the last two days turned her muscles to Jell-O, and she sank into the chair. Too bad it was the middle of the day—she felt like she could sleep for a week. Maybe she should take a nap. Her phone rang, and she told herself to hold on to that thought as she glanced at the ID. *The hospital.* She punched the answer button and identified herself.

"This is the case manager at Pearl Springs Regional Hospital. I just spoke with Dr. Wexler, and he would like to discharge Mrs. Richmond to a rehab facility, but she is insisting on going to her home, and that isn't feasible."

"I'll take her home and stay with her." Dani looked around for her purse. "In fact, I'm on my way there now."

"Oh. Well, I'll need to apprise Dr. Wexler of the change."

"Thank you." Dani ended the call and turned to Judith as she stood. "The hospital is discharging Mae. I'll be back as soon as . . ." Slowly she sat back down. "I forgot I don't have wheels, and I'm leaving tomorrow."

"Mae can stay here until you return—or as long as she needs to. And Alex wouldn't want you to drive alone to the hospital." Judith pointed to Dani's phone. "Call her—she'll know what to do."

"Thanks." She stared at her phone. The problems were piling up faster than Dani could take care of them.

"Do you want me to call her?"

She shifted her gaze to Judith and Carson at the table, touched by the look of concern on their faces. "Would you?" She handed Judith the phone.

"She's on her way," Judith said when she hung up.

"I can't thank you enough for your help."

"Mae is my best friend," the older woman said. "And knowing Alex, she will not want you isolated on Eagle Ridge."

When Alex arrived, she agreed with her grandmother. "And now we have to convince Mae."

Dani stood, and so did Lizi. "You don't mind if Lizi stays while we go to the hospital?"

"Of course not," Carson said. "And while you're back in Montana . . . unless you booked Lizi a seat on the plane."

Dani gasped. "I never thought about it, and I got the last two seats."

"Then it's settled. She'll stay here."

"Let me show you where you'll be sleeping tonight . . . and when you get back from Montana." Judith led them to a room painted light blue and accented with ceiling-to-floor gray curtains. "There's a bathroom here." She pointed to a door on the right.

Dani took one look at the bed and wanted to crawl in. Maybe when she returned with her grandmother.

"Mae's room will be right next to this one," Judith said. "It only has a half bath."

Dani followed the older woman to the next bedroom that mirrored hers, then she returned to the kitchen where Alex waited.

"Mark—"

Alex stopped her with a raised hand. "He's fine and should be here when we get back with Mae," Alex said.

As she rode to the hospital, Dani couldn't help but worry.

"I know what you're thinking," Alex said. "You aren't the first to stay with my grandparents for safety reasons and you won't be the last. And Mark was just doing his job. Danger comes with the territory."

"Maybe I should just stay in Montana," she said.

"I doubt that would make you or your grandmother any safer. Not that staying at my grandparents' will guarantee your safety, but at least there you'll have support."

Dani didn't want to leave, not after just meeting her grandmother. "All right, you've convinced me," she said.

Alex grunted. "Now to convince your grandmother."

Convincing her turned out easier than either of them expected but came with a condition. A condition her grandmother didn't mention until they were pulling away from the hospital in Alex's SUV. "I'll stay with Judith and Carson three days, then I'm going to my home on Eagle Ridge."

"But, Nonny." The name came out before Dani had time to think. "That may not be long enough."

"She's right, Mae. It's not like we have a suspect or anything. And you can't stay up on the ridge by yourself."

"Maybe we can lure him into a trap."

"Using you and Dani for bait? I don't think so."

"Not Dani—just me," she said firmly.

"Definitely not," Dani said. "If this person killed Keith, he means business."

"You think I don't know that?" Mae replied. "I'm truly sorry about Keith. I was upset with him for a long time, but I finally realized he wouldn't have done what he did if he hadn't been afraid something would happen to you, Dani. I just wish he'd told us what happened that night."

"But he didn't."

Mae turned to Alex. "Do you think you could spare a deputy long enough for me to see if anything is missing from my house?"

"That's actually a good idea, but let's give you a day or—"

"I was thinking right now. I feel fine."

Dani started to say no when Alex glanced at her in the rearview mirror. "That might not be a bad idea." She turned to Mae. "If you're sure you're up to it."

"I'm sure."

Dani had to admit her grandmother sounded strong. And it would be good to know if the person who broke in had actually stolen anything. Twenty minutes later, her Navigator came into view along with several deputies. "Is this where someone shot at Mark?"

Alex nodded and pulled over as Mark approached their vehicle. She lowered her window. "We're going to Mae's house to see if anything is missing."

He glanced at Mae. "You up for that?"

"I'm good."

Mark smiled. "You'd say that even if you weren't. We'll be through here soon, and I'll see if I can borrow someone's vehicle and join you."

Alex nodded and pulled away from the scene. Soon, she turned into Mae's drive and pulled the SUV close to her front porch. Her grandmother was out of the vehicle before Dani could climb out.

"I was going to help you," Dani said.

"I'm not an invalid. Dr. Wexler said I could do whatever I felt like doing."

Alex chuckled. "He hasn't known you long enough to know better than to tell you that."

Mae grinned. "That's not my fault." She sobered at the top of the steps near the bullet holes from Saturday night and studied them before turning to Dani. "Too high—whoever fired this wasn't trying to kill you."

"You think he was trying to scare me away?"

"Possibly." She pushed open her door and walked inside. After a few minutes in the living room, Mae shook her head. "I don't see anything missing here. How about fingerprints?"

"There weren't any unknown prints anywhere—he probably wore gloves."

"Let me check the rest of the house."

Dani lingered behind while Alex and her grandmother moved on. Something about the room called to her. She walked to the mantel. There was a photo of a man that Dani instinctively knew was her dad. Next to it was one that looked very much like herself. *Mom.* She picked that one up and hugged it to her chest as she closed her eyes briefly, soaking in the atmosphere.

She'd been here before. Her mom worked at a factory in Pearl Springs and her dad worked construction . . . was it possible she'd stayed here more than she had stayed at home? She tried to return to the memory, but it was gone. Maybe more memories would come in the rest of the house.

Dani returned the photo to the mantel and joined the other two in her grandmother's office, where Alex stood in front of a whiteboard like Dani had seen in cop movies. She turned to her grandmother. "Is that a crime board?"

"It is," Alex said, answering for Mae. "And a good one."

Dani stepped closer and examined the board, recognizing her dad's photo and her mom's. She shifted her gaze to a girl who looked to be nine or ten standing on a front porch. With the red ponytail and freckles, it had to be Dani, but she had no recollection of ever looking this young. The only photos of herself she remembered were taken by Laura, and Dani had been almost a teenager.

She turned as Alex tapped the board. "Can I borrow this?"

"Sure, just don't lose it," Mae said absently. She brushed her fingertips. "Why is there such a mess?"

"Taylor and Dylan dusted for prints."

She nodded. "Did they move anything?"

"If they did, they would've put it back like it was. Why?"

"I left my journal here Friday night after I wrote in it." She pointed to a place on the other side of the computer. "And the magazine with Danielle's article and photo is missing."

"Are you sure?" Alex asked.

"Yes. I laid the magazine to the right of the computer, where the journal is now, when I returned from your office Wednesday." A smile curved her lips up. "I took a couple of photos with my phone so I could look at Danielle's picture while I worked in the studio."

"I didn't read your journal Saturday. Would there have been anything in it about Dani or Keith?"

Mae nodded. "I wrote down everything Mark told me. That she was in Cincinnati and that she was coming Sunday."

"If someone read the journal entry, they wouldn't expect anyone to be around your house Saturday night," Alex said. "They were looking for something besides you."

Dani wasn't so sure. "Did you mention my name was Collins?"

Her grandmother picked the journal up and handed it to her. "I did, but see for yourself. There's nothing I wouldn't want either of you to see."

Alex took the leather-bound book and flipped to the last page. "There's nothing in here about where Dani and Keith lived, or any other pieces of information he could've used—just that she was coming Sunday."

"It's probably why he didn't take it," Dani said.

"The magazine had your name and website in the article."

"But he couldn't have found Keith that way—our location is nowhere on my website."

"But the name of your business is, and the murderer could've checked state records and found the address," Mae said.

Alex laid the journal back on the desk. "Would you mind booting up the computer so I can see the website?"

Mae woke the machine and put her password in, then Dani brought up her website. Alex scrolled through it. "Wow. You have some beautiful pieces."

"Thanks. And this reminded me—I need to check my phone messages and email when you finish."

Alex scrolled back to the top of the page. "Is that a photo of the Badlands?"

"Yes. They're not far from where we live." *Where I live.* Keith was gone. A lump formed in her throat. The life she knew was over. "But why kill him?"

"Maybe for the diamonds that never surfaced," Mae said.

"What diamonds?"

"The ones Bobby stole the night before they were killed."

Alex checked her watch. "Why don't we discuss that on the way home?"

"I need to check my kiln while we're here," Mae said. She turned to Dani. "Why don't you check your messages and email while I do that?"

Dani nodded. "It won't take me long, and I'll come help you. I'd like to see some of your pieces."

First she checked the messages on the landline. More orders. A couple of people had left condolences and inquired about arrangements. Dani sighed. She hadn't thought that far ahead. That was something else she would have to do this coming week.

She logged on to her email and groaned. Over a hundred emails. She quickly scanned through them, deleting the obvious advertisements and spam. Her heart stilled when Keith's email address showed up.

Dani glanced at the date. Saturday. With shaky fingers, she opened it and noticed there was an attachment. First she read the email.

Dani. I don't know how many times I've sat down and tried to write down the details of what happened when we left Tennessee, and after Laura died, I knew I had no choice. If anything happens to me, you need to know you have family. It's all in the letter I've attached. I'm emailing it because if I wait until you return, I'm afraid I won't have the courage to give it to you.

I love you, Punkin. I'll be glad when you get home.

P. S. There is more that I hope to tell you, but now is not the right time.

Dani hesitated before she downloaded the attachment. Maybe she should get Alex to read it first . . . or with her. No. She should be the first one to see it. She opened the attachment. She immediately recognized Keith's sprawling handwriting. Evidently he'd handwritten it and then scanned it into the email.

This is hard, Dani, but you need to know your history, and when you return, we'll talk more.

Twenty-five years ago—I can't believe it's been that long—we lived in Russell County, Tennessee, just outside of Pearl Springs. Your father, Bobby, and I did something stupid—we got involved in a burglary ring and we pulled poor Toby Mitchell into it.

After breaking into five stores, we decided one more store and we were done. Bobby had learned the store was receiving a load of DeBeers diamonds, and we planned to take the diamonds and money we had stashed and leave Pearl Springs.

Bobby and I cased this last store on the pretense of buying a ring for your mother. She knew nothing about what we were doing. It was me, your dad, and Toby Mitchell—he was the lookout. Bobby made a mistake when he turned off the alarms, and they went off. Toby disappeared, and

Bobby snatched one bag of the diamonds and I snatched some jewelry.

The plan had been to lay low for a few weeks and then head out for Montana, but the next day we learned Toby had been arrested. I knew Toby wouldn't rat us out—you just had to know him to understand that—but we were afraid the cops would put two and two together. We planned to leave that night, but sometime that afternoon, Bobby called and said we had to leave right away—just for me to get to their house now.

When I got there, to my horror and disbelief, I found that someone had gotten there before me and shot both your parents. Your dad lived long enough to tell me he'd hidden the diamonds, but not where.

This is the hardest part. Your mother . . . she was still alive, and with her dying breath she asked me to keep you safe.

Sirens were approaching when I found you in the hall closet, traumatized. I grabbed you and took off, didn't even take time to look for the diamonds. Using the money I had from the break-ins, I was able to make us disappear. We eventually landed in Clifton, where I changed our last name from Bennett to Collins and got a job doing what I knew best—construction. It changed my life. My boss was a Christian, and he introduced me to Jesus. I turned my life around. My only regret is it didn't happen before we left Pearl Springs. Your mom and Bobby might still be alive. I wouldn't be a thief. I've lived with that knowledge for twenty-five years.

Eventually I started my own construction company. You have to know that I always wanted to return to Russell County and make amends and to find the diamonds Bobby hid so I could return them to the rightful owners.

He'd written a line after that but had scratched through it. Maybe the original was at home, and she could decipher it . . . Dani returned to reading.

I hope one day you can go home and reconnect with your family there. I wish I could tell you that your Bennett grandparents are still living. Unfortunately, they passed not long after you were born, but Mae Richmond, your grandmother on your mom's side, will help you. I've always regretted not letting her know where you were. But I was afraid whoever killed Neva and Bobby were looking for you, thinking you could identify them.

I don't know who killed your parents. While I've always believed it was the leader of the burglary ring, I don't know for certain. I never knew who he was—Bobby wouldn't tell me, said I didn't need to know. Be careful, though. Don't trust anyone, and don't ever let on that you know anything about the diamond heist.

And Dani, I've never been one to show emotions, but I want you to know I love you. And I'm proud of you.

Dani stared at the computer screen. If only he'd told her all this before.

26

Mark parked at the bottom of Mae's drive and jogged up the hill with Gem by his side. She'd been ecstatic to see him. He took the steps two at a time and pushed open the front door. "Where are you?"

Silence.

"Anyone here?"

"Back here."

Dani's shaky voice came from Mae's office, and he quickened his pace. "What's wrong?"

She looked up from the computer and turned toward him with a dazed stare. Mark shifted his gaze to the screen and then leaned closer. "What is this?"

"It's a letter from Keith. He . . . before he died . . ." She swallowed and raised her gaze, her blue eyes filled with pain.

Without stopping to think, he pulled Dani up from the chair and wrapped her in his arms. At first she stood board stiff, but as he rubbed her back and murmured that everything was going to be all right, she buried her face in his chest. Her shoulders shook as tears wet his shirt.

Mark held her until she stilled.

"I'm sorry," she said, wiping her nose with the back of her hand. "Probably ruined your shirt."

"Nah. It's been through worse." Gem whined when he grabbed a tissue from a box on Mae's desk and handed it to Dani. "Sorry, girl." He turned to Dani. "You haven't met Gem."

Dani blew her nose, then knelt beside his dog. "She's beautiful."

"She likes to think so." Gem held her paw up. "And she likes you."

Dani gave a little laugh. "Got another one of those tissues?"

He handed her the box.

"I'm sorry. I feel kind of embarrassed crying on your shoulder like that."

"Don't be. You've had a lot happen in the past few days."

Gem followed Dani as she reclaimed her seat and nodded toward the screen. "I wasn't expecting that."

"May I print it out?"

Her nod was so slight he almost missed it. Mark pulled another chair over, sat beside her, and sent the letter to Mae's printer for two copies.

"Where're Alex and Mae?" he asked while they waited for it to print.

"Her studio. Checking on her kiln."

The printer finished, and Mark removed the sheets. "May I read it?"

Again, she nodded instead of verbally responding.

Mark quickly scanned the letter, the information in it hitting him like a blow. He could only imagine how it'd made Dani feel. Then he went back and slowly reread it.

"This changes everything," he said.

"What do you mean?"

"What if this person comes after you in Montana?"

Her eyes widened. "We really need Lizi to go with us, but I didn't book her a seat and she's not a service dog."

"No, but Gem is." He hadn't wanted to leave Gem behind anyway. He tapped the letter. "I need to give this to Alex."

"The letter says that my parents' killer had left before Keith arrived at our house. So why kill him?"

"The diamonds. Last week, before you called me back, I researched the case, and they've never shown up. The killer could've thought Keith had them. He'd probably been trying to find him for years."

Dani slowly shook her head. "I had no idea my father and Keith were criminals."

"It's no reflection on you."

The look she gave him said she felt otherwise, then she dropped her gaze to the letter. "At least Keith turned his life around."

Mark gently lifted her chin with his knuckle until her blue eyes met his. "Believe me, no one is going to judge you by your father."

"You knew," she said, her voice barely above a whisper.

He nodded. "Like I said, I researched the case. Mae is the one who told Carson, but it was after the murders."

"She never said anything to me."

"You haven't had much time to talk."

A text sounded on Dani's phone, and she checked it. "They're ready to go."

"I'll walk out with you." He picked up the second copy of the letter. "I made two. Do you want to keep that one?"

"Thanks."

When they reached Alex's SUV, the two women were already inside, waiting. Mark handed Alex a copy of the letter while Dani crawled in the backseat and explained what it was.

"Oh, honey," Mae said. "I'd hoped to talk to you about that before you heard it somewhere else."

"I don't remember him," Dani said, "but it did something inside me when Keith confirmed they both were criminals."

"It's no—"

"Reflection on me. Mark's already told me that, but it doesn't change the facts. They might have suffered the consequences of what they did, but their actions cost my mother her life and changed mine forever."

Anger laced her voice. Mark wished he had a good answer for her, but if it had happened to him, he would feel the same way.

"I know," Mae replied. "I'm praying you can forgive him."

Her words pierced Mark like a rapier. Had Jolie's family forgiven him?

27

It was midafternoon Monday by the time they landed in Billings and claimed their baggage. True to his word, Sheriff Crider had a deputy waiting for them, and they piled into his car. When they reached the ranch, Dani punched in the pin number for the gate keypad, although the deputy probably already had it—she imagined the security company gave it to them when they responded to the alarm.

Her stomach cinched as the wrought-iron gates swung open and they drove through. She wasn't ready for this.

"Always liked this place," the deputy said as they drove toward the house. "Hope you don't have any trouble selling it."

Dani grunted as Mark shifted in the backseat of the deputy's cruiser. Levi, that's what he'd said his name was.

"I doubt she wants to think about that right now," Mark said as Gem sat curled beside him.

"Didn't mean no disrespect. Just sayin'."

She'd seen Levi around the area but didn't really know him. Not until today. The poor guy seemed to think any silence had to be filled and had talked nonstop from the airport to the house. Now, she and Mark knew all about him, his family, his wife's family . . .

"I'm sorry. I probably shouldn't have said that." He shot an apologetic wince her way. "Lots of people don't mind living where someone died."

Give it a rest, she wanted to tell him. "I don't know what I'm going to do with it."

She'd gotten a call from Keith's attorney during their layover in Dallas, telling her that she was her uncle's only beneficiary and asking if they could get together while she was in town.

Dani had scheduled an appointment for Tuesday morning. She hoped she could take care of everything and book a return flight for Thursday. Four days was surely enough time to look through the house and make arrangements. Keith had wished to be cremated, so she could return at a later date for a memorial service.

Levi pulled in front of the house and parked. "You folks staying here while you're in town?"

"I don't know yet." She still had her apartment in town, but it was only one bedroom, and that might prove awkward. And there were no hotels or even motels in Clifton.

"I'm sure we'll still do drive-by checks."

"Thank you," Dani said. "And thank you for all you've done. Keith always bragged on the sheriff and you deputies."

He beamed. "Always liked your uncle." He climbed out of the cruiser. "I'll get your bags out."

"I can do that," Mark said as he crawled out of the backseat. Gem bounded out behind him and immediately began sniffing the air.

They all turned as an SUV came through the gate and sped toward the house.

"Sheriff said he'd be coming by, so you won't be needing me any longer?" Levi asked.

"No, and thank you again."

"I didn't expect this," Mark said as the deputy pulled away from the house and then stopped to talk to the sheriff.

She glanced at Mark, surprised at how thankful she was that

he was here with her. Gem as well. "What? That the deputy would talk your ear off, the sheriff being here, or the house?"

He laughed. "All three, but especially the house and . . ." Mark swept his hand toward the vista. "It's beautiful."

She followed his gaze. He was right. In the distance were banded cliffs and sandstone formations of buttes and tabletops and what looked like mushrooms that had all formed by thousands of years of wind and water erosion. Harsh but beautiful. "Funny how you get so used to seeing something that you forget to appreciate it."

They both turned toward the sheriff as he pulled beside them and parked. Sheriff Crider climbed out of his SUV. Once a rodeo bulldogger, he kept himself in shape. Dani would hate to be a criminal going one-on-one with the former steer wrestler.

"Welcome home," he said to Dani, his hand engulfing hers before he turned to Mark and studied him. "I gather you're the deputy I spoke with on the phone."

"Yes, sir." Mark shook the hand Crider offered.

Evidently Mark had passed some unspoken test because the sheriff relaxed. "Glad she didn't have to make the trip alone. This your dog?"

Mark nodded. "Her name is Gem."

"Wish we could afford one, but a county this size doesn't have much budget. It's all I can do to get a decent salary for my deputies."

"I think every county has that problem," Mark said.

"I talked with your chief deputy this morning and couriered the bullet the medical examiner took from Keith's body to the Tennessee State Police to see if it matches the .45 caliber bullet that was recovered the night your parents were killed."

Her respect for the sheriff grew. "You think there's a possibility the killer used the same gun twenty-five years later?"

"I've learned criminals like to hold on to their guns. Alex Stone also emailed Keith's letter to me. Did he ever mention any diamonds?"

"Never. Everything in his letter is news to me. I'm still processing it." She looked up at him. "Did you find the original letter?"

"Afraid not." Crider nodded toward the house. "So, if you're ready, I need you to go through each room and tell me if anything is missing."

"Could this wait a couple of hours? We just got here," Mark said.

"I considered that, but I want to be here, and I have an appointment in two hours that will probably take the rest of the afternoon. Besides, the sooner she does it, the sooner we can figure out who might've killed Keith."

"I'll do anything I can to help," Dani said.

"I figured you would. I'll need your prints to send to the state boys, and Stone mentioned that you had recently provided a DNA sample to her. She offered to share the report with me."

"I have no problem with that at all, and now is fine to go through the house. Oh, and if it's okay, I'll stop by your office tomorrow for you to take my prints . . . unless you have—"

"Tomorrow is fine."

While the men collected their luggage, Dani keyed in the pin for the door lock. She hesitated, then pushed the door open and walked inside the foyer.

Familiar scents met her. The cypress paneling from the den, lemon wax that the weekly housekeeper used . . . She almost lost it when she identified the cherry smell from the pipe tobacco her uncle smoked.

Dani wasn't certain she could do this.

Memories assaulted her as she went through each room, but she plowed through the task, clenching her jaw when she found her dresser drawers riffled through. No amount of washing would ever clean the contamination from the murder, and she wanted to grab a garbage bag and stuff the clothes inside, but she doubted that would go over well with the sheriff.

When she came to the den, she averted her eyes from the dark stain in the middle of the room. Dani stared at the wall safe standing ajar.

"Do you know what he kept in there?" the sheriff asked.

"No. He never shared the combination with me. And I don't know how he did it, but whoever killed Keith made him open the safe."

Crider eyed the empty box. "Why do you say that?"

"The company he bought it from assured my uncle it was burglar-proof. He didn't believe it and hired a 'reformed' safecracker to try and break into it. He couldn't."

"What would have made Keith open it?" Crider asked.

"That's easy," Mark said. "The killer threatened Dani."

28

Do you mind?" Dani asked as she placed two frozen meals in the microwave and set the cook time.

"Not at all." Mark had noticed two vacuum-sealed steaks in the refrigerator, but he didn't question her when she put them in the freezer.

She pulled ingredients from the refrigerator and set about making them salads. Their dinners were almost ready when she set a colorful salad beside each of their plates. "Maybe this will make up for not cooking the steaks, but I just couldn't eat one."

"Don't worry about it. What we're having has to be better than MREs."

"MREs?"

"Meals ready to eat."

"I forgot you were in the military."

He nodded. "I wish I could sometimes."

"Want to talk about it?"

He tried hard to focus on the dark irises in her blue eyes, but the flashback came all the same. Gunfire. Blood. Jolie . . . The soft dinging from the microwave brought him out of it. That or her hand as it covered his.

"Mark?"

"Sorry. Just a bad memory."

She immediately moved her hand. He wished she hadn't.

"Let's talk about something that doesn't deal with death," he said. "How about if I take you out to eat tomorrow night when you finish whatever you have to do. Then I want to see your studio."

She looked surprised. "You like working in the clay?"

"Never tried it, but I saw some of your pieces on your website, and they're different."

"We can do that as soon as we finish tonight. The sheriff said he didn't think anything in the studio had been disturbed, but I'd like to make sure."

Half an hour later, Dani tossed her half-eaten dinner in the trash. MREs couldn't be any worse. "Sorry about that."

"It was fine."

"Thank you. You are being more than kind," she said. "Ready to walk out to my studio?"

He opened the back door. "Yes, ma'am."

An almost full moon lit the eastern sky as they walked the short distance to the studio. When Mark glanced up at it, Dani said, "It's the Pink Moon."

"I never heard a moon called that before. It's not pink."

She laughed. "No, I can see that, but April's full moon is still called the Pink Moon."

"And you know this how?"

She stopped. "I . . . I don't know, but it feels like I've always known it. Maybe I heard Nonny say it when I was a kid."

"Sounds like something she would say."

Dani stiffened and glanced over her shoulder toward the mountains.

"What is it?" Mark moved closer, catching barely a whiff of a light floral scent that he'd noticed when they drove to Chattanooga.

"I don't know. Suddenly it felt like someone was watching."

He turned and slowly scanned the area. "I don't see anything."

She reluctantly brought her gaze back to him. "It's probably nothing more than I'm tired. Let's check the studio so we can get some rest."

As they continued on to the studio, he placed his hand on the small of her back, pleased somehow that the gesture seemed to ease some of her tension.

Dani punched in the code. "Not sure what we'll find. Hopefully nothing."

"Gem and I will go first." Mark stepped around her and opened the door. "Search."

He followed Gem as she shot ahead into the small front room that appeared to be a showroom of some sort. He followed her into a larger room with a couple of pottery wheels and several tables. Must be where she worked. Gem disappeared inside a side room before quickly reappearing. The dog sat down and looked expectantly at him. "Good girl." He patted her on the side, then returned to get Dani. "Looks good. Come on in."

Dani looked around the showroom and nodded, then walked into the workroom and surveyed it. "Just my usual mess." She turned to him. "I'm really glad you came with me. I don't know that I could have done this alone."

"You could have, but I'm glad I came along. I like getting to know you better." He nodded toward the showroom. "You have some beautiful pieces. I've never seen anything like them."

She blushed. "Thanks. At least now I know where I got my talent from. I wish I'd had time to check out my grandmother's work."

"You'll see it when we get back." Mae's work was good, but her pieces ran more to utilitarian vessels. Dani made those too, but judging by the vases in the other room and those scattered around the studio in various stages, she focused more on the artistic side.

He carefully picked up a vase that resembled a carved flower. "This is just . . . amazing."

"That one is an order and came out of the kiln just before I left." She ducked her head, then shyly looked up at him. "What do you see when you look at that vase?"

He tilted his head. "It makes me think of a flower, a tulip maybe? Except I've never seen one that was light green . . ."

"The color is celadon—I wanted the piece to look like jade. What else do you see?"

He studied the piece. "There's a . . ." Mark struggled to find the words he wanted. "A smoothness of motion in it."

Her full lips spread in a broad grin. "That's what I'm always going for—I want people to think of fluidity in motion."

"You certainly accomplished that." He glanced around the room. "All the pieces I see have that look."

"I love working with porcelain even though it's the most difficult clay to work with. I like to push the envelope—you know, like a teenager pushing their parents' limits." She laughed. "And before you ask, I've had more than one disaster. I never know when I open the kiln if it's going to be Christmas or Halloween."

With a low growl, Gem suddenly scrambled to her feet, the hair on her back raised. Mark thrust the vase into her hands and pulled his gun as headlights flashed across the window. "Stay here. You too, Gem."

She hugged her arms to her waist. "There's a back door."

He eased to the back of the room and out the door, then around the side of the studio.

"Anybody here?"

Mark relaxed and holstered his gun. He never thought he'd be glad to hear Levi's voice again. The deputy stood in front of the house. "Over here," he called.

"Oh, there you are. When nobody answered the doorbell . . ."

Mark stuck his head inside the studio. "It's Levi."

"Aren't you out late?" Dani asked when she and Gem joined the two men.

"Last run for the day, and if you folks are okay, then I'll be on my way."

"Thanks for checking on us," Dani called after him as he climbed into his cruiser.

Once he was out of sight, she pulled the door shut. "I don't know about you, but I'm beat, and tomorrow is a long day."

He agreed, and they walked back to the house. Mark glanced up, and his tension melted away. "I never get tired of seeing the night sky."

She raised her gaze and sighed. "Me either. Van Gogh got it right with *The Starry Night*."

She stumbled, and he grabbed her hand, steadying her. When she didn't pull away, neither did he. *Not a biggie. She just doesn't want to stumble again.* At least that's what he told himself.

"My bedroom is upstairs. There are guest rooms on either side of me or you can sleep in the guest room downstairs."

"I think I'd prefer downstairs."

"I'll get sheets and make up the bed, but first I'm going to set the alarm."

"Will I set it off if I ramble around?"

"Not as long as you don't open a door."

She showed him how to make either a pot of coffee or a cup, then went upstairs.

Mark showered, then called Alex.

"Stone."

She sounded groggy, and he checked his watch. Ten thirty. "Sorry, I forgot it's two hours later there."

"Everything all right?"

"Everything's fine. Met the sheriff. Seems like a decent sort. He said he talked to you."

"Yeah. I got the same impression of him. He mentioned he

planned to ask Dani for a DNA sample to compare hers to the fiber evidence the Montana State Police collected at the crime scene, but I told him she'd given me one. I've requested a copy of the results be sent to him."

"Any idea when it'll come back?"

"Shouldn't be long. The company I submitted it to usually gets the results back to me within a week. How is Dani holding up?"

"As well as can be expected. She's taking care of Keith's arrangements tomorrow and talking to his attorney. How is Mae?"

"Improving. She's a little anxious about Dani. I think she's afraid Dani might not want to come back."

"She does, trust me. I think she's shooting for Thursday to return."

"Great. I'll let Mae know. And keep me updated . . . but check the time first unless it's an emergency."

"Will do. And sorry, again." He disconnected and crawled into bed. Mark ran through what he knew about Dani's case. That was where he needed to keep his focus—on the case and not her. And that was the problem. Somehow it had subtly switched.

And Keith's death. He didn't understand how the killer got inside this place. The house had a security system that rivaled that of a bank. There was no way the killer just walked into the house unless Keith let him in. But why would he do that? He finally drifted off into a troubled sleep . . .

Mark lay flat on a rooftop as he kept overwatch, providing support as Marines went from building to building, clearing the town.

Hot. He was so hot.

Sweat trickled from his brow into his eye, and he knuckled it away. Suddenly, gunfire erupted and the enemy spilled into the street. His Marines took cover in an empty building. Mark and another sniper opened fire, driving the enemy inside a house . . .

He jerked awake, gasping for breath. Gem jumped up on the bed and pressed her body against his with a whimper. "It's okay, girl. Just another bad dream." She'd witnessed many of them. At least this time he woke before the worst of it.

Mark focused on calming his heart with measured breathing. But nothing could erase what happened to Jolie. His Jolie. She'd been dead when he reached her.

He tried to go back to sleep, but his mind wouldn't let the dream go. What if he let someone else down? Mark sat up on the side of the bed. Maybe a cup of coffee would help, but since he wasn't familiar with the kitchen, he'd probably wake Dani. She needed all the rest she could get.

Whenever I am afraid, I will trust in you. He'd almost forgotten the verse he'd repeated so often in Afghanistan. Mark took out his phone and opened his Bible app and found the Psalms, then he turned to Psalm 91. "Whoever dwells in the shelter of the Most High will rest in the shadow of the Almighty . . ." He read the rest of the psalm and let the words wash over him. Maybe he'd just read the Psalms the rest of the night.

Daylight was peeking through the curtains when Gem nudged Mark. Was that coffee he smelled? And bacon? He quickly dressed and followed his nose to the kitchen, where Dani stood at the stove.

"Good morning," he said. "I didn't know you could cook."

She laughed. "I can see why after your dinner last night. Cups are in the cabinet over the coffeepot."

He grabbed a cup and filled it. "This is good," he said after taking a sip.

"Thank you. Couldn't find any eggs, but there are biscuits. They're in the covered dish to go with the bacon, and no, I didn't make them, I found a can in the fridge. My biscuits can kill at thirty paces."

"I doubt that."

"Trust me. Laura tried her best to teach me how to make them, but I never got the knack."

He filled the plate she handed him with biscuits and bacon. “Did you cook a whole pound?”

She joined him at the breakfast table. “I wasn’t sure how much you would eat. We’ll save what’s left for tomorrow.”

“What’s up for today?”

“I thought I’d go by the sheriff’s office and leave my prints, and I have an appointment with Keith’s attorney at ten. Then, we’ll go from there.”

A little after nine, they pulled through the gate in Dani’s RAV4. “So this is what you drive around here?”

“Yeah. It’s easier on gas mileage than Keith’s Navigator or his pickup,” she said, then turned pensive. “Which I suppose are mine now.”

“This can’t be easy.”

“You’re right. It just . . . feels so surreal.” Then she shook her head. “I forgot to tell you—I talked to Mae before you got up, and she *said* she was feeling fine.”

“Sounds like her.”

Fifteen minutes later they arrived in town, and she left her prints at the sheriff’s office. At ten, she parked in front of a brick building in downtown Clifton, and he walked into the attorney’s office with her. The secretary looked up. “Ms. Collins, I’m so sorry about your uncle,” the sixtyish Ms. Banks said. “Mr. Kellum is on the phone, but he shouldn’t be a minute. Can I get you a cup of coffee?” She shifted her gaze to Mark. “And maybe one for your handsome friend here?”

He shook his head, and Dani answered for both of them. “Thank you, but no. I’ll show my . . . friend Mr. Kellum’s photos of the Badlands while we wait.”

When they’d moved out of her range of hearing, she whispered, “What did you do to Ms. Banks? She’s never been that friendly before.”

He shrugged. "I seem to have that effect on older women, babies, and dogs."

She rolled her eyes at him, but before she could answer, Ms. Banks said, "Mr. Kellum will see you now." Then she turned to Mark. "You're welcome to wait in the lobby here."

Dani lifted an eyebrow and shot him an amused look.

"I think I'll wait in the car—I have a few calls to make."

An hour later Dani returned to the RAV4, looking more than a little dazed. "You okay?" he asked.

"My head is spinning—a case of TMI to take in."

He knew what it was like to have too much information to take in. "You'll need to have time to process whatever he told you."

"That's what Mr. Kellum said." She took a deep breath. "Hearing all the details kind of shook me. Mr. Kellum gave me the name and contact information for Keith's financial planner, but I'll do that another day. Right now all I want to do is grab a cup of coffee in the little coffee shop around the corner and figure out what kind of spell you put on Ms. Banks."

29

First Ms. Banks and now Dani's favorite barista was fawning over Mark. A stranger would've thought he was a movie star. When she mentioned it, his face turned red. "I told you I had that effect—"

"I know. On older women, babies, and dogs," she said, laughing.

He took a swig of his coffee. "What was it like growing up around here?"

Dani wasn't sure she was ready to let him off the hook, but she relented. "Probably a lot like growing up in Pearl Springs was for you—both are small towns."

"Pearl Springs is much bigger than Clifton. Where's the school you went to?"

"A couple of blocks over. When we finish here, do you want to walk there?"

"Absolutely."

She'd been hoping he'd say no. He paid their bill and left a generous tip. When Dani raised her eyebrows, he shrugged. "Just want to make sure she remembers me."

"I don't think that'll be a problem."

It was a beautiful warm day as they walked toward the school with Gem at their side. When Clifton Public School came into sight, she tried to imagine how Mark saw the structure that hadn't changed since she was a student—a one-story white brick building with wings on both sides. There was a wing behind, but he couldn't see it.

"I thought it would be bigger," he said.

"We only had 550 students in the entire school."

Mark nodded. "I bet you had more boyfriends than you knew what to do with."

"Hardly." She didn't like to think about those days. "I was so shy, boys thought I was stuck-up."

"No way!"

"Way." She nodded. "They called me the Ice Maiden—never understood that. The Invisible Woman, maybe." She'd never let anyone know how much that had hurt.

"You didn't date at all in high school?"

Dani shook her head. "I didn't even attend our senior prom because I refused to go without a date and no one asked me."

"I bet it was different when you went to college."

"Ha!" The laugh burst out before she could catch it.

He tilted his head toward her. "You're kidding."

"College opened a whole new world up, but not many men were willing to get past the obstacles."

"Well, I still bet when you went to school here, if you'd wanted to you could've been the star of the senior play and maybe a cheerleader . . ." He stopped because she was laughing. "What?"

"You just aren't listening, are you? Get it in your head—I was shy and didn't have any desire to do any of the things you mentioned. I was the girl no one saw. The one who helped paint the sets, not the star of the show. And certainly not the cheerleader, although I tried out once because Laura insisted it would help get me out of my shell. The sponsor stopped me in the middle of my second cheer and told me to try again next year."

"Did you?"

"Are you kidding? Why would I ever ask for that embarrassment again, even to please Laura?" Then she gave a rueful chuckle. "I've discovered as embarrassments go, it wasn't the worst I would experience."

"What—"

She palmed her hands. "Don't even bother asking."

"I'm sorry you had a tough time at school, but look at you now—you're a successful potter and artist. I bet when you went back to your ten-year reunion—"

"Didn't go."

He frowned. "Don't you ever think about going back and thumbing your nose at all those people who didn't notice you?"

"If I ever gave them any thought, I might." She sighed. "I think most of them were like me, just trying to get through school so they could move out of this small town."

"But you didn't. You stayed."

Yes, she had. Because she'd known it would crush Keith if she left.

And now he was dead.

30

It was late Thursday before Dani wrapped up her business in Clifton, and Friday morning Mark rested his hand on the gun at his waist as he surveyed the land beyond Keith Collins's property that bordered the Badlands. He'd read about the stunning rock features, but nothing he read compared to the actual area. Keith could not have disappeared into a more austere landscape.

Footsteps came toward him, and he turned as Dani and Gem approached. "I think you've stolen my dog," he said.

Dani knelt and patted Gem on the side. "She's a sweetheart."

He agreed. "All of your art pieces packed and loaded in the FedEx truck?"

Mark wished he could afford one of the vases or bowls, but the thousand-dollar price tag was a little over his budget.

"I disabled the gate lock and they're pulling out now. I'll decide later what I'm going to do with the property and the rest."

"The house might be a little hard to sell, but who knows—if that's what you want to do."

"I could never live in it now, not after . . ." She shook her head. "This was harder than I thought it would be . . ."

His heart ached for her as she looked toward the mountains and closed her eyes, the muscle in her jaw pulsing.

"Come here." He gently wrapped his arms around her, and she leaned into his chest, awkwardly at first and then a gradual lessening of tension. If only his hug could heal Dani's pain.

"I feel so guilty," she said, stepping back.

"Why?"

"Because . . ." She took a deep breath. "I was so angry with Keith. It hit me just how much I'd missed because he kept my past from me. I keep thinking if I'd answered his phone calls as I drove from Cincinnati to Pearl Springs, if I'd told him what I learned, he might still be alive."

"That's assuming his death is connected to your past."

"You know it is—he's dead less than twenty-four hours after someone breaks into my grandmother's house, reads her journal and the magazine—there's no other answer."

"I told you before—you are not responsible for the evil someone else does."

"That's easier to hear than to internalize."

"You have to, otherwise it'll eat you alive." He ought to know. A text dinged on his phone from Levi letting Mark know he was almost there. He showed it to Dani.

"Guess we better close up the house," she said. "And thanks for coming with me."

"I'm glad I came along. I've enjoyed getting to know you better."

And he had. Dani had continually surprised him this week, whether it was going through Keith's things, or tending to the hundred and one details one had to take care of when a family member died, or patiently dealing with the sheriff, who was looking for a motive behind Keith's murder or details about her uncle that Dani couldn't provide. She had no knowledge of Keith's finances or business dealings and had pointed the sheriff to Keith's attorney.

Dani had met each hurdle with a patience Mark envied. She'd even handled the sheriff's doubts when she didn't find anything missing other than the original letter Keith had emailed her. She also hadn't found Keith's smartphone. Mark figured the killer took it.

They both turned as Levi's cruiser pulled through the gate. They started toward the house. "Guess we better get our luggage."

"And some earplugs."

31

You want to grab something to eat?" Mark asked as they walked past the food court in the Billings airport.

Dani checked her watch. An hour before their two o'clock boarding. They'd had a late breakfast and no lunch, and she was hungry. "Sure. You choose."

He glanced at the kiosks. "Looks like it's a sandwich or a bowl of soup."

"Make it a bowl of soup—that's hard to mess up. I'll get us a table." She took Gem's leash and found a spot at the edge of the kiosk.

While she waited, Dani dialed her grandmother's number just to hear her voice, something she'd done each day.

"Are you at the airport?"

"We are and will board in an hour. How are you feeling?"

"Better than I should."

Dani laughed. Nonny had said that each day.

"If that's Mae, tell her hi," Mark said from behind her.

Another voice chimed in at her side. "And tell her that her pastor says hi as well."

"Who is that?" her grandmother asked.

"I don't know." Dani didn't recognize the voice and swung around. A man, not quite as tall as and stockier than Mark, stood beside him holding a Styrofoam cup. She quizzed Mark with her eyebrows.

"Tell Mae it's her pastor."

"I guess you heard that," she said into the phone.

"What in the world is he doing in Montana?" Nonny asked.

That question popped into Dani's head as well. "I'll ask him and get back to you."

She ended the call and slipped her phone in her pocket as Mark set her soup on the table. He nodded toward the pastor. "Dani Collins, Rick Adkins. He's the pastor at Community Fellowship, where Mae and a few others that you know attend, me included. Believe it or not, he's on our flight. I asked him if he'd like to join us—that okay?"

"Of course." She was curious to know what he was doing in Montana.

Rick sat across the table as Mark took the chair beside her. "I've been meaning to ask if you would rather I introduce you as Dani Bennett," Mark said.

After considering the question, she shook her head. "Let's leave it at Collins for now. It's what I'm used to." Dani turned to the pastor. "So how long have you lived in Pearl Springs?"

"I actually grew up there." He sipped the liquid in the cup. "Left for college and then seminary and returned in the mid-nineties when my daddy decided to retire."

"Then you would've known my parents."

He nodded slowly. "Your mom more than your dad, since he rarely came to church. And I remember you. You were a quiet little thing."

"I'm sorry I don't recall you, but then I remember very little of my past in Pearl Springs."

"But you do remember some things?"

"Fragments, nothing concrete."

"I figure your memories will come back to you eventually." He smiled. "My door is always open if you'd like to talk sometime."

"Thanks."

"You know," Mark said, "a lot of the people who left Pearl Springs have come back. Me included. And Alex. And the mayor's uncle, Craig Tennyson."

"And now me," Dani added.

Rick smiled. "Mae will be so happy to have you home. We've talked extensively about you. She never gave up hope. I understand she's staying at the Stones'?"

"Yes." It warmed Dani's heart once more to know her grandmother had been searching for her. She removed the lid from the soup. Chicken noodle. Her favorite. "Thank you," she said to Mark, then turned to the preacher and casually asked, "Why were you in Montana?"

"I wasn't actually in Montana. I was fly fishing in Sheridan, Wyoming—I'm flying out of Billings since it's the closest major airport." He raised his brows. "And you two?"

"We were in Clifton," Mark said. "Dani's uncle died, and she had business to take care of. Alex sent me along."

"My condolences on the loss of your uncle," Rick said to Dani. His gaze dropped to Gem.

"Did you get to visit the Badlands while you were here?" she asked before he could ask the question on his face—like why would Alex send her K-9 officer and dog with Dani.

"Which ones? The Dakotas or the Montana Badlands?"

"The ones near Clifton."

"I'm not sure where that is, so I'm sure I didn't."

Another question popped into her mind, but she focused on eating her soup. "This is pretty good," she said to Mark. "How's your sandwich?"

"Bread's tough. I wish I'd gotten the soup." He glanced toward the kiosk. "And a plane must've come in—there are too many people in line now."

Rick checked his watch. "I need to make a couple of calls. I'll see you two at the gate."

After he left, Mark asked, "What was that all about?"

"What do you mean?"

"I don't know . . . you just seemed suspicious of Rick."

She thought through her answer. "It just seems odd that he happened to be in the area about the time Keith was murdered."

"Coincidences are rare, but they do happen."

"I know that. And there's no reason for me to even go there—Rick seems so nice, it's hard to believe he would be involved." Dani shook her head, trying to clear it. "I know, it's ridiculous. I'm seeing conspiracies everywhere. Just forget I said anything."

"Will do."

They caught up with Rick during their layover in Dallas. This time they found more substantial food, and while they ate, Rick kept them entertained with humorous stories of his congregation without naming names. Most of the people Mark seemed to figure out, and the stories created images of some of the people she'd heard Alex and the Stones talk about.

After the plane touched down in Chattanooga, they caught up with Rick again at the baggage area while they waited for their suitcases to be unloaded and sent to the carousel.

"I, for one," Dani said, "will be glad to get to Pearl Springs."

"Well, y'all be careful on that drive," Rick said. "Some of those curves can be bad."

"You're not following us?" Mark asked.

"No. My wife and her sister are flying home late tomorrow night, and I'd just have to turn around and come back to pick them up. I'm staying over with my sister, Roxanne. Gives us a chance to visit."

The first bags appeared on the carousel. "There's mine," Dani said. Before she could get it, Mark had it and handed it off to her while he grabbed his. "Thank you, sir."

They waited until Rick had his bag and then they walked out of the airport together to the parking area with Gem trotting beside them.

"Glad you're driving to Pearl Springs," she said as they walked to Mark's SUV.

"I'm glad I'm not hitting that long road tonight," Rick said with a chuckle.

"Lucky you." Mark whistled when they reached the pastor's vehicle. "Nice wheels," he said, admiring the black pickup.

"Thanks. It was a gift from the church on my thirtieth anniversary."

Mark shook his head. "I didn't realize you'd been there that long. Don't imagine it's easy shepherding a small-town church."

He didn't answer right away, then he shrugged. "Somebody has to do it."

"Does your sister live in this area?" Dani asked.

"She does. I just texted her I was on my way." He put his luggage in the bed. "It was good talking to you guys in between flights."

"Yes," Mark said. "And as soon as my schedule changes, I'll be back to church."

"I'll probably see you there too," Dani said.

Mark's SUV was parked another row over, and they soon had their luggage loaded. Dani settled in the passenger seat as Mark pulled out of the Chattanooga airport parking lot.

Traffic was light as they drove to Pearl Springs, and she leaned her head back against the rest. "It was nice meeting Rick," she said.

"Yeah, for someone who never wanted to become a pastor, he's a pretty good one."

"He didn't want to be a pastor?"

"I don't think so. I've heard Carson and Judith, Mae too, talk about how his daddy pushed him into it. They said Adkins Sr. was one of those fire-and-brimstone preachers. Hard to say no to."

Now she felt sorry for Rick and hated that she was suspicious. "He must like it now or he'd just leave."

"Sometimes that's easier said than done," Mark said.

"Especially if the parishioners are buying expensive gifts for you." Dani nodded her head and yawned.

"You must be tired," Mark said. "Why don't you take a little nap?"

"I might just do that," Dani said.

She was surprised she actually dozed off, and awakened when they crossed the bridge that led into Pearl Springs. She remained still, pretty sure he knew she was awake, but he didn't offer to intrude into her solitude. That was one of the many things she liked about him.

Mark had turned out to be different from what she'd first expected. It'd been her experience that a man as fine-looking as he was often traded on that fineness. Mark was different—it was like he had no clue that women found him handsome, from the barista at the coffee shop in Clifton to the sixtyish secretary at the attorney's office when he accompanied her.

He'd been a perfect gentleman all week, not that she hadn't expected that—Mark Lassiter was an honorable man, and he'd been assigned to protect her.

But . . . she was certain he was aware of an undercurrent of chemistry between them that neither seemed willing to address. Dani knew it was there. She just didn't know what to do about it. One thing she'd learned this week—she could trust Mark. Right now, he was turning out to be a good friend, and maybe that's all he should be right now.

Dani sat up. "What's next?"

"What do you mean?"

"Where do we go from here to find Keith's murderer?"

"We don't—that's not our jurisdiction. We'll be focusing on who fired at you, and then at me when I was in your SUV. And who killed your parents."

"Isn't it the same thing?"

"Only time will tell that."

"I want to go to my parents' house tomorrow. It might help me to remember."

He turned his blinker on. "I'll talk to Alex about it."

She recognized the street that the Stones lived on. They were almost home. She smiled when they turned into the drive that circled around to the back of the Stones' house and she saw that lights were on. "Looks like somebody waited up for us."

Lizi shot out the back door that Mae opened before they had time to grab their bags. The Puli dropped her pull toy and launched herself at Dani, almost knocking her over. "I've missed you too, girl." She patted Lizi's side and picked up the toy, then played with the dog for a minute. "Was she good?" Dani asked as she rose to her feet.

Her grandmother nodded. "Perfect angel." Then she wrapped her arms around Dani in a tight squeeze. "You're home, safe and sound!"

"It's good to be here."

Her grandmother released her and hugged Mark as well. "Thank you for keeping her safe."

His face colored and he ducked his head. "No problem. I'm going to give Gem a potty break and then I'll be in."

She followed her grandmother inside the house and nodded a greeting to Alex before pointing to her luggage. "I'll be right back."

By the time she returned to the kitchen, Mark was pouring a cup of coffee. "Anybody else?" he asked, holding the carafe up.

"Is it decaf?" Dani asked. When Alex nodded, she grabbed a cup.

"I don't guess it'll kill me to drink unleaded," Mark said and filled her cup.

"How were the flights?" Alex asked as they all took a seat around the table.

"Good." Dani sipped her coffee. "You two didn't have to wait up."

Her grandmother and Alex exchanged glances, and Dani's insides squeezed. "Is something wrong?"

Alex smiled. "Not at all. The DNA test results came back."

"And you are officially my granddaughter, Danielle."

"Oh!" Dani caught her breath as tears sprang to her eyes. "I don't know why I'm surprised."

There was another round of hugs and congratulations. Even though there'd been no doubt in Dani's mind that Mae Richmond was her grandmother, it was like a cloud had lifted. Even the kitchen was brighter. Alex stood and brought a covered dish to the table. "Mae made this for us to celebrate with." She removed the decorative cover, revealing a pineapple upside-down cake.

Dani stared at her favorite dessert. "How did you know?"

Nonny beamed. "It's always been your favorite."

Her grandmother remembered that from twenty-five years ago? It was like the last puzzle piece slid into place. Dani sat back in the chair. Then a shiver ran through her.

No. There was still a piece missing. The person who killed her parents and wanted her dead.

32

Either it was the coffee, even though it was decaf, or the cake, or just the excitement, but Dani couldn't go to sleep. Like a pinball, her thoughts bounced everywhere except toward relaxing. Images popped in and out of her mind, including one of the man at Mae's house that first night. She'd never drawn it for Alex like she promised.

Dani threw back the blanket and grabbed her sketch pad and pencil from her case. She stared at the blank page, reliving last Saturday night, until her fingers sketched what she saw. When Dani finished, she tilted her head, studying the image, then made a few adjustments to the eyes around the ski mask the man had worn. That was the best she could do. She didn't know if it would help Alex, but it'd certainly calmed her down. She put the pad and pencil on the nightstand, turned off the light, and soon fell into a fitful sleep.

"Danielle! Get in here!"

She flinched.

"Now!"

If she didn't go, he would come after her. She laid her Barbie on the floor and trudged to the kitchen, slipping inside the room quiet as a cat.

Her dad pushed her mama toward their bedroom. "Get packed. We have to leave. Now!"

Mama turned and crossed her arms. "Why is he coming here, Bobby? What does he want?"

"His share of the diamonds," he said. "We need to leave before he gets here. Now get to packing!"

"No! You have to take the diamonds back!"

"Don't you understand? They're our way out—" He cocked his head as tires crunched in their drive. "He's here!" He slammed his fist against the table. "If you'd done what I'd said, we'd be out of here."

"Me? You're the one who broke the law! And now you're even stealing from your partner."

His face was so red Danielle thought he might explode. Then his face changed, and he didn't look so mad. "I'm sorry. I'm just . . ." He swept her up in his arms and turned to her mother. "You stay here. I'll see if I can talk our way out of this. But first, I'll hide Danielle."

Suddenly someone else was there. And she heard yelling. A man turned, his eyes getting mean when he saw her. Mama was still . . . Daddy too.

Dani bolted upright in the bed, sweat clinging to her body. She touched her face and wiped away the tears that streamed from her eyes. Lizi nudged her, and she wrapped her arms around the dog, burying her face in the corded hair.

This was a dream unlike any she'd ever had, weighing on her like a heavy blanket. Never had she seen her parents so clearly. In the past, their faces had been obscured. Maybe it wasn't a dream at all. Maybe she was reliving something that had happened.

Could she capture the face of the man with the mean eyes in a sketch before the image faded entirely? Dani grabbed the sketch pad and pencil she'd placed on the table by the bed and began sketching a man's face.

Dani drew an oval. Too narrow. She widened it around the

temples, and then filled in the eyes. When she tried to fill in the rest of his features, she had nothing—her pencil refused to fill in any details. This man her mind refused to see . . . had he killed her parents?

She suddenly found herself drawing her parents. Not the frightened faces she'd seen in the dream, but a sketch of her mom and dad smiling.

When she finished, Dani stared at the drawings. She hadn't noticed in the photos she'd seen at Nonny's that her dad favored Keith so much. A tiny smile pulled at her lips. And while her sketch of her mother was different from the photo on the mantel, she looked like Nonny just the same.

Then almost on their own, her fingers began to sketch a scene. When she finished, Dani stared at it, trying to make sense of what she'd drawn. Her dad again, sitting on a porch. Beside him was a younger man. Dani had no idea who it was, but he was familiar in a distant sort of way. She didn't think he'd been in the dream, at least not tonight's.

Why could she see this man's face and not the other? Maybe if she concentrated harder . . . after a few minutes, Dani shook her head and sighed. She couldn't force it. At least she had the sketch of the man at Mae's house Saturday night to give to Alex.

Lizi nudged her hand, and Dani scratched her head. "You want to go back to sleep, don't you, girl?"

She put her art supplies away. The truth of what happened the night her parents were murdered was locked away in her mind. If only she could find the key to unlock it.

Maybe the key was at the house where she grew up.

33

A low growl took Mark from sleep to awake in seconds. Gem stood at the foot of the sofa bed, the hair on the back of her neck raised. "What is it, girl?"

She ran to the door that provided privacy for the living room and scratched to be let out. Mark grabbed his gun and followed. He opened the door, and she shot through it to the kitchen door. He let her out and followed as she ran in a zigzag pattern, sniffing the air as Mark scanned the backyard under the security lights.

Soon she returned and sat at his feet, cocking her head—Gem's signal that she'd found nothing. Whoever or whatever had disturbed her was gone. "Good girl."

After Mark and Gem checked the perimeter, they returned to the kitchen to find Alex sitting at the kitchen table. Gem circled and lay down in the corner.

"Everything clear?"

"Yeah." He checked his watch. "What are you doing up at five o'clock on a Saturday morning?"

"I heard you go out and decided to get up since I was awake. Chattanooga PD is couriering over the burglary ring files this morning—they're paper, and as soon as they're scanned, I'll send you a copy." She nodded toward the counter. "I made a pot of coffee if you'd like some."

"Sounds good." He poured a cup and took it to the table, where he sat across from Alex. "What're we doing about Dani?"

She sipped her coffee and set the cup down. "It won't take long for word to get out that she's Danielle Bennett, and I figure the killer will double down on silencing her. So, I need you to stick with Dani when she leaves this house, and when you can't, call in Jenna Hart."

He nodded and took another sip of coffee. "Dani wants to go to her family home today. Thinks it might jar her memory."

"We can only hope. Knowing who we're looking for would greatly simplify everything. I can spare Hayes to go with you as backup."

"Good."

Alex wrapped her hands around her cup. "I located the murder files in our archives and reviewed them with Gramps. I'd like for you to talk to Kyle Peterson, see if you can get any information out of him about Bobby's last burglary—he was the manager of the jewelry store where the DeBeers diamonds were taken and lost his job right afterwards."

"You think he had something to do with the murders?"

"He would've known Toby Mitchell was arrested for the burglary. It would've been easy for him to put Toby with the Bennett brothers."

Mark leaned back in his chair. "You think that would've been motive enough to kill Dani's parents and Keith?"

"People have killed for less."

"How did Toby get involved in the burglary ring?" Mark asked.

"Nobody knows. Toby never would talk about it to Gramps. But he and the Bennett brothers worked in construction together. After Toby's wife left him, he started drinking and hanging out with them all the time, and Gramps believes he joined the burglary ring thinking if he flashed enough money, his wife would come back. Instead, he went to prison."

Everyone in town knew Toby. "So he had a drinking problem then?"

"I think it's worse since he got out of prison—he pled guilty and served five years with time off for good behavior. He probably could've avoided prison altogether if he'd given the Chattanooga district attorney the names of everyone involved in the burglaries, but he refused."

"Did they keep working the case after Toby's confession?"

"Not really. According to Gramps, Chattanooga PD believed the ring broke up after the murders because the break-ins stopped, as well as the pattern, and they moved on. You know the drill—there'll always be more cases than you can solve, and at least they could point to some success with the arrest and confession of Toby."

He completely understood. Not that Russell County had anything like the cases Chattanooga worked, but they had enough. "Have you interviewed Toby?"

She shook her head. "Haven't been able to find him—he's not at that shack he calls home or at the beer joints."

"I've seen him hanging around Peterson's Grocery. Maybe Mr. Peterson knows where to find him?"

"That's a good idea. You have good rapport with Mr. Peterson. See what he'll tell you about Toby when you go see Kyle."

"Don't know it's me he likes as much as it's Gem." They both laughed. "Did you know Dani's parents?"

"About as well as any nine-year-old knows the parents of their friends," she said. "I don't remember seeing her dad that often. I do remember her mom. She was really sweet. I was just so shocked, not just by the murders but that Dani disappeared."

Mark didn't remember Dani's parents or her uncle at all, but like Alex, he too would've only been nine. He probably wouldn't remember Dani except for her parents' murders and her disappearance. "Was any of the jewelry from the break-ins recovered?"

"Some of it was, but not the DeBeers diamonds." She checked her watch. "I guess I better get dressed."

Peterson's Grocery opened at eight—but it was closer to eight thirty when Mark looked for a parking space in front of the store and found one on the next block. The grocery store was practically an institution in Pearl Springs, started by Mr. Peterson's father back in the 1920s. From its inception, the store had offered biscuits with ham, sausage, or bacon to its early morning customers. Originally everything had been freshly made, but after Mr. Peterson's wife passed, he'd switched over to frozen fare. Not that it seemed to matter judging by the lack of parking space.

The bell over the door jingled as he and Gem entered the store, and the tantalizing aroma of bacon and biscuits had Mark's stomach growling.

Mr. Peterson stood behind the counter, and at least six people waited in line. The older man glanced up. "Sorry, Mark, but if you're here to get one of these"—he held up a white paper bag—"they're all spoken for. But when I'm done, I have a treat for Gem if it's all right."

"Thanks," Mark replied. If the biscuits were sold out, then the customers should clear out soon. Gem followed as he wandered around the store looking for Kyle. When the last customer left, Mark approached the counter. Gem looked at him expectantly. "Free," he said, and the dog bounded around the corner to the older man. Once Mr. Peterson gave her the treat, Mark said, "Where's your grandson?"

"He'll be in around ten."

"And you run the store all by yourself when he's not here?"

Before he could answer, the door jingled opened, and Mark turned. Toby Mitchell. Good, a twofer. He took stock of the man. Judging by the way the dingy white Henley hung on him, he'd lost weight.

Toby eyed Gem, but she ignored him as he gave Mark a curt nod. He walked past them and around the counter, stopping a few feet from the older man. "Kyle said you needed me to help out here at the store this morning."

"I'd appreciate it." Mr. Peterson pointed to a stack of boxes. "You can start by stocking the shelves with what's in those boxes."

"Pay?"

"Same as always." He named a figure.

"Cash?"

The older man nodded. "When you finish."

The two men shook hands, and Toby's hand engulfed the older man's. Mark had never noticed how large-boned Toby was. If truth be told, he'd never paid much attention to Toby, period. But he did now and noticed a cross crudely tattooed on a knuckle of his left hand. A prison tat.

Toby pushed the sleeves of his shirt up as he walked to the stack of boxes. Mark waited until he carried a box to a back aisle. "Be right back," he said to Mr. Peterson. "I need to talk to Toby."

"Would you mind waiting until he finishes? If you start questioning him, he'll run, and I need those shelves stocked."

The older man seemed to know Toby pretty well. Maybe he could get a little background information first. "I'm surprised you hire him."

"Why?"

"Well, he's been in prison for burglary—aren't you afraid he might steal from you?"

"Toby paid his debt to society. And it's hard to get help to do what he's doing—it's not like it's regular work." Mr. Peterson crossed his arms. "And to answer your other question, no, I don't believe he'd do that. He was as much a victim in what happened twenty-five years ago as Kyle."

"How's that?"

Mark kept eye contact as the older man studied him. Mr. Peterson looked away first and took out a briar pipe from his coat and filled the bowl. Mark waited while he tapped it down and then refilled it. Mr. Peterson looked up, a twinkle in his eye.

"The doctor told me this is bad for my health, and I told him that at ninety-two, it didn't matter. So we compromised. I can have my pipe as long as I don't light it."

Mr. Peterson was playing him. "I'd still like to know why you said Kyle was a victim."

"Kyle was the manager of the store that they broke into, and because he's from Pearl Springs, the same hometown as Toby, Kyle's bosses thought he was involved and fired him the next morning after the burglary."

"Chattanooga PD didn't charge him."

"It didn't make any difference to his bosses that there wasn't any evidence pointing to him."

That made it even stranger that Mr. Peterson would hire Toby. "I would think *Kyle* wouldn't want him around the store."

"My grandson feels sorry for Toby."

Or Toby was holding something over Kyle's head. "How long has he worked for you?"

"I wouldn't rightly call it working for me—more like a day laborer. Toby drinks too much to hold down a nine-to-five job. Reason his wife left him."

"Because he drank too much."

He pointed his pipe at Mark. "You already seem to know a lot about him."

Mark shrugged. "So, he's been doing odd jobs for you since he got out of prison?"

"He has, but why are you so interested in Toby? He served his time."

"We're reopening the investigation into the murder of Neva and Bobby Bennett, and I think Toby knows something about it."

"He won't tell you anything. First question you ask him, he'll clam up tighter'n bark on a tree."

"I have to try."

Mr. Peterson glanced toward the back of the store, then leaned toward Mark. "Tell you what. Toby and I have talked about what happened over the years, mostly after he'd been drinking. He's talked about how he got involved in the ring and what happened that night. Pretty sure I already know more than you'll get out of him. So ask me whatever you planned to question him about, and I'll tell you what I know."

"Okay, then." Mark took out a pad and pen. He still planned to question Toby, but if he talked to him at all, Mark would at least have something to compare his answers to. "Do you know if Toby left Pearl Springs in the past week?"

"I can't answer that other than I haven't seen him all week until today. But that's not unusual."

Mark noted that. "How did Toby get involved with the burglary ring?"

"Bobby Bennett recruited him. He needed someone to be a lookout in case an alarm went off or the police showed up. Someone who didn't ask questions and would do what Bobby said."

"Toby fit the bill."

"Yeah. And he's loyal—never told the police anything, even after they pressured him."

"Do you think Toby knows the ringleader's identity?"

Mr. Peterson hesitated. "I do, and I've asked him who it was more than once, thinking if I could discover who he is, I could clear Kyle's name. He always just shakes his head and clams up. One thing he did say—Kyle's name was never mentioned around Toby. When he gave the police that information, they didn't believe him."

"Did he see the diamonds that night?"

"According to him, he never saw the loot from any of the

stores. His job was to watch and warn them if a cop drove by, or if the owner or manager showed up. Bobby paid in cash, except for that last job."

"Why do you think Toby wouldn't give the names of the other people involved in the ring?"

A sad smile creased Mr. Peterson's face. "Because being loyal is written into Toby Mitchell's DNA." He tilted his head. "You asked why I hired Toby. Have you wondered why Toby works for me or why he would confide in me?" Before Mark could answer, the older man continued. "It's because I befriended him way before all this happened—back when he was being teased in high school for his mama being on drugs and for being in foster care after she died. I gave him a job and helped him buy decent school clothes."

Toby Mitchell wasn't the first kid Mr. Peterson had helped out. "Like you did a lot of other boys."

"Cheap labor," he said.

But Mark knew better.

The grocer crossed his arms over his belly. "Not many people have ever bothered to look beyond the surly, given-to-drink person with a prison record that he's become—that's all people see when they look at Toby. They're missing a good friend who is loyal and will do anything to protect those he cares about."

Mark tapped his pencil. Judging by Mr. Peterson's closed-off stance, he'd gotten all he was going to get from the grocer. "Thanks for your help."

"Any time," Mr. Peterson replied.

Instead of walking to the door, Mark headed toward the aisle where Toby stocked groceries.

"Hey! You said—"

"I'm not going to hinder him from his job." Just ask him a few questions. Toby ignored Mark when he stopped beside him. "Morning, Mr. Mitchell."

"The only people who call me that want money."

"I don't want your money. Just information."

"Sorry, fresh out, Dep-u-ty."

"You don't know what I was going to ask."

"You're the law. Judging by the buzz that Dani Bennett is back in town, I figure you think I had something to do with her parents' murders." He looked up, his dark eyes hard.

"Did you?"

He snorted. "Like I'd tell you if I did."

"How about this—do you know who committed the murders?"

A shadow flashed across his face, then was gone. "Same answer."

"Where were you last Sunday, and the rest of the week, for that matter."

"Sunday I was out flying my plane, then I came in and grilled filet mignon, medium rare, and went to bed—after spending an hour in my jacuzzi. As for the rest of the week, it's none of your business unless you're ready to read me my rights."

Mark took a card from his wallet and handed it to Toby. "Whoever killed the Bennetts plays for keeps, and if you know anything, I can promise you're expendable. Give me a call if you decide to cooperate."

Not that he thought Toby would. Mark hurried out of the store, almost running into Morgan. "Sorry!"

She held up her hand. "Probably my fault."

He smiled. "How's the job-hunting coming along?"

"It's promising." She nodded toward the store. "Especially if I can work up a story to take to one of the news stations."

"What? Are you doing a story on Mr. Peterson?"

"Mr. Peterson?" She frowned. "No. After we moved to Texas, every time my dad drank too much, he started talking about the Bennett murders, and Toby's name always came up. I always wanted to know what happened. When I saw Toby at Pete's Diner,

I followed him, thinking he might talk to me. Then he went in the grocery store, and I've been waiting out here for him to come out so I can interview him."

"You may be in for a long wait—he's working for Mr. Peterson today putting up stock."

"I'm patient." She rubbed her jaw, then raised her eyebrows. "Maybe he'll talk to me while he's working."

"Good luck on that," Mark said.

"Luck will have nothing to do with it," Morgan said. "And I plan to ask Alex if she'll share the case files, but I wanted to talk to Toby first."

Morgan had what all good investigative reporters had—confidence and determination. "I hope you'll share any information you get out of him."

She opened the door to the grocery. "Why not? Especially if it's a two-way street."

Before he could warn her that Alex might not share, she slipped inside the store.

34

The aroma of bacon frying pulled Dani awake. Lizi raised her head from her spot at the foot of the bed when Dani raised her arm to check her watch. Almost eight thirty? She hadn't slept this late in years.

The Puli hopped to the floor as Dani climbed out of bed. After a stop-off in the bathroom, she slipped into her jeans and pullover and grabbed Lizi's leash before the two hurried to the kitchen. Her grandmother sat at the table, drumming her fingers. Dani hugged her. "Good morning."

Nonny hugged her back. "You too."

Judith looked up as she placed a strip of bacon on a platter and smiled. "Coffee's on the counter," she said.

"Thanks, but I better take Lizi out first."

"I'll take her," Sheriff Stone said as he entered the kitchen.

"Thank you, but she's my responsibility."

"Today's she's mine," he replied with a smile. "Mark isn't here, and Alex is in the shower—she gave me explicit instructions that you weren't to step outside the house unless one of them is available. Besides, I need to get the morning paper from the box."

She quirked her mouth to the side. Even though Dani understood, she didn't like being hovered over, but judging by the set of the sheriff's jaw, there was no changing his mind. Might as well be gracious. She handed him the leash. "Thank you."

"Now you know how I feel," Nonny said.

"What do you mean?"

"Judith won't let me do anything. Expects me to sit here like the Queen of Sheba, getting waited on hand and foot."

"You know better than that. I just don't want you to overdo." Judith winked at Dani. "Coffee's still on the counter."

"Thanks." Dani poured a cup and refilled her grandmother's. "How did you sleep?"

"As well as can be expected, seeing how it's so noisy here. Cars running all over the place, honking horns and the like. I miss my mountain. How about you?"

"I had crazy dreams." Details of the dream came flooding back along with the sketches she'd done afterward. "Be right back. I have something I want to show you."

Dani hurried to her bedroom, grabbed the sketch pad, and returned to the kitchen. She flipped to the drawings of her parents and showed them to Nonny.

Her grandmother pressed her fingers to her lips as she gasped.

Judith looked over her friend's shoulder. "It's Neva and Bobby," she whispered.

"I couldn't sleep after my dream," Dani said. "My hand seemed to work of its own accord."

"I love the way you've sketched them." Nonny looked up, her eyes shiny.

"Sketched who?" Alex asked as she came into the kitchen, her damp hair pulled up in a ponytail.

Nonny held up the sketch. "She drew Neva and Bobby."

Alex's eyes widened. "I barely remember Bobby, but this looks just like the picture of Neva you have on your mantel."

"I know."

"I also drew the man from last Saturday night." Dani turned

to the sketch of the man in the ski mask. "There was some light with the full moon, but not enough to see details. It's the best I could do. The body is a general impression. The dark eyes and the gun he had pointed at Lizi made a stronger imprint on my mind."

"The mask was camouflage?"

"Yes."

Alex studied the image. "Looks like you think he had wide shoulders. Was he as tall as Mark?"

Dani closed her eyes briefly. Her face warmed as she brought up Mark's image in her mind and quickly shifted her thoughts to what the other man looked like. "About the same."

Alex nodded. "Good job."

"I have a couple more sketches." She flipped to the man she hadn't been able to see. "This one"—she pointed to the drawing that didn't have facial details—"I got the shape of the face, but that's all. And the other is my dad and someone on a porch. I don't know who the other person is."

Alex stared at the drawings and then tapped the one that was completed and frowned. She showed it to her grandmother and Mae. "Who does this look like?"

"Ben Tennyson." Both women answered together. All three looked up at Dani.

"Why did you draw him?" Alex asked.

Dani lifted one shoulder slightly. "I don't know. I draw what I see up here." She tapped her head. "Maybe I saw him at some point when I was a kid."

35

Mark turned into the Stones' drive and pulled around to the back just as Sheriff Stone came around the corner of the house with Lizi on her leash. He climbed out and released Gem from the rear seat harness. When traveling short distances in town, it was his preferred method of transporting her. Besides, she liked to look out the window.

"Did you get dog duty?" he asked.

The sheriff laughed. "More like mop duty, but don't tell Dani I said that. Lizi is a sweet dog—makes me wish we had one again. How'd the interview with Kyle Peterson go?"

"He wasn't there, but I talked with his grandfather, and I found Toby."

"Good. Let's go inside and tell Alex what you learned."

The four women turned as they entered through the back door. Alex handed Mark the sketch pad. "Dani drew these—I think her memory is starting to return. Look through them and see if you can identify anyone, then tell me what you learned from Kyle."

He nodded and flipped through the drawings. He'd seen prints of her drawings at her studio in Montana, and the sketches reminded him just how good Dani was. Both drawings of her parents were perfect, but was she drawing them from a deep memory or the photos she'd seen at Mae's? "Not saying her memory isn't returning, but Dani saw the crime board, and there are photos of Neva and Bobby on it."

"I'd forgotten that," Alex said.

"May I see Neva's again?" Mae asked and studied the sketches he handed her. She looked up with a smile. "I'd say memory—see this mole?" She pointed to a mole just above her daughter's lip on the right. "It's not in the photo on the crime board. Neva had the mole removed a year before that photo was taken."

Mark bumped fists with Mae, something they'd done for years when one acknowledged the other was right about something. He looked through the other sketches and frowned. He turned to Dani. "Is this Ben?"

Alex answered for her. "She hasn't seen Ben since she returned—the drawing is of someone from her memory, but it looks like Ben to me. What did you get out of Kyle?"

"Nothing. He wasn't there. But I talked to Mr. Peterson and Toby Mitchell."

"You found Toby? Where's he been?"

Mark glanced at Mae and Dani. "Do you want to talk about this here or your dad's office?"

"Now just wait a minute," Mae said before Alex could answer. "I want to hear what you have to say. After all, I tracked Danielle down, and it's my crime board you're using down at your office."

Mark ducked his head to hide the grin that spread across his face. But Mae had a point.

36

Calm down," Alex said. "I planned to discuss it here. Let me grab my tablet and Gramps's files." By the time she returned, they'd gathered around the table. Alex opened her tablet and turned on the recorder on her phone. "Go ahead—where has Toby been?"

"Sunday he was flying his plane, eating steak—blowing smoke. He informed me the rest of the week was none of my business unless I was arresting him. I gave him my card in case he wants to talk."

Mae snorted. "That boy'll die before he'll talk to you—I know. I tried to talk to him after what happened to Neva."

"What did you learn from Mr. Peterson?" Alex asked.

Mark quickly went over their conversation. "He claims Toby never told him who was running the burglary ring, but I think Peterson either knows or suspects more than he's telling." He nodded to Alex. "He might open up to you."

Gramps lifted the Russell County Sheriff's Department cap he wore and smoothed his hair. "Mark's right. Peterson has a soft spot for you."

"Ha! He has a weird way of showing it if he does."

"Trust me," Gramps said.

"I'll try him." She turned to Mark and Dani, who'd been quiet to this point. "When do you two plan to drive to the Bennett place on Eagle Ridge?"

"What?" Mae sat up straighter. "I don't think that's a good idea."

"Nonny, I want to go there. Seeing the house might jar loose more memories."

Mae shook her head. "But will it be safe?"

"I'm sending Deputy Hayes as backup," Alex said. "And we'll check Mark's vehicle for a tracker. That way no one will know where you're going unless they follow you, and Mark's good at spotting tails."

The older woman crossed her arms. "If they're going, I want to go."

"No!"

Five nos rang out. Gram's the most emphatic. "You just had a stroke," she said. Mae opened her mouth. Gram held up her hand. "Hear me out—I know you think you've recovered, but this will be a highly emotional and tiring trip. You don't need that."

"But—"

"No buts, Nonny." Dani turned to Mark. "And I want to stop by this Peterson's Grocery on the way. There's something about it that rings a bell."

"It should," Judith said. "You kids generally went there every day in the summer."

Dani's eyes widened. "The Three Musketeers . . . we walked there." She pointed to Alex. "You, me, and . . . Morgan. She has dark hair. Right?"

Alex grinned. "You remembered."

"Oh!" Mae tapped her hand to her head. "I forgot—Morgan called just before breakfast. She and Ben want to visit later today. I'll call and let her know to wait until after church tomorrow."

"Speaking of Ben," Gramps said, "he and Toby are distant

cousins. I remember being surprised that Ben's dad, Ralph, didn't take Toby in after his mom died."

"I don't know why," Gram said. "Ralph Tennyson always thought he was better than the Mitchell side. When he discovered Ben was hanging around the pool hall with Toby and Bobby and Keith Bennett, he yanked the whole family up and moved them to Texas."

Alex jotted notes on her iPad and looked up. "Any chance Ben was involved in the burglary ring?"

"That's a question that bears looking into," her grandfather said. "Ralph wouldn't admit it, but Ben was a little wild back then."

Alex tapped her pen on the tablet. "I don't remember any of that."

"You wouldn't with Ben being ten years older—he didn't hang around home much. I'm glad to see he got his priorities straight, though. He's been a good mayor so far."

"If Ben was nineteen, Bobby would've been eleven years older and Toby even more . . ." Alex leaned back in her chair. "Why would they let anyone that much younger than them hang around?"

"Good question," Gramps said.

She looked over her notes and saw one on Ben's uncle. "How about Craig Tennyson?" Alex turned to Mae. "He was with Ben at the hospital. Do you know him?"

"He was friends with Bobby and Neva, but I probably haven't seen him more'n ten times since then. As for why he was there, you'll have to ask Ben that. That day is fuzzy." She stared down at her hands. "Oh, wait, seems like Ben said they were together when Ben found out I'd had a stroke."

"Craig moved to Chattanooga about twenty years ago," her grandfather said. "You say he's back now?"

Alex nodded. "Opened up a real estate office downtown about three months ago."

"I'd heard he did real good in real estate in Chattanooga," he said. "Is this a satellite office?"

"I don't know. I'll ask next time I see him." She put down her pen. "Can you see any of the men we've mentioned being involved in the burglary ring? Or even the head of it?"

Her grandfather thinned his lips. "Sober, Toby could've been the ringleader . . . except he wasn't usually sober. Ralph got out of here in a hurry after the Bennett murders, so there's that, and he certainly had the brains for it. Craig too. Ben was too young to have what it took to plan and execute the robberies."

Mark leaned forward. "How about Chattanooga PD? Did they have any suspects?"

"The detective I worked with thought Bobby was the ringleader, but I always disagreed with him on that." He rubbed his jaw. "There was a pawnshop dealer I always suspected of being involved, but I never had any proof. I'm not sure he had the wherewithal to be the ringleader."

"Who was he? Is he still in business?" Alex asked. If he was, he could be the one after Dani.

Gramps nodded slowly. "Joe Yates. Still runs the pawnshop down in South End. I have a file on him in my office if you want to see it."

"I do." Alex knew the man. Didn't like him, but that didn't mean he was involved in the burglary ring. She would ask Nathan about him as well. "Okay, I think this pretty well sums up what we know. Mark, let me know when you and Dani leave."

Alex followed her grandfather to his office, where he pulled Joe Yates's file from his cabinet.

"Here you go," he said. "And be careful dealing with Toby Mitchell. You never know which way he's going to jump. I know he's on Mae's list of suspects."

She frowned. "I've never gotten that impression of the man.

According to Mae's crime board, he was out on bail the night the Bennetts were killed. Do you have a file on him?"

"It's in the Bennett case file I gave you."

"I read most of it but must have missed it when I scanned the rest. I'll have Jenna check Yates out."

The sheriff nodded. "How's she working out?"

"Good. She's so organized it's scary. We're lucky to have her."

Her grandfather leaned back in his chair. "Have you given any more thought to qualifying for the sheriff's race next year?"

"Some. This job has a lot more paperwork than I expected." She wasn't ready to make a decision. Part of her still wanted to be the first female police chief in Chattanooga. Being the first female sheriff of Russell County was no small thing, though.

"Tell me about the paperwork," he said with a chuckle, then turned serious. "You'll have your year residency in October, and if you want the job, it's a lot easier to run as the incumbent."

"Are you saying you're resigning in September?"

"Thinking about it." He took a deep breath and released it. "Going in to the office even one day a week is too much some weeks."

She walked to his chair and put her arms around him. "Gramps, your deputies understand."

He patted her arm. "That's not the point. I haven't gotten the fire in the belly back after the heart attack, and that's a disservice to you and my deputies. They need to be able to look to you as the sheriff, not the chief deputy."

It looked like she wouldn't have a year to decide. Alex kissed his cheek. "Can I give you an answer after this case is solved? I don't have a lot of time to think about it now."

"Of course."

She walked to the door.

"One more thing," her grandfather said. "When are you going

to let Nathan put that wedding band on your finger? He's not going to wait forever, you know. At least I wouldn't."

Alex glanced down at the solitaire he'd given her at Christmas. That was another thing she was dragging her heels on, and she didn't know why.

"Has he been talking to you?" she asked.

"More like I've been talking to him. If you don't know your own mind by now, will you ever?"

Alex pressed her lips together. She expected this line of questioning from Gram, but not him. "I'll see you tonight—I need to get to the office."

37

By the time Mark parked in front of the white building in downtown Pearl Springs, Dani was second-guessing her decision to stop at Peterson's Grocery. What if this Kyle Peterson was the man in the mask who shot at her a week ago and maybe murdered her parents? But Mark would be with her, and a Pearl Springs police officer would be nearby.

"You ready?" Mark asked.

Dani wiped her hands on her jeans. "As I ever will be."

"Let me come around and get your door."

Normally she would object, saying she was perfectly able to do that herself, but it was different with Mark. She enjoyed his thoughtfulness, and there was something so reassuring about him. She felt safe in his presence. Almost cherished.

Dani jerked her mind away from those thoughts. What was wrong with her? Mooning over a man she'd met only a week ago? Still, she couldn't deny he ticked all her boxes—thoughtful, kind, brave . . . handsome. Not that the last had ever been one of her boxes, but it didn't hurt that he was easy on the eyes.

At least Mark was better than the last man she'd mooned over—the one who broke her heart in college. All he'd wanted was another conquest he could brag about, another notch on his belt. But the college experience hadn't been without its advantages—it had toughened her up. She never let herself be that vulnerable again.

"I'm capable of opening the door," she said and pushed it open before he could come around.

He held his hands up and backed off. "I wasn't suggesting you couldn't. I figure you're nervous."

It was easier to let him think that than to explain. "You're right. Sorry."

"I know." He winked at her.

She felt herself blushing. *Stop it!* "Let's get this over with."

Dani followed Mark inside the store and gasped as the scent of the oiled floors sent a rush of emotions surging through her. A memory teased her brain . . . She glanced to the right and caught her breath when the glassed-in candy display was exactly where she remembered it.

How many times had she pressed against that glass with a dollar clutched tightly in her hand and picked out two candy bars? Always at least one Three Musketeers that she shared with . . . Alex and Morgan. She remembered! Dani stood straighter.

"May I help you, Miss?"

That voice. She raised her gaze. "Mr. Peterson?"

"No one around here calls me anything but Kyle. You must mean my grandfather." He turned. "Granddad. You busy?"

An older man shuffled to the candy display. He looked at Dani and took off the black-framed glasses and rubbed his eyes before he slipped them back on. "Neva? No, that can't be . . ."

"You're right, Mr. Peterson," Mark said. "This is her daughter, Danielle Bennett."

"Oh, my goodness . . ." The older man shook his head. "You're the spittin' image of your mother when she was young. Grandmother too."

"Danielle Bennett?" Kyle's gaze narrowed. "You have a lot of nerve, showing yourself in this store after what your family did."

The venom in his words was like a slap in the face, and Dani took a step back.

"Kyle!" Mr. Peterson scowled at his grandson. "What is the matter with you?"

He turned to his grandfather. "Her thieving family cost me my job at the jewelry store. If just one of them had come forward and told authorities I had nothing to do with the burglaries—"

"But Neva and Bobby were dead, and we know now Keith was running for his life. And Danielle's." Mark eyed him. "Maybe you're the one who killed Bobby Bennett."

"Are you kidding? Why would I kill him? I needed him to exonerate me."

Dani swayed, and she pressed her hand to her head.

Mark immediately put his arm around her. "You okay?"

"I think we need to leave." She hadn't expected a confrontation when she came into the store, and she wasn't prepared for this man's anger.

Mark turned to Kyle. "I'll be back to discuss this further with you."

"You do that, and don't bring her in here again."

Was Kyle guilty of killing her parents? Dani stiffened her backbone. "Are you afraid I'll remember seeing you kill my mama and daddy?"

His nostrils flared. "That's one thing I don't have to worry about, Missy." He pointed his finger at her. "And those diamonds they stole—they never showed anywhere. Maybe you have them."

She gritted her teeth. "And maybe you're the one who shot at me."

"Not me. I didn't even know who you were when you walked in."

"And maybe you're lying." She pulled away from Mark and marched to the entrance.

"I'm sorry," he said once they were back in his SUV. "I didn't think it'd turn out this way."

"I guess I better grow a thick hide—Kyle Peterson probably won't be the last one to throw the past in my face."

"No inkling that you saw him that night?"

She shook her head. "Why can't I remember?"

"What you saw was a terrible trauma for a nine-year-old. You've blocked everything about your life here."

She looked back at the store. "When I first entered the store, I remembered being there before."

"Good. Maybe seeing some of the places where you hung out will unlock those memories."

Dani bit her bottom lip. "Maybe it'll happen when we go to my parents' house. That's where it all started."

"After what happened at Peterson's, are you sure you still want to go to Eagle Ridge?"

"Want to? No. But I don't have any choice. What happened there is the source of my memory loss. Maybe seeing the house, being inside it, will jar something loose."

"You're really brave to do this."

She gave a mirthless laugh. "Not brave. It's a survival thing. In my heart of hearts, I believe I saw the man who killed my parents. I'm willing to do whatever it takes to find out who it was."

38

Mark turned onto the road to Eagle Ridge and checked his mirrors to make sure Hayes was following. The deputy's sedan was behind them. He glanced at Dani. She'd been really quiet since they left Peterson's. "It's a beautiful day."

"Beautiful mountains too," she said quietly. "So different from Clifton and the Badlands."

"Definitely." The Badlands were desolate, yet beautiful too. "Growing up there would've been different."

She fell silent again, and Mark concentrated on the curvy road. When it straightened out, he took his eyes off the road long enough to glance at her. Tears dampened her cheeks. "I'm sorry if I said something wrong."

"You didn't." She sighed. "I missed so much."

"Were Keith and his wife good to you?"

She wiped her face with the back of her hand. "Keith treated me like a daughter. Laura too. But it was lonely. We never had company or friends over, and I never felt like I fit in."

"That had to be hard."

"I always felt like an outsider. You know what I mean?"

"Sort of." All he'd felt growing up was love and acceptance

from his family, and that may have made what happened in Afghanistan harder. He wasn't prepared for failure or the harsh realities of war. "Is that why you became a potter and artist—it was something you could do alone?"

"Drawing and painting, yes. I didn't fall in love with clay until I went to college." She held up her hand. "And that's enough about me. Your turn. What was it like growing up here?"

"That's hard to answer. For the most part good."

They passed a sign that read "Watch Out for Falling Rocks." She glanced out the window at the mountainside. "Does that happen much—falling rocks?"

"Sometimes, especially after a rain." He checked his rearview mirror to make sure Hayes was still behind them.

"Can I ask you something?"

"Sure."

"When Laura was sick for so long, and then died, Keith talked about how God gave him peace. And you seem to have that same peace even though you went through terrible times in Afghanistan. How do you get that peace?"

He gripped the steering wheel. He hadn't been expecting that. How to explain it to Dani? "You'd have to have known me when I came home from Afghanistan to understand. I was seriously messed up."

Mark slowed for a deer bounding across the road and sorted his thoughts.

"You don't have to tell me."

"No, I need to. Seven years ago, I was in my last year before I mustered out of the service. There was a guy at the base who trained dogs like Gem. I started working with him and the dogs. Saved my life.

"He was a Christian and got me started in a Bible study about how to have peace. He also made me see how good God had been to me." Mark laughed. "That took a while, but the more I studied my Bible, the more I understood what he was talking about." He glanced at her. "Does any of that make sense?"

"I want it to," she said. "How was God good to you?"

Mark didn't have to think hard on that one. "He got me out of Afghanistan in one piece."

"But it was bad that you had to go in the first place, and evidently bad things happened to you over there."

"Being a Christian doesn't mean we won't encounter bad things. I've learned that the bad things that come my way make me depend on God more."

She bit her lip. "You sound like Keith."

He hesitated. "I don't know where you are where God's concerned, but when life gets overwhelming for me, I talk to God about it, give him whatever it is that's bigger than I can handle. I usually start repeating a verse in one of the psalms—'Whenever I am afraid, I will trust in you'—and that gives me peace."

"I've never felt the peace Keith talked about his God giving him."

"Maybe that's the problem," Mark said quietly. "You have to make him your God."

39

Alex parked in front of Peterson's Grocery. Nathan was meeting her at Pete's Diner for lunch in half an hour, which gave her time to interview Kyle Peterson. And she didn't look forward to it.

As a kid, she'd been scared of Kyle. He'd been close to thirty when he came back to Pearl Springs to help his grandfather in the store, and he was always so grumpy, talking mean to the kids who came into the store—never when a parent was around, though. Kyle no longer frightened her, but she still didn't like to shop at the grocery when he was there.

She liked his grandfather, though, even if he had tattled to Gramps that she'd pranked him. Alex climbed out of her SUV and entered the store, smiling at the jingle of the bell over the door that had been there as long as she could remember. Mr. Peterson was behind the counter in his usual place, and the store appeared not to have any customers at the moment.

Or any sign of Kyle. If he wasn't here, she could talk to Mr. Peterson. The older man's memory was sharp, and he might've heard something around the time of the Bennett murders. "Good morning, Mr. Peterson. Do you still keep Prince Albert in a can?"

He laughed. "Actually, I do. Can't tell you how long I've had it, though. Not many people roll their cigarettes these days."

"Do you still get calls telling you to let him out?"

"Been years since that happened. Can't say as I'm sorry either," he said with another chuckle. "But it's good to see you looking as lovely as ever."

She grinned. "And you need new glasses."

He leaned on his cane as he shuffled to the cash register. "Bah! You know you're the vision of loveliness."

She wished. Now Dani, on the other hand . . . "You might not be Irish, but you certainly have the gift of gab."

He laughed. "Oh, but I am—on my mother's side. Now what can I do for you?"

Alex looked around the small store. "Is Kyle here?"

"Gone to the bank, but he'll be back soon to help with the lunch rush—a lot of people drop in around noon to get a sandwich—I make a mean ham and cheese."

Looked like it would just be Mr. Peterson. Alex propped a foot on the railing at the bottom of the counter. "I know Mark told you we've reopened the investigation into the Bennett murders. I'm looking for any information that someone might have that would help crack the case."

"Thought that might be why you're here. I've been searching my memory ever since Danielle and your nice K-9 officer left." His face grew somber. "Such a sad thing to happen."

"I know. I was too young to know much about it, but I've been getting familiar with the case through my grandfather's files."

He perched on the stool beside the counter. "Then you know, of course, that my grandson lost his job over that robbery?"

"I do," she replied. "Did Kyle have anything to do with the burglaries?"

Mr. Peterson didn't answer right away. "I don't rightly know how to answer your question. I asked him after the Bennett girl left, and Kyle said he didn't. Can I prove he didn't? Other than he's never lied to me before, no."

"Did you ask him about the Bennett murders?"

The older man shook his head. "No need to. My grandson did not kill the Bennetts. And his girlfriend at the time said he was at her apartment the night the murders took place." His mouth turned down. "Not that I approved of him staying the night with her."

"Do they still stay in contact?" Alex knew they hadn't married because Kyle was single, or at least they weren't married now. And from the gossip she'd heard since she'd returned to Pearl Springs, he didn't have a very active dating life.

"You'd have to ask Kyle that. I don't even remember her name."

"I'll do that." She glanced down at her notes. Chattanooga PD had included an address in the file, but Alex didn't know if it was current. "Do you know if she's moved?"

Mr. Peterson lifted an eyebrow and peered at Alex over his round glasses. "It's been twenty-five years. If I don't remember her name, I dare say I won't remember where she lived."

"Her name is Crystal Davis," Alex said. Mr. Peterson was touchy about his grandson, which surprised her. They never seemed that close the few times she'd shopped in the store, always snapping at each other. Alex made a note to check with Chattanooga PD for a current address. "Do you mind telling me what you remember about the murders?"

He stared at the floor. "The Bennett murders . . . sad thing. I'll grant you, the brothers made bad choices, but that was a terrible price to pay. The whole thing was a bad affair. First to find out they were involved with those burglaries—Bobby, yeah, but I never figured Keith to get involved in anything like that. Then Bobby and Neva getting killed, especially since Neva had nothing to do with the burglaries. I worried that Mae Richmond wouldn't get over her daughter dying like that and then her granddaughter disappearing."

The bell over the door rang, and a customer hurried in. Alex waited while she picked up a loaf of bread and lunch meat and paid the grocer.

"Any thoughts on who might've killed them?" Alex asked when the customer left.

"Not a one . . . except it wasn't Kyle. He had an alibi."

"The girlfriend."

"Not just the girlfriend—he'd had his car serviced the day before and had a record of his odometer reading. The day of the murders he'd only put fifteen miles on his car. Should be in your grandfather's files—Sheriff Stone questioned him."

Alex made a note to check the files. "Any other thoughts?"

Mr. Peterson shifted on his stool. "I figure whoever headed up that ring was mighty upset when Bobby Bennett took off with those diamonds."

"How did Kyle feel about losing his job the very next day?"

"Like he was tried and convicted without a jury. It's eaten at him like battery acid, and I don't blame him for being bitter."

"I can see how he would feel that way," Alex replied.

"I do recall thinking it a little strange when Ralph Tennyson pulled his family out and relocated to Texas right after it happened. There's no law against that . . . but Ben was pretty wild back then. I've always wondered if he got involved in that mess someway."

Her grandmother had mentioned the same thing. "Anything else?"

Mr. Peterson glanced toward the ceiling. "I heard about somebody buying stolen goods around here not long before it happened. Never found out who it was, though. I imagine that's all in your grandfather's files."

"What can you tell me about Toby Mitchell?"

"I told your K-9 officer what I know."

"Where does he go when he doesn't want to be found?"

"He likes to hunt and fish when he's not at the pool hall or bar."

"Where does he do that?"

"Pearl Lake for fishing, and any place around here that doesn't have a 'No Hunting' sign."

"And when he's not at any of those places?"

"Sometimes he hangs out at the county airport."

"Why would he hang out there?"

"You'd have to ask him."

Her cell phone dinged with a text. Nathan. He was leaving his office for the diner, and Peterson was stonewalling her. Her time would be better spent brainstorming with the police chief. "Thank you for your time, Mr. Peterson. I'll come back later and talk to Kyle."

"Anytime, Chief Deputy," the grocer said.

She nodded and walked to the door. Mr. Peterson was hiding something or protecting someone. Alex didn't know if it was Toby or Kyle. Or both.

40

Mark's heart hurt for Dani. If she only knew what God could do for her, the peace he could give her. That peace was what got him past Afghanistan and what happened there. He wanted Dani to have the same peace.

But it was more than that. Dani pulled at his heartstrings in a way no other woman had, not since Jolie. Mark brought himself up short. He couldn't go there with Dani—she was depending on him to protect her. Mark needed to get his head in the game.

He checked his mirror. Where was his backup? "Do you see Hayes?"

"What?"

"The deputy. He was behind us when we went into that last curve." He handed his phone to Dani. "Call Hayes—he's in Favorites. See where he is."

"There's—"

His side window exploded. Mark barely heard the buzz before cracked glass spiderwebbed across his windshield. He slammed on the brakes.

Dani screamed, and the phone flew from her hand. Another bullet took out their back window, barely missing her. "Get down and stay there!"

They were sitting ducks on the road, and someone was using them for target practice. Mark floored the gas pedal, shooting the SUV forward. The steering wheel jerked to the left when a tire exploded. Another bullet took out a back tire.

With his heart thumping like a kettle drum on steroids, he manhandled the SUV to the side of the road. "Get out and stay near the motor." Nothing else would stop a bullet.

She scrambled out of the SUV, and he followed on her side. They knelt near the front of the vehicle. He checked out Dani. Ghostly pale as though every drop of blood had drained from her face—probably the same way he looked. "You okay?"

"Yeah," she croaked.

He'd pulled the SUV off the road next to the metal railing that kept motorists from plunging into the deep gorge below. "Where's my phone?"

"On the floorboard. But there's no signal—I was trying to tell you when all of this happened."

He sidled around her, opened the door, and grabbed his phone. *Where is the shooter?* The bullets had come from the west, and he turned and scanned the mountains. Nothing. No sun glinting off metal, no anything. "Stay here. I've got to find a signal."

"I'd feel safer with you."

He hesitated, then nodded. "Stick close."

"You don't have to worry about that."

For the time being, he left Gem in her crate. Which way to go? There were no trees along the road in either direction. While he was trying to decide, his cell phone rang and he checked the ID. Hayes. And one service bar that blinked off and on. "Where are you?"

"Half mile back . . . got a . . . call. Someone . . . shooting and pulled over. You . . . okay?"

"You're breaking up. The shooter took out my SUV. Call Alex and bring her up to date. And don't try to get where we are—

there's a sniper shooting at us." Mark hoped Hayes's connection was better than his.

"Sure thing . . . get to me?"

"No." They couldn't risk the road—there was absolutely no protection from the sniper for the half mile between Mark and Hayes. And they were at the top of the next highest ridge on the mountain. He'd hiked the whole area, but in this particular section, the gorge was so steep he'd given up.

He peered over the railing at a narrow ledge six feet from where they stood. If they missed it, the hundred-foot drop beyond meant certain death. They simply could not miss it. Once they reached the ledge, they would be out of the line of fire, and the hike to his house was doable.

He spoke into the phone again with no idea if his words were reaching Hayes. "We're going over the railing and then walking to my cabin to get my four-wheeler."

With the all-terrain vehicle, they'd be able to come around the mountain on the other side of the gorge. By that time, Alex would have a team in place. Mark disconnected and glanced at Dani. "Guess you heard we're going to my cabin."

The wind whipped her hair, and she brushed it away from her face. "How do we get there?"

He nodded toward the railing, and her eyes widened. "We can't walk up the road?" she asked.

"I'm afraid not. I don't know where the shooter is."

"You don't think he's gone?"

"I doubt it."

"But he's not shooting at us."

"We're out of his line of sight." Mark scanned the hills around them. Other than the wind being a little high, it was a perfect place for a sniper, and he'd picked the perfect spot to blow out their tires. Dare Mark risk checking to see if the shooter was still out there?

There was no question in Mark's mind that the shooter was using a high-powered rifle and scope, which meant he was probably a good distance away and would take a second to zero in on a target. A quick look should easily be possible with minimal danger.

He crouched beside the fender and popped up just long enough to scan for a reflection. Yes! A light glinted on the hill across from them. Mark dropped to the ground just as a bullet whizzed by and embedded in the metal railing.

Another bullet kicked up dirt not a foot from the front of the SUV.

Dani hugged her arms to her waist. "I'm sorry! If I hadn't wanted to come—"

"Not your fault." He opened the rear door and grabbed Gem's harness and leash before he released her from the crate. "Good girl," he said as she stood for him to put her in the harness.

He hadn't heard a single rifle report so the shooter must have a suppressor. The brief flash of light had given Mark only a general sense of where the shots originated.

Another bullet shattered his side mirror. Again no report, but with the angle, he had a better idea of the direction. "He's moving and we'll be sitting ducks." He grabbed her hand. "Come on!"

For now, the SUV blocked the shooter from seeing them as they inched their way to the metal railing. His heart pounded in his chest as more bullets rained around them. He had to get Dani to safety.

Mark peered over the edge at the six-foot drop to a narrow ledge, and tried to keep his mind off what would happen if they missed it. He glanced at Dani, alarmed at her paleness. "Can you make it?"

She swallowed hard, then squared her shoulders and nodded.

He looked down at Dani's feet. Athletic shoes. Hiking boots

would've been better. He decided not to tell her to watch for rattlesnakes, at least not yet. "I'll let Gem down first, using her harness and leash, then I'll follow. You'll come last."

That way if she stumbled when she jumped, he could catch her before she plunged over the side of the ledge.

41

The lunch rush was just starting when she entered Pete's Diner, and Alex quickly spotted Nathan in their corner booth.

"Any luck with the Petersons?" he asked as she slid across the vinyl seat, facing him.

"Not really." Alex had emailed Nathan the files on the Bennett case and told him she planned to interview the Petersons. "Kyle never showed up, and Mr. Peterson didn't give me as much as he gave Mark. Did you get a chance to read the files?"

Nathan nodded. "The files indicated there wasn't any proof that he was involved in any aspect of the case."

"I know. It's just a gut feeling that he might have been. And it could be hunger pains."

"I've already ordered chicken salad on a wrap. It's such a pretty day—do you think your hunger could hold off long enough to take our wraps to the park to eat?"

"Fresh air and sunshine and seventy-degree temps? Absolutely."

"You want to ride with me or follow in your SUV?"

"I'll follow."

He nodded. "How about we pray before it gets here?"

She nodded, and he took her hand, his thumb resting on the engagement ring he'd given her at Christmas. After he said the blessing, Alex looked up, and he was smiling. "What?"

"You haven't seen the email?" he asked as Ethel approached with their meal.

"Here you go, folks." Ethel set the sandwiches down with a flourish.

"Do you mind boxing it up for us?" Nathan asked. "We're taking it to the lake."

"Give me a second." She hurried away to the kitchen with the food.

"What email?" Alex demanded as soon as Ethel was out of hearing range.

"The one from the venue you wanted for the wedding. They had a cancellation."

Her eyes widened. Alex had never thought she'd want to have her wedding at a venue, but this one was on top of a mountain. "When?"

"June first."

She swallowed hard. "That's so soon. I couldn't possibly plan a wedding in a month."

He frowned, but before he could respond, her cell phone rang. She checked the ID. "It's Hayes. I better see what he needs."

Nathan nodded, and she punched the answer button. "Stone."

"Someone's shooting at Mark. They disabled his SUV and have me pinned down."

"Where? And are you okay?"

"I'm fine. It happened on the road to Eagle Ridge."

"Mark and Dani?"

"He was okay when I talked to him. Said he was going to hike to his place and get his ATV, but Mark kept breaking up. He doesn't answer when I call. I'm hoping it's because his reception is terrible."

"I'll be there in twenty minutes."

"Good."

Alex gritted her teeth and disconnected. "There's been another attempt on Dani's life." She relayed Hayes's information. "I should've sent more deputies with them."

"You couldn't have known."

"But I should've anticipated it." She scrolled her contacts and punched a number.

TBI Special Agent Maxwell Anderson answered. "Alex? What's going on?"

"I have a witness and K-9 officer under fire on Eagle Ridge. I need a chopper. How soon can you get here?"

"I'll be at the sheriff's office within forty-five minutes."

"I'll be waiting. And thanks." A good working relationship with the Tennessee Bureau of Investigation always came in handy.

42

Dani's head swam as she peered down at Mark. He looked impossibly far away as he stood on the narrow ledge. She should've told him she didn't like heights. What if she missed and fell to the bottom of the gorge? And what was he doing with his phone?

"Jump!"

At least he'd put his phone away. She tried to swallow, but her mouth was too dry. Maybe she could just stay here.

A bullet pinged off the railing.

Not an option. Dani took a deep breath and jumped. As soon as her feet hit the ledge, Mark grabbed her, and she collapsed against him.

He wrapped his arms around her.

With her head against his chest, Dani felt Mark's heartbeat. Slow and steady. How could he be so calm? She didn't want to move away from the safety she felt in his arms.

"You did great," he said.

"Thanks," she replied in a husky voice that matched his.

He brushed a strand of hair away from her face, then he released a tight breath. "We don't need to stay here."

She glanced around, and once again her heart leaped into her throat. How did he expect to get off this ledge? "Wh-where are we going?"

"My cabin." He pointed to the east. "That ridge leads to my house."

"I hope you know what you're doing," she muttered.

He laughed. "Trust me. I do."

"How will we get off this ledge?"

"We're not for a while. It runs along the side of the gorge here until we reach the ridge my house is on."

She shifted her gaze from Mark to the ledge. Didn't he see how narrow it was? But he'd said to trust him. He lived here and probably knew this area as well as she'd known the land around their ranch in Montana. "Is this one of those times you're trusting God?"

"You better believe it."

"Okay, lead on," she said.

"Actually, why don't you go first, after Gem," he said as he unhooked the dog's leash. "That way I can cover our backside."

Her knees turned to water. "What if he comes after us?"

"I expect him to, but if he was set up where I saw a flash of light, it'll take a while to reach us. We'll be long gone by then, hopefully at my cabin or on the four-wheeler headed around the mountain."

"There isn't any other way to get there?"

"Sorry."

"Then I guess we better get to walking."

"That's what I like about you—no matter what happens, you don't stop. You keep on going."

"Like the Energizer Bunny," she said dryly.

He laughed. "You're funny too. Okay, Gem, let's go home."

The dog barked, and Dani watched as she loped along the ledge. "I swear, I think she understood you."

"She did. And she'll alert us if there are any rattlesnakes on the ledge."

"Rattlesnakes?" She looked down at her feet. Of all times not to wear her boots.

He nodded solemnly. "It's April and getting warmer, especially where the sun hits the rocks, so when we get to a sunny patch, watch for them."

She cocked her head. "Why can't you call for a helicopter to come pick us up?"

"I tried. No service. I have a booster at the house—it's the only way I have service. I'll try again when we get there."

Gem loped back to where they were and barked. "We're coming," Mark said. "You ready?"

"Might as well be."

Dani followed Gem along the path, always conscious that Mark was close behind.

Doubts assailed her. What if the shooter had been close instead of far away? He could be on them before they knew it. Her thoughts circled back to the bullets pinging off the SUV, then to the possible rattlesnakes Mark mentioned. She tried to corral her wild imagination, but it was no use.

Maybe this was when she should focus on a Bible verse like Mark said. She did know one . . . right? The verse he'd told her about earlier popped in her mind. *Whenever I am afraid, I will trust in you.* Dani silently repeated the words, seeking that peace Mark talked about.

The walking grew harder now that they'd left the ledge and were climbing. Sweat beaded her face. She turned to check on Mark.

"I'm here," he said. "You want to stop and rest a minute?"

"How much farther?"

"Probably another hour."

"What do you mean, probably?"

"If it were just me and Gem, it'd take about forty-five minutes to reach my house from here . . ."

"Are you saying I'm slowing you down?"

"It's always slower with two people. Plus, we don't have any water with us."

What she wouldn't give for a drink of water. But Mark was kind to try and make her feel better. She *was* slowing them down. "I'm fine—let's keep going."

She'd barely gotten the words out of her mouth when she tripped over a rock. Dani grabbed a bush to keep from falling, but Mark was faster and grabbed her around the waist.

"We're stopping to catch our breath," he said when she was steady.

His tone brooked no arguing, not that she wanted to. She sank to the ground. A minute later, Gem bounded up and sniffed her before plopping next to her. "Why do you live way out here in the boonies?"

He sat on the ground near her. "I like seeing the stars at night. And it's quieter than in town."

"You're a lot like my grandmother."

"I'll take that as a compliment."

She smiled at him. "Now, what are the other reasons you like living out here?"

He was quiet a moment. "Even though Pearl Springs is small, there's still a lot of noise—cars passing by, sirens, neighbors yelling. When I first came back from Afghanistan, I couldn't stand to be around any noise."

"How many times did you go to Afghanistan?"

Mark shifted and turned toward the valley below. "Three tours."

"Is being a sniper the reason you're always super vigilant?"

"Hadn't thought about it, but I guess it is."

It also explained why he was so calm when most people would be running scared. "Was that a sniper shooting at us?"

He gave a short, ironic laugh. "Not a trained one. A trained sniper would have killed us."

She shivered at the deadly calm way he spoke. "So you think he missed because he isn't a good shot?"

"Not saying that at all. He probably didn't take the wind into consideration, and even if he did, it's hard to judge just how much to adjust your aim sometimes. And it takes a second to find your target with a high-powered scope." He stood and held out his hand. "You ready to hike again?"

Dani took it, and he pulled her up, his hand lingering a little longer than necessary.

An hour later they walked out of the woods into a clearing with a neat frame house in the middle. Just off the back porch was a stack of firewood, and not far from the firewood sat a four-wheeler. "Your place?"

He hurried her across the yard. "Yep. Give me a minute. We need to get a couple rifles. You know how to shoot?"

She nodded. "But—"

"Good, and don't worry. We should be out of here before the shooter arrives."

"You don't know that. What if he's already here?"

Mark turned toward the road, and she followed his gaze as he scanned the woods. Dani had hunted in Montana when she was a teenager, and she hadn't forgotten how to look for telltale signs that other hunters were in the area. But this hunter was tracking them, not deer. The only movement was Gem trotting back and forth from the front porch to the back.

"Come on," he said. "You grab the bottles of water in the refrigerator."

Suddenly Gem's hackles raised, and she started a barking

frenzy. "What is it, girl?" Mark bent to pet the dog just as a bullet plowed into the post on his back porch. "Get behind the well!"

He pointed to a brick well that was a short distance from the side of his house, and she ran for it while he disappeared inside. When he returned, he held a rifle and ammunition in his hands and another rifle slung over his back. "Catch," he yelled and tossed a box of shells to her. "I'm going to throw the rifle easy-like behind you. Don't try to catch it."

The rifle landed in the grass behind her, and she quickly grabbed and loaded it. "Got it ready."

"Cover me!" Mark ran a zigzag pattern to the well.

Dani squeezed the trigger on the rifle, then tugged the bolt handle up and back, ejecting the spent casing. She fired again. Too slow!

The shooter obviously had an automatic, as he fired in rapid succession.

She screamed as Mark went down.

43

Mark felt no more than a sting when the bullet hit him and didn't understand how it brought him down. Another bullet kicked up dirt two feet away.

He had to get behind the well. "Did you see where the shots are coming from?" he yelled.

"Generally." Relief sounded in her voice.

"Then keep him down long enough for me to get to the well."

Dani fired one round after another with barely a second between shots. Then she stopped and helped him as he crawled behind the brick.

"Good job. Might want to talk to you about becoming a deputy."

"I don't think so, but thanks. Where're you wounded?"

"My thigh, but I think it's just a graze."

"You're lucky it didn't hit an artery. Does it hurt bad?"

He had too much adrenaline to feel pain. That would come later. "Not too much. Where's our shooter?"

She pointed to a hill across the road from his house. "If he hasn't moved."

"Where's Gem?" He hadn't seen her since the shooting started, and that wasn't like her. He frantically searched the area, his heart almost stopping when he saw her still form near the front porch. "Gem!"

She raised her head barely an inch, but she was alive! He had to get to her. "Cover me!"

"You got it."

He ran a zigzag pattern again as Dani fired the bolt-action rifle toward the hill. Gem thumped her tail when he drew near. "I'm here, girl."

She yelped when Mark pulled her under the porch behind the concrete steps. A branch dug into his good leg, and he shifted away from it. Mark's thigh throbbed, and he examined the wound. It looked like just a graze, and the bleeding had checked. Then he gently examined Gem and found a graze wound near her ear. Another half inch . . .

The shooter had tried to kill his dog. Thank God, it had only stunned her. They needed backup and quick. Alex could commandeer a medical helicopter and fly a few deputies to Mae's house. From there it was only a mile or so to where they were pinned down—if he could reach Alex.

Mark checked his cell phone for service. One bar. That shouldn't be—why wasn't his booster working? Then he saw why. Half the receiver was on the ground. How could the shooter hit something no bigger than a frying pan and miss them? Maybe because the receiver wasn't a moving target.

He tried calling Alex anyway, but as he expected, the call failed. Time to switch to plan B—get to the brick well and from there to the back of the house and the four-wheeler. Mark smoothed Gem's coat, murmuring encouraging words to her, then crawled to the edge of the porch where he could see Dani. "Gonna need cover again," he shouted to her.

"Say when. Is Gem all right?"

"I think so." He urged the dog to stand, and she clambered to her feet. Mark glanced toward the road. The shooter hadn't fired for at least five minutes.

Was he moving in closer for the kill . . . or had he left? "You see anything moving?"

"No. I was just wondering where he was."

Maybe he was conserving his ammo. Mark shrugged out of his jacket and attached it to the branch he'd crawled over and then stuck the branch out from the house, waving it up and down. Two shots from the shooter answered his question. He was moving closer.

"Get ready," he said and turned to Gem. "Let's go, girl."

They dashed from the porch to the well as Dani peppered the hillside with bullets. There was return fire, and while closer, it wasn't by much.

"You two okay?" Dani asked.

"The bullet grazed the side of her head, but I think she'll be fine." Mark nodded toward the hillside across the road. "He's moving closer."

"I know."

"If we can make it to the back porch, we'll have the house to protect us while we get to the four-wheeler," Mark said. "Can you drive a four-wheeler?"

"Yes, but I don't know the terrain. I'll sit behind you—you need to be the one steering and handling the braking and throttle."

With a shooter behind them, that was the most dangerous place. He hated putting Dani in danger, but that was their only option. He nodded. "Let's do it."

"What about Gem?"

"I'll strap her in the front rack."

They ran for the back of the house. He worried when the gunman didn't immediately open fire. What was he doing?

Mark had his answer when the gunman started firing from

a different angle. He'd anticipated they would try to escape and had moved into a better position.

"He's closer," Dani said.

"Yeah. Get to the other side of the house!" When they were out of the shooter's line of fire, he said, "See if you can distract him with your rifle. I'm going after the four-wheeler."

"Where is he?"

Mark pointed to a stand of woods to their left. "He's still on the other side of the road and will have to cross the ravine to get here. Should give us time to get away."

Dani opened fire as Mark dashed for the four-wheeler. Less than a minute later he drove the all-terrain vehicle to the back of the house and secured Gem in the front rack. Then he straddled the machine, and Dani climbed on behind him.

"Say a prayer." Mark gunned the four-wheeler, and they shot past the house. They'd almost reached the edge of the clearing when the gunman opened fire again. A bullet lodged in a tree as he wheeled to the left, away from the gunman, then back to the right.

The shooter was still far enough away that he needed a scope, and with Mark not driving in a straight line, he wouldn't be able to get a bead on them. Seconds later the woods hid them from his view, and Mark released the breath he'd been holding.

They weren't out of danger yet—anyone as prepared as the shooter probably had an ATV with him. It wouldn't take a rocket scientist to figure out they were making a run for the road back to town. If the gunman knew the mountain, he'd know the best way to get there.

44

Adrenaline pulsed through Dani's body as the ATV flew out of the trees into a valley. She looked over her shoulder. No sign of the shooter.

The four-wheeler hit rough terrain, almost unseating her. Dani wrapped her arms around Mark's waist and held on as the ATV climbed a rock trail.

He turned his head. "Do you see him behind us?"

"No." The wind almost whipped the word out of her mouth. "How's your leg?"

"Okay."

She didn't know why she asked—he wouldn't admit it if it was about to fall off.

"Once we top this ridge, we'll be going slower as we descend, but hold on tight."

He didn't have to worry about that. "How much farther?"

"Barring trouble, an hour."

Trouble as in the shooter catching up with them or trouble with the trail or ATV? She wasn't sure she wanted to know. "How's Gem?"

"Fine—she's trying to get out of the restraint."

The four-wheeler hit a rock and kicked up, almost throwing Dani off.

"Sorry. Just hang on tight."

If she held on any tighter, she'd probably cut off his breath. And she couldn't help noticing the rock hardness of his abs. There was no question that he worked out. Probably ran too.

Running. That was her thing. Or it had been in Montana. So far staying alive was her thing in Tennessee. Maybe when this was all over, Mark would consider letting her tag along on his runs sometimes. Dani shivered. If she was still alive.

Mark steered the ATV up the mountainside over rocks and dirt. At the top of the ridge, he stopped and killed the motor. For a full minute he said nothing, just cocked his ear toward the trail they'd just climbed.

"I don't hear anything," he said. "Maybe our shooter doesn't have an ATV with him."

"You think he's still following us?"

"Not on foot. He may be waiting on the road somewhere, thinking we'll try and get back to it." Mark dismounted from the ATV and winced as he put weight on his wounded leg.

Blood stained his pants leg. "You—"

"I'm fine." He helped Dani off. "You probably need to walk around a little."

Then Mark unstrapped Gem and lifted her off the rack. She shook herself and stretched, then looked expectantly at Mark. He ruffled the fur on her neck. "Free, Gem."

She barked and ran in a small circle.

"Looks like she's going to be okay," Dani said.

"I hope so. When we get back to town, I'll take her to the vet to get checked out. Right now, I need to find water for her."

They'd left the bottled water at Mark's cabin when the shooting started. "If you do, can we drink it as well?"

"At this point I'd wait—we should get to the highway soon. If something happens and we don't, then we'll talk about drinking what water we find."

Dani kept an eye out for the shooter as she walked over the ridge away from the ATV and did a few yoga stretches while Mark searched. She was still stretching when he returned. "Find anything?"

He shook his head. "Maybe we'll run across a stream soon, but right now, we need to get moving." He took her hand and pulled Dani toward the ATV with Gem trotting beside them. "Watch your step."

He didn't have to tell her that twice. She focused on where she put her feet as well as for any rattlesnakes sunning themselves on the rocky terrain.

They were almost to the four-wheeler when a bullet ricocheted off a boulder beside her.

Mark practically tackled her to the ground. "Get on the other side of the rocks. And Gem, down!"

Another bullet pinged off the rock right where she'd been standing. Dani scrambled around the boulder followed by Mark and Gem. "How did he get ahead of us?"

"He has to be tracking one of us, and it's not me. Give me your cell phone."

She pulled it from her back pocket. "But Alex disabled the family app—"

"If Keith thought you might turn it off, he could've installed a hidden one." He quickly opened her settings and scrolled through them. "I don't see anything—wait. Here's one with an odd name." He opened it. "It's a find your phone type of app."

Suddenly she wanted to throw up. Keith's phone. That she never found. The murderer had it and was using the app to track her. Mark tapped on the app and then looked to the southwest. "We're running parallel to the road right now, and his location is less than a quarter of a mile from it."

He showed her the shooter's location. She clenched her jaw. "He's been tracking us the whole time."

"Yeah. It's why he was waiting for us at the house."

"What do we do now?"

For an answer, he took out the SIM card in her phone and stomped it. "This ought to buy us a little time. You ready?"

She nodded.

"Stay low and beside me until you reach the crest—whatever you do, don't run ahead of me. After you're on the other side, you'll be safe."

She knew what Mark was doing—he was protecting her by putting himself between her and the shooter. Dani followed his orders and crawled to the crest of the ridge. Once they were over it, they ran to the four-wheeler. He quickly strapped Gem to the front again. "Sorry, girl, but I don't want to risk you getting shot."

"Do you think he has an ATV?"

"Maybe." He held his phone up again.

"Still no service?"

"No."

Dani flinched at his curt tone.

"I'm sorry." He pulled her into his arms. "We're going to make it."

Mark's voice held conviction, and his words from earlier popped into her mind. *Whenever I am afraid, I will trust in you.* Was the verse running through his mind? Silently she repeated it. Hope flickered, and she repeated the verse again. When they got out of this mess, she wanted to know which psalm that verse was in.

45

Alex paced outside her office as she waited for the team from the Tennessee Bureau of Investigation to arrive. *Come on.* Finally the *whop-whop* announced their arrival. Relieved, she looked up. Alex waited until the pilot set the bird down in the middle of the parking lot before running to it, ducking under the rotor blades.

She'd been in contact with Maxwell again. The plan was to pick Alex up and first check at Mark's house. If he wasn't there, they would search Eagle Ridge. She climbed on board, and Maxwell high-fived her as she buckled in.

"We need to quit meeting this way."

She grinned. They'd worked a kidnapping case while she was in Chattanooga and had formed a mutual respect. "Thanks for coming, Max."

"It's always a pleasure to play Captain America." He nodded to the other agent, a woman about Alex's age. "Alex Stone, Gina Fielder."

Alex offered her hand. "How do you put up with him?"

Gina pointed to her head. "Use earplugs all the time."

Max laughed with them. "Y'all wound me. Put on your headset and tell me what happened."

Alex donned the headset as the chopper lifted off, but even then, it was difficult to communicate. She gave them the basics of the case. “Mark tried to communicate with the deputy following him, but he kept breaking up.”

“Which way?” the pilot asked.

She directed him to the road to Eagle Ridge. “His house is on the road, so just follow it. We should come to his SUV first.”

Ten minutes later she spotted Mark’s SUV, the front bumper against the railing and all four tires flat. “There.”

“Do you want to set the chopper down?”

“No. Go on to his house.” Minutes later, the house came into view.

The pilot’s voice sounded in her earpiece. “There’s a clear spot about half a mile from the house. I can set down there.”

She gave him a thumbs-up. Once they were on the ground, Alex and the other two agents jogged to the house with their weapons pulled. “Mark!” Alex called out when they reached the front porch. “Are you here?”

Silence answered her. She tried the door. Locked. “Before we break it down, let’s try the back door.”

They found the back door open.

“Hey,” Gina yelled. “Bullet hole here.”

Alex turned. The TBI agent pointed to a hole in the post. Alex’s stomach churned. What if they found Mark and Dani inside, dead?

Max banged on the door. “TBI. Coming in!”

She followed the agent inside. Her stomach settled a little. “Mark? Dani? You here?”

Room by room, they cleared the house.

“His rifles are gone,” Alex said.

Max turned to her. “You sure?”

She nodded. “He showed them to me once. A Browning .270 and a Springfield .30-06. Both belonged to his dad.”

They returned to the backyard. "Found quite a few bullet chips and several casings here by the well," Gina said. "Looks like there was a shoot-out."

Alex scanned the area. "His four-wheeler isn't here!"

"Which way would he have gone?" Max asked.

She frowned. "I don't know the area like Mark does, but I do know this is the only road to town. Pretty sure he would head down the mountain and come out on the other side of the gorge where the shooting took place. I just don't know exactly how he'd go."

"At least we have a direction. Let's find out what we can see from the air."

Once they were back in the helicopter, they swept back and forth over the area. "I see something moving!" Alex yelled, pointing to a four-wheeler that disappeared into the trees.

"Where?" Max leaned toward her.

"It's hidden in the thicket."

"I have eyes on a four-wheeler carrying two people over here," Gina said.

Alex quickly shifted in her seat as the chopper swung closer. The rider on the back waved frantically. "That's them!"

46

Never had the sound of a helicopter sounded so sweet to Mark as the bird set down on the top of the next ridge.

"They won't leave us, will they?" Dani asked over the sound of the motor.

"No. Pretty sure they scared off our shooter too."

Mark gunned the ATV toward the ridge, his heart thudding heavily in his chest when she wrapped her arms around his waist and leaned into him.

He'd made a mess of things, and Dani could've been killed. He should've thought about her cell phone having a tracking device . . . but he hardly ever saw her use it.

The helicopter came into sight as the ATV topped the ridge. Alex and a man and a woman he didn't recognize stood outside the chopper.

He released Gem from the restraint, then helped Dani off the ATV before he climbed off, wincing when he put his weight on his leg. He'd all but forgotten the gunshot wound in his thigh. The adrenaline was wearing off. Alex and the other two approached.

"I don't think I've ever been happier to see the cavalry," he said.

"I was pretty happy when I spotted you too." Alex turned to

Dani. "Are you okay?" When Dani assured her she was, Alex introduced the two with her.

"This is Max Anderson and Gina Fielder, TBI agents. They already know who you two are. We found bullet holes and casings at your house. What happened?"

"We had a shooter," he said. "How far are we from the road? I'd like to get Gem to the vet."

"It's at least a couple of miles," Alex said. "We'll fly you out of here. What's wrong with Gem?"

"One of the shooter's bullets grazed her. If you'll take her and Dani in the chopper, I'll use the ATV to get to the road."

"Mark was shot as well," Dani said.

He waved his hand. "It's just a scratch."

Alex jerked her head toward the helicopter. "We'll all go in the chopper."

Mark shook his head. "There's not enough room for all of us."

"They sent the big chopper—there's room," she said. "We'll go straight to the hospital, and I'll have a deputy waiting to take Gem to the vet."

Mark groaned. He did not want to see the ER again.

47

A tantalizing aroma filled the Stones' kitchen as Dani paced the floor. "And that's how we didn't make it to the house and Mark ended up in the ER again."

She quit pacing and sat in a chair across from her grandmother. Lizi rose from her place in the corner of the room and plopped down next to her chair.

"I'm just glad you're safe. Do you know how Mark is?"

"No. He hasn't let me know." She'd debated whether to tell Nonny any of the details as Jenna Hart drove Dani to the Stones' from the hospital. In the end, she didn't have to—Nonny had heard about it by the time Dani and Jenna arrived.

What she didn't tell her was how scared she'd been when they'd been running for their lives. Or even how relieved she'd been when the helicopter landed. Or how worried she was now that Mark hadn't called her with an update. According to the last check of her watch, which must have been at least five minutes ago, it was close to six.

"You haven't heard anything, have you, Jenna?" Dani casually lifted to her lips a steaming cup of Lady Grey that Judith had brewed. She resisted checking her watch again.

The deputy shook her head. "He's going to be fine—he always is."

Lizi raised her head as the back door opened, and Dani turned toward it, hoping it was Mark. No. Just Alex. "Do you know how Mark is?"

"He's going to be fine." Alex repeated Jenna's words. "The doctor cleaned the wound, and Mark was waiting on an IV antibiotic when I left. But it'll be a couple of hours before he's released—you know they don't get in any hurry there."

"How about Gem?"

"The vet treated her for the graze and didn't find anything else wrong. But, like Mark, she'll have to take a round of antibiotics."

She sagged against the chair. Dani had been terrified the vet might find a bullet lodged in the dog's body somewhere. "Good. Where is she?"

"She's still at the clinic and probably will stay the night for observation."

A car door slammed, sending Dani's heart through the roof. Lizi jumped to her feet, growling, while Alex and Jenna unsnapped the straps over their guns. Alex eased to the back door.

"It's probably Kyle Peterson delivering the groceries I ordered," Judith said as she came into the kitchen.

Tension in the room went down a notch even though the dog continued to growl.

"At ease, Lizi," Dani said. The dog obeyed the command, but the look she gave Dani said the Puli wasn't happy. Dani wasn't either and wasn't sure how much more yo-yoing of her emotions she could take.

"One of us could've picked them up." Alex's voice was tight—evidently Dani wasn't the only one on the yo-yo string.

"It was after five when Jenna and Dani got here, and Kyle had already closed the store and left with the order."

"I'm sorry, Gram. I'm just a little tense."

There was a knock at the back door, and Dani grabbed Lizi's collar when she went on alert again.

Judith hurried to the door. "Come on in, Kyle."

"Yes, ma'am." He set the groceries on the island and surveyed the room, his face flushing. "None of these folks could've picked these up?"

"They weren't here when I called the order in. I tried to cancel the delivery, but you'd already closed," Judith said. "I'm sorry if it inconvenienced you."

"Didn't mean no disrespect, but it just seemed strange." Kyle handed Judith the bill.

"Oh dear," she said. "I forgot my purse. I'll be right back."

"Here, I've got it." It was the least Dani could do after all the Stones had done for her. She took the ticket from Judith and fished two twenties from her purse. "Keep the change."

Kyle's face turned even redder. "My grandfather would skin me if I took a penny more than what's on the bill." He pulled a roll of bills from his pocket, peeled off a ten, and handed it to Dani. "But then, you'd probably like that. Your uncle would've too." Kyle's eyes hardened. "I heard at the store he was dead, and I can't say I'm sorry. He ruined my life."

"You seem to have a lot of animosity toward Dani." Alex crossed her arms. "Where were you this afternoon?"

"Not that it's any of your business, but I was running the store. I took Mrs. Judith's order, and I waited on . . ." He shrugged. "I don't know how many others stopped in to shop. Several paid with a credit card—I'll get their names and you can check with them. They'll tell you I was there."

"I'll do that," Alex said. Once Kyle was out the door, she said, "If Keith had been killed in Pearl Springs, Kyle would be my number one suspect."

Dani wasn't so sure the chief deputy should strike Kyle off her list. "I think I'll take a shower."

"Don't be too long. My grandmother made one of her chicken and rice casseroles." Then she called after her, "Oh, I almost forgot—Morgan and Ben are coming to visit tomorrow afternoon."

Dani nodded.

Before she showered, Dani was certain she wouldn't be able to eat anything, but cleaning up made a world of difference . . . or at least enough to be able to eat Judith's delicious casserole. She'd even resisted checking her watch every five minutes. But by the time her grandmother turned in, a slow boil had started, and by eight thirty, Dani was set to blow.

She checked her watch again.

"It's ten minutes past the last time you looked," Alex said.

Heat rose in Dani's face. Was she that obvious?

"What do you think is taking him so long?"

"I'm sure he went to check on Gem."

"But he's not answering your calls."

"His phone might be dead—he probably doesn't have a charger with him."

"Oh, right." She stole another look at her watch.

Alex sighed. "Did . . . uh . . ."

Dani raised her gaze to the chief deputy's concerned gaze. "Did what?"

Instead of answering, Alex stood and took her cup to the coffee maker and refilled it.

"Did what?" Dani repeated.

Alex turned toward Dani. "Is there something going on between you and Mark?"

"No." From the way Alex looked at her, she'd spoken too quickly.

"'Cause if there is . . ." She took a sip of coffee, then looked at Dani over her cup. "I'm afraid you're setting yourself up for heartbreak."

She bit her lip. "Why do you say that?"

"I've heard him say he isn't husband material."

"I'm not looking for a husband." Dani wasn't, was she? No. And she definitely hadn't been thinking along those lines with regard to Mark. So why did Alex's words hurt? "Like I said, there's nothing between us."

Dani raised her cup to her lips only to realize it was empty.

"More coffee?" Alex asked, holding the pot up.

"Sure." She leaned back as the chief deputy refilled her cup. Even if she wasn't looking for a husband, what were her feelings for Mark?

Alex sat across from her at the table. "I shouldn't have said anything, but you don't seem to have much experience with men. I don't want to see you get hurt."

Was she that transparent? Dani set the cup down. "You're right. I've never dated much. I don't know how I was when we were friends, but growing up in Montana I was very shy. I would have much preferred to be homeschooled, but Keith thought I needed social interaction and insisted I enroll in public school. He was probably right, but I hated it."

Alex nodded sympathetically. "From what I remember, you were quieter than either Morgan or me, but I never thought much about it." She chuckled. "If I had, I probably would've just thought you couldn't get a word in edgewise—Morgan and I usually did all the talking and planning, and you did what we said."

Dani gave her a rueful smile. "That didn't change, except it was my uncle doing the talking and planning. And being the good little soldier he said I was, I never argued with him, just went along." She rubbed her thumb on the cup handle. "By the time I was in high school, my classmates thought I was stuck-up."

"I'm really sorry—you deserved better than that." Alex squeezed her hand. "You've mentioned before that you don't remember anything about your life before Montana. What's your first memory?"

She didn't have to think twice. "Keith telling me to never mention anything about our lives before we came to Montana, never mind that I couldn't remember one thing about that life."

"That must've been strange to you."

"It was." Then Dani grinned. "But you'll laugh at my second memory."

"No, I won't."

"A schedule. I didn't talk for a year after we moved to Montana, and evidently Keith took me to a doctor, actually a psychiatrist, and told her that the move had traumatized me. She prescribed a schedule. Said that routine would make me feel safe."

"That kind of makes sense. What kind of schedule was it?"

"Everything I did was on a board in the kitchen. School schedule, then when I was home, it was meals, snacks, playtime, bedtime—you name it, it was on that board, even down to when I brushed my teeth. I got up by the schedule and went to bed by it."

Alex stared at her. "I can't imagine what your life was like."

"Me either now. But it worked and I started talking again." She shook her head. "A few years ago, I figured out the reason I stopped in the first place was because of Keith's warnings. I was afraid someone would come and do something terrible to us if I said anything . . . subconsciously, I was probably remembering my parents' murders."

A car door slammed, and they both looked toward the back door. "Probably Mark," Alex said as she stood and pulled her gun.

A text dinged on her phone, and she glanced at it. "It's him," she said, holstering her pistol before she unlocked the back door.

His presence filled the whole room when he came through the doorway with Gem at his side. The dog padded over to the table and put her paw on Dani's knee.

"You really are okay." She gently scratched behind Gem's ear, being careful not to touch the wound. Dani looked up as Mark limped into the room, and her heart ached at how pale his face was.

"Doc said she'd be fine."

"How about you?" Alex asked. "Much pain?"

"Enough." His expression was grim. "Where's Jenna?"

"Home. I told her we could hold down the fort tonight."

He nodded. "Any more coffee?"

Alex pointed to the coffee machine. "Half a pot, but don't drink too much and not be able to sleep."

"It won't be coffee that keeps me awake." He poured a cup and brought it to the table and sat across from Dani. Gem followed and lay down beside his chair.

"Did they give you anything for pain?" Alex asked.

"They wanted to, but I told them Tylenol would be enough."

She nodded. "Now that you're here, I'm going to bed." Alex stopped at the door. "Oh, Gram moved your belongings from the living room to the guest bedroom this side of Dani's room."

"If you don't mind, I'd feel better about sleeping in the living room—that way if anyone tries to break in, I'll hear them better."

"Suit yourself," she said. "See y'all in the morning."

Dani stood as Alex disappeared down the hallway. "I think I'll turn in too."

Mark stilled her with a look. "Don't go just yet."

He wanted her to stay? "Why didn't you let me know how you were?"

Mark rubbed the stubble on his face. "I can't rightly say. I was pretty busy in the ER."

"How long does it take to send an 'I'm okay' text?"

Mark ducked his head. "You're right. I should've let you know."

"You're darn right you should've." Heat climbed up her neck. Evidently the head of steam she'd worked up had spread to her whole body. "I need some air." She walked to the back door. "Come, Lizi."

The night air washed over Dani, cooling her. What was wrong with her? She had no reason to be upset because Mark hadn't called. Except . . . there was a spark between them. She'd felt it and believed he had too, and she just didn't want to hear him tell her he wasn't interested. Lizi leaned against her leg. Oh, Mark would've couched it in pretty words like "it's not you, it's me" or "you deserve better."

What was wrong with her? She'd only met the man a week ago . . . Falling in love didn't happen that fast. She froze. *Falling in love?* That couldn't be what she felt—love was supposed to be happy and fun, not painful like this. She'd been right in the first place about keeping their relationship strictly professional.

The back door opened, and she swiped at the tears on her cheeks before she moved into the shadows of the trees in the backyard.

A cold nose touched her hand. Gem. Lizi tried to nudge the other dog away, but Gem stood her ground. Halting steps sounded behind her.

"What do you think?" Mark asked softly.

"About?"

"The stars."

Dani raised her gaze and caught her breath at the sight. As far as she could see, stars twinkled against a black expanse. The same sky and stars she'd seen in Montana. There had to be a lesson in that, but all she could think of right now was how close Mark was. She drew in a deep breath.

"It's almost magical." Awe filled his voice.

If she turned and looked at him, her resolve to keep their relationship on a professional level would blow away like dust in a sandstorm.

Mark slowly turned her to face him. He ran his thumb along her jaw. "I've never met anyone like you," he said, his voice low, husky.

Her knees turned to water, and she looked away.

He drew Dani closer and turned her face toward him, his blue eyes dark in the moonlight, holding her captive. Then he dipped his head, his lips hovering above hers briefly before he claimed them.

Dani moaned, giving herself to the moment. He deepened the kiss, slipping his hands behind her head, pulling her even closer.

She sighed when he released her and laid her head on his chest. Good. His heart pounded as hard as hers. No one had ever kissed her like that before. And she'd never responded like that before.

A car backfired, and Mark stiffened. "I shouldn't—"

"Mark Lassiter, don't you dare apologize for kissing me."

"I wish it were that simple."

His abrupt tone made her look up. Dani's heart stuttered at the steely determination in his eyes, replacing the softness that had been there just moments ago. She stepped back.

"I'm sorry, Dani. I have a job to do and that's what has to come first."

She squared her shoulders. "I get it that you regret kissing me, but it's not like you professed your undying love."

His eyes grew round. "I didn't say I regret—"

"You didn't have to—your actions say it for you." She steepled her fingers. "Why don't we go back to the way we were this morning and pretend the kiss never happened."

"Is that what you want?"

Was that disappointment in his eyes? "It's probably for the best. Alex pointed out earlier that I don't have a lot of experience with men, and I don't care to have my heart broken, not by you or any other man."

48

Mark winced. Dani's words cut deep. Not that he didn't deserve them. "It's not you—"

"Please, don't give me that 'it's not you, it's me' line," she said, palming her hands.

"But it's true. You're an amazing woman, and you deserve someone so much better than me."

"What's so terrible about you? I don't get it."

He rubbed his forehead. "I can't let another Jolie happen."

"What are you talking about. Who's Jolie?"

"Never mind." He took his hand back. "I'm sorry. We just can't get involved."

Her eyes narrowed. "Where's the man who told me God gave him peace? I believed you. When we were running from the shooter, I even kept saying that verse in Psalms over and over—'Whenever I'm afraid, I'll trust in you.' And where is it in the Bible, anyway?"

He looked startled. "Psalm 56."

"Oh. Why do you say God gives you peace if it isn't true?"

He turned away from her and closed his eyes. Boy, he'd made a mess of things. "I told you I was a work in progress."

"That's a cop-out and you know it."

Mark stared down at his hands. He had to make her understand how what he'd been through changed him. That sometimes he could claim those verses and peace flooded his soul. And other times, the darkness had such a hold on him, he froze.

He raised his head and locked gazes with Dani. Why couldn't things be different? It was simple. Because she was everything that was good and beautiful, and he wasn't.

But he owed it to her to at least try and explain. Mark took a deep breath and released it.

"It takes a certain type of person to be a sniper," he said softly. "To look through a rifle scope at someone and not see that person as a human being but as a target. An enemy."

He pulled his bottom lip through his teeth. "Don't get me wrong. I'm proud of my skill with a rifle. I kept my squadron safe against enemies who intended to kill as many Americans as they could." His shoulders slumped. "Until I didn't."

Could he tell her what happened with Jolie? Maybe if he did, it would help her see he wasn't what she needed. "We had intel a bomber who'd blown up a barrack was hiding out in this village. There were two squads and they'd spread out, preparing to make an assault on the house where the bomber was located.

"I was providing overwatch. Five or six soldiers had taken position in an empty building across from the house when this kid, couldn't have been more than ten or eleven, came running toward the building with a grenade . . ."

She squeezed his hand. "Don't relive it."

He gave her a sad smile and pulled his hand away. "You won't understand unless I tell you. I couldn't kill the kid. He threw the grenade, and it landed right next to Jolie. It went off before she could move. I couldn't save the woman I loved."

Dani reached over and gently covered his hand again. This time he didn't pull away and allowed the warmth to travel all the way to his heart.

"The choice you had to make was a horrible choice to have to make," Dani said softly.

"It was war." He blew out a deep breath. "When I first came home, I didn't want to sleep because of the nightmares every time I closed my eyes. They're down to only once a week for the most part now."

"I'm so sorry."

"Me too."

"Have you—"

"I've tried everything—drugs, alcohol, therapy . . . It was God and Gem and dogs like her that have gotten me as far as I am. Which, unfortunately, isn't very far."

At the sound of her name, Gem stood and nuzzled Mark's hand. "Good girl." He looked up. "I don't think I could have made it without the dogs."

"What do you mean?"

"Working with them touched something inside me. Then I returned to Russell County, and Sheriff Stone hired me as a deputy and gave me the freedom to train first Gem, then several other dogs that have gone to small police forces around the country."

Dani leaned toward him. "You're a good man, Mark Lassiter. Don't let the darkness rule you."

He held her gaze. "You just don't realize how much darkness is there."

She shook her head. "What you don't realize is how much light is there."

49

The next morning Dani lay curled in a ball, halfway between sleeping and waking. She wasn't certain where she was, but the smell of bacon tickled her nose, and sunlight peeked through the blinds. It was a place she'd been before. A place she didn't want to leave.

"Good morning, sweet pea."

"Mama?"

"Hmmm. Always remember Mama loves you . . ."

Something inside her broke, and tears filled Danielle's eyes and spilled down her cheeks.

Dani's eyes popped open. For a minute she didn't move, other than to breathe. She wanted to hold on to the dream. But had she been dreaming? It'd seemed so real. And the tears had brought relief.

Her mind had taken her back home to her mother. But why?

Justice. That's what her mind was seeking. She would not rest until she got justice for her parents, and now Keith. But first she had to jar those memories loose.

Dani climbed out of bed, and her gaze fell on the sketch pad. She picked it up and flipped to the drawings of people she'd felt compelled to draw before leaving Montana. She hadn't shown these to Alex and Nonny. She would today.

After dressing, she grabbed the sketch pad and her computer and took them to the kitchen, expecting to find Judith frying bacon. Except the kitchen was empty, and no one had been cooking. The smells had been part of the dream.

But where was everyone? It was seven thirty. Then she remembered everyone was going to the late church service, and they'd all insisted that Judith stay out of the kitchen—everyone would eat cereal this morning.

She set the computer on the table. *Coffee first.* Dani made a pot, and while she waited, she typed *dissociative amnesia* into a search engine, hoping to find something new.

Dani looked up as Mark came into the kitchen, and her heart did the flipping thing it'd done last night when he kissed her. And then he'd ruined it all by trying to take it back.

Mark was so wounded, though, and she wanted so badly to help him. No. She wanted to heal his heart.

"Oh, good, you've made coffee." He grabbed a cup from the cabinet, then filled it. "Looking up something?"

"I was trying to find a therapy to help me remember what happened that night."

"Did you?"

"Not really. It's about the same as what a psychologist in college suggested—hypnosis as a therapy. When that didn't work, she suggested art therapy and perusing old photos of my family and revisiting my roots to see if places I knew as a child might trigger memories."

Mark brought the cup of coffee to the table and sat across from her. "And . . . ?"

"I was already into sculpting, so that obviously wasn't working. And considering I had no photos and no clue of where I was born, I couldn't do that. When I decided to come to Pearl Springs, I expected it would unlock my memories."

"And it hasn't." Mark rubbed his thumb over the top of the cup handle. "Why don't you talk to Mae again? And Ben and Morgan will be here this afternoon. Ask them what they remember about you."

"Morgan may remember something, but Ben would've been practically grown when I was a kid. I doubt he remembers anything."

The door opened, and Alex entered the kitchen. "I thought I smelled coffee."

She soon joined them at the table with a full cup in her hand and nodded toward the computer. "Searching for anything in particular?"

"New therapies for regaining memories."

"And?"

"What I found was basically what my psychologist told me years ago." Dani shared what she'd told Mark.

"Photos, you say?" Alex sipped on her coffee. "Mae should have some . . . and Gram may have some of the three of us—you and me and Morgan." She raised her eyebrows. "And Morgan may have photos. I'll call her and tell her to bring any she can find when she comes today."

"Do you think we could go to my parents' house after they leave? I still think seeing it is the key."

"We'll see—this time I'd like to go with you along with a couple more deputies, and I'm short-staffed on weekends."

"Tomorrow, then?"

"That should work. There'll be a briefing on the case tomorrow afternoon. Would you like to sit in on it?"

"I think that's a great idea," Mark said.

"Could I really?"

"Definitely. I'll send a deputy to pick you up." Alex checked her watch, then drained her cup.

"Someone made coffee." Dani's grandmother cinched the belt on her housecoat as she came into the kitchen. She poured a cup and brought it to the table and joined them.

A few minutes later, Mark and Alex scattered to get dressed for church, but Dani lingered behind with her grandmother. She hadn't spent nearly as much time with her as she would've liked. "How are you feeling?"

"Better each day, but I've discovered I have my limitations—I'm not as steady on my feet as I was."

"Maybe you need to use a cane?"

"I have a walking stick at the house. When you go to Eagle Ridge, maybe you could bring it back?"

"Of course." Dani tilted her head. "Do you have any photos of me?"

"A whole box full. You can get them as well—they're under my bed. Maybe that will help you remember."

"That's what I'm hoping." She picked up the sketch pad she'd laid by her computer. Dani flipped to the older sketches. "When I showed you my sketches the other day, I didn't show you these. I sketched them before I knew about you or Pearl Springs."

She scooted the chair beside her grandmother and waited while Nonny looked at them. Dani pointed to a sketch of a girl with light-colored hair. "I figure that's Alex. And this is probably her with Morgan." She pointed to the same girl with a dark-haired girl.

"Oh, my goodness." Her grandmother looked up at her. "How . . . ?"

"I don't know. These faces came to me randomly, and after the second or third time, I started sketching them."

"God was opening your mind even then."

"Maybe so." Dani flipped the page and pointed to a woman with short hair who looked to be in her fifties. "Is that Judith?"

"It is."

She flipped the page again. "Is this you?"

Nonny pressed her hand to her mouth, then she turned to Dani, her eyes bright. "That's the way I looked when you were nine. I hadn't cut my hair yet and wore it in a braid."

"How about these people?" She turned to another page. "I think the older man is Mr. Peterson. The younger one looks a little like Kyle . . . but not."

Her grandmother leaned closer. "That's probably Kyle's dad. He died maybe a year before everything went bad." She pointed to a younger man. "That is either Ben's dad or his uncle—they favored a lot at that age." Then Nonny looked at the clock. "We better get dressed if we're going to church."

"I'll be ready." Dani studied each of the men she'd drawn before she closed the sketch pad. Was one of them the person trying to kill her?

50

Dani grabbed her robe and slipped into it when someone tapped on her door. “Who is it?”

“It’s just me,” Alex said.

“Come on in, then.”

“I meant to give this to you earlier.” She handed Dani a light-colored vest.

She examined it. “Body armor?”

“I’d like you to wear it anytime you’re outside the house, including church today.”

“Do you think someone might come after me there?”

“I don’t think so, but why take the chance?”

“Maybe I should just stay home.”

Alex shook her head. “It’s important to Mae for you to go. Take it into the bathroom and try it on.”

In the bathroom, Dani slipped into the vest. It was remarkably light. She stepped back into the bedroom. “Do I have it on right?”

Alex tightened the tabs, giving a snugger fit. “How’s it feel?”

“Odd, but not too bad.”

“Good. See you in a few.”

Dani pulled on black pants and a flowing top that covered the vest well, and half an hour later joined the others in the kitchen, where Alex assigned Dani to her SUV. "Mark will be riding with us," the chief deputy said.

Dani enjoyed the service, especially standing beside Mark as he joined the congregation in singing hymns she remembered from her childhood. She'd gotten out of the habit of attending church after she moved into her apartment in Clifton. And when she moved back into Keith's house during Laura's illness, Dani always volunteered to stay with Laura so he could attend.

Pastor Rick was a good preacher, but she'd expected that after meeting him in the airport—he was the type that never met a stranger. The sermon was more anecdotal than hellfire and brimstone, linking the story of David and Goliath to modern-day problems.

Pastor Rick was at the door as they were leaving the church. He took Dani's hand. "It's so good to see you here. I hope you'll come back next week."

"Thank you." Dani wished she knew what next week promised.

His warm brown eyes bored into hers. "My offer is still good if you want to talk about your parents . . . actually anything. I'm a really good listener."

He'd known them, and it might be good to have someone she could discuss her parents with. Someone who remembered them but wasn't part of the family or a close friend. "I'll think about it."

Mark and Alex flanked her as they walked to Alex's SUV.

"Alex," a voice called from behind them. "Wait up!"

They turned as one person. "Morgan!" Alex said as a dark-haired woman hurried toward them.

Dani studied Morgan, hoping for . . . recognition. Then her attention switched to the man trailing behind her. Even though he was older, it had to be Ben. She caught her breath. Dani couldn't be certain, but he looked like the man in her dreams.

"You have to be Danielle!"

Before she knew what was happening, Morgan swept her up

in a hug. And just as quickly backed away. "You're wearing a bulletproof vest."

"Morgan!" Ben scolded.

"I'm sorry." She looked around. "But no one heard me. I brought the photos Alex called about. Why don't you and Alex go to lunch with us? And Mark."

"We're meeting my grandparents at the salad place," Alex said. "Why don't you join us? We can look at the photos there."

"That sounds like a good idea," Ben said. "We'll see you there."

A few minutes later, Dani looked out the window as Alex pulled away from the church. "So that was Morgan and Ben."

Mark, in the front passenger seat, nodded. "Morgan only has one speed, and that's wide open."

Alex laughingly agreed. "Did seeing the two of them jar any memories loose?"

"No . . ."

Mark turned and looked at her. "But?"

"I have dreams sometimes, and Ben's in some of them."

"And that's why you sketched him the other night?" Alex asked.

"I'm sure it is."

An hour later, Dani laughed with the others as Morgan related another story from their childhood. Why couldn't she remember *any* of them? "You have a good memory."

"She does," Alex said. "I don't remember half the stuff she's talking about."

"I do," Nonny replied dryly. "So how long will you be in Pearl Springs?"

Morgan shrugged. "Not sure. I'd like to stay close—I have feelers out at the different TV stations in the Chattanooga, Nashville, and Knoxville areas. I'm an investigative reporter and what I'd really like to do is a crime documentary." She took a deep breath and glanced around the table as if debating what to say next.

Dani swallowed hard. She hoped Morgan wasn't about to suggest—

"I don't want this to come off wrong, but I'd love to document Dani's case and what happened twenty-five years ago."

"Are you crazy?" Ben snapped. "What gave you that harebrained idea?"

"It is not crazy. I always wanted to know what happened, and maybe I could help find out."

Alex shook her head. "I think you need to stay out of this case."

Silence fell around the table.

"I disagree, Alex," Nonny said. "I think we can use Morgan."

Everyone, including Dani, turned to her grandmother. "What?"

"Think about it. I've been checking her out, and she has a huge following on social media."

"I do." Morgan leaned forward. "When I was in Houston, people sent me tips all the time, and one of those tips was instrumental in helping the police catch a killer."

"You talked to Toby in the grocery store. Did he tell you anything at all?" Mark asked.

She shook her head. "Not really. When I pressed him on it, he said to meet him later at the coffee shop and we could talk. Only he never showed."

Nonny turned to Alex. "She needs to see my crime board."

"Where is it?" Morgan asked.

"At the sheriff's office."

She turned hopeful eyes to Alex, and Dani held her breath. *Let her say no.* The idea of sharing her story with the world went against everything in Dani.

"Let me think about it," Alex said.

"I think it's a bad idea," Ben said. "You could get yourself killed."

Ben's voice . . . a brief memory . . . Dani turned to him. "Were you friends with my parents?"

He shifted his gaze to her. "I knew them, of course. I mean, in a town this small, you tend to know everyone. Your mom was a great cook."

"How about my dad?"

The mayor shrugged. "I hate to admit it, but back then I hung out at the pool hall a little too much, so I knew him. I wouldn't say we were friends, though." He checked his watch. "It's getting late. I have an appointment with a client."

"I need to leave as well," Morgan said. "I'll be waiting to hear from you, Alex."

"I'll let you know something later this afternoon."

Alex would agree. Dani knew it. And it was a mistake—she felt it in her bones.

51

The next morning, traffic was light on the main road out of Pearl Springs. Even so, Dani noticed as Mark kept checking his rearview mirror. She glanced over her shoulder at Gem buckled into a harness in the backseat. "Will Gem be okay like that?"

"Yeah. But I'll be glad to get the Expedition back with her crate."

"Do you know how long it'll take to repair it?"

"Depends on how long they have to wait on the parts. One of the bullets took out the radiator." He snapped his fingers. "Look in the console. I have something there for you."

"What is it?"

"Look and see."

She opened the console and took out a package. A flip phone? "Oh! Thank you!"

"I remember you saying you hated the smartphone. This is actually a burner. You have to buy minutes, but at least it's not something new for you to learn right now."

The phone was just like the one she'd had before Keith gave her the smartphone. Dani turned toward him in the passenger seat. "What do you think about Morgan's idea?"

"I'm against it. You?"

Mark had taken patrol yesterday afternoon and evening, and they hadn't had a chance to discuss the subject. "I have a bad feeling about it. This person plays for keeps."

"I agree." He checked his mirrors again.

She glanced in the side mirror. Alex followed in her SUV, and Hayes and another deputy were behind her—they looked like a caravan.

"Morgan will be at the briefing this afternoon."

"Alex told me." Sweat bloomed on Dani's palms as Mark turned off the main road onto a road barely wide enough for two cars to meet. Going to the place where she grew up was harder than she expected.

On her side of the road, a narrow shoulder gave way to steep drop-offs. On Mark's side, huge oaks and hickories butted up to the gravel. If they met another car, someone would have to back up.

"I haven't been over this way in a while," Mark said. "I'm glad to see the county is keeping the road passable. I think the house is only about a mile away."

The image of a neat, white plank house popped into her mind. "Is my parents' house the only one on the road?"

He shook his head. "There are several cabins beyond their place that people rent, usually in the summer and fall."

"That's probably why the road is this good."

"Yeah."

Dani stared out the window, looking for anything that seemed like it didn't belong. She didn't think the shooter would attempt an attack with four deputies present, but after Saturday's encounter, she couldn't keep from being a little nervous.

They rounded a curve, and the house she'd just seen in her memory stood to her left in a clearing. "It looks freshly painted," she said, surprised.

"Your grandmother keeps this place up," Mark replied. He parked in the drive and the other two vehicles pulled in behind them. "She used to mow the grass herself, and then hired Toby Mitchell to do the job, but that didn't work out too well. Now she hires one of the teenage boys in town. He keeps the shrubs trimmed and the woods from encroaching on the yard, as well."

"Why go to all this trouble? Why not just sell it?"

"I asked her that very thing one time after someone offered her a really good price for it. She let me know she didn't need the money. It belongs to you, and to get a clear deed, the court would've had to declare you legally dead. Mae never gave up hope that you might come back one day." He sighed. "But I think the real reason is this house is her last link to her daughter. Mae told me one time that Neva had poured her heart and soul into this house."

Part of her brain understood that. She was finding it hard to think about selling Keith's house. She cocked her head. "How do you know all of this?"

He smiled. "She told me. Your grandmother and I are pretty good friends."

She'd noticed the bond between the two but hadn't realized just how much Nonny confided in Mark. "How far is her place from here?"

"As the crow flies, less than a mile. The road is another matter—all uphill and about fifteen minutes away by car."

Dani stared at the plank building. She'd hoped when she saw the house, it would trigger a tsunami of memories. But so far, nothing.

He nodded toward the two vehicles behind them. "The others are going to wait until you walk through before they join us."

"Good." That lessened the pressure a little, plus she could concentrate better. With a deep breath, she opened the SUV door. "Will we need a key?"

He pulled one from his pocket. "Mae gave me one before we left."

Mark released Gem from the harness, and Dani laughed as the dog hopped out and shook herself. "I'd like to do that myself."

As Dani climbed the steps to the porch, she tried to imagine herself playing on it, maybe sitting in the swing to the right, but no . . . Mark unlocked the door. It creaked as he pushed it open.

An image flashed in her mind but was gone before she could pin it down.

"You remembered something," Mark said.

"Only a fragment." A familiar scent wrapped around her as she stepped over the threshold into a large room. She couldn't identify the scent, only that it was one she'd smelled before.

She turned toward the window, where dust motes swirled in a narrow beam of light. That, too, was familiar. Dani glanced around the room. Sheets covered a sofa and several chairs and tables. Small roses on cream-colored paper covered the walls. Dani touched them.

The image of a man and woman hanging wallpaper popped into her mind. She knew what the scent was now. "This paper covers up cedar walls," she said. "My mother wanted Daddy to get rid of them, but he wouldn't do it. So she made him paper over the wood."

Mark beamed at her. "You're starting to remember!"

Dani nodded and pointed down the hallway. "Their bedroom was at the end on the right." She walked through the doorway to the hall with Gem following. Dani stopped at the first room they came to. "Mine was here."

"Do you want to go in?"

She stood rooted to the floor. "Not yet."

"How about the kitchen?"

Dread filled her stomach. That was where her parents' bodies had been found. *How do I know that?* She couldn't remember Mark or Alex discussing the crime scene.

"You okay? We can come back later if you want."

What she wanted was to leave and never come here again. *"You are made of sterner stuff than that."* Nonny's voice echoed in her head. Another memory! But when had she told her that?

Dani stood stock-still with her eyes closed while a movie played out in her head. Alex's sixth birthday party . . .

There was a girl in a pretty black-and-white-checkered dress . . . Dani didn't know who she was.

"Where did you get your dress?" the girl said to Dani. "I wouldn't let my dolly wear anything that yucky!"

Dani smoothed the material in the yellow dress her mom had made. It was an exact replica of one of Belle's dresses in *Beauty and the Beast*. Well, maybe not exact. Her mom hadn't been the best seamstress and hadn't wanted Dani to wear it to the party. But she loved the dress. It made her feel like a princess.

Her grandmother had brought her to the party, and Dani ran to her in tears. That's when Nonny had told her she was made of sterner stuff . . .

"No. We'll stay." Dani straightened her shoulders and opened the door to her bedroom. She caught her breath and covered her mouth with her hand.

"What is it?" Mark asked.

Instead of answering, she walked around the room and touched the blue gingham bedspread that covered a white twin bed, then ran her fingers over the white chest. "I remember this room."

A bench abutted the wall under the window, and she sat on it. Mark joined her and slipped his arm around her waist, and she leaned into him.

"I used to look out this window at the moon and stars, and sometimes Mama or Daddy or even Uncle Keith would tell me the names of the constellations." She sighed, and Gem laid her head on Dani's knee. "Why do people have to be so evil? We had a good life here."

Mark pulled her closer. "I know this isn't easy."

She jutted her jaw and stood. "No, it isn't, and sitting here thinking about the good times isn't getting the job done."

"You said your uncle told you the constellations. Was he here much?"

She looked at him. "I don't know, but if he took me with him, we must have been close." Dani turned to the door. "Let's go to the kitchen."

Mark and Gem followed her down the hallway. When she stepped into the kitchen, the temperature seemed at least ten degrees cooler than the rest of the house. Maybe because a huge oak shaded the back of the house? Or was it because her parents had been killed here? Beside her, Gem whined.

"Are you all right? You look as though you're about to pass out."

"I'm not all right, but this has to be done." She walked around the kitchen, looking for anything familiar.

Angry voices. Someone was here, and he was yelling at her dad. She tried to pull the memory out, but only bits and pieces came.

"Dani?"

The memory fled, and she looked up into Mark's concerned eyes. "Another fragment." She dropped her head and studied her feet. "I just don't remember enough of anything to make sense. I know that whatever happened that night happened in this room, but some of the memories I have could be from other times." She sighed. "Why don't you have Alex join us? Maybe she can help prod—"

Gem barked, and Dani jerked her head toward the tires that sounded on the gravel road. Scenes flashed through her mind. Nothing she could pin down . . . but she'd heard tires that night . . .

"Let me see who that is." Mark glanced out the back door. "I don't see anyone other than Alex and the deputies, but it sounds like a vehicle is coming from the summer rentals up the road. I'll check and tell Alex to join us." He turned to Gem. "Stay."

When he left, Dani slowly turned in a circle. The yellow curtains on the window seemed familiar, and then she scanned the painted white cabinets, the coffee cups hanging from little hooks. Her gaze stopped on the bottom cabinets. "Why can't I remember, Gem?"

She opened the one nearest the door. Her uncle had said he'd found her in a cabinet . . . had it been one of these? Somehow, she didn't think so.

A memory tugged at her subconscious. She closed her eyes . . .

It was afternoon. Dani was supposed to be resting, but her mama and daddy were arguing. She'd slipped out of the house and was practicing walking quietly through the woods like the Native Americans they were studying in school.

The back door to the house slammed and she looked up. Why was her daddy running? He never did that. Maybe he was looking for her, and Dani stepped back into the shadows of the trees. She'd just seen deer tracks and didn't want to go inside yet.

Instead of looking for her, he went to the well house and pulled out a shovel. Then he hurried to the edge of the woods. She almost called out to him, but something held her back. Instead, she followed him, being careful where she stepped so she didn't make any noise. In her heart, she knew he would be upset if he saw her.

He started digging in the ground with the shovel, and Dani edged closer as he buried a small box.

She stepped on a dry branch, and it snapped, turning her ankle. "Oh!" she cried as she fell.

"Who's there?"

Dani scrambled up and her eyes widened. Her father held a gun in his hand. "It's me, Daddy!"

"Danielle?" He slipped the pistol in his front pocket. "What are you doing here in the woods?"

"I-I was just walking in the woods and pretending—"

"It's okay. I didn't mean to scare you."

She hopped on her good foot. "What was in the box?"

"Nothing that concerns you . . ." He bent down and picked her up. "You know what this place is?" When she shook her head, he said, "It's where my grandfather built his house when he first came to Russell County."

"But there's no house, just woods."

"Yeah, I know. The house burned down when I was about your age. I like to come here when I'm troubled. It's peaceful." He hugged her and set her back on the ground. "We're leaving in a bit. You need to go pack your Barbies."

"Where are we going?"

"You'll see. Now hop to it or your mama will throw the snack she made you out the back door."

She giggled. He was always saying things like that. Her mama wouldn't ever throw out food. Nonny would fuss at her . . .

Dani opened her eyes. The memories were coming back ever so slowly. The box her daddy buried must have been the diamonds. Gem followed as she walked out onto the back porch and stared toward the woods. Could she find the place where he buried them? Her great-grandfather's old homeplace?

She glanced toward the road for Mark, but he was busy with Alex. Dani looked toward the woods. With Mark and Alex and two other deputies here, it should be safe enough to see if she could find the old homeplace.

She started to call to Mark, but he and Alex had walked to the edge of the road and were talking to someone in a tan SUV. If her memory was right, she and her dad had gone only a short distance in the woods—she should be back before anyone even missed her.

52

An SUV coming from the vacation rentals had pulled off the road. Mark frowned, then relaxed as he recognized Ben and his uncle, Craig Tennyson. They were probably checking out the summer cabins beyond the Bennett house.

He joined Alex as she walked toward the SUV. "Dani's ready for you to come in," he said.

"Has she remembered anything?"

"A little, but nothing major. I don't think it will be long before she remembers what happened, though. Dani wants her life back, and she's one determined lady." Mark kicked at a rock, then raised his gaze to Alex. "In fact, next to you, she's probably the strongest woman I know."

Alex stopped, and his neck grew hot under her intense scrutiny.

"You're protecting her," she said. "Don't do anything to jeopardize her life."

Like lose his focus because he was falling for her. Might be a little late for the falling-for-her part. "I won't lose my focus."

"See to it that you don't." They'd reached the road, and she turned to the two men climbing out of the SUV. "Morning, Craig, Ben," Alex said.

"Morning, Chief Deputy," Craig said. "Surprised to see anyone here."

"Why's that?"

"Well, Mae's just had a stroke. Who else would be here?"

"Ben didn't tell you Mae's granddaughter is back in Pearl Springs?"

The older man jerked his head toward Ben, who shrugged. "Why didn't you say something? You know I've been trying to find that little gal. Thought if Mae wouldn't sell, she would."

"I can tell you now, she won't be selling," Mark said. He was pretty sure Dani would want to hang on to the property. He eyed Craig. While Mark liked Ben well enough, Mark didn't care for his uncle.

Craig cocked his head toward him. "Now how do you know that? You don't even know what I'd be willing to offer."

"Because you never buy anything unless it's a bargain," Mark said. "I've heard you make Ebenezer Scrooge look like a spendthrift."

Ben laughed. "He got you there."

Craig gave him a sour look. "Nothing wrong with a man trying to save money." He turned toward the house. "Is the Bennett girl in the house?"

Alex stepped forward. "Yes, but we're here on official business. If you want to talk to her about buying the place, you'll have to catch her some other time."

"What kind of official—"

"Nooooo!"

The scream jerked Mark's attention toward the house. Dani!

She screamed again, sending chills down his back. It was hard to pinpoint the direction of the scream, but he'd left Dani in the kitchen. He spun around and dashed toward the house, taking the steps two at a time with Alex on his heels. Hayes and the two Tennyson men ran toward the back of the house.

"Dani! Where are you?"

No answer.

"I think it came from the woods," Alex said.

Mark raced through the kitchen and out the back door, almost plowing into Ben and Craig. "You two need to leave," he said.

"What's going on?" Ben asked.

He ignored him. "Dani! Where are you?" he yelled.

"There's someone crying over that way. And a dog barking." Craig pointed toward the other side of the well house.

Mark cocked his ear. Craig was right. He was about to tell the two men to stay put when Alex did it for him.

"You two need to stop right here," she said. "This could be a crime scene, and I don't need you two traipsing all over the place."

Craig held up his hand. "But—"

"No buts," she said. "Go back to the road, or I can arrest you. Your choice."

Mark didn't wait to see what they did and sprinted through the woods toward the sound of crying and Gem barking.

The scent of death hit him before he found Dani rocking on her knees beside freshly turned dirt, a shovel on the ground, and Gem beside her. There was no doubt the scent came from the body attached to the partially exposed arm.

"Oh no," Alex muttered as she caught up to him. "Let me see if I can reach Max." She took out her phone and walked out to the clearing.

Mark swallowed down the bile that rose up in his throat. It wasn't his first body to deal with, but it never got easy. He knelt beside her. "Dani," he said softly. "I'm here. It's okay."

She shook her head and pointed toward the dirt. "I-I first thought it was K-Keith." Dani burst into tears.

Mark breathed through his mouth as he looked past her to the shallow grave. "But you know he died in Montana."

"I know . . . it's just . . ." She swallowed hard as her face took on a gray tinge.

Mark yanked a handkerchief from his pocket and handed it to Dani before she could throw up, wishing for some Vicks VapoRub to put under her nose . . . his too. She pressed the cloth to her face, and he helped her to her feet.

Her chest rose as she took in a breath. "I saw some fresh dirt, and without thinking . . . the first thing I uncovered was his arm with that watch on his wrist." Dani took a shuddering breath. "Laura gave Keith one like it last Christmas."

"Let's go talk to Alex," he said as the chief deputy pocketed her phone.

When they reached her, Alex hugged Dani. "I'm sorry you had to find this. Tell me what happened."

Mark turned to examine the grave closer, but Dani grabbed his arm. "Sorry, I'm dizzy," she said as he steadied her.

"Why don't we do this at the house?" he said.

"Good idea." Alex motioned Hayes over. "I'm going to let Hayes take you to the house, but—"

"Can't Mark take me?" Her blue eyes searched his face. "He . . . makes me feel safer."

That she felt safe with him touched something deep inside him. Maybe he was doing something right. He squeezed her hand. "Hayes is a good man, and I'll send Gem with you. They'll keep you safe until Alex and I secure the crime scene."

"He won't be long," Alex added. "But I need to talk to him before we get your statement."

Reluctantly Dani agreed, and after she and Hayes left with Gem, Alex turned to Mark. "I called the CSI team. Shouldn't take Dylan and Taylor long to get here." She rested her hand on her belt. "We know it's not Keith. Any guess who it might be?"

He nodded. "Maybe. How long do you think the body has been here?"

Alex rubbed her temple. "Daytime temps have been in the seventies, so it wouldn't take that long for the body to break down.

I'd say from the smell, no more than thirty-six hours and probably more like twenty-four to thirty."

"About the time Toby Mitchell has been missing." Mark knelt, staring at the exposed hand. It did look familiar even though it was swollen . . . "I noticed Toby's hands the other day, and he has big hands like this and a cross tattooed on his left knuckle—like here." He pointed to the cross with his pen.

Alex studied the hand. "You're probably right. He's not going anywhere, so we'll wait for the CSI team so we don't run the risk of disturbing evidence."

Mark stood and scanned the area. "But why bury the body here? The killer had to know that with Dani back in Pearl Springs, if he buried the body this close to the Bennett house, we'd find it sooner rather than later."

"Maybe the killer was sending Dani a message," Alex said. "Or Toby and the killer were here together and got into an argument that Toby lost."

Mark nodded. "He's a big man and easier to bury than to move."

"Good point." Alex took out her phone. "Guess I better call the medical examiner's office over in Hamilton County."

They walked to the edge of the woods to put distance between them and the body. "I'd like to get Dani away from here," he said. "Instead of hanging around here while we wait for the ME and the TBI agents."

"That's a good idea, once I get her statement."

"Actually, I had in mind to take her to Mae's house first. She told us where to look for the family photos. Hayes could go along for backup."

Alex chewed the bottom of her lip.

"We got rid of her phone, so it should be safe enough to drive up to Mae's, maybe stop at my house so I can check out the damage from yesterday."

"Why can't you do that by yourself?"

"You saw how she reacted to just going to the house without me. I don't think she'd like it if I left."

"Let me think about it, and I'll let you know once Dylan and Taylor arrive." Her phone rang. "It's Hayes," she said and slid the button. "What's wrong?"

Mark was already sprinting toward the house. He burst from the woods to see Dani on the ground with Gem standing guard, keeping Hayes and the Tennysons away. "Free, Gem!"

He knelt, and once he rewarded the dog with soothing words and a gentle pat on the head, he shifted his attention to Dani. Mark pressed his fingertips to her wrist, checking for a pulse. It was fast. He stood and scooped Dani up in his arms just as Alex jogged up. "I'm taking her inside."

"What happened?" Alex asked.

"She came out of the woods and just fainted," Hayes said as he opened the back door.

Dani's eyes fluttered open as Mark carried her into the kitchen. "W-why are you carrying me?"

He smiled at her. "I was hoping you could tell me." Mark set her in a chair in the kitchen. "What do you remember?"

She frowned and slowly shook her head. Abruptly she stilled and her eyes widened. "The body!"

He knelt in front of her. "Yes, and Hayes was bringing you back to the house . . ."

A strand of her golden red hair had slipped out of the tie, and she hooked it behind her ear. "Gem came with us . . ." Dani turned toward the window, then she shook her head again. "That's all I remember."

"Maybe it'll come back to you." He stood and walked to the back door, where Alex spoke with Craig and Ben. Alex raised her eyebrows, questioning him.

"She's okay now," he said. He turned to Craig and Ben. "Did either of you see what happened?"

"I just saw her fall," Ben said, and Craig agreed.

Mark felt pressure at his elbow and turned. "You should still be sitting in the chair," he said.

Dani pushed past him and pointed her finger at the man with Ben. "You were here, and you argued with my dad."

53

Dani stared at the man with Ben, who was shaking his head.

"I don't know what you're talking about," the man said. "If you're talking about the night your dad died, I was in Chattanooga."

"Whoa." Ben held up his hand. "You have it wrong about me too. I was with Craig."

Dani pressed her lips together. Was she wrong? Was she having false memories? Like the memory of her dad burying something? She'd been almost to the woods when she remembered he'd been digging up a box, not burying it.

She'd read about false memories in her research. And Ben was the Pearl Springs mayor . . . What was she thinking? "Did you ever come here to see my dad?"

"Well, yeah." Ben lowered his hand. "I told you yesterday your mama fed me sometimes. And your dad and I . . . well, I'd never kill either one of them."

"And I knew both your parents," Craig said. "I'd never intentionally hurt them."

They sounded sincere. Why couldn't she remember? She pressed her hand to her forehead. It wasn't right for her to accuse someone with nothing to go on. Dani sighed. "I'm sorry. I shouldn't have said what I did. I guess I'm just tired."

Mark squeezed her shoulder. "It's okay."

She leaned into him. It wasn't okay to go around accusing people of murder.

"Why don't you take her back inside," Alex said. "I'll talk to Craig and Ben."

"Want me to carry you?" Mark asked.

"I can walk." Once they were inside the house, she asked, "Who was that man with Ben?"

"That's his uncle, Craig Tennyson. He's the one who offered to buy this place." Mark led her to the kitchen table and pulled out a red and white vinyl chair.

She sank into it. Like she had so many times before. Dani ran her hand over the Formica table, remembering how excited her mom had been when the used furniture store delivered the table and chairs and took away the old wooden set. She scanned the rest of the kitchen. It was coming back to her—the dishes that were guaranteed not to break that Nonny had given them for Christmas, and how had she missed the bowl of fake fruit on the table?

She took a pear from the bowl. Not even dusty. Dani could not believe how her grandmother had kept the house in pristine condition, waiting for her to return. Or maybe it was a way to honor her daughter?

"You want some water?"

"The faucet works?" Why did she even ask? Of course it did.

"Yeah, but I planned to grab a bottle from the car."

"I'm sure the water is fine."

"Maybe so, but I'll be right back."

Mark was barely gone a minute before he returned with a bottle of water and uncapped it. "Why did you go into the woods?" he asked after she'd taken a long sip.

"Before I tell you, why don't you record it on your phone. I'm sure Alex will want to know and that way I only have to tell it once."

"Good idea," he said.

Once he punched the record button, she began. "I remembered I followed my dad that day." She told him what she'd remembered. "I couldn't tell what he buried. I thought maybe it was the diamonds. That's why I went into the woods, to see if I could find the old homeplace where he buried a box. But before I reached the woods, I remembered he wasn't burying something—he dug something up. It must have been the diamonds."

"And you found a body instead."

"Who is it?"

"I don't want to say until we have a positive ID."

She understood that. "Can you still take me to my grandmother's house?"

"If Alex approves."

They both turned as Alex entered the back door. "Craig and Ben have gone back to town," she said.

Mark nodded. "I have Dani's statement on my phone. I'm sending it to you."

"Good. I'll listen to it later. The Hamilton County medical examiner is on his way," Alex said. "I called Max, and he's bringing the state forensic team to help our crime scene investigators."

"What about us going to Mae's house?" Mark said.

She sat at the table across from Dani. "Once Dylan and Taylor get here, you can take Hayes and drive over there. Max and his people should be here by the time you return, so I'll have enough deputies to escort you back to town then."

Dani clasped her hands. "I hate being so much trouble. After I get the photos, why don't I stay here and look at them until you're ready to go back to Pearl Springs? Everybody can go at the same time."

"I appreciate your willingness to do that." Alex cocked her head. "And that sounds like it might be our CSI team now."

Dani's heart went into double time as Mark and Alex unsnapped the straps over their guns. Both eased to the back door and then relaxed. "It's Dylan and Taylor," Alex said. "I'll go with them to the grave and send Hayes to accompany you to Mae's."

Fifteen minutes later, Hayes followed as they drove to her grandmother's house and got out. Mark released Gem, and she bounded from the SUV to the house.

Dani couldn't keep from searching out the bullet hole in the post and shuddered when she found it. Maybe she should've gotten in the Navigator that night and driven straight back to Montana.

No. She didn't regret for one second staying and meeting her grandmother. And Alex and her family and . . . Mark. Warmth spread through her chest. Other than Evelyn, she'd never had real friends before, and it was nice. But even nicer was to have someone who made her heart beat faster. She just wished Mark felt the same way.

Hayes waited outside while Mark unlocked the door and entered the house. Dani followed him inside to the small living room. She remembered staying at Nonny's while her parents worked, her mom at a factory, her dad in construction. "Did you tell me where my mom and dad worked?"

"What?"

She repeated the question, and he shook his head. "I never knew where either of them worked."

Yes! Dani wanted to do a happy dance. Her mind was slowly releasing the memories locked in it. "They worked in town. I think I must've stayed here with my grandmother a lot."

She scanned the room, taking in once again the rich cedar walls, blue sofa, two gold chairs, tables . . . framed photos of the mountains and a photo of a small girl over the sofa. Dani at seven or eight, taken by her mother.

She hadn't gone to Nonny's bedroom when she'd been here the other day. "My grandmother's bedroom is down the hall. Right?"

"Right," he replied.

In Mae's room, Mark knelt beside the bed and pulled out a cardboard box with a strip of gingham tied around it. Her heart thudded as he slid the cloth off and lifted the lid. The box was packed full of photos. She picked up one on top and caught her breath. "Oh, my goodness," she said. "This is my mother and me at Easter."

"You remember."

She did. Dani looked up at him and smiled. "I told you the photos would make a difference."

Mark replaced the lid. "Let's take them to your parents' house. You can go through the box while we wait for Alex to finish up at the crime scene."

She followed Mark to the SUV, where he opened her door. "Mind if we stop by my house to see if everything is okay?"

"Sure. I'd love to see your bachelor pad anyway."

"Where'd you get the idea it's a bachelor pad? It's our home—mine and Gem's."

"From the articles I read in magazines, I thought single guys had bachelor pads."

"You've been reading the wrong articles," he said and called Hayes to relay what they were going to do.

A few minutes later, they pulled into Mark's drive, and the deputy pulled in behind him but didn't get out. Dani climbed out of Mark's vehicle and looked around. "I was so scared yesterday I didn't notice you live in a log cabin."

He nodded. "My grandfather built the original four rooms, and I've added a couple more, a loft, and another bathroom."

Dani took in the house and yard. "What are those?" She pointed to several bushes that were blooming along the front of the house. Beside them was a freshly dug plot of ground.

"The ones with blooms are azaleas, and the others are rhododendrons—they'll bloom in June. And I just put out deer-resistant wildflower seed in that patch of ground that's broken up."

He seemed pleased that she noticed. "I wouldn't have figured you for a gardener."

"And why not?" His voice was teasing.

Dani felt her face getting hot. "I don't know."

"Maybe instead of reading articles about men, you should get to know some *real* ones." He flexed his muscle.

"Be still my heart," she said, patting her chest. "Don't you think we need to finish checking your place out?"

He sobered. "You're right."

Mark surveyed the outside of the house, pointing out the splintered post near the back porch. "That looks like damage from a .270 or .30-06."

Deer rifles, meant for long-distance shooting. "He meant business."

Mark's jaw muscle worked furiously. "We have to find him before he makes good on his threat."

"Yeah, but he's like a ghost, and what happened was twenty-five years ago." If there ever was a cold case, this one was.

"He'll make a mistake, and then we'll have him." Mark ran his hand through his dark hair and then nodded toward his car. "You ready?"

She nodded. "Lead the way."

When they returned to her parents' house, Alex was ready to leave. "The state forensic team doesn't want our help, but I'm leaving Dylan and Taylor anyway," she said. "I forwarded Dani's statement to Max, and he'll contact you if he has more questions. So, if you two are ready, we'll go back to Pearl Springs and have the briefing like I'd planned before this happened."

As Dani walked to Mark's SUV, the sun ducked behind a cloud, sending a shiver down her back. There were so many places someone could hide with a rifle between here and Pearl Springs. What if the person who'd shot at them earlier was lying in wait?

The thought cut off her breath.

What was that verse Mark had told her? *Whenever I am afraid, I will trust in you.*

Her breathing became a little easier. She said it silently again. *Whenever I am afraid, I will trust in you.*

The bands around her chest loosened a little more, and she kept repeating the verse until the Russell County Sheriff's Office building came into sight.

54

Later that afternoon Alex rolled the whiteboard next to Mae's crime board. She preferred to call it an evidence board, although she'd have to give Mae credit for the thorough job she'd done. The board carried more information than the files she'd been poring over. Mae would've made a good detective.

She scanned the seven faces staring intently at the whiteboard—two outsiders—Dani and Mae—and her deputies, Mark, Hayes, and Jenna Hart. CSI team members Dylan and Taylor had arrived just moments ago. Then Alex turned to the whiteboard and divided it into three columns. At the top of the first column, she wrote "jewelry store burglary ring and suspects," then moved to the second column where she wrote "murder victims and suspects." She hesitated at the top of the third column and walked over to Dani, who had tension radiating off her. "Are you certain you want to sit in on this meeting? You're already stressed, and some of what we will discuss may be painful."

"What do you mean?" Dani asked.

"You're jiggling your foot. If this is stressing you out too much—"

"You don't have to stay." Mark leaned into Dani. "Hayes can take you home."

"No! I'll be fine." She glanced toward Mae on the other side of her. "If my grandmother can take it, so can I."

"You sure? I can give you a condensed version later."

"I'll be all right. I promise."

If she were Dani or Mae, Alex wasn't sure she'd want to hear what they were going to discuss. She studied Dani a minute and nodded. "If it gets to be too much, you can leave." Alex turned to Mae. "You too."

Both women nodded, and Alex returned to the front of the room. As she wrote Dani's name at the top of the third column, the door opened and Morgan burst into the room.

"Sorry I'm late. Had an interview with a Chattanooga TV station."

"Promising?" Alex certainly hoped so. She'd regretted giving Morgan permission to sit in on this as soon as the words were out of her mouth. But her friend was hurting. Losing the job in Houston ate at her, and from the articles she'd read online about Morgan, she was a good investigator. If Alex had the money, she would hire her as a deputy. Not that Morgan would take the job—she loved being a reporter.

She turned to her deputies. "Here's what we have so far. According to the files Chattanooga PD sent over, they believed the burglary ring consisted of at least one other person, and possibly more than the three names I have up there."

She aimed a laser pointer at each name she'd written. Keith Bennett, Robert (Bobby) Bennett, Tobias (Toby) Mitchell. Below those three, Alex had written Kyle Peterson with a question mark.

"The Bennett brothers and Toby Mitchell were captured on video at the jewelry store Kyle Peterson managed. The stolen diamonds have never surfaced. Max Anderson with TBI called before I reached the sheriff's station and confirmed the victim in the grave is Toby Mitchell, so all three are dead now."

Alex shifted her attention to Mark. "You spoke to Mr. Peterson, Kyle's grandfather. You want to fill everyone in on that conversation?"

"Okay to do it from here?" Mark asked from where he sat. She nodded, and he continued. "As Alex said, I went to Peterson's Grocery early Saturday morning. I intended to talk to Kyle, but he wasn't there."

Mark related the information Mr. Peterson shared and then the brief conversation with Toby.

"I spoke with him around nine." He turned to Morgan. "What time did you talk to him?"

She opened her iPad and tapped on the screen. "At 10:05. I caught him at Peterson's. We talked about ten minutes, then he told me he had to get the stock up and then meet someone, and we set up a meeting at the coffee shop." She looked up. "It was like he wanted to get something off his chest—one of the last things he said to me was, 'It's time the truth came out.' But he never came."

"I've asked around, and no one saw him after that."

Alex steepled her fingers. "Toby went to prison rather than roll over on his accomplices. What could have changed his mind?"

Mae sat up straighter. "I figure he knows what happened that night, and he got tired of carrying the guilt around. He did some odd jobs for me through the years, and more than once I thought he wanted to tell me something."

Alex could buy that. Guilt was a heavy load to carry, especially for twenty-five years.

"He wasn't going to tell me anything," Mark said. "I think he was just being smart with me about the plane."

Mae reached for her water bottle and uncapped it. "I don't believe he had a plane either, but he did like to hang out at our little airport."

"I don't see him having a valid license either." Alex nodded to Mark. "Call the manager out at the airport. See if she can tell you anything about Toby."

"I'll do it right now."

"While Mark's doing that," Alex said, "we'll discuss Kyle Peterson. He swears he had nothing to do with the burglaries, and Chattanooga PD never found any evidence that pointed to him. Even without evidence, he lost his job, something he is still very angry about twenty-five years later. That will play into the third column involving Dani. Thoughts on the burglaries, anyone?"

Jenna tapped her pen against her tablet. "Did the Chattanooga PD ever consider Mitchell or the Bennett brothers as the mastermind of the ring?"

"According to their files, Chattanooga didn't believe it was any of them. Toby pled guilty and received a six-year sentence. Served five years with a year off for good behavior. Even though he denied it, Chatt PD believes Toby knew the identity of the ringleader."

"What do we know about Toby?" Jenna asked. "Who were his friends? Associates?"

"He lived here in Pearl Springs," Alex said. "You've probably seen him around. Back then he worked in construction with the Bennett brothers."

The door opened, and her heartbeat quickened when Nathan stepped inside the room. Their gazes lingered a second before he sat in a nearby chair.

"Glad you could make it," Alex said, managing to not sound breathy. She'd already gone over the previous information with him, so he hadn't missed anything. "The police chief here has had more contact with him than the county."

Nathan raised his brows. "Who are you talking about?"

"Toby Mitchell."

"Oh. Bad thing, what happened. He was a frequent resident in our little jail. What do you have on his murder?"

Alex glanced over her notes. "Not a lot. TBI and the Hamilton County medical examiner will send me a report when they finish the crime scene. But according to a preliminary report I received from the ME, the body didn't show signs of being transported a long distance, indicating he was killed on-site."

"You're going to let TBI handle it?"

"Yeah. They have better resources than we do, but we're assisting. I think it'll point back to the case we're working." She nodded at Mark as he stepped back in the room. "Learn anything from the airport manager?"

"Just that she often saw Toby cleaning up an old two-seater biplane at the airport but never had heard of him having a pilot's license."

"Good work. Anything else, anyone?"

When no one spoke, Alex pulled the crime board front and center. "From here on out we'll be considering the murders of Bobby and Neva Bennett." She eyed Mae and Dani. "Are you two sure you want to stay?"

"I am," Mae said.

"Me too."

Dani didn't sound as sure. Alex turned to the older woman. "Mae, I'd like for you to explain who you have on your board, then I'd like for Hayes to take you home."

"We'll see about Hayes when I finish." Mae stood and used a cane to steady herself as she walked to the board. "Confounded doctor said I had to use this thing." She pointed the cane to the right side of the board. "He didn't say how I had to use it."

Everyone laughed, breaking some of the tension.

"And before you ask how I came up with this, I'm no Jessica Fletcher, but I saw enough true-crime programs before you were born to put one of these together.

"I'm going to focus on the left side here that deals with Bobby. Neva and Danielle have nothing to do with what we're discussing today." She tapped Bobby's photo. "I have him listed and all of his known acquaintances and friends." She named each one.

"Toby Mitchell, Kyle Peterson, Keith Bennett, Rick Adkins, Ralph Tennyson and his brother, Craig, and Ben Tennyson."

Her cane landed on the mayor's name. "Looking at him now, it's hard to believe, but my great-nephew had already gotten in trouble at the casino over in Murphy, North Carolina. Underage drinking and gambling. Cost his dad a pretty penny to get him out of it. Thankfully, he turned himself around."

Mae tapped the board. "All have one thing in common. None of them have an alibi for the night Bobby and Neva were murdered." Alex started to interrupt, and Mae held up her finger. "I know—Craig and Ben alibied each other, but that doesn't count in my books."

She had a point. Alex turned to the others in the room. "You have a list of these names and the research Mae did in your folder. Look over the material when we take a break."

"How do you know they don't have alibis?" Dylan asked.

"Some I flat out asked, others, like Pastor Rick, were by accident. He wasn't in Chattanooga visiting his sister like he told the church secretary—not that I believe for a minute that he has anything to do with Neva's death. But he and Bobby had been seen together several times at the pool hall before Bobby was killed, and he wasn't in Chattanooga, at least not seeing his sister. The very first time I saw her after Neva died, she told me how sorry she was that she hadn't come to the funeral. Turns out she'd been in Kentucky helping her daughter who just had a baby when Neva died."

"How about the diamonds?" Mark asked.

Mae pointed to a photo on the board of diamonds she'd cut from a magazine. "Neva called me the day they were killed and told me what Bobby had been doing." She turned to Alex. "I should've called your granddaddy as soon as I hung up, but I didn't. I told him afterwards, but then it was too late."

Silence filled the room. "I think now would be a good time

for a break," Alex said as her cell phone rang. Sheriff Crider in Montana. "Stone," she answered, stepping out into the hallway. "Do you have anything on the bullet?"

"The bullet is a match for the murders in Tennessee."

"So the cases are related."

"Yes."

They discussed the case for a few minutes, then she hit the end button and slipped her phone in her back pocket.

"Anything wrong?"

She hadn't heard Mark come up. "Depends on how you look at it. That was Crider. The slug found in Keith matched the ballistics here in Tennessee."

"Okay, so we know for sure that the two cases are connected."

"Yes."

Half an hour later they reconvened in the room, minus Mae. She'd acquiesced to Alex's request. "Any questions?" she asked the group.

"Do you know if Toby Mitchell was shot?" Nathan asked.

Alex nodded. "He was. Max didn't know the caliber of the gun used yet. Once an autopsy is completed, we'll have that information. Max indicated we might get an initial report tomorrow that will hopefully include the caliber of the gun used. We just received information from Sheriff Crider in Montana that the bullet that killed Keith came from the same gun that killed Dani's parents."

Taylor raised her hand. "Are any of the people on Mae's list considered suspects in the Montana killing?"

"That investigation is ongoing and has now expanded here." Then Alex nodded at the board. "Other than Toby, most of these people are upstanding citizens. It's hard to imagine someone like Ben and his dad and uncle or Pastor Rick being involved."

Nathan cleared his throat. "Just between us, I find it a little disturbing that less than a week after the murders twenty-five years ago, Ralph Tennyson moved Ben and the rest of the family to Texas. And Carson said he quit his job at the plant without a notice."

Her grandfather hadn't mentioned that to her. Alex turned to Morgan. "What do you know about that?"

Morgan shook her head. "Nothing. Daddy never talked about why we moved, and he wasn't someone you could easily ask. Craig or Ben might know something."

"Was Ralph ever considered a suspect in the murders?" she asked Nathan.

"No. According to your grandfather, Ralph had an air-tight alibi, and as Mae said earlier, Ben and Craig alibied each other."

Alex frowned. "When did you and my grandfather discuss this?"

"When I was his deputy. He and I were going over a few cold cases and this was one of them."

"It appears we might need to interview Ben more in-depth. Craig too. Anything else?"

Jenna raised her pen. "Was Kyle Peterson ever a person of interest in the murders?"

"Gramps had a file on him, but since there wasn't any evidence he participated in the thefts, there didn't seem to be a motive, so my grandfather didn't pursue it. I haven't interviewed Kyle myself, but I did talk with Mr. Peterson, and the version he told me tallied with Gramps's—the night of the murders, he spent the night with his girlfriend, plus he'd just gotten his car serviced and the odometer reading was on the receipt. The car hadn't been driven enough to put him in Pearl Springs and back to Chattanooga." Alex looked over her notes. "He also claimed he had a flat tire on his vehicle, and AAA confirmed a service call on the day of the murders."

"He could have taken the girlfriend's car," Jenna said. "Maybe someone needs to interview her again, see if the alibi stands up."

"Good idea. *If* he was in on the thefts, and he thought Bobby Bennett was withholding the diamonds, he could've confronted him and things got out of hand. See if you can get a current address for her."

"Do we have a name?"

Alex shuffled through her papers. "Here it is. Crystal Davis."

Jenna jotted the name on her tablet. "I'll see what I can find on the internet."

"You might call Chattanooga PD. I've been talking to Detective Todd Madden. He might have a number."

"Anything else before we move on to Dani?" Alex asked. When no one spoke up, she said, "There have been attempts made on her life. She thinks, and I agree, it's the person who killed her parents, and now her uncle. He either doesn't know she has no memory of that night and thinks she can identify him, or he knows and is afraid she'll get her memory back."

55

Dani wasn't sure how much more of this she could listen to. Hearing all the details . . .

Alex's phone rang and she said, "It's Max. Excuse me a minute."

As she stepped out of the room, Jenna turned to Dani. "How much of your memory have you regained?"

"Not a lot." Dani liked the deputy. She'd heard Alex say Jenna was a rock climber, and she'd enjoyed rock climbing in Montana. Maybe when this was all over, they could take a day and the deputy could show her some good places to climb. "And certainly nothing concrete about that night, but I'm hoping some of these pictures will do the trick."

Dani rubbed her hand across the box of photos they'd gotten at her grandmother's.

Photos. She stilled.

Mark was sitting across from her and covered her hand with his. "Did you just remember something?"

"No, but . . ." She turned to Alex, who had stepped back into the room. "Are there crime scene photos in the files?"

Alex's eyes widened slightly. "Yes, but I don't think you should see them."

Dani pressed her lips in a thin line as a band tightened around her chest. "What if they could shock my brain into remembering?"

Mark spoke up. "I don't think it's a good idea either."

She took a deep breath. "It's not that I want to see them, but maybe that's what I need to do. Where are they?"

"In my office with the rest of the files on this case," Alex said. "Would you rather I bring them to the house?"

If she waited, she might back out. Dani shook her head. "It'd be better to look at them here."

"If you're sure . . . but first, Max just told me his CSI team used a metal detector to search for spent bullets and casings, and they found a small black box."

"What?" Dani leaned forward.

"It's probably the box you saw," Alex said. "It was empty—I assume your dad took what was in it and dropped the box in the hole he dug, and it filled in over the years."

She'd been right to question her memory of what happened in the woods that day.

Dani felt Alex's eyes on her and looked up.

"Would you rather put off looking at the photos until tomorrow?"

Dani concentrated on breathing to keep from hyperventilating. Could she do it? The thought of looking at the photos ratcheted her heart rate off the charts. "No. If I wait . . ."

"What if I went through them first," Mark said. "And removed the close-ups of . . . the victims?"

Her heartbeat settled a little. "Would you stay with me?"

"Of course."

Dani took in another deep breath through her nose. "Let's do it."

"We're all leaving," Alex said. "Why don't I bring the file in here?"

"That would be better." She didn't think her legs would carry her down the hall to Alex's office. Mark stayed with her while Alex went to get the files.

"I wish there was some other way to do this," he said.

"So do I." She closed her eyes and concentrated on calming her nerves. The door opened, and her pulse jumped again. So much for biofeedback.

"I only brought the photos." Alex laid the envelope on the table. "You don't have to do this."

"Yes, I do."

"You want me to stay too?"

Dani shook her head. It would be bad enough if she came unglued with Mark here. She didn't want Alex to see it as well.

Once they were alone, she waited while Mark went through the photos. Maybe she should stop him, tell him she needed to see them all.

"Okay, I have them separated."

His words sent a rush of light-headedness, and Dani swayed slightly.

"I still don't think you should do this," he said.

"We've already been through this. I just need to breathe." Dani closed her eyes and gave herself a minute of deep breathing, then she lifted her chin and reached for the first photo. It shook in her hand.

She willed her hand to stop shaking and viewed it. The photo was taken in the kitchen. She looked everywhere but at the bodies on the floor.

Dani licked her dry lips and plowed ahead, picking up another photo, similar to the first one. One by one she went through them, numbness settling into her brain until there were no more photos.

"You okay?"

"No. And it was for nothing. I still can't remember what happened." She looked up and couldn't stand to see the sadness in his eyes. "I'll be all right. I just need a little time."

"No, what you need is a little fun."

She tilted her head. "What are you talking about?"

"We're going to my uncle's place to do some rock skipping. And don't look at me like I'm crazy."

"You are. What if someone follows us?"

"Got that figured out. I'll pick you up at the sally port and you can get in the backseat and lie down. That way if someone sees my vehicle leave, they'll only see me."

Maybe this would work. She would love a distraction. But rock skipping? Her doubt must've shown on her face.

"What? You don't think that will work?"

"It's not that. I just never thought of throwing rocks across a pond as fun."

He grinned. "Then you've never been rock skipping with me. Besides, my uncle's is the only place I can think of that would be private."

Five minutes later, Dani lay down in the backseat beside Gem in her harness.

"Don't get up until I'm sure no one is following us. Okay?"

"Whatever you say. Does Alex know what we're doing?"

"Yep. I called her before we left."

"And she was okay with this?"

"I wouldn't say that exactly, but since it's at my uncle's fenced-in farm that has only one way in and one way out that you have to access through a locked gate, she agreed."

Her instincts still said no, but the idea of getting away from everything overruled them.

56

Twenty minutes later, Mark hesitated before he climbed out of his SUV to open the metal gate. Why was he suddenly second-guessing himself? He'd waited until they were on a stretch of road with no houses and no traffic before he pulled over for Dani to get in the front seat. After that they hadn't met five cars. No one could possibly know she was with him.

Mark climbed out of the SUV and turned in a full circle, scanning for anything out of the ordinary. Everything looked fine. He jogged to the metal gate and keyed in the code on the lock, then dragged the gate across the dirt road before he jogged back to Dani.

This should work fine. No one knew they were here except Alex. But what if it didn't?

The passenger door opened. "You okay?" Dani asked.

"Yeah. Coming." He hopped back in the SUV. "Wish I'd asked you to drive through," he said as he pulled through the gate and stopped.

"I'll get the gate this time," she said.

"Wait!"

But it was too late—she'd hopped out before he could stop her.

He scrambled out, scanning the area again. And again, everything seemed fine.

Dani frowned when she saw he'd gotten out of the truck. "Did you think I couldn't do it?"

"Didn't think that at all." He couldn't shake the anxiousness that had settled on his shoulders.

"Then why are you checking the lock?"

"Sometimes it doesn't catch."

Once they were back in his SUV, he relaxed a little and drove to the far side of his uncle's land. "One day I hope my uncle gets an automatic gate."

"Do you come out here often?"

"Not really. When I do, it's usually to see my aunt and uncle. The entrance to their house is about a quarter mile up the road—don't have to go through the gate for that."

He wound around the pasture road to the river and was surprised to see saplings growing where only grass had been in the past. "My uncle must've quit bush hogging along the riverbank."

"How long has it been since you've been down here?"

He rubbed the back of his neck. "A couple of years, or five."

"A place can change in that length of time."

His uncle was getting older. Mark made a mental note to check and see if he needed help with the farm. He parked the SUV at the edge of the trees and let Gem out of her harness after they got out. She sat and looked expectantly at Mark. "Free," he said, and she bounded toward the trees and river. "She remembers being here," he said, laughing. "Let's see if we can catch up with her."

The sun was warm, and the scent of damp earth and green grass floated on a breeze out of the south.

"It's so peaceful here," Dani said when they'd been walking a few minutes. "Thank you."

"Maybe you can enjoy a little bit of tranquility since it doesn't look like there'll be any rock skipping." He swept his hand to the left. “There used to be a sandy beach here. We’d bring our girlfriends and have picnics, spend the day, maybe even have a bonfire after it got dark.”

“So, you haven’t always been anti-dating?”

Mark bristled. “I’m not—” The twinkle in her eye stopped him short, and he chuckled. “You like to push my buttons, don’t you?”

“Hmm. Maybe. What do we do here?” she asked when they came to a ditch with water.

“This.” He jumped it, then held out his hand.

“No way. You’d probably let go and I’d fall in.”

“Me?”

“Yes, you.” She laughed and jumped it as well. Then she looked around. “How do you get to the river? There’s water everywhere.”

He hadn’t realized that the recent rains had overflowed the banks of the river, leaving ponds of water. “We probably should go back to the SUV.”

“We can walk the log.” She pointed to a tree that had fallen across the water in front of them. “Last one across is a rotten egg.”

Dani hopped up on the fallen tree, and using her arms for balance, she practically flew to the other side of the water. “Coming?” she asked, looking back at him.

Mark followed suit, and when he reached her, she asked, “Where’s the river?”

“Probably two sloughs over. I think we’d better head back. We can come again when it dries up.”

“It’s a date!” Then she froze. “I mean, we can come back.”

He softened his voice. “I like the idea of a date.”

Dani raised her gaze. The way she looked at him made it hard to breathe. She wasn’t tough and adventurous in a military sense like Jolie, not that Dani wasn’t tough. And she was beautiful in a girl-next-door way.

She was . . . Dani. At that moment, he knew if he let his fears keep him from loving her, he would miss something very valuable. But what if . . . *Whenever I am afraid, I will trust in you.*

Mark sighed and tucked the verse in his heart. Then he smiled at a streak of mud on her cheek and gently tried to wipe it off.

"What are you doing?" she asked, her voice breathy.

"Trying to clean the mud on your face."

"Where?" She raised her hand to her cheek.

He captured it with his hand and pulled her closer. "I got it," he said softly.

"Don't start something you can't finish," she whispered.

"I'm not." Mark lowered his head and gently kissed her fingers, then the palm of her hand, then he brushed her lips with his. Dani slid her arms around his neck. With a groan he deepened the kiss, sending a shock wave through him. All awareness of time and their surroundings disappeared as Dani leaned into the kiss.

Suddenly they were falling . . .

57

The cold water shocked Dani's senses. It was deeper than she'd thought, midchest on her but only coming to Mark's waist. "Are you okay?"

"The question is, are you? You fell when . . . we . . . you know."

The Kiss with a capital K. Heat rose in her face. "Yeah. Well, Keith always said I was klutzy, and this proves his point. Pretty sure my foot slipped."

Mark brushed a strand of wet hair from her face. "Come on, let's get out of the water and get you dried off."

He took her hand as they waded a short distance to the edge of the water. Once they were on solid ground, Dani looked up at him and saw a grim expression on his face. "What's wrong?"

"I shouldn't have kissed you." He shook his head. "You mess with my head. What if the killer had followed us?"

"But you said it was safe—"

"That's just it. When I'm around you, I don't think straight. I was so concerned about making you feel better that I could've made a bad judgment call. I even brushed away Alex's concerns, lost total awareness of everything around us, and because of that you could've drowned."

"I hardly think I could've drowned in four feet of water, and besides, I can swim."

"But you shouldn't have gone into the water in the first place. I should've kept that from happening, and I would've if I hadn't been so caught up in . . . And what if the killer had somehow followed us? I can't let what happened to Jolie happen to you."

"But—"

"What we have can wait—your life is too important."

58

Tuesday, Alex stepped inside the Bean Factory and glanced around. She'd asked Nathan to meet her at twelve forty-five, and she'd managed to beat him here. She didn't have much time to waste, not if she wanted to catch Crystal Davis, Kyle Peterson's former girlfriend and alibi, before she left for her 3:00 p.m. shift.

She ordered a cappuccino for herself and a black coffee for Nathan and took it to their regular table just as he opened the door to the coffee shop. An older woman was leaving, and he held the door for her before entering. That was one of the things she admired about him—Nathan always noticed what someone needed and took care of it.

Alex grinned at his raised eyebrows when he spied her and then ambled over to the table.

"You're seeing right," she said. "I have to leave for Chattanooga in about fifteen minutes. Want to tag along?"

"Depends on how long you'll be gone."

"An hour there, an hour back, and thirty minutes to interview Kyle Peterson's former girlfriend. Will that fit into your afternoon schedule?"

He laughed as he took out his phone. "I don't know. Let me check with Peg and see if she'll let me go."

Peg doubled as his office manager and part-time dispatcher. Alex sipped her coffee while he stepped away and called. She hoped he could get away. Lately they hadn't had much time together.

When Nathan came back to the table, he was smiling. "It seems things are quiet enough for me to take the afternoon off."

"Great. Give me a minute while I get a refill."

Five minutes later, Alex programmed the address Jenna Hart had gotten from the Chattanooga PD into her GPS. "Says we should arrive in forty-five minutes."

"Must be on this side of the city."

"It is," Alex said. "And it's the same address in the files from twenty-five years ago. She even has the same last name."

"Does she know we're coming?"

Alex shook her head. "I didn't want to give her a chance to say no to our visit."

"What if she's not home?"

"She is, or was fifteen minutes ago." Then Alex added, "I asked Todd Madden to have a black-and-white check and see if her car was in the drive, and it was."

He nodded. "I wonder if she and Kyle still see each other?"

"I asked Mr. Peterson that question a couple of days ago, but he *said* he didn't know."

"You don't believe him?"

"I get the feeling he would do or say anything to keep Kyle out of trouble, whether it was true or not."

"You're probably right," Nathan said. "In other news, I found a great place for our honeymoon and will book it once you set the date."

Alex's breath caught in her chest. She wasn't the only one who could spring a surprise announcement. "O-kay."

"I'm assuming you called the venue and booked our wedding?"

She'd like to say it had slipped her mind, but that would be a lie. It was all she'd thought about when she wasn't working on the case. "Not exactly."

"Not exactly? What does that mean?"

"I called the venue to see if they have something later than the first of June, but they haven't gotten back to me."

He was quiet for a minute. "Do you want to back out?"

"No! But no woman wants to try and put a wedding together at a venue in a little over a month."

"We don't have to have a venue, you know. There are plenty of beautiful places right around here. I just get the feeling . . ."

She pulled over to the shoulder of the road and killed the motor. The hurt in his eyes almost undid her. "I . . . I don't know what's wrong. But every time I pick up my phone to check with the venue, I . . ." She shrugged. "I don't do it."

"Do you love me?"

She stared straight ahead as she took in a breath to slow the pounding of her heart. Loving him—she was sure of that. But marriage was forever. "I'm scared," she whispered.

Nathan unbuckled his seat belt and shifted toward Alex. "You think I'm not?"

She turned and stared at him. "You are?"

"It's a big step, Alexis. And if you're not sure . . ." He took her hands in his. "You're shaking."

"That's what you do when you're scared." Then she giggled. And that was so not like her. A second later, Nathan laughed. And not just a chuckle but a belly laugh.

He traced his thumb along her jaw. "It's okay to be scared," he said softly. "But you can't let fear keep you from moving forward in life."

He cupped her face, and she leaned into his hand. "I do love you, but what if I snore and you can't stand it?"

"I don't think you snore—your grandmother would have told me before now. And even if you do, we've got God on our side—we'll work through it, and any other problem that comes up."

Peace settled in her heart. She took a deep breath. "You know what? You're right—we don't need a venue. We can say our vows on Eagle Ridge and then have a small reception at the house."

His eyes widened. "You sure?"

She nodded. "I think just thinking about what all needed to be done overwhelmed me, and it's not supposed to be that way. We'll keep it simple with just family and a few friends."

"I don't care where it is as long as we're married." He took out his phone and opened the calendar app. "How about June the eighth? It's on a Saturday."

Alex looked at the calendar on her phone. "Let's make it the twenty-second at 6:00 p.m. That's the day after the Founders Day Picnic and the extra work that will take will be behind us."

"Are you sure?"

She took a deep breath and released it before giving him a firm nod. "Done deal." Then she smiled. "And my grandparents will be so happy."

"Not as happy as I am."

She grinned again. "Me too. Now let's get this interview done."

The miles flew by, and they were soon turning into Crystal Davis's neighborhood. It was an older area with well-kept houses and yards.

"Did you say she's a nurse?" Nathan asked.

Alex nodded. "Works the three-to-eleven shift and lives here with her daughter who is a schoolteacher. The officer who checked earlier said she drove a light-colored Honda Accord." She nodded at the taupe Honda sitting in a drive on the right just as the GPS indicated they had arrived. "I think we've been blessed."

Alex pulled to the curb in front of the brick, single-story house. A fiftysomething blond in blue scrubs answered the door.

"Ms. Davis?"

"Yes?" Crystal Davis said cautiously. She fingered a gold cross as she looked past them to Alex's SUV with the Russell County Deputy Sheriff logo on it.

"I'm Deputy Alex Stone with the Russell County Sheriff's Office, and this is Nathan Landry, Pearl Springs's chief of police." They both showed their badges. "May we come in?"

For a second, Alex thought Crystal was going to refuse, then she sighed.

"I suppose, but I have to leave for work soon." She stood to the side and allowed them inside.

"We won't take up much of your time. It's about Kyle Peterson," Alex said.

"I figured that." She crossed her arms. "Look, I told that Chattanooga detective who called two days ago, I don't know anything, and I don't know how I can help you."

That was in the report Todd Madden had emailed her, but Alex wanted a face-to-face. She wanted to read Crystal Davis's body language. "We'd still like to talk with you a few minutes."

"Fifteen minutes, then I have to leave for work." She turned and led the way to a small living room with furniture reminiscent of the nineties.

"Sit wherever you want." Crystal waved to a chair and sofa as she sat in a dark brown leather recliner and clasped her hands together. Alex chose the overstuffed sofa while Nathan settled in a floral chair.

Alex took out her pad and pen and flipped to a clean sheet as she quietly observed the woman. It was normal for someone to be uneasy when the police showed up at their door unannounced, but Crystal held herself so rigid Alex feared she might shatter. And her face was even paler than when she opened the door. Her red lipstick was like an angry slash across her face.

She needed Crystal to relax. "Lovely house you have here,"

Alex said, glancing around. She nodded to a desert painting. "Is that a Georgia O'Keeffe?"

Crystal followed her gaze. "A print. She's my favorite artist."

Alex smiled and leaned toward her. "One of my favorites too. I've always wanted to go to Santa Fe, to see her house and the museum of her works."

"Oh, so have I." Crystal's mouth softened. "I've been to the gallery in Cleveland, Ohio, but they only had six of her paintings. The one in New Mexico would be better." She raised her chin, and her eyes narrowed. "But you didn't come here to talk about Georgia O'Keeffe's paintings."

"You're right," Alex said. She caught the other woman's gaze and held it. "Are you still friends with Kyle?"

Crystal stilled like a marble statue. Alex waited her out. It was a few moments before she said, "I haven't seen him in a long time."

"Can you define 'long'?" Nathan asked.

Crystal turned to him and lifted her shoulder in a half-hearted shrug. "Twenty years, maybe?"

The *maybe* gave a lot of leeway, but Alex let it pass for now. "How long were you two together?"

She rubbed her tongue along her top lip as she looked up. "Four or five years—we weren't that serious."

"That's a long time to date someone you're not serious about," Nathan said and shifted in his chair. "Do you mind telling us why you stopped seeing him?"

Again she shrugged. "Our relationship just ran its course."

"No big problems?" he asked.

Crystal started to shake her head. "Well, just one. Kyle was . . . he didn't like kids, and I had a three-year-old. She got on his nerves."

"That had to be difficult," Alex said, softening her voice. If Kyle was the same then as now, everything probably got on his nerves.

She fingered the cross, sliding it back and forth on the chain. "Shelly didn't like him, still doesn't. Not that he ever comes around, just, you know how kids are."

Alex glanced at Nathan, and he gave her a barely perceptible nod. "Having to decide between your child and someone you love . . ." she said. "I'm sure that had to be difficult."

Crystal's shoulders relaxed. "It was . . . but it wasn't just Shelly. Kyle could be very demanding and heavy-handed, and I got tired of it."

"Understandable." Alex glanced at her notes. "What can you tell us about the night the jewelry store was broken into?"

"Not a lot. Kyle was here that night when the police called him a little after midnight to come to the store. When he came home, he was really upset. The police had insinuated Kyle was involved in the crime because he was acquainted with the man they'd arrested—he was from Kyle's hometown.

"They questioned me, and I told them the truth—Kyle was here from the time the store closed until they called."

Alex made a few notes on her iPad and looked up. "How about the next day? Was he here then?"

She fingered the cross again. "Yes."

"Did he ask you to give him an alibi?"

"No." Crystal frowned. "I assume this is about those murders that happened after the robbery. Why are you opening a twenty-five-year-old case?"

"Someone is trying to kill the victims' daughter."

Crystal gaped at Alex. "Why?"

"We don't know, other than the daughter probably saw the murderer that night."

"Then why don't you arrest him?"

"Her mind has blocked all memories pertaining to the murders," Nathan said.

Crystal nodded. "The murderer is afraid she'll remember."

The front door opened, and a young woman entered. "Mom? What's going on? Why is there a police car out front?"

"Shelly, what are you doing home?" Crystal had turned even paler, if that was possible.

"The water main broke at school and everyone, including teachers, were sent home. Who are these people?" she asked again.

Nathan stood and introduced himself and Alex. "We were just asking about Kyle Peterson."

"I hope you told them what a sorry—"

"Shelly!" Crystal jumped to her feet. "That's enough."

"Mom, you know how controlling he was. Just tell them the truth. I'm grown now. He can't force you to do any—"

"Please, just be quiet." She turned to them. "I told you she didn't like him. And I have to leave for work."

Nathan was already standing, and Alex joined him. "One last question." When Crystal didn't say no, Alex continued. "Was he here the afternoon after the break-in?"

"It's like I told the cops then, he was here." Crystal's watch beeped, and she checked it. "I'm sorry, I have to leave or I'll be late for work."

"Thank you for talking to us and verifying Kyle's alibi." Alex took out a business card and handed it to Crystal. "If you think of anything that might help us with this case, give me a call. My cell phone number is on the back."

Crystal tucked the card into the pocket of her scrubs. "I don't think I'll remember anything."

"You never know. You could have buried information that may save Dani Bennett's life."

Worry showed in the furrow between Crystal's eyes. "I don't see how . . . and now I really need to get to work."

After Alex and Nathan exited the house, they watched as Crystal shot out of the drive, her tires screeching as she gunned her car toward town. Evidently she hadn't wanted to hang around and talk to her daughter either. "That went about as well as a three-second bull ride."

"She certainly wasn't happy to see us."

Alex stopped at the traffic light. "I got the feeling a couple of times that she wanted to say more than she did."

"So did I. Maybe she'll call you when she has time to think it over."

"Don't hold your breath waiting."

59

Mark parked outside Peterson's Grocery. He'd spent the earlier part of the day with Dani and Mae. He couldn't believe that a little over a week ago Mae had a stroke. He did see small changes in her. She wasn't as steady on her feet and she tired easily. But she was determined to return to her home on Eagle Ridge and her pottery studio.

Of course, that would depend on whether they caught the man trying to kill her granddaughter. Mark couldn't understand why they couldn't catch a break. Well, actually he could. The case hadn't been solved twenty-five years ago, and the trail was as cold as an Alaskan mountain.

Their only hope was that Dani would regain her memory. He'd suggested trying hypnosis again—it'd been ten years since she tried it the first time. She was researching it while he interviewed the Petersons again. Since he had a good relationship with Mr. Peterson, Alex had assigned him the task of talking to the grocer again, and to Kyle.

"Come on, girl." He released Gem from her harness in the backseat of the SUV. Mark ruffled her neck. He would certainly be glad to have his Expedition back with Gem's crate and the alarms that let him know if the cab got too hot. Since it was so warm, she'd be going with him inside the store. And Peterson liked Gem, so that might make getting information easier.

He said a quick prayer for Dani's safety as he climbed out of the SUV. Even though Alex had assigned a deputy to guard the Stones' house, Mark was uneasy about leaving Dani. It didn't help that Alex was an hour away in Chattanooga.

He tried to shake off the worry. Sheriff Stone was there, and even though he still had health problems, he was a dead shot with his Glock. Mark had almost left Gem at the house, but Lizi appeared to be as good a guard dog as his German shepherd. The Puli had been formidable at Mae's house the first time he met Dani.

The bell over the door jingled as he entered the store and approached the cash register. Mr. Peterson sat at his customary place behind the counter.

"Hey, Mark. I'm so glad you brought Gem."

Gem thumped her tail and looked up at Mark.

"Free," he said with a laugh, and the dog bounded around the end of the counter. "How are you today, Mr. Peterson?"

He looked up from petting Gem. "Got a little indigestion. Must've been the spaghetti I had for lunch."

"I'm sorry to hear that. Is Kyle around?"

Mr. Peterson's smile faded. "Here I was hoping you'd come just to visit. Kyle was sick, took off again today."

Mark blinked. He'd never known the man to take a day off, and it sounded like he'd taken more than one. "Is he sick?"

"A customer mentioned Toby's death yesterday afternoon, and it shook him up, and—"

Mark hadn't realized word had gotten out about Toby. "Do you know what customer told him about Toby?" he asked.

"He didn't say, just told me to come, that he had to leave."

"Why would Toby's death upset him?" Mark asked.

"Can't tell you that, just that by the time I got here, he was all worked up about losing his job again—I think it was seeing the Bennett girl last week. It didn't help that his old girlfriend called to tell him the Chattanooga police had questioned her again about the night of the murders at the request of Alex Stone." Mr. Peterson looked at him over his glasses. "Know anything about that?"

"I knew she was going to be questioned. Dani Bennett is still in danger, and we believe it's tied to the murders of her parents. We're looking at everyone and everything."

"If you're looking at Kyle, you're wasting your time. He didn't kill those people." The older man absently rubbed Gem's head. "I wish you'd leave him alone. He was really down and out this morning when he called. He said he wasn't able to get out of bed."

Mark didn't want to push anyone over the edge, but maybe it wasn't him pushing. A guilty conscience could make a person sick. "Hopefully we'll get this wrapped up soon."

Mark scanned the notes he'd taken the last time he'd been here. He didn't see where he'd asked about Kyle's whereabouts a week ago. "Has your grandson taken any other days off lately?"

"I'm done talking about Kyle. You got any other questions?"

Mark had never seen this side of the old man. He'd come back to this question before he left. Besides, he still had a few questions about Toby he wanted to ask. "Did Toby ever tell you what went wrong during the burglary?"

Mr. Peterson glanced toward the back of the store almost like he was looking for the man. "Yeah, he told me several times, and it never changed.

"Toby met them at the jewelry store and waited at the back door after Keith picked the lock. Bobby and Keith entered the store and got into the safe, and Toby stayed by the door. Toby thinks they had the combination. As soon as they had the safe opened, an alarm went off. They all took off, but Toby got caught."

"They let him take the fall?"

"Same thing I asked him, but Toby insisted that was the way

it was supposed to be. If anything went wrong, everyone was supposed to scatter. Toby just went the wrong direction and met a police car in the alley coming to investigate the alarm. They arrested him on the spot."

Mark tapped his pad. "Why do you think Kyle's boss fired him?"

"I don't know. Maybe the boss was the inside man and saw an opportunity to put the blame on someone else. But to tell the truth, I was glad Kyle lost that job. He was in over his head—got promoted beyond his abilities. Working twelve, fifteen hours a day. He was losing weight, had ulcers . . ." Mr. Peterson rubbed his left arm. "Even though managing the store was killing him, he never would've quit. I needed him here, to help me run the store."

And he still needed him. Anything he told Mark would be filtered through that lens. He'd always known Mr. Peterson as an honest man, but then how well did Mark actually know him? The man was sweating bullets right now. "You've said that Kyle didn't kill Bobby and Neva Bennett. What do you base that on, other than him being your grandson?"

Mark had taken a risk, asking more questions about Kyle.

Peterson flexed his fingers, then slid his hand in his pocket. "You don't live to be nearly a hundred without learning a thing or two about human nature. I know my grandson, and he never killed anyone." He pulled a tiny amber bottle from his pocket and fumbled with the cap. "I think you better leave. I'm not feeling good."

Mark's phone chimed, and he checked it. His breath caught in his chest. Dani had sent the text five minutes ago, and he hadn't heard the first alert.

I think someone is in the house.

His heart almost stopped. "I'll be back—I gotta leave!"

Before he could move, the old man clutched his chest and fell forward onto the counter. Mark ran over and eased Mr. Peterson to the floor. Not a heart attack now. Dani needed him.

"Nitro pills . . . bottle . . ." Mr. Peterson held out the amber bottle.

Mark grabbed the bottle and shook out a small white pill. While Peterson put it under his tongue, Mark called dispatch and asked for an ambulance to the grocery store. Then he asked for her to send deputies to the Stones' house.

"Can you go? I've dispatched every available deputy we have to a tractor-trailer accident on the highway."

He stared at the old man. He'd turned ashen, and sweat beaded his face. If Mark left him and he died . . .

The bell over the door jingled.

"Mr. Peterson?"

Judith Stone's voice was like an angel's. Mark looked over her shoulder. Carson and Mae were with her. "Behind the counter. He's having a heart attack." Mark stood and ran for the door. "There's an intruder at your house."

"Go!" Carson knelt beside Peterson. "We'll take care of this."

Mark raced for his SUV. He'd been counting on Carson being at the house. What if he was too late?

60

They were halfway to Pearl Springs when Nathan's phone rang, then Alex's. She glanced at the ID on her SUV screen. Marge. She wouldn't call unless it was important. Alex answered her phone and listened as her dispatcher advised her that she'd dispatched all the available deputies to handle a tractor-trailer accident on the highway. "Good call. I should be at the location soon."

As the call ended, she overheard Nathan tell his dispatcher the same thing.

"Sounds bad," he said after he hung up.

She nodded as her phone rang again. Alex answered on the hands-free as she flipped on her flashing lights.

"This is Crystal Davis," the voice on the other end said. "Is this Alex Stone?"

"Yes," she responded. "Did you remember something?"

"No . . . but I can't lie anymore . . ."

"Go ahead."

"Okay," she said and took a deep breath. "The day after his boss called and fired him, Kyle got really angry. He said if this Mitchell guy was involved, that meant somebody named Bobby Bennett was behind it, and they'd set him up to take the fall. He tore out of my house, said he was going to Pearl Springs and find out what was going on. But then his car had a flat, and he made me let him use my car. He was so angry, I didn't want him to go, but I couldn't stop him.

"When he got back, he was scared, kept saying 'They're dead.' Then he told me I had to give him an alibi. I didn't want to, but he said if I didn't, he'd file a report to child protective services that I was doing drugs around my daughter. I wasn't, but social services tend to act first and investigate later. I couldn't risk losing my daughter.

"And to tell you the truth, I was afraid of Kyle, still am. He's crazy when he gets mad."

Alex braked as traffic slowed in front of her, then she pulled off onto the shoulder. "Thank you for telling us now."

A number beeped in on the call. Mark.

"Crystal, can we talk later? I have another call I need to take."

Crystal agreed and Alex switched the call over. "Mark, I need you to—"

"Where are you? I need backup. Dani texted there's an intruder at your house!"

Her heart sank. All of her deputies except the one at the house were tied up. "Everyone's caught up in an accident on the highway," Alex said. "Nathan is with me, and we'll be there as soon as we can."

"I'm almost there. Get here ASAP!"

61

Lizi stood, and a low growl came from her throat. Dani cocked her ear toward the kitchen. She was pretty sure she'd heard the funny noise the back door made when it was opened. She checked her watch. Judith had gotten a call from Mr. Peterson about an unsigned check she'd written, and she and Carson had headed to the store.

They hadn't wanted to go, but Mr. Peterson was worked up and Judith said he sounded funny. She was afraid he might be having a stroke or something. Dani had told them to go and for Nonny to go with them since she hadn't been away from the house in a while. Besides, Dani had Lizi and a deputy sitting outside the back door.

But they hadn't been gone long enough to be back yet. And if they were, Judith would've let her know.

Dani shivered at the total silence. Had the deputy guarding the house stuck his head in the door and that's what she heard? She started to call out but instead texted Mark that someone was in the house.

She put her phone on silent. "Come," she whispered to Lizi.

With her hand on the dog's collar, Dani eased down the hallway to the kitchen. Empty. Maybe she'd just imagined the noise. Feeling a little foolish, Dani scanned the room. Lizi pressed toward the living room door.

It was open. She stood rooted to the floor as the mirror over the sofa reflected Kyle Peterson coming toward the kitchen. In his hand was a gun. That was no match for Lizi.

Her mind screamed at her to run. But where to? He was too close for them to escape out the back door. She crept back to her room and eased the door shut, then frantically searched somewhere for them to hide. Her gaze stopped at the closet . . . No. That would be the first place he would look. The bathroom, the second. Her bed—she prayed the prowler didn't hear her as she scooted under the bed.

Why hadn't Mark answered her text? And where was the deputy assigned to guard the house? Knife-like pain gripped her stomach. What if Kyle had killed him?

Dani stilled herself as a board creaked in the hallway outside her bedroom door. Beside her, Lizi tensed. Dani tried to swallow, but her mouth was too dry.

Her phone vibrated in her hand. A text from Mark saying he was on his way. What little relief she felt at this news fled when the door to the bedroom opened. She and Lizi could be dead by the time he got here.

"I know you're in here, and that you're alone. I don't want to hurt you. Just give me the diamonds."

The closet door opened and closed. Then the bathroom door. Should she run for it? No. He'd catch her before she got out the door.

A sudden light blinded her. Lizi lunged toward it.

"Keep that dog away from me unless you want it dead."

She gripped Lizi's collar. "Down."

"Now get out here."

She didn't move.

"I can wait until the Stones and your grandmother get back. They'll make good hostages."

Dani clenched her jaw. She couldn't let him harm anyone. Slowly she slid out into the open. Kyle jerked her to her feet and held a gun at her head. Lizi growled. "I told you—"

"Down, Lizi."

"Put her in the hallway."

He held the gun at chest level as Dani put Lizi outside the room. The dog barked as she shut the door and turned to face Kyle.

"That's better." His voice shook and his bloodshot eyes darted around the room. "Where are they?"

"What?"

"The diamonds," he said through gritted teeth.

"I-I don't have them." Kyle showed all the symptoms of someone about to explode. Chest heaving, sweat running down the side of his red face, tight voice.

"You know where they are, then."

"But I don't!"

"Stop lying. You owe me. Your family ruined my life. Now hand them over or I'll—" He jerked his head toward the door as Lizi stopped barking.

A board creaked outside her door. *Mark!* The man grabbed her, wrapping his arm around her neck. "Don't say a word or I'll kill whoever it is."

Dani fought for air as his hold tightened on her neck. She had to stop him before he shot Mark. He stepped to the back side of the door, forcing Dani to move with him. If Mark opened the door, he wouldn't see them until it was too late.

The doorknob twisted. Dani couldn't let Mark get hurt again. She bunched her legs and lunged back, ramming the back of her head into Kyle's chin and nose. He screamed, and his grip loosened on her neck.

Dani twisted away and kicked him in the groin. He staggered, and the gun went off. The bullet went wide just as Mark threw open the door and Lizi burst into the room with Mark and Gem right behind.

Kyle grabbed for Dani just as Mark tackled him. She wrenched away from him as the two men went down. Mark slugged him in the jaw. Kyle scrambled away and turned his gun toward Mark's chest.

Dani screamed. "No!"

Lizi and Gem lunged at Kyle as Dani kicked his hand and the gun sailed across the floor.

"Free!"

"Release!" Both dogs released their hold on the man, and Mark quickly subdued him and slapped on handcuffs.

"Why, Kyle?"

"I got nothing to say. I want a lawyer."

62

Blood dripped down Kyle's nose as Mark sat him in a chair in the kitchen. "Guard," he said to Gem, then turned to Dani. "Can you and Lizi check on the deputy that was guarding the house? He was out cold when I got here."

Mark's heart had almost stopped when he saw the deputy slumped over his steering wheel. He barely took time to check for a pulse. Mark checked his phone. *All emergency vehicles dispatched to accident.*

One of the minuses of living in a small town. He looked up as the back door opened and Dani returned inside.

"The deputy is dazed and said his head is killing him, so he probably has a concussion. You want me to call an ambulance?"

"There aren't any available—there was a big wreck on the highway into town," Mark said. "I need to get Kyle to the jail."

"Why don't I take the deputy to the hospital in his SUV and you take Kyle to jail?"

He hesitated. Kyle had lawyered up, and Mark couldn't question him about any accomplices.

"Okay," Mark said. "Just be careful. We don't know if Kyle has any accomplices out there."

Mark prayed Dani's ordeal was over. His heart skipped a beat. If it was, then they could get on with their lives.

63

A week later, Dani inspected the heating and air-conditioning unit the contractor had installed at Mae's house. She had no idea what she was supposed to be inspecting, but both the contractor and Mark seemed pleased with the unit. All Dani cared about was that it worked.

She handed the contractor a check. "Thanks for installing it so quickly."

"Thank you, Ms. Bennett. Good to see you again, Mark." The man shook hands with Mark, then pocketed the check and climbed into his pickup.

Dani turned and surveyed her grandmother's house. With Mark's help, she'd cleaned out the flower beds and added a few rosebushes and azaleas along the front of the house.

Mark nodded toward the front porch. "I really think we should build a ramp."

"I agree, but Nonny insists that it isn't necessary."

He shook his head. "Why does that not surprise me? But I suppose she can manage the steps since she's only using a cane."

She chuckled. "A cane that she carries half the time instead of relying on it. Has she always been so independent?"

Dani still hadn't recovered any childhood memories of her grandmother, or . . . anything.

"I've always thought *independent* was just a nice word for *stubborn*, and yes, she's been that way ever since I've known her."

Mark followed Dani as she climbed the steps to the porch and entered the living room.

"At least with the new central heat and air, you won't have to cut firewood for her," Dani said.

"I'm still surprised she agreed to let you put that in."

"I didn't exactly ask her. This is a surprise, but since I'm going to be staying with her for a while, we'll need it."

"Think you'll be okay here? It's pretty isolated—not many neighbors."

"Well, there's you."

Mark grinned. "This is true."

She picked up the photo of her mom. "Has Kyle broken his silence?"

"Still not talking. Arraignment is next week, and he refuses to see anyone except his lawyer, not even his grandfather."

"How is Mr. Peterson?"

"He's better. They got him to the hospital before his heart sustained damage."

"Do you know what Kyle's being charged with yet?"

"Right now, your kidnapping and attempted murder. The DA is still putting together a case against him for the murder of your parents."

"What's there to put together? Isn't the gun he used when he tried to kidnap me the same one that killed my parents?"

"We know it was the same type—.45 caliber—but we won't know for sure until the ballistics report comes back."

Dani sighed. If only she could remember what happened that night. Then there wouldn't be any question of Kyle's involvement.

He took her hand as they walked to his Expedition. "Are you ready to head back to town? I have to take Gem to the vet for a follow-up visit. She keeps biting at something on her side."

"And I need to get back too. Judith and Carson are leaving for an appointment with his cardiologist, and I don't want to leave Nonny by herself for long. I don't care what she says, she's not fully recovered."

Forty-five minutes later, Dani parked the Navigator behind the Stones' house. Out of habit, she looked for the deputy stationed outside the house before she remembered that Alex had pulled him once she was confident that Kyle was the killer. She grabbed her purse and hurried inside the house. "I'm back," she called.

No one answered, not even Lizi. Maybe Nonny was taking a nap. Dani tiptoed down the hallway and peeked inside Nonny's bedroom. The bed hadn't been disturbed.

Dani fumbled for her phone, and her legs threatened to buckle when she saw something dark on the other side of Nonny's bed. Lizi, and she wasn't moving.

She rushed to the dog and knelt beside her, placing her hand on the dog's chest. A rush swept over Dani when her hand rose and fell. Lizi was alive.

Dani jerked her phone out to call 911, and a text from her grandmother's phone popped up. She quickly opened it, and her breath stilled.

I have your grandmother. If you want to see her alive again, come to her house on Eagle Ridge.

They'd just come from Nonny's house. How had she missed them?

She punched in Mark's number, and the call went to voicemail. No! Dani quickly left a message, laying out what was happening and telling him she was going to her grandmother's house.

Then she replied to the text.

What do you want?

You. And the diamonds if you have them. You might can buy your grandmother's life.

She buried her face in her hands. *Lord, if I ever knew where those diamonds are, please let me remember . . .*

She raised her head and tried Mark again. Nothing. It was up to her. Dani closed her eyes, willing herself to be still. Her parents' house, where it all started, filled her mind.

Mentally she walked through each room. Nothing. Maybe if she went to the house . . .

Sheriff Stone's gun. He wouldn't have taken it with him to his doctor's appointment in Chattanooga. Dani ran to his office. The gun was hanging in its holster on the back of his chair. She grabbed it and ran to the Navigator.

Lord, please don't let whoever this is harm Nonny . . .

64

X-rays show a bullet fragment under the skin next to her leg. I don't know how I missed it before," the veterinarian said, rubbing his hand along the dog's side. "I can remove it this afternoon, and you can take her home around six, but I will have to sedate her."

That's what the biting had been about. "Let's get it out, then."

"Bring her back to the surgery," the doctor said. "And you can stay while I take it out."

An hour later, he breathed easier when Gem roused from the anesthesia. "You got it all?" he asked the vet.

"Yep. She'll be good to go in a couple of hours."

"Thanks, Doc." He took out his phone to call Dani.

"No need to even try to make a call in here."

"What do you mean?"

The vet pointed to the ceiling, then the walls. "Metal roof, and the rest is thick concrete—calls just don't get through. It's why I leave my cell phone by the window."

Once Mark was in his SUV, he tried to call Dani and noticed he'd missed a call and voicemail from her. Evidently the vet was right, but before he could check the message, his phone rang. Alex. "What's up?"

"Kyle's .45 didn't match the gun that killed Dani's parents."

"That means—"

"I don't know that it means anything. He could have a dozen guns, but his lawyer swears he didn't have anything to do with their murders."

"You know how that goes. I have a voicemail from Dani. Let me call you right back," he said.

His heart seized when he listened to the message. Mark called Alex back. "Dani's in trouble. Someone's holding Mae. I'm on my way to Eagle Ridge."

"I'm putting you on hold." A minute later she came back on. "Where are you?"

"At the vet."

"That's about ten minutes from the hospital. There's a medevac helicopter waiting to take you to Eagle Ridge, and I have every available unit headed that way now."

"Thanks! Do I wait on you?"

"No. I'm on the other side of the county, and it would take me too long to get to the hospital. I'll head to Eagle Ridge now."

65

Dani pulled into her parents' gravel driveway and climbed out of the Navigator. The hairs on the back of her neck raised. She stopped and scanned the woods, the yard, and finally the house, where deep shadows hid the evil in it.

Where did that come from? It wasn't the house that was evil, but the man who had done horrific things there.

He wanted her dead.

Something within had pushed Dani to come here, to her parents' house. Her subconscious or God? Was God giving her a plan?

If he was, she wished he'd let her in on it. Maybe he wanted her to find the diamonds. If she did, could she buy Nonny's freedom?

Maybe she should try Mark again in case he'd missed the voicemail. She took out her phone . . . No. He would try to talk her out of meeting with this person, and then Nonny would die. No one else could do this but Dani.

Except . . . when the killer got what he wanted, he would probably kill Nonny anyway. She felt the gun in her pocket. She would have to stop him.

She climbed the front porch steps and walked to the door, shivering as the boards creaked. Dani used the key Mark had given her to unlock the door. Inside the house, the familiar scent of cedar gave her strength. She could do this.

In the kitchen, she stood stock-still, willing herself to become that nine-year-old girl again. *Let the memories come*, she prayed.

Dani didn't know how much time had passed before an image formed . . . her dad, and he was taking her down the hall.

"I want you to get in this cabinet, and no matter what happens, you stay here until Mama or I come get you. Can you do that?"

"Why, Daddy?"

"Because it's very important." He knelt and pushed a board on the wall, and it slid open. Then he put something inside, but she couldn't see what it was before he closed it. Her daddy motioned her inside the cabinet. "Climb in."

Once she was settled, he stood and stared solemnly at her. "Promise me you'll stay here no matter what you hear. Will you do that for me?"

She nodded.

"I want to hear you say 'I promise.'"

"You're scaring me, Daddy."

"I'm sorry, honey, but you have to promise."

Tears burned the back of her eyes. "I promise."

Dani walked to the cabinet she'd hidden in and opened the door. She stared at the small space, and suddenly her brain released the memories hidden for so long . . .

Tires crunched on the gravel outside the house. "No, Daddy! I don't want to!"

"I'm sorry, but you have to, and Danielle, don't say a word. Remember your promise."

She nodded.

He shut the cabinet door. Then darkness except for a tiny beam of light from a small hole. Dani pressed her ear against the hole. She could hear them talking, but what they said didn't make sense . . .

"Where's Neva?"

"I told her to stay in the bedroom."

"Call her."

"There's no need to involve her. This is between me and you. We can split the diamonds."

"I don't trust you. You were going to skip town—"

"Just leave Neva out of it."

"You think she didn't recognize my voice? Neva! Get in here."

"Pastor Rick? I-I don't understand!"

Dani held her breath. That was her mama's voice.

"No!"

It sounded like someone was rolling around on the floor. Then there was a loud noise, like when her daddy shot his gun.

"I want my diamonds."

"You shouldn't have killed her!"

Suddenly there were more loud booms. Then it was so quiet.

Danielle's heart beat so fast she thought it'd jump out of her chest. She looked through the small hole and didn't see anyone. Slowly, she eased the cabinet door open and crept down the hallway to the kitchen.

Her daddy lay on the floor beside her mama. A man knelt next to them. Dani must have made a noise because he looked right at her with mean black eyes. She turned around and raced down the hall to the cabinet and pulled the door closed.

Footsteps stomped down the hallway.

"Where did she go?" he muttered.

Danielle barely breathed, fearing he would hear her. Way, way off, she heard a horn like the one Sheriff Stone had on his car. The man swore, then it sounded like he ran down the hall and slammed the back door.

Danielle's body started shaking and tears ran down her face. The back door opened again, and she tried to stop her tears. Whoever it was said something, but she couldn't hear what it was.

Footsteps came down the hall, and suddenly the cabinet door flew open.

"Danielle?"

Dani sank to the floor and took a shuddering breath. She remembered it all now. Keith had taken her out the front door to his car, then they had driven for what seemed like days, and probably had been.

She leaned her head back against the wall as quiet settled around her. At least now she had answers. It had been Rick Adkins she'd seen kneeling over her parents.

And now he wanted her. He would kill Nonny if she didn't do what he said.

Where were the diamonds? She'd thought her dad had buried them, but he hadn't. *Think!*

Her father had put something in the wall before he made her get into the cabinet. Was that where he'd hidden the diamonds?

She got on her hands and knees and leaned inside the cabinet, running her hand over the wood. There. A small hole in the back wall. She stuck her finger in the hole and something clicked, releasing a small section of the paneling. She pried it open and pulled out a small bag. Her hands trembled as she opened it.

Dani caught her breath as light reflected off the glittering diamonds. She didn't know much about diamonds, but she'd bet even the smallest ones were bigger than a carat.

Could she use them to buy her grandmother's life?

A text dinged on her phone.

You must not care about your grandmother.

She texted back.

On my way.

You better hurry if you want to see her alive again.

If you hurt her, you'll never see me . . . or the diamonds.

She poured the gems on the floor, snapped a photo, and sent it to him.

A minute later another text chimed on her phone.

Bring them with you.

No. A plan formed in her mind. Maybe she held an ace in the hole.

Answer your phone.

Dani tapped on the number at the top of the message and pressed the button for a call.

Rick answered with a growl.

"I want to talk to my grandmother."

"She's fine."

"Then you won't mind putting her on the call."

A second later she heard her grandmother's voice. "Danielle?"

"Nonny, are you all right?"

"I'm fine, but his father would be so ashamed."

"My father is to blame for all of this."

Please don't agitate him more. "Nonny, do you think you can drive a car?"

"Drive?" Her grandmother sounded unsure. "I can try."

"I believe you can do it. In a few minutes you are going to get in the car with Rick, okay?"

"Are you sure?"

"Yes." A call beeped in on her phone and she checked the screen. Mark. She ignored it. "Let me talk to Rick."

While her grandmother handed off the phone, Dani shot off a text to Mark.

Rick Adkins holding Nonny. Come to my parents' house.

"You have five minutes to get here," Rick said.

"No. If you want me, you're coming to my parents' house, and you're bringing my grandmother with you."

The line went quiet.

"Just remember—if you harm her in any way, you lose me and the diamonds. And you'll blow your chances of getting away, of starting a new life somewhere."

Silence stretched between them. "What's the deal?"

Good. Greed had reared its ugly head. But she wanted some answers first. "Tell me why you killed my mom and dad."

"I hated that Neva and Keith had to die. Bobby, not so much."

She frowned. What was he talking about? "What do you mean?"

"Neva was an accident—Bobby's fault, actually. He pulled a gun on me, and we were struggling for it when it went off. If he'd just given me the diamonds . . ."

"If you want the diamonds, they're here waiting for you," Dani said.

"You'll give them to me, just like that?"

"After my grandmother safely leaves. When you arrive, you'll stay in your car while my grandmother gets out and leaves in my car. Once she's gone, you and I will do business."

She didn't want to think what might happen if he said no. "And don't think you can double-cross me. By the time you get here, the diamonds will be back where they've been all these years. No one's found them in twenty-five years, and you won't find them now without my help."

Suddenly he ended the call, and she was left staring at her phone.

What had she done? What if he wasn't as greedy as she believed?

Please, Lord, work this out.

While she waited to see if Rick and Nonny would arrive, she turned her Navigator around so Nonny could make a quick getaway on the off chance he let her grandmother go. In her heart, she didn't believe he'd leave a witness behind to identify him. Their only chance was to stall to give Mark time to get here.

Dani grabbed some dollar bills from her wallet and stuffed them in the bag with the diamonds. Something to sweeten the pot without having to lie about it. Then she returned the bag to its hiding place.

Tires crunched on the drive. He'd taken the bait! She hurried to the front window, watching as Rick's truck pulled into the drive and parked beside the Navigator. When no one got out, she called out to him. "We're not doing any business until my grandmother is in my car and driving down the road."

Rick lowered his window. "This is an exchange," he yelled, his voice tight. "She's not moving until you're walking toward me."

In other words, until she was under his control. "You don't trust me."

"No way."

"And I don't trust you. Let's start off with her getting out of the car and walking to my SUV. Once she's there, I'll step out on the porch."

He didn't respond, but a minute later, the passenger door opened and her grandmother climbed out, then Rick. He held a gun in his right hand.

Dani cringed as Nonny leaned on her cane to walk the short distance around Rick's pickup. Had he hurt her in some way? What if she couldn't climb in the Navigator?

"All right, your turn!" he yelled.

She stepped out onto the porch. "I'm here. We'll do business as soon as she drives off."

"No, we'll do business now. You stay put." He pointed the gun at Nonny, then turned back to Dani. "I want to see the diamonds."

"I want answers first—why did you do it?" She had to stall for time.

"What? You want to know why I killed your parents or why I planned the burglaries?"

"Both."

"Do you really want to know?"

"I do. Maybe it'll help me to understand why a pastor would do what you did."

"Pastor." He laughed, but there was no humor in his voice. "I never had any choice. From my first memories it was 'You're going to be the next preacher at Community Fellowship like your daddy and his daddy before him.'

"There was no talking about what I wanted to do. They never even asked." He stopped and looked at her. "Nobody's ever asked what I wanted."

"I'm asking."

"You don't count. And it's too late."

"No, really, I want to know."

He paced in front of Nonny, careful to keep his gun trained on her. Then he stopped. "I wanted something bigger than being a small-town preacher, and I had the chance, but your daddy and uncle ruined it."

"How?" Dani asked.

"They double-crossed me. Kept my share of the diamonds. I knew that's what they had planned after your daddy wouldn't answer my phone calls the next morning. When he finally did, he tried to tell me he left the diamonds at the store. He was lying. By noon all the news stations led with the theft of the diamonds. So I showed up at the house, and I was right—they were getting ready to leave."

He stopped pacing in front of Nonny. "Bobby pulled a gun on me when I got there, and we fought for it and it went off. Unfortunately, the bullet hit Neva."

Her grandmother stiffened. “You had no cause to kill my Neva! She thought you hung the moon.”

Rick went on like he hadn’t heard her. “As for Bobby, it was him or me, but I swear, I didn’t mean to kill Neva, even if she did start the whole thing.”

“What are you talking about?” Nonny said. “My Neva never stole anything in her life.”

“Maybe not, but if it hadn’t been for her, I wouldn’t be standing here with a gun today.”

“You’re crazy,” Nonny said.

“Am I?” Rick curled his lips in a sneer. “Your Neva came to me. ‘I’m so worried about my Bobby. Please, talk to him. He’s at the pool hall every afternoon,’” he mimicked in a falsetto. “You people always expected me to pull miracles out of a hat. Bobby didn’t want saving, I could’ve told you that.”

Rick fell silent and started pacing again. That frightened Dani more than when he was raving. “What happened then?” she asked.

He stopped and glared at her. “I couldn’t go to the pool hall like a normal man—the congregation wouldn’t have approved. My daddy would’ve had a stroke. But I could go if I was saving souls. Hallelujah!” He raised his hand toward the sky, then he laughed. “No one knew that I loved playing pool in that smoky room, that I felt normal there.”

Rick was so bitter and angry. Like a lit fuse—he could go off any minute. *Mark, where are you?* “I can understand that.”

“Don’t patronize me! Do you not hear me? I never had any choice. No, I had to go to the pool hall, not because I wanted to, but because it was *expected*.

“And there they all were. Toby. Bobby. Keith. They were all playing pool and having a good time. And I envied them. They were doing what they wanted to do. Then, as I kept going, I got to know them, and I really liked them.”

"How did you get involved in the burglary ring?" Dani kept her eye on Nonny, who seemed to be getting angrier by the minute.

"I wasn't *involved*, I created it. You don't really think one of those other three could've successfully robbed a jewelry store, do you? They couldn't think their way out of a paper bag."

Dani shook her head. "I still don't get it."

Rick gave an exasperated huff. "I always thought big, and when my cousin down in Florida called me about an investment opportunity that promised to pay 500 percent dividends, I needed buy-in money. A hundred thousand dollars to be exact, and my share of the diamonds would've given me that and more."

"You ought to be ashamed of yourself," her grandmother said.

"Shut up!" He grabbed Nonny and wrapped his arm around her waist, pointing his gun at her head. "I'm done talking. Get the diamonds or I'll kill her."

Dani took a calming breath. "I told you—not until you release my grandmother and she's driving down the road."

He hesitated, and Dani lifted her chin. "I just sent a text to Mark that you're holding us prisoner. You're wasting valuable time that you could be using to escape. Let her go, and I'll show you where the diamonds are."

He shook his head. "You know I can't leave you here to identify me."

"Mark knows who you are—it's over, Rick, unless you let her go."

"You'll get the diamonds now, or I'll kill her."

66

The pilot set the chopper down in a clearing near a trail that came out at the Bennetts'. Mark grabbed his bolt-action rifle and jumped out of the helicopter.

If he stuck to the road, it would take longer to get to the house than cutting through on the trail. He figured every second was important. Mark cocked his ear, listening for sirens. Nothing. No telling how long before Alex and the other deputies would arrive.

He carried the rifle in his right hand and jogged through the woods, being careful not to trip on a root. At least it was mostly downhill. Mark heard voices before anyone came into view. When they did, his heart crashed.

Rick Adkins was holding a gun to Mae's head. And Mark didn't have a clear shot.

67

Dani folded her arms over her chest. "What's more important to you? Killing us or escaping while you can? This place will be crawling with deputies soon. If you leave now, you can still get away."

He stared at her, indecision on his face.

"But if you harm one hair on my grandmother's head, those deputies will track you down, and I'll be leading the way." Time to play her ace and pray God would forgive her for any lies she might have to tell. "There's more than diamonds in the bag."

"What are you talking about?"

"There's cash as well. Enough for you to make a fast getaway."

"How much?"

"I didn't count it." She cocked her head. "So, what's it going to be? Are you going to waste your time standing here arguing with me until Alex Stone and the rest of the Russell County deputies get here? Or do we have a deal?"

"On one condition. I'll exchange the old lady for you and then you'll take me to where the diamonds are."

He wanted a hostage, and she'd do anything to keep her grandmother safe. "Deal."

"You come to my truck, and I'll let her leave."

"No, she leaves first." When he started to protest, she pointed to her sandals. "I can't outrun you with these on, but I want my grandmother safe."

He stared at her for a minute, then released her grandmother but kept his pistol trained on her.

"Nonny, get in the car," she said. Her grandmother crossed her arms over her chest. "Trust me. Please."

Her grandmother looked at Dani, and her shoulders squared as she took a step away from Rick.

"She's free." He turned his gun toward Dani. "Get down here!"

"You're not hurting my granddaughter!"

68

Mark's finger was on the trigger as he waited for an opportunity to fire. Mae took a step away from Rick, but she was still in his line of fire. Suddenly the scene seemed to unfold in slow motion as Mae reared back and brought her cane down on Rick's arm.

He yelled but managed to hang on to the gun. Dani jumped off the porch and raced toward them while Mae drew the cane back to hit him again. Rick backhanded her with the gun, and she fell to her knees. He turned his pistol on the kneeling woman.

"No!" Dani screamed.

It was now or never. Mark squeezed the trigger, feeling the recoil of the .30-06. Rick staggered back, a red stain appearing on his chest. He didn't go down, instead lifted the gun and pointed it at Dani just as she tackled him.

Mark sprinted toward them and held his gun on Rick. The faint sound of sirens was music to his ears. "Help's on the way."

"I think he's dead," Dani said as she climbed to her knees.

Mark handed her the gun. "Watch him while I check."

She waved him off and pulled a .45 from her pocket. "I have Carson's."

He shook his head and felt Rick's neck. "He's still alive, but barely." Mark quickly took out his phone and dialed Alex. "Is the medevac standing by? Rick Adkins is critically wounded."

"I'll contact the pilot, and if he isn't, he'll be back there in ten minutes."

"Good deal."

Dani hurried to her grandmother and helped her stand. "Are you hurt?"

Mae dusted her hands. "I've been better, but I've definitely been worse."

"Well, you scared me to death." Dani wrapped her arms around Mae. "You're the bravest person I know. When you hit him with your cane . . ."

Mae patted Dani on the shoulder. "You're brave yourself—a little too brave."

"You both are something else." Mark enveloped both of them in a bear hug as flashing blue lights rounded the curve. "I believe the cavalry has arrived."

69

Dani paced in the ICU waiting room. For two days, it'd been touch and go with Rick since the surgery to remove the bullet. He wasn't out of the woods yet, but he'd asked to see Dani, and she was waiting for the nurse to come get her.

"You don't have to do this," Mark said. He'd brought her to the hospital after Rick's request.

"But I do. I still don't know why he killed Keith." She stopped and faced him. "He didn't give you *any* reason?"

Mark shook his head. "I only had a limited amount of time with him, so I only touched on the details of the crimes here in Russell County. I hope for another opportunity to interview him again."

Dani sat in the chair beside him. Piecing together the details that Mark had shared was like putting together a jigsaw puzzle without all the pieces. As best she could tell, Kyle Peterson had nothing to do with the crimes in the past. He'd spent his life blaming Dani's father for losing his job and the way his life turned out. He'd let it eat away at him until his bitter anger affected his mind.

"You said Toby Mitchell was the one who shot at me that first night. How did he even know I was in Pearl Springs?"

"He didn't," Mark said. "Toby always believed Bobby had given Mae the diamonds and that she hid them."

"Nonny would never have done that."

"I know, but that's what Toby believed. With Mae in the hospital, he thought it'd be safe to look around the pottery shop again—it wasn't his first time over the years to search her place. Then you came up, and he was afraid you could identify him."

Dani glanced at the ICU doors, wishing the nurse would come get her. "Did you ask Rick why he killed Toby?"

"Yeah," Mark said. "The night of the murders, Toby went to Bobby's house, looking for his share of the diamonds, but before he got to the door, he heard the gunshots. Then he saw Rick leave."

"Why didn't Toby tell? He could've traded that information for a get-out-of-jail-free card."

Mark rubbed his jaw. "You'd have to know Toby. He would've cut off an arm before turning in a friend, and he considered Rick a friend. But the truth had been gnawing on Toby for a while when Morgan approached him. Whatever she said to him that day in the store was the match in the powder keg."

"Why were they at my parents' house, though?"

"Rick lured Toby there. He saw him talking to Morgan and—"

"And Rick couldn't take a chance of Toby spilling his guts to Morgan," Dani said. "Was Toby the one who broke into Nonny's house the day that she had the stroke?"

"No, that was Rick. He'd heard Mae had found you, and he thought there might be information on Keith's whereabouts in her office."

Dani nodded. "Rick thought my dad and Keith had double-crossed him. He wanted his share of the diamonds."

The doors to the ICU opened and Rick's nurse stepped into the waiting room. "Ms. Collins, you can see him now."

Dani stood and Mark said, "Would you like me to come with you?"

She shook her head. "I want to go by myself."

Dani followed the nurse to Rick's door and pushed it open. He turned toward her. Oxygen flowed through a nasal cannula, but his lips were blue. That couldn't be a good sign. "They told me you wanted to see me."

He nodded. "They tell me I might not make it."

Dani didn't know what to say, so she said nothing.

"I've lived a lie for so long. Pretending to be something I'm not. Preaching forgiveness . . ."

She stiffened but couldn't turn away from his piercing dark eyes.

"I don't deserve it, but I don't want to die without asking for your forgiveness." He closed his eyes. "Don't say no yet."

"Why did you kill Keith?"

He shifted his gaze to a spot over her head. "I didn't mean to. Saw that picture of the Badlands on your website." He took a deep breath and coughed. "It didn't take long to find your business along with the address on the Montana Secretary of State website . . ."

He closed his eyes, and she waited. "When I got there and saw Keith's fancy house . . . I lost it. He . . . cheated me out of my share of the diamonds. We argued. I shot him." Rick coughed again. "You probably don't believe me . . . but I truly am sorry."

He was right. She didn't believe him. Dani balled her hands into fists. And she wasn't forgiving him. He'd taken her family and twenty-five years of her life from her. She turned to go.

"Wait . . . I'm not asking for me. See . . . I know what happens when you don't forgive. It eats away at you like a cancer."

Dani faced him again. "Who was it you didn't forgive?"

"My father. It was always about what he wanted. Instead of

forgiving him and moving on, I hated him." Rick held out his hand. "Don't let that be you."

Forgiveness wasn't something she could just turn on. "I'll think about it."

"That's all I can ask."

She turned to leave and stopped. "Your father. Did you ever forgive him?"

He nodded. "Today."

She was halfway to the ICU doors when an alarm went off. Nurses ran past her toward Rick's room. She kept walking and pressed the button. When the doors opened, Mark stood waiting for her.

Dani stared out the window of the plane, trying to see if she could recognize Pearl Springs from the air as the plane flew toward Chattanooga.

Two weeks ago, she'd flown to Montana to say her goodbyes and to bring Keith's ashes home. She'd been working on the forgiveness thing. She'd forgiven Keith for keeping the truth from her. She was still working on forgiving Rick. He'd taken so much from her.

The tires touched down on the runway, and she breathed a prayer of thanks. She was so anxious to see everyone. The Stones, Nonny . . . and Mark. Especially Mark.

They'd talked every day she was in Montana, sometimes twice a day. Without a murderer dogging their trail at every turn, it was like getting to know him all over again. He'd feared once the danger was past, she might find him boring. Never in a hundred years.

Fifteen minutes later, she rode the escalator down to the baggage claim, her heart jumping at the sight of Mark as he leaned against a pillar with his arms folded.

A slow grin spread over his face when he saw her, and two seconds later he wrapped her in his arms.

"I thought you'd never get here."

"Me either." She laid her head on his chest, liking the way his heart pounded. "I thought Alex was picking me up."

"Nope. You got me." He tilted her face up. "You know, we've never had a real date . . . or an understanding."

"Understanding?"

"Yep. Like maybe you'll go out on a few dates with me?"

Joy flowed through her body. She grinned. "I think that can be arranged."

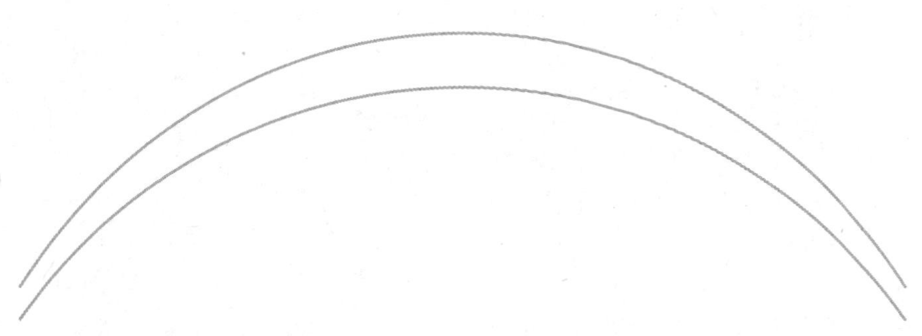

READ ON FOR

PATRICIA BRADLEY'S NEXT

ELECTRIFYING NOVEL

IN THE PEARL RIVER SERIES

COMING SOON

A little before midnight, he pulled his vehicle off the blacktop onto an abandoned logging road in the Cumberland Mountains in Russell County, Tennessee. Seconds later, he climbed out and shot a glance toward thick clouds that smothered the full moon. A gust of wind brought with it the promise of a storm. Hurriedly he slipped on the night goggles, adjusted the strap, and set out for his target.

Five minutes later, he emerged from the woods that abutted the property belonging to former Pearl Springs councilman Joe Slater. He couldn't see the back of the house, but darkened windows along the front indicated no one was up. The garage was connected to the house with a covered breezeway, and he crept toward a side door. Once inside, Slater's fancy pickup was easy to find parked on the other side of his wife's Escalade. The GMC Hummer was the only vehicle Slater drove.

He slid under the truck and found the nut assembly that held the tie-rod in place. Using tools he'd brought with him, he pulled the cotter pin locking the castle nut in place and let it fall to the floor while he tackled the nut. Once it was off, he wrapped it in a handkerchief.

Just as he started to crawl out from under the Hummer, his heart almost stopped at the opening click of a door. He snapped his flashlight off seconds before the door opened and overhead fluorescents lit up the room. Barely breathing, he slipped his hand in his pocket where he carried a Glock subcompact semiautomatic.

Footsteps approached the passenger side of the Hummer. Plaid pajamas and leather house slippers came into view and stopped so close, he could grab Slater's legs if he wanted to. The man muttered something under his breath about an insurance card as he opened the truck door and fumbled in the glove box.

"Told her it was there . . ." Slater grumbled and slammed the door. "Don't know why she couldn't wait till morning."

Less than a minute later, Slater killed the lights, plunging the garage into pitch darkness. Tension eased from his body, and he took a shaky breath. *That was close.*

He checked his watch and forced himself to wait thirty minutes before slipping out of the garage with the castle nut in his pocket. As tempting as it was to keep it as a souvenir, it might be better to toss the nut on the shoulder of the road for the cops to find—that way they would think it simply came loose and fell off.

Just as he started to cross the front yard, a dog yapped. An ankle biter—it figured that Slater would have the kind of dog that sneaked up behind a person and sank its teeth into their ankle when they weren't looking.

The front porch light flickered on, revealing a large "Harrison Carter for Senate" sign in the yard. He stepped back into the shadow of the garage, his jaw clenched so tight pain shot down his neck. After a few seconds, the dog quieted and the light went dark.

A whip-poor-will's lonely call filled the June night as he entered the woods. Legend said that the bird was an omen of death.

Slater had been given a chance to confess and repent.

Fool that he was, the former councilman had laughed instead.

Thunder rumbled as he turned and stared at the dark house. Slater had lined his pocket with taxpayers' money for the last time.

Jenna Hart sighed. A June morning should smell like sunshine and honeysuckle, not gas fumes and death. Or ninety-plus temperatures.

After four hours in the heat, several strands of wilted hair stuck to the back of her neck. While she waited for the wrecker attendant to attach the winch to the Hummer at the bottom of the gorge, Jenna removed her ball cap identifying her with the Russell County Sheriff's Office.

With quick movements, she gathered the strands, redid her ponytail, and returned the cap to her head. The visor didn't offer much protection from the sun, but maybe it would be enough to keep more freckles from peppering her nose. Not that she had many—freckles were a rare combination with black hair.

The black hair came from her dad, and the freckles and her blue eyes from her mother. The mother Jenna had never met as an adult.

She shook off the dark thoughts brought on by the unexpected deaths of Joe Slater and his wife, Katherine, and turned her attention to the road. There'd been a thunderstorm in the early morning hours, but according to Slater's sister, the roads had been dry when the couple left for the Chattanooga airport around seven.

The blacktop showed no sign he'd braked, only a scrape where the Hummer plunged off the road. What sent the sixtysomething Slater over the side of the mountain? Heart attack, maybe?

They should know soon enough since the local coroner had sent the bodies of Slater and his wife to the Hamilton County medical examiner in Chattanooga for autopsy. Jenna turned as Chief Deputy Alex Stone approached. Her heart hitched at the sight of Maxwell Anderson trailing her.

What was the Tennessee Bureau of Investigation agent doing here? She barely caught the words before they shot out of her mouth.

"Jenna, you remember Max, don't you?" Alex asked.

"Sure." Jenna tried to read his thoughts as his amused brown eyes caught her gaze briefly. "He was my supervisor in Chattanooga when I worked robbery."

"Not that you needed much supervising," he said.

Ha! She certainly hadn't gotten that impression. If anyone had asked Jenna, which they never did, she would've told them he'd been harder on her than anyone else in the department.

"So why do you think Slater tried to straighten a curve?" Alex asked. "Mechanical problem or driver error?"

Saved by a question. Jenna jumped on it. "Given this is a late-model Hummer, I doubt it was mechanical."

The whine of the winch drowned out her last words, and they all turned toward the gorge as the front of the SUV came into sight, the right front wheel jutted at an odd angle.

Beside her, Max whistled and nodded toward the vehicle. "I think that's our answer. Looks like the tie-rod came loose."

Why would the tie-rod come loose on a practically new vehicle? "It's possible it happened when the car went down the gorge," Jenna said. "But if it happened before the accident, when Slater entered the curve—"

"He wouldn't have had any control over the wheels," Max said.

She nodded. "What if someone loosened the nut assembly?"

"That's a big jump," he said.

Jenna tapped an electronic pen on her tablet. "The vehicle is less than two years old, and from what some of the deputies who knew Slater said, he took better care of that Hummer than he did his wife."

Max didn't say anything, just raised his eyebrows, and she couldn't tell if he approved or disapproved. Probably approved, given the bad divorce he'd gone through—and the fact that men liked their toys.

He looked toward the road. "If the nut that holds the tie-rod assembly in place came off before the accident, it should be around here somewhere."

Alex nodded to Jenna. "See if you can find it. I'll have the other deputies search the side of the gorge."

"I'll help," Max said.

Before Jenna could protest, Alex nodded. "Thanks—four eyes will be better than two, and I want to look at the crash site."

Jenna started to object and tell Alex she didn't need help, especially from her old supervisor, but the chief deputy was already walking toward the accident site.

Jenna knuckled sweat from her brow and grabbed a bottle of water from the cooler in her SUV. She started to walk away and caught a glimpse of Max. He looked hot as well. *In more ways than one.*

She squashed the thought and couldn't believe she'd even had it. *Really? Admit it. You've been attracted to him since day one.* No. She wasn't going there. Still, there was no need to let the man die of thirst, and Jenna grabbed a second water. "Here," she said as they backtracked on the path the Hummer had taken.

"Thanks. How far do you want to search? Quarter of a mile?"

He was asking her opinion? That was new. "Slater's house is a little over a mile from here—why don't we backtrack to it."

"I didn't realize the house was that close," he said. "Lead the way."

They walked in silence, Jenna on the right side of the road and Max on the left. She noted several potholes on the road as she searched—it'd been a bad winter and the county hadn't gotten around to repairing the lesser-traveled roads. Jenna kept her gaze glued to the blacktop and shoulder.

"Tell me what you know about the victims," Max said after they'd walked what looked like halfway to the house.

She stopped. "I don't know much—I've only been back in Russell County about nine months and don't remember either of the victims, although I heard Alex say Joe had been an alderman in Pearl Springs at one time."

"An alderman? When?"

"I'm not sure, but Alex can probably tell you."

Jenna started walking again, and Max followed suit. When

they reached the drive, she walked toward the attached garage and found it locked. "I wonder if there's a key hidden outside the house?" Jenna said and approached the back of the two-story house. She felt along the top of the door. Nothing. Maybe the Slaters had hidden one under a rock or a brick.

"Do you have a search warrant?" Max asked.

"Why would I need one? The people who live here are dead."

"But they didn't die here, so it's not part of the crime scene."

She hadn't considered the legal ramifications and texted Alex, asking if they needed a search warrant and explained they needed a key to get inside the garage.

The chief deputy's response was quick. *"Not if Slater's sister will let us in. She lives up the road. I'll call and see if she'll meet you there, although it might be a minute."*

Jenna pocketed her phone. "Alex is getting in touch with the sister to come. You want to wait here or walk back to the accident site?"

Max glanced toward the road. "Let's go back."

Jenna nodded and followed him down the hill to the road. Sweat ran down the side of her face as she continued to search the highway and shoulder. After half a mile, they came to an oak tree near the side of the road. She glanced at Max. His white dress shirt stuck to his body. "Want to cool off a minute?"

"I thought you'd never suggest it."

"You could've."

"And have you think I can't take the heat? No way."

Men. She wanted to roll her eyes but instead took a swig of water and stared at the ground, unable to think of one single thing to say.

"How do you like being a Russell County deputy?" he asked, tipping the water bottle she'd given him to his lips.

Jenna stiffened. Max had tried for offhand, but something in his voice told her it was more than a routine inquiry.

Max's gaze made Jenna even hotter than the sun beating down on her as he waited for an answer. She could deny it all she wanted, but she felt a current running between them. Always had. Just being in his presence made her heart beat faster.

Trouble was, he never gave her any indication he might feel the same thing. Of course, he'd been her boss. Then he'd left the police department. With a start, she realized he was waiting for an answer.

"I love being a Russell County deputy. Never a dull moment, and Alex is great to work for—I think I was her first hire." She tilted her head. "What made you ask?"

He hesitated, then palmed his hands. "When you worked robbery, you worked most holidays and volunteered to fill in when someone was out—I wondered if that had changed."

Jenna swallowed down her surprise. She had no idea he'd even noticed. She shrugged. "A lot of the deputies have families, and it's no big deal for me to work the holidays."

"So you're still doing it."

"Not as much." Jenna tipped the water to her lips and took a long draw. "How about you?" She capped the bottle and directed her gaze at Max. "How do you like being a TBI agent?"

He didn't look away, and that amused look popped into his eyes again. "Same as you. Never a dull moment."

She frowned. "Okay . . . so why are you here in Russell County?" It was the question she'd been dying to ask ever since she saw him.

A look Jenna couldn't decipher crossed his face, then he shrugged. "Harrison Carter is holding a big political rally for his US Senate race at your Founders Day picnic, and I've been assigned to check out the security protocols. I met earlier with Alex and Nathan Landry to discuss security arrangements."

Nathan was the Pearl Springs chief of police and Alex's fiancé. "But that doesn't tell me what you're doing *here*."

He nodded toward the accident site. "The accident interrupted our meeting, and I came along to help, thinking I might hurry the process. We'll still have our meeting as soon as Alex is finished."

Jenna frowned. She'd heard her dad mention that the former Pearl Springs mayor had announced his candidacy for the Senate seat. "Does the TBI check out every rally?"

"Not normally, but Carter has friends in high places, and they requested it after he received a threatening letter yesterday."

"What kind of letter?"

He took out his phone. "I photographed it."

Max held out his phone with the picture. Instead of typed words, someone had cut letters from newspapers and magazines to write the message. *You've lined your last pocket.*

"It's not exactly a threat," she said.

"With the way things are lately, we're not taking any chances."

She stared at the photo. "Does Carter say what the letter is referring to?"

Max shook his head. "Claims to not have a clue, and so far he's checked out clean, which is all the more reason to beef up security."

Jenna understood their caution. She felt his gaze and looked up. "What?"

"Alex indicated she wanted you and me to work together on security for the Founders Day picnic."

"But it'll be at the park. Isn't that Chief Landry's territory?"

He nodded. "Nathan is on board with it. He and Alex were already collaborating on security for the picnic." He glanced in the direction of the accident scene. "I thought Alex and Nathan were tying the knot soon."

"They are. They were supposed to get married the day after the Founders Day picnic, but after Carter decided to have his shindig, they decided on the next Sunday afternoon. Since it's only going to be a few friends and family at Mae Richmond's place on Eagle Ridge, it wasn't hard to move it." Jenna didn't know which of them was more disappointed—Alex or Nathan. "Guess we better finish searching for that nut."

Max nodded his agreement. "You want the left or right side?"

"Left," she said.

Ten minutes later the sun glinted off something silver, and she bent down to look closer. "Max," she called. "Come tell me if this is what I think it is."

He jogged to where she crouched at the side of the road and knelt beside her. "I believe you found it." He slipped his pen through the nut and held it up.

She squinted her eyes and studied it. "Can you tell if it was tampered with?"

Max turned his pen, looking at all sides of the nut. "It looks pretty clean. A deeper examination may show something."

The look he gave her indicated his doubt. Max dropped the nut into a paper evidence bag she handed him. Jenna turned and surveyed the road. If the nut belonged to the Hummer, and this was where the nut worked loose, the tie-rod wouldn't necessarily have come loose at this point.

When she worked with her dad on his old cars, sometimes they had to take a hammer to the tie-rod to get it loose. Her gaze landed on a pothole ten feet from where the vehicle veered off the road. That hole would do it.

Max turned and looked up the road. "The cotter pin would've come out first, so do you want to walk back toward the house?"

Jenna brought her attention back to him and nodded then inched forward, scouring the gray gravel on the side of the road.

"You'll never find—"

"I found the pin." Her gaze landed on a small, round piece of metal, and she stooped closer to the ground.

"Did you find it?"

Her shoulders drooped. "No. It's a finishing nail." Jenna looked up at him. "It could be anywhere . . . or nowhere. Even in Slater's garage if someone pulled it out to loosen the nut."

He frowned. "Don't start looking for criminal activity where there's not any evidence."

It wasn't the first time he'd accused her of jumping to conclusions. "But what if there is a crime?" she asked. Because something about this wreck seemed off. "It doesn't make sense for the tie-rod to come loose on a practically new vehicle."

He scanned the accident scene with his binoculars, recognizing each deputy at the site, except for the one with Jenna. White short-sleeved shirt, dark slacks—didn't look like a Russell County deputy. TBI, maybe, but why would Slater's accident attract the interest of a bureau investigator?

Shifting the binoculars back to Jenna, he watched as the two walked either side of the road. She had almost reached where he dropped the castle nut. *Don't miss it.* A smile stretched his lips as she knelt beside the road. He zoomed in the field glasses so he could see what she held in her hand.

Yes. She'd found the castle nut. *Good girl.*

They'd missed the pin he'd dropped about thirty yards up the road toward the house. He watched as they talked for a few minutes and then started walking back toward the house. She knelt to pick up something. Couldn't be the pin. No, a nail. She shook her head, and the other cop started walking ahead of her.

Now that they'd found the castle nut, they would backtrack to the house. He was still kicking himself for not picking up the cotter pin last night, but when Slater came into the garage, it'd blown his mind, and he'd forgotten dropping it. Until he woke this morning. He'd rushed over to search the garage, arriving just in time to see Slater deadbolt the door and set an alarm before they left.

Picking a lock, no big deal, but the alarm was a different matter, and there hadn't been time to figure it out. He'd rummaged around in the toolbox on the back of his pickup until he found a cotter pin and then planted it along the road.

Killing someone was the easy part. Manipulating the evidence was another matter.

ACKNOWLEDGMENTS

A special thanks to Bryan for always being willing to eat leftovers whether I'm on deadline or not, and to the rest of my family and friends who encourage me on this writing journey.

To my editors, Rachel McRae and Kristin Kornoelje, thank you for the hard work! You catch my mistakes and make my stories so much better. I'd be lost without you!

To the art, editorial, marketing, and sales teams at Revell, especially Michele Misiak, Karen Steele, and Brianne Dekker, who have to deal with me directly—thank you for all your hard work. And to the ones behind the scenes, you're awesome!

To Julie Gwinn, who always goes to bat for me, for your direction and for working so tirelessly with me and for being my friend.

To my readers . . . you are awesome! Thank you for reading my stories. Without you, my books wouldn't exist.

As always, to Jesus, who gives me the words.

Patricia Bradley is the author of *Standoff*, *Obsession*, *Crosshairs*, and *Deception*, as well as the Memphis Cold Case novels and Logan Point series. Bradley is the winner of an Inspirational Reader's Choice Award, a Selah Award, and a Daphne du Maurier Award; she was a Carol Award finalist; and three of her books were included in anthologies that debuted on the *USA Today* bestseller list. Cofounder of Aiming for Healthy Families, Inc., Bradley is a member of American Christian Fiction Writers and Sisters in Crime. She makes her home in Mississippi. Learn more at PTBradley.com.

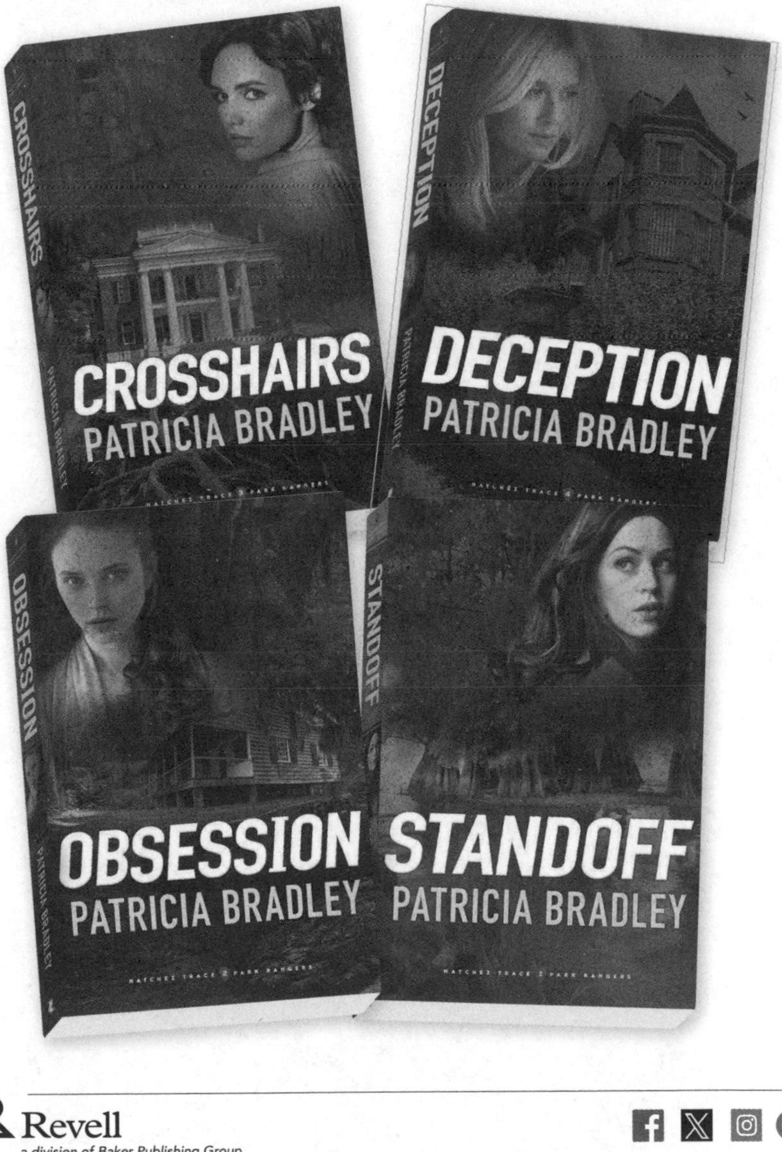

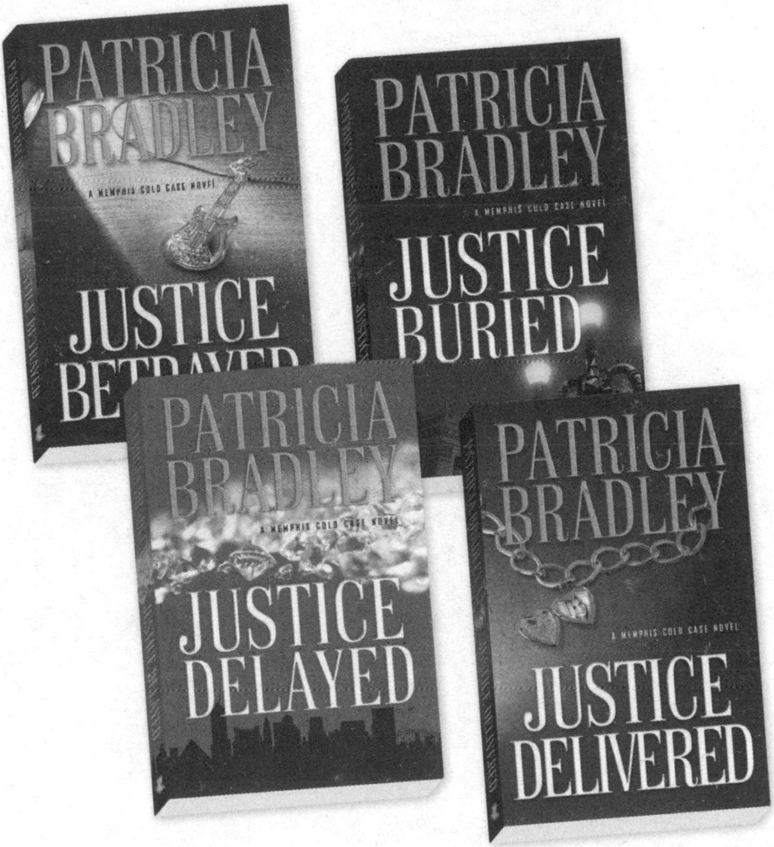

Meet

Patricia BRADLEY

PTBradley.com

PatriciaBradleyAuthor

PTBradley1

PTBradley1